also by Vickie McKeehan

The Evil Secrets Trilogy
JUST EVIL Book One
DEEPER EVIL Book Two
ENDING EVIL Book Three

The Pelican Pointe Series
PROMISE COVE
HIDDEN MOON BAY
DANCING TIDES
LIGHTHOUSE REEF
STARLIGHT DUNES
LAST CHANCE HARBOR
SEA GLASS COTTAGE
LAVENDER BEACH
SANDCASTLES UNDER THE CHRISTMAS MOON
BENEATH WINTER SAND

The Skye Cree Novels
THE BONES OF OTHERS
THE BONES WILL TELL
THE BOX OF BONES
HIS GARDEN OF BONES
TRUTH IN THE BONES

The Indigo Brothers Trilogy
INDIGO FIRE
INDIGO HEAT
INDIGO JUSTICE
THE INDIGO BROTHERS TRILOGY BOXED SET

Exclusively at Amazon in print and Kindle format

Ending Evil

The Evil Secrets Trilogy
Book Three

Vickie McKeehan

beachdevils
PRESS

Ending Evil
The Evil Secrets Trilogy

Published by Beachdevils Press
ISBN: 978-1-4524-0544-5 eBook
ISBN: 978-0-6156-6057-8 Paperback
Printed in the USA

Cover art design by Vanessa Mendozzi Design
www.vanessamendozzidesign.com

Visit the author at:
www.vickiemckeehan.com
www.facebook.com/VickieMcKeehan

For Carrol, sister by blood, the best mother
I know, and my best friend. You know all
my darkest secrets and manage
to love me anyway.

"She Walks in Beauty"
Poem Excerpt by **Lord Byron**

"Family isn't always blood. It's the people
in your life who want you in theirs.
The ones who accept you for who
you are, the ones who would do
anything to see you smile, and who
love you no matter what."
Anonymous

"To let evil go unpunished
is to breed more evil."
Anonymous

Ending Evil

The Evil Secrets Trilogy
Book Three

CHAPTER 1

Darkness descended causing shadows to fall around him, helping to conceal his movements. He quickened his steps as cop cars flew past him racing to get to the Medical Center.

It seemed to him the LAPD occupied the area in record time and from every direction. From the corner of his eye, Trevor Dane watched as uniformed cops blocked off the main entrance then scurried to get the entire hospital in lockdown mode in a matter of minutes.

He had only a block to go and he would make it off campus entirely. Knowing that, he lengthened his stride, notched up his radar, kept his pace brisk.

When he got to the end of the street, more black and whites screeched to a stop, cordoning off the last remaining access road into the parking structure directly to his right. Keeping his head down, he reached the first alleyway behind the Medical Center and the first path that wasn't out in the open. He hastily ducked into the narrow opening before the cops had a chance to get a good look at him.

Hidden now, behind a six foot wall of concrete, he continued putting one foot in front of the other toward his Chevy, which he'd parked several blocks over in a residential section of the neighborhood. After that close call, he didn't dare run. Running would only draw attention to himself. Old habits sometimes paid off.

Escaping from a risky area often called for simple action, like walking away rather than a problematic foot chase or worse, a do-gooder who took down the description of a vehicle fleeing the scene.

He wasn't far enough away, though, not by a long shot. He kept his steps brisk as he dared not steal a glance behind him. He didn't have time to worry about security cameras or what surveillance images he'd left behind.

Too late for that, he thought wearily.

He'd worn gloves, though, and he had another name to check off his list.

That list grew shorter by the day.

Right out of the box he'd taken care of the viper, Alana Stevens with a simple kitchen knife, ending her reign of terror for good. She'd never be able to hurt another innocent soul.

From there, he'd moved on to her cohort, Jessica Geller Boyd. A bullet to her temple from a nine-millimeter Glock had put an end to those soulless dark eyes once and for all.

Thereafter, he'd moved down his list to Jessica's sister, Eva Geller Gatz, then on to Sumner Boyd.

By that time, it had been sleazy Frank Geller's turn. Frank had met his fate with the standard suicide gun, a .22 caliber Smith and Wesson, the up close and personal model.

Now, the boot knife that went wherever he did had taken care of Connor Boyd.

That left two brothers still standing.

Throw in a cousin or two, which even now might need his attention before too long and he would complete the coup d'état, ending the regime of Boyd Boyd Geller &Gatz for good. He'd missed taking out Collin Boyd once before though.

He didn't intend to miss a second time.

Because he wore no shirt beneath his jacket, dusk made the June gloom marine layer cooler than it had been just an hour earlier. He'd left his shirt behind, the shirt he'd used to wrap up little baby Sarah, which obviously had Connor

Boyd's DNA all over it. But it was one of those things that couldn't be helped.

And the baby remained safe now back where she belonged in the arms of her mother, Baylee Scott, away from the violent and unstable man who'd fathered her.

The baby.

It had been a long time since he'd held an infant, especially one so young, so dependent on the adults around her. He remembered her smell, her little face, her little puckered mouth, the hiccupping, and her eyes brimming with so many tears.

Tears she should never have been forced to shed.

Not twenty minutes earlier, he'd slit the throat of the baby's father and left him on the dirty concrete of the fifth floor parking garage to bleed out. He would not soon forget Connor Boyd's cold eyes as the man lay dying at his feet.

Nor would he forget the man's attack on the young mother. Connor had used his fists to bring her to her knees. If Trevor had let the man escape with the baby, he wouldn't have been able to live with himself.

In the distance Trevor heard the sounds of even more sirens as they grew closer. He needed to put some miles between this place and the crime scene as quickly as he could. Even a professional, he reminded himself, with his years of experience, sometimes had to take risks.

He sighed. No sense beating himself up. Not every kill could be as meticulously carried out as one could hope or plan he thought bitterly. Even though the June night lacked a real bite to the air, he pulled his jacket collar up around his ears and hurried on.

From the moment Connor had kidnapped Sarah, ripped the baby out of her mother's arms, he had left Trevor few options. As he saw it, he'd been fortunate Connor had made his escape route via the parking garage. The place had been deserted enough that he had been able to take the man down without bringing much attention to himself or to the area.

When his rented Chevy came into view, Trevor pressed the remote key lock. Good thing he hadn't parked near the hospital. He hadn't spent years working as a paid assassin for nothing.

He thought of his bumbling counterpart, Uri Jankovic, and wondered if the Pacific Ocean had yet to give up his body to the land. Probably not, he decided, as he slid neatly behind the wheel of his car, quickly threw the vehicle in gear and took off down the quiet, residential side street.

As he drove toward the 101, he contemplated his next move.

He could simply leave L.A. now, wad up his list, discard it in the nearest trash can at LAX, and be on the next flight to Buenos Aires. He could find the first available warm body and spend the next two months fucking anything with a heartbeat.

Or, he could finish what he'd started. He still had two more names on his to-do list. Certain Cade and Collin Boyd weren't yet finished, he anticipated another attempt. He just wasn't sure where or when.

He pressed the accelerator, shot into the lane to access the 101 and made his decision.

Ending the evil, once and for all, was the only thing that made any sense.

Noah Parker wouldn't have wanted it any other way.

⚭ ⚭ ⚭ ⚭ ⚭

Two months into her first year of residency, Quinn Tyler realized chaos was about to erupt inside the ER. Having just finished stitching up a thirteen-year-old skateboarder's mouth-meet-sidewalk mishap, she quickly shed her pair of latex gloves and stepped back out into the common area some twenty feet away from the front doors.

She caught the last bit of conversation between one of the triage nurses who kept up a dialogue with the EMTs. They were bringing in a white male in his late thirties.

From the call Quinn learned that the victim was in distress because someone had slit the man's throat. He'd been found bleeding out on the fifth floor of the hospital parking garage.

Quinn heard the overhead pager repeat the same alert several times. "Code Trauma Now!" The litany brought every available shift resident on the first floor running, along with a respiratory nurse along with any attending physicians not working on another patient. That included Harold Mendenhall, chief of emergency surgery.

They all hovered near the ER entrance—anticipating the arrival of the EMTs.

A minute later the doors whooshed open and technicians wheeled in a gurney with the injured man. Quinn grabbed a gown, slipped it on, a pair of glasses, another pair of gloves, and prepared to go to work.

It wasn't until the man had been transferred from the stretcher to the table that Quinn recognized Connor Boyd.

But he didn't look anything like the dark, brooding man she remembered from her youth. This man lay white as the sheets around him. And dark blood already congealed around the six-inch-long slice to his neck.

As the paramedic reported on his vitals and what, up to now, they had done for him, Quinn listened, keenly aware the man looked more dead than alive.

"He had a faint pulse when we first got to him but loading him up...it got fainter." The EMT shook his head. "But I think we lost him on the way inside."

Dr. Mendenhall went to work, sizing up the man's condition and snapped out orders, "Ms. Tyler, don't just stand there. Cut these clothes off. Lopez, get me a blood workup. Stat! He's not breathing. Sullivan, intubate him. Once she has the tube in, somebody try to put pressure on that gaping wound and get the bleeding stopped. Jesus, this man's carotid artery has been severed. It looks like he's lost too much blood. But…who knows…? We might perform a miracle."

As the resident with the least amount of experience, Quinn went to work cutting off Connor's shirt and removing what was left of his clothing.

Out of the corner of her eye, she watched with a certain amount of envy as Angie Sullivan, third-year resident and Mendenhall's favorite underling, manually intubated Connor trying to get him to breathe.

It wasn't every day they saw a patient with his throat sliced open, let alone actually got to see the tricky procedure of intubating him with a fiber-optic laryngoscope firsthand. Quinn eagle-eyed Mendenhall in fascination, then watched Angie and Lopez while they worked together to get the airbag compressing air into Connor's lungs, trying to get him to breathe.

While they did their job, Quinn began to apply pressure to the wound. But there was no sign of life, no pulse and no heartbeat. After an eternal thirty minutes of trying, despite the fact that Mendenhall, Sullivan, Lopez, and Quinn worked frantically to save the man's life, even a brand new resident knew it was too late. He'd lost too much blood.

Connor Boyd was gone.

He had more than likely bled out in a matter of minutes. Whoever had done this to him had known what they were doing, at least in Quinn's mind they had. After another several long minutes, Mendenhall simply shook his head. "I'm calling time of death at…" He glanced up at the clock. "seven-twenty-five even though it was more like on the way in. By any chance, is there any next of kin around here?"

"You're goddamned right there is. Don't you dare stop working on him! Do something! You can't let him die!"

Quinn whirled around at the sound of Cade Boyd's voice and saw a disheveled man, standing holding the curtain that separated the attending rooms. He gripped the fabric like a drowning sailor held onto a life raft.

Unlike his brother, Cade wasn't pale but instead stood defiant and red-faced.

A pair of glassy, black, stormy eyes met hers.

The man looked very much like the last time Quinn had seen him—livid and arrogant.

He pointed an accusing finger directly at Quinn and screamed for all it was worth. "This is your fucking fault. What the hell did you do to my brother? Get away from him. Get out of here. You shouldn't be here. You don't know shit about being a doctor anyway. What you know about medicine is nothing more than a fucking nurse knows. And you hate my family."

He turned to the bank of police officers standing around and yelled, "Ask her. Tell them, Quinn, tell them all how you hate my family. Now, get away from him, get away from my brother. I'll sue your ass. I'll sue this entire fucking hospital. I'll own this fucking place before I'm done."

He began to sob uncontrollably as he finally took in the whole scene: Connor's face a whitish gray, all the blood, and the fact that his brother lay still, unmoving. Dead.

Dr. Mendenhall raised his voice an octave and demanded, "Get this man out of my trauma room!"

A rage built inside Cade, along with a sickening hard knot in his stomach. Acceptance brought another string of obscenities until he finally screamed and pointed at Quinn, "You fucking bitch, you killed my brother!"

He lunged for her then. A uniformed cop barely managed to peel him off her right before his fists could meet flesh.

☙☙☙☙☙

Reese Brennan strolled through the hospital doors that led to the ER and past a waiting area filled with people on his way to check up on Baylee's terminally ill father upstairs. As of two days ago, William Scott had become his client.

He'd been hoping to catch a brief glimpse of Quinn on his way, maybe exchange a couple of sparring words to tide her over until the end of her shift. But when he heard a man's voice that he recognized as Cade Boyd's coming from one of the trauma rooms, he hurried past the waiting area.

Even from this distance, the man sounded pissed.

After spending all day on the sprawling grounds of The Enclave, which was owned by the Boyds, Reese was exhausted. He'd been riding on adrenaline for the past twelve hours watching a team of forensic anthropologists scrape away enough dirt to bring up three human skulls buried under the cabana house near the reflecting pool, the exact location where William Scott had directed the police to look.

The cops suspected one skull belonged to Baylee's mother, Sarah Moreland, the other to her friend, the tennis player Luc Delaine. But at this point, they had no idea who the third one could possibly be; in fact, it was anyone's guess.

Reese had stopped by the hospital hoping William Scott might wake from his coma enough to talk more about how the bodies came to be entombed on Boyd property. Jessica Boyd and Alana Stevens had more than likely put them in the ground. But if those two held the answers as to why, the why would likely remain a mystery.

Right now, Reese just wanted five minutes with Quinn, preferably alone. Five minutes was usually all it took before they found something they could argue about—in spades.

The woman hated his profession. But in spite of that, she had a feisty side which for some reason he found appealing. Her sarcastic wit aside, though, it was more than likely her deep, chocolate brown eyes that drew him in. Or the fact that he wouldn't mind getting his hands in her hair, maybe slip that band from around her ponytail and let it drape down free.

And if he kept thinking like that he'd need a cold shower.

But before he laid eyes on Quinn, it became clear Cade's rant was beginning to take on an incoherent, crazy rambling. Knowing Quinn was somewhere around the ER, knowing what Cade was capable of doing, Reese followed the man's voice as it filled the air with a string of nasty threats.

At that point, Reese even considered the fact that Cade might have crossed the line entirely and brought a weapon with him into the hospital. He let his imagination run wild with that possibility, deciding Cade could easily be holding everyone hostage. The man was that irrational.

By the time Reese took in the scene, two uniformed cops were restraining a still-ranting Cade Boyd. But then he noted the look of sheer terror on Quinn's face as each cop held Cade back from going after her. It seemed they were trying to get him out into the hallway without much success.

Even Reese could tell the exotic-looking Quinn tried for a stoic expression but failed miserably. And the Quinn Tyler he had known over the past two months rarely failed at anything.

To Reese, her usual toffee skin looked a little on the pale side probably because Cade kept resisting the officers and trying to break away. But not before he let go another string of obscenities aimed at her.

"Goddamn it, I'm coming for you, Quinn. You and your fucking friends think you can get away with this but...I'll be there when you least expect it. I know people," he shouted as the cops fought to remove him from the area. "Let go of me, you bastards. Don't I get a chance to be with my brother before you take him away?"

Reese threw an anxious look at LAPD detective Max St. John, who had just appeared from the other side of the corridor where he was deep in discussion with his partner Dan Holloway.

Reese raised his voice and said, "Can't you get him out of here? Arrest him for threats like that for chrissakes."

Max sighed. "He needs to give me a valid reason, Brennan. And as a defense attorney you should know that. He's upset about his brother. Connor died on the table in there. You have any idea what Boyd was doing with Baylee Scott's baby?"

"No idea," Reese retorted, without feeling guilt for the lie. If Max wasn't going to arrest Cade on the spot, he'd be damned if he helped out the obstinate detective.

Max shrugged. "Well, if I were you, I'd watch the doctor's back," he cautioned before turning back to Holloway.

Reese intended to do just that. But first he had to get her attention.

☯ ☯ ☯ ☯ ☯

Like a beacon in a blustery storm at sea, Quinn spotted Reese through the bedlam and started moving his way. Unlike other times when she'd been around him, today she was almost glad to see him. She attributed her change of heart to Cade's tirade. After all, a friendly face always trumped a pissed-off rant from the next of kin.

Any time you lost a patient there was bound to be the chance a relative might go off on the staff, the same staff that had fought to save the loved one and failed. But Cade's furious outburst surpassed any she'd experienced, mainly because he'd aimed it solely at her.

Leave it to a Boyd, she decided, to embarrass her in front of every co-worker within earshot who would likely gossip about it for days, maybe even weeks.

She had to believe it was Reese's cool demeanor that pulled at her now and not the tall good-looking guy with penetrating soft, gray eyes flecked deep with bursts of golden brilliance. According to Kit Griffin, her best bud, the man had graduated law school at Berkeley at the top of his class.

Quinn had always been attracted to intellect and had to believe that's why Reese Brennan got her fired up in a way few men had over the years. She didn't want to be attracted to a lawyer though. But not even the doctors she rubbed elbows with on a daily basis got her juices flowing quite like the cocky attorney did.

And she wasn't happy about it.

She pulled out of the reverie and realized she must be more upset than she thought. She had to remind herself this particular man had a tendency to rub her the wrong way and usually it took no more than five minutes.

That had to be a huge red flag. And one she didn't dare ignore.

The fact that he made his living writing briefs and petitioning the court with arguments that surely affected the wellbeing of others gave her reason to push him away. She detested having to deal with anyone who held that kind of power. She'd been forced to rely on his kind most of her life, at least as far back as she could remember. In her experience, lawyers seemed to take control over anyone who had the money to hire them.

None had ever turned out to be in her corner, either.

So, why was she drawn to this particular man?

Eyeing the curious gazes from her co-workers, all of a sudden she wanted to be somewhere else. Unfortunately, she still had almost ninety minutes to go on her shift. Of course, that was if nothing else major happened.

Right now, all she wanted was to get out of there, away from Cade Boyd and get home to a hot bath and a bed.

She sidled up to Reese. Maybe basking for a few minutes in the serenity he always seemed to emit might give her the goose she needed to get through her shift. The man had a calmness she envied. She supposed all attorneys were like that. At least the ones she'd crossed paths with sported their frosty demeanor like heartless drones. Not only that, they were proud of it.

Okay, maybe she wasn't being entirely fair. Reese had helped Kit out of a jam when detective Max St. John had been ready to arrest her for killing Alana Stevens. And Reese was the longtime buddy of Jake and Dylan, two guys she had come to respect a great deal over the past two months.

The fact that Reese had a really nice ass gave him a few extra points in his favor, though. At the moment, he was in the middle of making a case to that same detective about why Cade Boyd should be locked up.

How could she turn a blind eye to that?

Lawyer or not, loyalty was high on Quinn's list. And she had to give him major points for looking out for her welfare.

So what if the man had an exceptionally fine set of abs to go with the ass? Why would she not take the time to appreciate such a lanky frame, or those sexy gray eyes that gave off enough bedroom vibes to make her mouth water? No wonder she felt that pull in the belly every time they crossed swords.

After his face-to-face with St. John, it took Reese a few seconds to realize Quinn was standing right next to him. He had to take a second look before their eyes locked and held.

No one else seemed to matter. Those usual energetic eyes told him she'd reached her limit.

She asked wearily, "What are you doing here?"

"Dylan called, told me Connor had kidnapped the baby. I got here as soon as I could."

"I was about to stitch up a kid when Baylee called to let me know Connor had taken the baby. I could barely understand her because he busted her lip, Reese. I haven't even had the time to make sure she's all right. Have you seen her yet?"

Reese winced at the idea that petite little Baylee had taken a punch. He shook his head. "I haven't been upstairs yet but I talked to Dylan not twenty minutes ago as I pulled into the parking lot. Now that Sarah's back, Baylee's fine. Battered and bruised, but Sarah's back with her mother and that's all Baylee cares about at the moment."

Quinn let out a breath. "You know we lost Connor. He was gone by the time he got here."

"Yeah, I figured. And I heard Cade pitching a fit from the front door. Not sure I can gut out any sympathy for Connor after what he did to Baylee."

"How bad is she? I need to go see for myself that she's okay. Things happened so fast down here, I never made it upstairs. Sarah's okay though, right? Dylan got her back and she's okay? They got a doctor to check her out, right?"

"I believe so." He didn't see any need to mention that Dylan had described Baylee as beaten up with bruises already starting to turn purple and black. Nor did he see any reason to mention that Sarah had been wrapped in a bloody shirt.

Why upset Quinn any more than Cade already had with his outburst?

Plus, Reese noted that the usual bouncing-off-the-walls Quinn looked done in. As he watched her, his heart did that little two-step it so often did whenever she came within ten feet. Those long legs, those Native American almond-shaped eyes, that creamy toffee skin, her high cheekbones, had captured his attention the moment she'd walked into Kit's hospital room several weeks back.

He hadn't been able to bank his lust ever since.

Quinn nodded toward St. John and his partner Dan Holloway as the two detectives headed for the elevators. "Do they know…? Do they have any idea who did that—to Connor?"

"Dylan says it has to be Mr. X."

"Mr. X?"

"Hey, leave it to Dylan to come up with a clever way to describe our mystery man. The way he figures it, Mr. X must've followed Connor to the parking garage, cut his throat, and grabbed Sarah before Connor could take off with her in his Hummer, coming to the rescue again just in the nick of time."

"It's been a zoo down here. But I'll tell you what I know from the cops. They found Connor not ten feet from his vehicle, bleeding out. They found Sarah in one of the elevators that services the parking garage. She was wrapped in a bloody shirt."

Okay, so she already knew the gritty details. "And inside the shirt pocket, Dylan found one of those gold cowboys, which tells us it is Mr. X because the cowboys apparently have become his signature."

"Jesus." Quinn rubbed a hand across her face. "Who is this guy?"

Before he could answer, before they could get on the elevator and head upstairs, Dr. Mendenhall caught up with Quinn and demanded, "Tyler, I need to see you in my office. Now!" He turned on his heels without waiting for a response and crossed to a counter, where he grabbed a chart, expecting her to follow him.

Quinn shot a quick glance back at Reese before going after Dr. Mendenhall down the hall and into a small room off the ER.

She had barely shut the door behind her when he asked, "What the hell was that out there? I want the truth, Tyler. And I want it now! Don't even think about lying to me or putting a pretty spin on it. This is serious. He threatened to sue the staff *and* the hospital. I need to know now if you're involved with Cade Boyd in any way, past or present."

God, would people ever stop throwing her relationship with Cade Boyd back in her face? "No! I'm not involved with him."

"But you know him, know the family—personally?"

"Some." She let out a tired sigh. "Okay, Cade and I went out for about six weeks...a very, long time ago. It's ancient history. It doesn't have a thing to do with what happened here today."

"That's where you're wrong. If you had trouble with this ranting maniac who just threatened a lawsuit, you shouldn't have been anywhere near treating his brother. You should have said something the minute you recognized him as someone you knew. You know the rules, Tyler. Any person you have conflict with is off limits in the trauma rooms. You've put the hospital in a difficult position. Sumner and Jessica Boyd were two of our biggest donors. The Boyd family wields a great deal of power in this town."

"From the moment the EMTs brought him in all I did was get his clothes off and assist in putting pressure on the gaping wound to stop the bleeding. I watched as Angie tried to get him to breathe! And you're the one who told me to apply pressure."

"I didn't know you knew him!" he snapped back.

"You were right there. You're the one who started working on him. Not me. You know that. I just tried to help as best I could, which I might add, is impossible since he looked as if he'd bled out by the time we got him. He looked... gone already. Dr. Mendenhall, don't you think you're overreacting to a hysterical relative of the deceased who might...if you ask me...might be a little deranged?"

"No one's asking you, Tyler. Do you have any idea how serious this situation is? The Boyd family can make a lot of trouble for this hospital. Lawyers have a tendency to sue hospitals."

Quinn had the urge to list the number of Boyds who were no longer able to practice law because they were all dead, but she didn't think pointing that out at the moment would be beneficial to her cause.

She of all people understood fully there were still plenty of lawyers at the family firm, Boyd Boyd Geller & Gatz, who would love nothing more than to bring a nice fat lawsuit against her and the hospital.

So typical, she thought, a bunch of money-greedy lawyers putting an end to her medical career before it ever really got started.

Wisely she held her tongue and listened as Mendenhall pointed out, "Going forward, we need to do everything by the book. That's why it pains me to put you on report. You have potential, Tyler, you really do. You care about the patients and it shows. Your medical knowledge is first rate. But like all first year residents your training needs repetition to get better. As of right now, you're suspended from this hospital."

Quinn's mouth dropped open. "What? No, you can't. But I didn't do anything wrong. Jesus, just because Cade threw a hissy fit, I'm suspended? That's bullshit and you know it. I did my best to get Connor Boyd to stop bleeding. I watched *you* treat him. I watched Angie intubate him. This is ridiculous." When she eyed Mendenhall's set jaw and how serious he was, she added quickly, "Please tell me this isn't going to put my residency in jeopardy?"

"Once the review board gets the facts, I'm sure everything will be fine."

"Review board? How long?" Quinn grumbled.

"Three weeks—minimum. That should teach you to notify your superiors whenever someone is brought into this hospital with which you have had prior conflict."

"Great. Fucking great. Three weeks! That's almost a month. I just got started!" She yanked the door open and stormed out—and ran right into Reese's chest.

"What's wrong?"

"I just got suspended. Damn Boyds," she tossed out as she stormed past him to the bank of elevators.

"What reason did they give?"

"Short version? Cade uttered the word lawsuit and Mendenhall crapped his pants. He thinks two minutes from now someone named Boyd, Geller, or Gatz will walk through those doors, serve him papers and sue the hospital for millions."

Quinn snorted. "Just because I was standing within two feet from Connor Boyd trying to stop him from bleeding, I get kicked out of the program."

Reese grabbed her arm, stopping her path. "Wait, they kicked you out? They can't do that without..."

She shook her head. "I got suspended for three weeks. Might as well be an eternity. Like I had anything to do with the asshole getting his throat slit." But then she realized for the first time that Mendenhall had never actually answered her question whether or not the suspension put her residency in jeopardy.

She glanced at Reese as he pushed the elevator button to head upstairs. "I knew Mendenhall didn't like me, but I never thought he'd suspend me over something as insignificant as this."

Reese re-evaluated the situation. A three-week suspension sounded harsh to him but it was a far cry from getting kicked out of the residency program for good. But knowing she needed to vent, he would willingly oblige. He draped his arm around her shoulders. "Buck up. I never saw anyone who needed a lawyer more than you do right now. It just so happens...I know one, an excellent one, the best. I think his brilliant legal mind can get you reinstated, work you back in to the rotation in record time."

She elbowed him lightly in the ribs. "Now is not the time to yank my chain, Brennan. This is serious! This is my career."

"One more reason you need the services of the finest..."

This time she poked a finger into his chest. "Just my luck, I'm at the mercy of an arrogant barrister with an ego the size of L.A."

When the elevator dinged, they waited for people to drift out of it before stepping into the empty car. "Arrogant is an awfully strong word there, Dr. Tyler. I prefer to think I'm confident and, as such, go the extra mile for my clients."

Once the doors clanged shut, Quinn grabbed him by the shirt collar, pulled his head down to her eye level. "You get me re-instated, I guarantee I'll make it worth your while."

"Really? Now that's the best offer I've had in..."

"Do you always yak it up so much?"

His arms went around her, tugging her into his chest. Her feet left the floor as he backed her up against the mirrored sidewall and took her mouth.

Lips, slick and wet, did the tongue tango. Instant heat ramped up.

Chest to chest, she felt the familiar tug in her lower belly.

The slow graze became a hungry feeding. He felt her body quiver the instant he took the kiss deeper.

Searing heat poured through her like a firestorm. The moment he plopped her feet back down on the floor, her knees wanted to buckle.

"Well..." The jaunty comeback died on her lips.

"I don't believe it. For once I've managed to put a muzzle on Quinn Tyler's mouth." She had that look on her face that said she'd just been thoroughly kissed and—was a little scared of taking that next step.

He saw her wall go back up like a laser shield.

"Oh, shut up. Just like a damn lawyer to tout his own skills. Should I hold up a sign giving you a seven-point-five?"

"A seven-point-five? Is that all? On the Richter scale that might be a full magnitude earthquake. I could do better. Who knew you'd be such a harsh judge."

She couldn't very well admit it had been a helluva lot more potent than that. Reese Brennan hardly needed encouragement in the tonsil-dive department. Instead, she shot him a steely glance and said, "Get me reinstated and you get another shot at proving me wrong, how's that?"

CHAPTER 2

Upstairs on the twelfth floor, Quinn and Reese stepped off the elevator into a waiting area and a different kind of chaos. There were more police officers than medical staff still milling about.

Max St. John, as well as another dozen or so cops, gathered around an injured Baylee Scott as she stood holding her infant daughter, Sarah. She was doing her best under the circumstances to give them her statement about Sarah's kidnapping while everyone crowded around to listen.

It was obvious she was still distressed but grateful to have her daughter back safe and sound.

Quinn had to give it to the cops. They seemed to hold back a little, waiting for Baylee to compose herself. Although they still surrounded her they put off their questioning because the woman looked like she'd gone six rounds with Sugar Ray Leonard and lost.

Her split lip had some glossy ointment spread on it now and what looked like a butterfly stitch or two. Quinn wasn't sure how Baylee could even talk with her lips so swollen and puffy. Her cheeks and eyes were a collective mass of bruises and bumps already beginning to turn a nasty purplish black.

Quinn had never seen the laid-back Dylan Burke so upset. Even though he stood next to Baylee, clutching her to his side as if he didn't want to ever let the woman go, she could tell he was getting more agitated by the minute because the cops wouldn't leave Baylee in peace.

Reese decided that maybe he needed to get over there and run a little lawyer interference. It didn't look like Max St. John intended on going anywhere anytime soon either. Knowing the players like he did, the bulldog detective wouldn't give up until he got what he wanted. And Dylan simply wanted the cop to keep his distance so he and Baylee could get past this ordeal.

As Reese made his way across the room, he knew compromise was a critical part of his profession. Realizing Max needed to get his questions asked and be on his way, Reese intervened. If Baylee had to answer questions, it would be done with a lawyer at her side.

About that time, Max's partner Dan Holloway stepped off the elevator into the madhouse. And just as Reese suspected, as soon as Baylee took a breath, Max pounced.

"Let me see if I understand this, Miss Scott. You're standing vigil beside your terminally ill father. Mr. Burke here goes down to the cafeteria to get coffee with your housekeeper, Tanya Lincoln. You're left alone in the room. Connor Boyd bursts in, assaults you, and kidnaps your six-month-old child? Why? Why would he do that? Why would Connor Boyd of all people be interested in kidnapping your baby?"

And just as Reese knew he would, Dylan exploded, stepping into Max's face. "Who the hell knows what motivates a psycho bastard like Connor Boyd? Baylee certainly doesn't have a clue. He kidnapped a baby, there's no denying that fact. Doesn't that settle this mess enough for you, detective?"

"It does. And seems to be at the core of what started all of this today." Max paused and pointed out, "Right now Mr. Burke, you need to take a step back before I arrange to have you spend the night locked up away from this woman who needs you the most right now."

Reese knew Dylan could be as cool as anyone, but where Baylee was concerned he wouldn't hesitate to do something stupid, like getting arrested to shield Baylee from answering any embarrassing questions. So Reese quickly grabbed Dylan by the arm, pushing him back out of the cop's face.

"Take a step back, Dylan. Cool off. This won't help Baylee."

But Dylan shook Reese off. "Look, St. John, Baylee didn't beat herself up, and I sure as hell didn't kidnap my own daughter. No one here has anything to hide, but you're standing here wasting our time questioning us, and to what purpose? Don't you see Baylee's upset? We almost lost our child to Connor Boyd. It's time you faced facts. Boyd is your bad guy here."

But Max was persistent. "Mr. Burke, I'm simply trying to get at the truth. You claim to be the child's father. But downstairs, not fifteen minutes earlier, Cade claimed Connor had been certain he was the baby's father."

Reese saw Baylee take a visible step backward away from all of them. She probably wondered if this mess would ever have resolution. For Dylan and Baylee's sake, Reese wondered if Max intended the interrogation to be a long, drawn out process.

Connor was dead. So what was the point?

Reese, like Dylan, was afraid Max's suspicious nature might open up a different can of worms entirely. Looking at Baylee's face, he flinched. Thank goodness Connor hadn't broken her nose. He watched as Quinn took up a position on the opposite side of Dylan, as if both of them were all that was holding Baylee up.

Reese noted Quinn took hold of Baylee's chin to assess the damage, female to female. The look on her face told him she was pissed.

Quinn might be suspended, but she intended to take care of her friend in more ways than one. "Isn't it enough the bastard beat the shit out of her? And it's difficult to believe you'd put much stock in anything Cade Boyd told you at this point. You saw him downstairs, witnessed firsthand how he lost it. He's as much a psycho as his brothers. If that display down in the ER fails to convince you, then maybe we should talk—officially. There's a side to Cade Boyd you might not know about."

At the sound of Quinn's words, Baylee recovered somewhat to set the record straight. If Quinn were ready to talk to them about what Cade had done to her, then she could do the same.

"Look, Detective, Connor was obsessed for some reason with my child. He mistakenly thought he was Sarah's father. He isn't. I tried to tell him that, tried to set him straight. But when Connor Boyd got something in his head, it was difficult to persuade him that he was wrong about anything. And he was flat out *not* Sarah's father."

Insistent, Dylan snarled, "I am this child's father. I'm listed on her birth certificate. Any more talk about Connor Boyd fathering this baby from you or anyone else and you will have to answer to my lawyer."

Okay, thought Reese, Dylan was still sticking to the role he'd chosen to play several weeks earlier. For his friend, he'd take up the crusade.

"And you'd need a court order for anything above that," Reese reminded Max. "As well as justification, and I'll fight you on that Max, every step of the way. Count on it. There is no legal or moral justification for getting a court order to determine paternity at this point."

Max stared at Reese before taking a long, hard look at Dylan and Baylee. He glanced in the direction of Jake Boston and Kit Griffin and decided a unified wall was a tough thing for a cop to overcome.

"Okay. For now, that's none of my business. I'm just trying to plug a few holes here, trying to understand why Connor Boyd decided to kidnap a six-month-old infant that had no apparent connection to him. Not to mention trying to understand who the hell slit his throat."

Dylan and Baylee looked somewhat relieved at that, and it didn't go unnoticed by Max. At this point though he wasn't certain anyone in the room was leveling with him. Satisfied for now though, he sought out his partner, Dan

Holloway, who was on the other side of the reception area, deep in a discussion with Jake and Kit.

Max reluctantly headed that way.

In mid-sentence, Dan explained, "No denying it now. We hit upon the skulls first, two of them buried together on Boyd property near the reflecting pool, just like the old man told us. It wasn't until about an hour ago the third skull came into view about five feet away from the others. By that time, they'd found the rest of the skeletal remains, leg and arm bones, the rib cage. Might take a while for the forensics team to excavate the entire perimeter, though; the grounds are huge and we intend to use ground-scanning sonar to go over every inch of the place. If we're patient we might get some answers now. Groundskeeper said he worked on the reflecting pool himself back in the late '80s with the help of a local contractor. We're trying to find the contractor now. Of course, we suspect two of the victims are Sarah Moreland Scott, the actress, and Luc Delaine, her lover, the tennis player."

"Luc was not her lover," Baylee corrected from ten feet away. "He was a friend, nothing more. Those two hags, Jessica and Alana, spread rumors about Sarah at the country club, made up lies about her running off. She didn't. So many people bought into the story, though. My father admits to that now, admits that Jessica and Alana made up the whole thing. For reasons only he knows, my father didn't bother setting the record straight."

About this time, Tanya Lincoln appeared in the waiting area and took Sarah out of Baylee's tired arms. "You need a breather. You're exhausted. If you aren't ready to go, then I'll take Sarah and sit down here with her until everything settles down and these officers leave. Getting this upset isn't good for you or the baby."

"Thanks, Tanya. I just want to make sure I'm around when they find out for sure about…my mother."

"I know, honey, but it won't do any good if you push yourself until you collapse."

Dylan watched as Sarah settled into Tanya's lap on the waiting room couch. Tanya soothed the child as only a grandmother could. He turned to Baylee and whispered. "The sooner we get rid of these cops, the sooner we can get this day behind us. We can do this, Baylee. We're halfway there. Now, put on your 'I've got nothing to hide' face and let's get these cops out of here for good so we can get on with our lives."

Baylee took a deep breath, nodded and sent Quinn a knowing look before reaching for her hand.

The three of them left Sarah in the capable hands of Tanya and sidled over to join the conversation with Jake and Kit just in time to hear the last of Dan's assessment. "That third body may be difficult to ID. Right now, those remains belong to someone not on our radar, another missing person, maybe, we just don't know."

"Probably another poor soul who no doubt happened to have the misfortune of crossing paths with Jessica and Alana," Baylee offered. "After all, those two decided to end my mother's life out of spite, out of jealousy, out of revenge. No one may ever know what exactly the motivation was to kill her or anyone else who happened to cross their paths for that matter."

"A deadly attraction if there was one," Quinn agreed. She turned to eye St. John. "Doesn't finding all this out make both of them a pair of female serial killers? I mean first there are the Parkers, then Baylee's mother, the tennis player, and some poor unidentified person as yet unnamed."

"It's chilling," Reese agreed. "They got away with five murders for an awfully long time without anyone ever questioning them."

"Well, someone has taken exception to their murderous ways and decided to exact his revenge, enough to wipe out the entire founding members of Boyd Boyd Geller & Gatz while managing to play rescue again. That makes twice now he's saved the day for our side," Quinn threw in.

"It sounds to me like our Mr. X is set on ending the evil once and for all, making sure it stops with generation number two," Reese decided. When they all turned to stare at him, his lips curved in a slight smile.

For two months now, he'd been a reluctant passenger on their mystery train. They'd been trying to prove their revenge theory all that time. In fact, he could admit he'd been the last one to board, skeptic to the very end, convinced all of his friends were overreacting.

But after Collin had kidnapped Kit, after he'd learned the gun found in Alana's attic had been used in the Parker murders, he'd started to suspect his friends were onto something. Then they had discovered three bodies buried at the Enclave. After what Connor had done to Baylee and Sarah, after listening to Cade downstairs threatening Quinn not more than fifteen minutes earlier, it was time to board that train for good, maybe ride it to the next stop, see if he could prevent it from touching any more of his friends and destroying more lives in the process.

Jake slapped him on the back. "It took you long enough."

When Quinn aimed that hundred-watt smile in his direction and moved a little closer, Reese stuck out his hand. "What do you say to a truce, Tyler?"

"Sure, I suppose that stubborn nature of yours is what keeps your clients off death row. But it's about time you used some common sense where these guys are concerned," Quinn reasoned as she placed her hand into his. She would simply ignore the little vibe she got skin to skin, just like she intended to do with that searing tongue-tag in the elevator.

But when she left her hand in his, Reese simply tugged on her fingers until hers were entwined with his.

Max, however, was in no mood to hear them wax poetic about the professional killer he knew was stalking BBG&G's law firm under the guise of meting out justice or what he considered justice. And it didn't sit right with him, none of it.

"The guy's a cold-blooded killer, no better than Alana and Jessica. Talk about serial killers, he might be one for the record books. You shouldn't dismiss that one critical point."

"I'm not," Baylee said. "But I want you to understand the man has my undying gratitude and respect. What he did today to get Sarah away from Connor and back to me is nothing short of a miracle in my book."

Looking into Dylan's eyes, she corrected, "Back to us." She slid her hand neatly into his. "Some good the restraining order did. Connor waltzed in here and just snatched her out of my arms."

"I've come to realize that with the Boyds restraining orders are useless," Quinn acknowledged. "Nothing but a worthless piece of paper that seems to piss them off even more, gives them another excuse to ramp up, to take even more drastic measures. And I'm with Baylee on this. No one's saying he's a hero. But he prevented Collin from killing Kit. And now, he's prevented Baylee from losing Sarah…"

"To a fucking monster," Dylan finished. "I don't care who the hell he is. If he were standing in front of me this minute, I'd throw my arms around his neck and kiss him on the mouth. He saved Sarah. That's all that matters to me. He didn't let Connor make it to his car with her. If he'd driven off…"

Baylee agreed, "God only knows what Connor would have done, where he would have taken her. I don't even want to think about it. Fucking rapist."

Max cocked a brow in her direction. "Rapist?"

Baylee's lips tightened, but it was too late. She'd carelessly tossed out the word. But it didn't mean she had to explain a thing unless Max forced her. "Rapist," she said quietly, jutting out her chin, daring Max to ask. "I'm thinking I'd like to pin a medal on our mysterious stranger."

When Max didn't pursue the subject, Dylan picked up Baylee's sympathetic attitude. "Right there with you on that score. Merely thanking the man isn't nearly enough."

Reese weighed in with his take. "I'd say, whatever he is, we are all grateful to a man we wouldn't recognize if we passed on the street."

At Reese's comment, Kit turned to lock eyes with Jake. Picking up on the group's mindset, she wanted them all to know, "Hey, no one's more grateful than I am. As one who got rescued, I'd have to vote 'yes' with the big kiss on the mouth thing."

Not one cop in the room suspected that the knowing look between Jake and Kit masked a deliberate agenda. As far as Kit was concerned, she had no responsibility whatsoever to tell the police she might know exactly what their Mr. X looked like.

He had, after all, come in to the Book & Bean. She'd had a conversation with him about a painting he believed resembled his late wife. Since he'd saved them from some guy the Boyds had hired to blow up the coffee shop, she decided to keep her mouth shut. No matter what he'd done in the name of a body count on his own, Kit felt she owed the man something for having saved her—twice.

And when Jake gave a curt shake to his head, he seemed to be telling her he agreed with her silence. To her, the man's description wasn't important anyway. Coming clean now with what he looked like would help no one.

But they all politely listened as Max St. John continued to make his feelings known. "Oh, for god's sake, I don't believe you people. This man is a professional killer."

"Don't doubt that," Jake agreed, never taking his eyes off Kit. "But because of him, I have Kit standing here with me now and a six-month-old baby is back with her mother. I'd say, Max, I'm officially signed on to the guy's fan club. Hell, I might even be president."

"Remember, every single thing he's done up to this point has been self-serving. Every step he's taken, his body count goes up. Nine by my count, and those are the ones we know about," Max grumbled.

Fed up listening to such talk, Max turned to leave. "This investigation will move forward. I'm headed out now to review surveillance cameras from the garage. This time your mystery hero made a mistake—a big one. In fact, that shirt the baby was wrapped in is headed to the lab. Connor Boyd's blood isn't the only DNA we hope to find there."

When Jake and Reese followed him to the elevator, Max simply waved them back and said, "I'm on it already. I'll see to it that Connor's DNA is taken at the morgue and sent to the lab for testing before we release it to the funeral home. As soon as the coroner gets me a swab, I'll send it off for comparison to the samples we took at your wife's crime scene. I've talked to the forensics people, already given them a heads-up."

Jake slapped Max on the back. "That's all I ever wanted, Max. I need to know who killed Claire. If that was Connor Boyd I can put this to rest."

When the elevator dinged and the doors opened, Max strolled inside, pushed the button. "You will, Boston. We both will. You have my word."

CHAPTER 3

Not five miles away at the Malibu Terrace Resort, a distraught Cade Boyd sat in his room at his laptop and plotted his own course for revenge.

While Collin sat on the leather sofa in the two-bedroom suite the brothers were sharing, drinking and doing lines of cocaine, Cade was stone cold sober, and—seething.

He had another goddamn funeral to plan.

The son of a bitch had gotten to Connor, taken his beloved older brother so quickly there hadn't been time to get to him to help, to save him. And that bitch had hovered over him in the ER pretending to be a doctor, pretending to help him.

But he knew better. She might fool those assholes at the hospital, but she couldn't fool him. Quinn didn't know shit about being a doctor.

It was no comfort knowing at this very moment a contingent of police and forensics investigators were stationed at the Enclave, destroying everything, tearing up what belonged to him and his family, digging up the beautiful grounds, ruining everything his parents had worked so hard for over four decades.

"Maybe we should leave the country, get the hell out of town, Cade. You know and I know the guy's coming for us. We're next. It's just a matter of time before he finds us. How about we go down to Tahiti?"

Cade thumped his brother on the head, a little side slap much like he'd seen Connor give him in the past. "Stop the drugs, Collin! Get a grip! Grow up! You aren't thinking straight. I need you sober. I need you off the booze and drugs—now. Connor isn't here to take care of everything like he always did. We have to do this for him. We aren't running anywhere."

"I know, I know," Collin agreed, as he rocked back and forth trying to convince himself there was truth in his brother's words. "But I'm scared. He's out there, waiting, watching. He seems to know our every move."

"Yeah, probably tracking us some way. I think that's how he got to Connor. Jacob says the cops want to get a court order and confiscate our vehicles, all of them. They've already got Connor's Hummer. I'm thinking it's not such a bad deal to let them have our cars. We get new ones, ones without GPS. That way we know for sure there are no devices in them to give away our location."

Cade took a deep breath, eyeing the fear in Collin's eyes before admitting, "You think I'm not scared. I am. But we can't let this all go down without putting the fear of god into Kit and Quinn. I have it all planned. And we start with the bitch that let Connor die in the ER."

When he noticed the terrible physical shape Collin was in because of the drugs he'd snorted, he decided to level with him. "You gotta stop shaking so hard, bro, clean up your act. I'm depending on you for backup." He gripped his brother's shoulders. "Connor needs you. I need you. We're both counting on you. It's now or never."

"What about Baylee? What if the baby is our niece?"

"I don't give a damn about that squalling brat. That was Connor's deal, not mine. I've got too much other stuff going on now to worry about some little bitch of a bastard that may or may not belong to our dead brother. And Dylan Burke keeps insisting the kid's his. I saw the birth certificate. Yeah, the document was amended, but that means nothing these days. For all I know, Burke could've had a change of heart, decided to own up to his own kid. Either way, it isn't worth my time."

He shook Collin's shoulders. "Come on, bro, snap out of it!"

"Okay, okay. I'll go shower. I won't let you down, Cade. You'll see I can carry my own weight in this."

Cade's rage had him plotting the demise of the woman who six years earlier had promised she loved him—for about six weeks. He sneered at that. He'd made her pay even back then for laughing at him. Since the day she'd had him arrested, he'd vowed to get his hands, once again, around her throat.

No Hollywood slut would get the better of him. Trash like Quinn had to be dealt with and disposed of in the proper manner. She'd never appreciated the fact he was practically L.A. royalty. Hadn't she known he'd had dreams of running for political office one day? His parents had assured him it was a done deal after he got a couple of more years at the firm under his belt. He had been so close to getting what he wanted, and now…

Quinn Tyler had ruined everything. She'd even let his brother die.

He thought back to how his life had gone downhill after the arrest for domestic violence. Even though his father had convinced Quinn to drop the charges, he'd been disappointed in him. His mother had simply slapped him across the face for his stupidity at not finishing the job and leaving Quinn alive to file charges.

He wouldn't make the same mistake twice.

He didn't know how he could have been so wrong in thinking Quinn cared about him. But it was a miscalculation he had not made since.

He would take care of her now, though, once and for all. He just needed to look up what he needed to know on the Internet.

He should have finished her years ago when he'd had the chance. Recalling what it had felt like to be inside her, what it felt like to have his hands around her throat, he went hard.

Like the other ones, he thought now.

The ones no one knew about.

⚛ ⚛ ⚛ ⚛ ⚛

As things wound down in the waiting room, as cops began to find better places to go than hassling a beaten-up single mother, Baylee got everyone's attention. "Okay, Tanya is willing to sit with Dad for a while. I'm taking Sarah and going back to Dylan's, getting something to eat, and then sleeping for about twelve hours. You're all welcome to follow us home for food."

Dylan wiggled his eyebrows up and down. "But don't. We'll let you know when we're in the mood for company, say, maybe in a couple of months, around August."

Reese smiled affably at his friend. Dylan had blood on his shirt, no doubt Connor's blood. No one deserved a breather from all of this more than Dylan and Baylee did.

"Understandable, but just remember, Dylan, there are two more Boyds out there who have it in for all of us." He thought again about Cade's threat.

"So don't drop your guard," Reese reminded as he watched Quinn say goodbye to little Sarah and realized that in another two years or so, the woman would make a helluva pediatrician.

And Jake tossed in for good measure, "Kit and I are still scheduled to testify against Collin on kidnapping charges. He'll do his best to make sure that doesn't happen. He may not be very bright, but that doesn't make him any less dangerous. They hired someone to try and blow up the Book & Bean. That person could still be out there…waiting to make his move."

"I know, I know. But is it too much to ask for one damn night where Baylee isn't scared out of her mind." With that, Dylan winked. "She doesn't know it yet," he said as he shot a glance toward Baylee saying her goodbyes to Tanya. "But I am taking her to an undisclosed location where we plan to get all the sleep she wants and some much needed downtime. How about we meet up tomorrow and take a look at this whole mess with fresh eyes?"

"Sounds good," Reese agreed as he realized it was time for him to make his move toward the doctor. She faced three weeks of suspension. Did the others know about that yet? They didn't act like they had a clue, mainly because with everything else going on Quinn hadn't seen fit to come clean and disclose the seriousness of what had happened downstairs with Cade.

Odd, he thought now. But then he'd spent more than a few conflicting moments over the last months mulling over why she seemed so unwilling to share any personal tidbits about herself to anyone, least of all to him.

But not letting her friends in on the scene in the ER seemed—off.

He knew one thing, though. The woman would surely go crazy with that much time on her hands. Reese knew exactly which buttons to push where Quinn was concerned. He hadn't been studying her for the past two months to go brain dead now.

He decided to take on the doctor, one on one.

When she ambled back over to where he stood, he told her simply, "You look wiped, Tyler. Why don't we go get some dinner? Celebrate our truce."

"Why?"

Skeptical to the very end, Reese decided. "Because I have an angle on how to get you reinstated. Did they mention taking you before the review board?"

"Yeah, I'll have to answer a bunch of stupid questions. And won't that be a delightful way for them to grill me— about nothing!" Even she recognized when she was backed into a corner and needed all the support she could muster. Wasn't it good to show the review board she had a lawyer on her side?

She sighed in frustration. "All right, it's about time one of your kind did something constructive instead of wreak havoc on the public filing useless restraining orders and petitions."

With that, she gave him her sweetest smile and headed to the elevators.

As he watched her walk away, Reese decided he could get used to that hundred-watt smile when she decided to send it his way, even if it had been totally insincere. He reminded himself he wasn't completely without appeal to the opposite sex. In fact, most women found him easy to talk to, a good dancer, generous to a fault on a date, an all-around engaging guy.

So why did he have to work his ass off to get Quinn Tyler to give him a break?

⚭ ⚭ ⚭ ⚭ ⚭

At a restaurant in Marina Del Rey over pan-seared salmon, Reese and Quinn took their newfound accord and sat outside on the patio under a patch of stars with a night view of the moon glistening on the water. Sharing a bottle of merlot they chatted, all the while listening to gentle waves slap against the concrete pilings below them near the waterfront.

It wasn't the first meal they'd shared, but it might have been the first solid hour they hadn't spent sniping at one another.

"There's a better chance of fighting your suspension if they think you've hired a lawyer." His eyes twinkled with amusement and his grin spread. He almost loved yanking her chain as much as she did his.

Those dark almond eyes of Quinn's grew wider. "Then I expect you to use any angle. Do you need a retainer or something?"

He cracked up with laughter. "Define 'or something.'"

Those chocolate eyes flashed with temper. She tossed the paper coaster at his head. "Bite me."

"Absolutely." He picked up her hand and nibbled a couple of fingers. "I'll start here and work myself down. How would that be?"

It suddenly got very hot on the patio. "You like to use that mouth of yours—a lot."

He chuckled. "Relax, Quinn. I'll press our advantage until the other side shouts uncle. That's what I do. And I'm good at it."

She made a derisive sound and looked out into the blackness of ocean meeting night sky. "I've had enough of lawyers to last a lifetime."

When she finally looked over at him again, she propped her chin in her hand and groaned, "The thing is I was just getting started, finally getting over that lump of nerves every time I walked into the ER, just at that point where I'd stopped being intimidated by Mendenhall every time he asked me a question.

"I was just getting comfortable leading rounds, too. And now, I'm out on my ass thanks to a rich boy who brought his temper tantrum to my public workplace. Ah, well, what am I so mad about anyway? A vacation is what it is. Maybe I'll use the time to go to a spa and get one of those fancy masks put all over my face, a facial, or a pedicure, or maybe I'll schedule me one of those indulgent mud baths."

Reese didn't buy her attitude for a minute. In the short time he'd known Quinn Tyler, she had no more chance of relaxing, let alone spending time inside a spa, than she did playing wide receiver for the Raiders. "And do you like mud baths?"

"I don't know. That's the thing, I might. I could get use to all the pampering they do there. I could certainly use a massage. Kit and Baylee and I keep promising ourselves to take a run at one. Maybe we'll see how the other half lives."

"My sister certainly loves going to one."

"There you go."

As much as he hated to put an end to the first banter they'd shared without ripping into each other, he bluntly asked, "Quinn, aren't you worried about what Cade said in the ER?"

"Of course I am. I'd be crazy as a loon not to be. But at this point, what options do I have? Another restraining order?" She snorted. "Come on, Reese. Is that the best you can do? It's a waste of paper."

Reese ignored the dig and asked, "What happened between you two?"

She took several calming breaths to keep herself from getting worked up about it. She picked up her wine, took not a sip but rather a gulp as if she found courage in the liquid enough to talk about it.

"He beat the crap out of me. There, is that what you wanted to know? Kit and Baylee had warned me, multiple times. But he had this way about him back then. At the time he made me feel so...special." She'd been nineteen and looking for that certain someone who made her feel as if the universe revolved around her for the very first time in her life. She'd been incredibly inexperienced and naïve about men and relationships.

That much she could admit now.

She shook her head. "He was generous to a fault, always bringing me little cards and gifts, even sending me flowers. He gave me the full court press. He was the first guy to show me any real attention, like maybe I was his world. And I fell for it. It was an act, of course. But after two months of saying no, one day, I suddenly said yes. When Kit found out, I thought she was never going to speak to me again, even thought she might pack up and move out of our apartment; she was that upset. But at the time I honestly thought Cade might be the one, you know." She sighed audibly. It sounded so insane now.

"That lasted six weeks, lasted until one night we were at his place, inside The Enclave. We'd had a lovely dinner prepared by his personal chef. One minute we were discussing which movie to go see. The next, out of the blue, he thought I'd laughed at him about something. The next thing I knew, he picked me up and threw me against the wall. After that, he hauled off and slapped me, grabbed me around the throat. I went down for the count." She paused, remembering the nightmarish scene.

Reese flinched. Just thinking about Cade having his hands around her throat had him wanting to rearrange the man's face. And he'd never considered himself to be a violent sort, had never been the jealous type either, but now he had to admit this might be a different facet to his personality.

He didn't believe in hitting a woman, couldn't imagine doing so. He'd seen too many bruised and battered faces at the women's shelters early in his career when he'd counseled wives and girlfriends who were hiding there trying to find the legal means to leave behind a violent home life.

Quinn went on before she lost her nerve. "I tried to hit him back. He pushed me down face first on the bed. I was wearing a short skirt at the time. He ripped off my underwear, started to…" She shifted gears.

"Because I had an idea of what he planned to do, I kicked my legs out, caused him to fall back enough to let go. As soon as he hit the floor, I got up and started running. But he caught me by the hair and dragged me backward. He threw me around some more, knocked me into a wall face first. Before I knew what was happening, I was on the floor again and his hands were around my throat. I guess I'd been screaming down the house because one of his cousins, Adam Gatz I think it was, came running in and pulled Cade off me. I got out of there and never looked back."

"This is the first time you've shared those kinds of details with anyone except the police, am I right?"

Her mouth dropped open. "How did you know that?"

"Doesn't matter. Go on, I didn't mean to interrupt."

"I'm convinced if Adam hadn't shown up when he did, Cade would have killed me. I pressed charges. And yes, I told the police everything. Later, the son of a bitch tried to butter me up with flowers and presents for several weeks afterward. I sent the gifts back, threw the flowers in the trash."

"Jesus, Quinn." Reese reached across the table and took her hand in his. For the second time in as many hours, she left it rest there.

"It took me about six months to stop remembering how it felt when he had his hands around my throat, about how he might have finished me off right then and there if Adam hadn't shown up to stop him. That's why I got a restraining order against him."

"Was he prosecuted?"

She looked away, dropped her eyes to the floor. "Sumner Boyd talked me out of going through with it."

Reese cocked his head. "You know that's never the answer."

"Of course I do. But I have to admit, I was scared of him. I told Sumner if I dropped the charges I wanted assurance Cade would never come near me again."

Reese lifted a brow. "And? How could Sumner Boyd make that kind of assurance and have you of all people believe it?"

"Maybe because I refused to cancel the restraining order. I wanted it to remain in effect. Plus, I demanded Cade make a deposition to a police officer with no ties to the Boyds that could be kept on file in case he got—any ideas about revisiting our brief time together."

Impressed, he said, "Smart girl."

"The strategy worked until recently. "

"What about taking out another TRO?" He put up a hand in a gesture that said he knew she'd object. "I know it didn't work for Kit and Baylee. But getting one makes it official. You already know it's the one thing that makes the authorities aware of the situation through proper channels. I'll take care of it."

She put her head in her hands. "Thanks. Since this afternoon, my life went from normal to this mess thanks to Cade. Up until today I was pretty much concerned with Kit and Baylee's situation, not mine. But Cade has a way of weaseling himself back into my life whenever he finds a crack in the door."

"Then we need to weasel him right out."

Amusement flickered in her eyes. "Aren't you going to offer to beat him up again? I could seriously get on board with that."

"I could, but I'd rather see him in San Quentin for about twenty years."

"I can't say I haven't dreamed about that myself. God, Reese, you're so calm, cool, and collected all the time, like you've never had a hair out of place before. I envy that."

Just to show her he wasn't as calm as she thought, he reached over, grabbed her chin, and covered her mouth.

He meant the kiss to be light and feathery and quick. Yet at the first taste he realized nothing about Quinn's mouth made him want to rush. Instead, he teased her lips open, deepened the kiss. In no time, the light press of lips became a ball of heat that punched a hole in his system.

Caught up in the warmth, Quinn simply surrendered to his onslaught. She whooshed out a breath. "Is that mouth legal?"

He chuckled. "Tyler, I've wanted to do that ever since the Sunday afternoon you walked into Kit's hospital room. But you were too busy railing on me."

"That day I could see through your veneer, Reese. You didn't approve of Kit, it showed. And it pissed me off considerably. You were a..."

"Lawyer," he concluded.

"A horse's ass," she corrected, her lips curving in playful scorn.

He poured her another glass of merlot. "I've taken a lot of crap from you these last few weeks. And yeah, I was skeptical about Kit at the time. If you'd known the money-hungry Claire Boston, you'd have felt the same way about any woman a friend was obviously falling for—and fast. Way too fast."

"In your opinion it was fast. Doesn't mean it was. You do know those two have known each other since she was a kid."

"Sure, but I didn't know the grown woman. For all I knew she could've turned into a top ten most-wanted grifter."

Quinn shook her head. "You thought Kit was after Jake's money? Get real. Kit loved the guy before he took his company gold, before he made a fortune. She cared for him, loved him for *who* he is, not for what he has."

"I know that now, but I didn't know it then. Besides, I've seen you cynical plenty times yourself, holding that cool veneer together in your own way. At least you were that day."

But there was a time she hadn't known to project a cool veneer or perfect her cynical nature. Her early years had been chaotic and pathetic. "Now maybe, but it wasn't always like that. Let me ask you something. What were your parents like growing up, Reese? Did you have a stable home life? Were you able to eat regularly? Did your mother read to you at bedtime?"

He lowered his eyes for a moment before meeting hers again. "Yes to all that."

"That's what I thought. People who've lived Norman Rockwell childhoods like you couldn't possibly understand what it's like to grow up the way Kit, Baylee, and I did. Never knowing if that instability you faced everyday might get worse with just one little reaction on your part, the *wrong* response. Never knowing if you might get a backhand for a slip of the tongue. Suffice to say the three of us have had our—challenges over the years."

She looked into those piercing gray eyes. "You think you know most of it because of the last two months, but you don't know a thing about it. Don't presume to know."

He thought back to the conversation he'd had with Kit. She'd given him the short story about Quinn's parents. Like the fact she'd never had a real relationship with her father, Nick Tyler, the rock legend and the lead singer for the Irish band Shatter. Not only that, but her mother, the flakey artist Ella Canyon, had pretty much come and gone in her life without sticking around for very long, either.

Reese picked up his wine glass, motioned for her to go on. "So tell me. No one's stopping me from knowing the real Quinn Tyler but you. Remember, I listened to Kit have to go on record about her abuse—in detail. Listening to her take me through the cruelty she endured in that Beverly Hills horror chamber Alana called a house was painful. Was living with your stepfather as traumatic as Kit's living with Alana Stevens?"

She eyed him over her glass. "I see Kit's infamous loose lips have been flapping in the wind again. What else do you think you know about me, Reese? Because I can assure you there are varying degrees of trauma."

He sighed. Sometime during the last two minutes the prickly pear had shown up. "Look, Kit simply took five minutes to try and explain to me why you hate my profession so much. I know Tyler's lawyers pretty much handled any communication you tried to have with him over the years. And that your mother was never around much. Don't beat Kit up because she was trying to explain away your rude behavior at the time."

She took another sip of wine, set down her glass. "Okay, that's fair enough." She put a fist under her chin as if contemplating whether or not she should tell him anything. She never talked about those neglectful childhood years before she came to live in Beverly Hills. Ever. After all, what was the point?

Kit and Baylee were the only two people on earth who knew her life story. But even they didn't know a hundred percent because she'd locked those memories away so deep down she didn't like going there, especially with a lawyer, and particularly not tonight after the kind of day she'd had.

But staring at the man sitting next to her, she supposed he did deserve some type of explanation.

"I was a financial responsibility to Nick Tyler, nothing more. Look, my early years were kind of messed up. When life finally settled down for me, everything I needed, everything I wanted from my sperm donor father had to go through a ridiculous array of tedious channels. The stuffy barristers obviously had their client's best interests at heart, certainly not that of a child. I got sick and tired over the years of listening to their excuses. At some point, he eventually started owning up to his responsibility and sent the checks each month. At least I assumed he did. I certainly never saw much money floating my way aimed just for me."

She took another sip of wine. "His lawyers must have hit the stall button plenty of times. And then when he did cough it up, what money Ella didn't use to snort up her nose, she spent shopping on Rodeo Drive like a crack whore, which she was, by the way.

"But if I happened to need something extra for school or if I'd outgrown my two pairs of jeans, those extra requirements had to be put in writing—and justified. Hoops had to be jumped through. When I was younger, around ten or so, I was still in the hopeful stage, that naïve kid daydreaming about the rock star they said had fathered me, thinking he might be curious enough to want to come see his daughter."

She snorted. "Instead I got letters from the lawyers making up excuses why he couldn't come for a visit. I'd make him a card on Father's Day and Christmas then wait for him to get in touch. At the very least I thought he'd respond with a card, write a one-line sentence."

She set her glass down. "What I got was a big fat nothing for my trouble, nada from Nick-fucking-Tyler.

"Then when Ella married his record producer I was about eight. Our lives changed dramatically after that. We moved to Beverly Hills after years of living in the car or whatever rundown cheap motel she could find where she could pick up a few extra dollars cleaning out rooms or hustling johns. Sometimes she'd be so strung out from the snow, she couldn't function. When that happened..."

She threw out a sigh. "You see, Reese, before Beverly Hills, Ella hooked, with some regularity, too. I was never sure exactly where we'd spend the night. We might crash at some friend's house in the valley, or maybe on the couch somewhere in Riverside, or maybe sleep in the car near the beach. I never knew what to expect until it got dark."

Reese looked at her as if she might be making this up just for him, maybe playing him. But gauging her demeanor, her huge chocolate eyes said it all. She was serious. Kit hadn't mentioned any of this to him. Then he realized Kit, by her own admission, knew nothing solid about Quinn's life before she'd arrived in Beverly Hills.

"Why in the world would Nick Tyler's daughter be living hand-to-mouth with a hooker if she were getting monthly checks of support from his lawyers?"

"Good question, lawyer Brennan, and if you happen to find out that answer from Mr. Rock Star Legend, you be sure and let me know, okay? Because I always suspected it was during his stall session fully supported by his lawyers. But I've wondered that very thing for most of my life. I even fired off a letter once asking. I was about fifteen then, rebellious as hell. I asked where all the bastards had been those first eight years of my life when I was lucky to get a peanut butter and jelly sandwich for supper."

She tossed back her head and laughed. "Naturally there was no response."

She sucked in a breath. "Those early years were the worst though. After we came to live with Ross Jennetti at least I got to go to school regularly. No more going hungry at night either."

She picked up her glass and made an air toast. "I'll say one thing for good old Ross, he always kept a damn fine cook on staff that could and did make delicious food. I used to hoard the food just in case I ever had to get out of there in a hurry."

Reese shook his head, mortified. Something wasn't adding up. "Why would you have to leave in a hurry?"

She whooshed out a laugh. "Spoken like a man who has never lived amidst daily turmoil."

"That's unconscionable for Nick Tyler's daughter to be living such a precarious existence. The man's worth millions." Not for the first time Reese realized how much Kit, Baylee, and Quinn had overcome in their lives.

Living in Beverly Hills hadn't afforded any of them with stability or the luxuries associated with the address. "You and your friends have managed to rise above all of that."

That was an understatement. She wondered if he realized just how much. "That's right. And the Boyds are just one more thing the three of us have to conquer—together."

"You can't do it by yourself."

"That's where you're wrong. I've been doing things by myself my entire life. With the help of the only family I've ever really known, of course. My sisters, maybe not by blood, but by choice, our choice. Kit and Baylee are my family, my true family. And we've been on our own for a long time now, Reese. The three of us moved in together at sixteen. Even before that we were a tight unit. And I'm not used to being a unit with anyone else."

Before he could say anything she went on, "Which brings me to a question for you, what exactly are you looking for here, Reese? Because I recognize you're putting the moves on me. I'm not sure what you expect, either. Go out? Sure. We could go see a movie. Is that still part of date night? Having a relationship? Now that's totally different. Resident doctors don't have a lot of downtime for anything serious. So I tend to avoid anything long-term."

She wasn't even sure what a serious relationship looked like, let alone long-term. She bit her lip, took another sip of wine. "Not to mention one with a lawyer." When she noted that questioning look on his face, she added, "Although there are times when you do get me all jazzed."

His lips curved. "There's not a single doubt in me, Quinn, that I couldn't have you jazzed and on your back in record time. Give me an hour and you'll be at my mercy." He toyed with her fingers before he said, "What I'm looking for is to get to know you better. Is that so difficult to understand?"

She rolled her eyes. "Pair up?" She laughed. "Now that is *so* lame."

"Good to know you aren't after jumping my bones then."

"Now see, saying stuff like that will definitely get you a certain amount of play time."

"How much play time?"

"We hit the sheets with no intent of getting serious, I'm in. Residents don't make the best people to date. But we could get to know each other, sure. After all, we've got this Boyd thing to ride out, make sure our friends don't end up dead. Just don't expect too much from me, Reese. I want to do well as a resident. That's priority one. I'm not blowing this opportunity for anyone. That is as soon as I get the damned suspension behind me and get reinstated."

Maybe it was ego, but he felt like telling her he didn't mind a challenge and she had definitely been more of one these past two months than any other woman since Brie Peterson in his first year of law. Brie had been a prickly pear, too.

But since he watched Quinn's eyes light up every time she talked about anything to do with medicine, he went another way instead. "Why a pediatrician, Quinn?" When she gave him a cutting look, he shrugged and said, "Kit mentioned it."

"I like taking care of kids. They are usually the innocent ones who get the short end of the proverbial stick when it comes to the circumstances in life. They get dumped on whenever things take a turn for the worse. And the worse can be pretty damned ugly."

"Private practice?"

"Yeah, but not Beverly Hills. I want to open my own clinic where all kids from all walks of life can get treatment when their parents can't afford things like shots, stitches, medicine for an ear infection, stuff like that."

He reached to take her hand. "Then let's get this Boyd business behind you and focus on getting you back on duty."

"What about you, Reese? Why law?"

"My father was a lawyer." It was said simply and without further clarification.

"And?"

"He died, last year of law school. Sudden heart attack. The plan had been for father and son to practice law together. I'd looked forward to doing that. Then..." Somewhere inside, his own heart wrenched a little just thinking about the loss he'd never quite adjusted to.

"I'm sorry, Reese. You loved him. It shows in your eyes. And after all these years, you still miss him."

No one had ever picked up on that little chunk about him before. He titled his head toward the doc, moved in to take her mouth again. This time he moved slower, lingered longer. She tasted like the sweet merlot, so he took the time to tug at her lower lip until he got a nice little moan out of her.

"You do that very well."

"You know what they say, practice makes perfect."

"Did I say perfect? Very well is a distant second to perfect. You've got an ego there, Brennan."

He shook his head. "Parsing words again. Such a hard-ass, Tyler."

She grinned as they got up to leave. "Are you kidding? I'm a sweetheart."

"Prove it."

As soon as they got outside, she grabbed his jacket by the lapels and kissed him hard on the mouth. A burst of white heat ramped up. The kiss went on, a tonsil-dive that turned red-hot.

Reese nipped her around the waist and brought her closer, whispered in her ear, "Wanna make out in the parking lot, Tyler, and show me whatcha got?"

She sneaked out a giggle, feeling like a fifteen-year-old teen on her first date. While he playfully backed her in the direction of her car, his arms kept her wrapped up. Meanwhile their mouths continued a steamy byplay.

As soon as they reached her little red Miata, Reese suddenly lifted her off her feet, plopped her down on the fender of the car. He slid in between her legs and bent his head to cover her mouth again.

Quinn parted her lips, met the assault with a force of her own. The mating of tongues took her on a slow path inside a furnace. Her belly danced with lust. She felt him harden like iron.

"Let me take you to bed," he whispered as he trailed little nips and bites down her jaw.

"Hmm, okay. Let's get out of here."

"How about I follow you home?"

"We could go to your place."

"Westlake Village? Too far away," he muttered, nibbling that tender spot under her ear.

She tilted her head, giving him better access, and said, "Since you've been so un-Reese-like all night *and* not so annoying, I guess my place *is* closer. Wherever, let's just get someplace. I want you; Reese." Her hands crawled up his chest in anticipation.

With Cade's earlier threat on his mind and after listening to Quinn's account of what he'd done to her, Reese already planned on spending the night wherever they ended up. He also knew they had to figure out a way to put an end to the Boyd madness once and for all. Even though he believed in the law with all his heart, Reese wasn't a delusional man.

He knew a restraining order at this point would do little to impede Cade or Collin's momentum into further malice.

But now was not the time to mention that to Quinn. She looked as relaxed as he'd ever seen her. He intended to do everything in his power to keep her that way for as long as he could.

Instead of bringing up Cade, he prompted, "Then by all means, let's get the hell out of here. I'll follow you home."

CHAPTER 4

Cade and Collin crawled out of the Mercedes at the same time.

One glance at his brother told Cade that Collin was one hundred percent on board now with the plan. He had to be.

Tonight would be a simple but quick strike. If she happened to be home, together as brothers they'd finally take care of her. If she weren't, then this little raid would, at the very least, make a statement, pay her back for her part in what had happened to Connor.

The way Cade saw it, the sneak attack was a win-win.

But as he approached Quinn's building from the alleyway, he needed to find out for certain if she were home. Once out of the car, Cade peered into the rear entrance of the parking garage and scanned the dimly lit area. Her Miata wasn't parked in its dedicated spot.

There had been no light coming from her condo either. At least from here, the place looked dark. But if he got lucky and she happened to be in bed asleep, he'd send Collin out in the hallway to keep lookout and have a little fun with her.

Gripping the wrench he'd brought, he took the stairs two at a time up to the second level, walked down a narrow hallway as if he knew exactly where he was going. Because he did know, he soon found himself standing in front of Quinn's front door. The fact that she could she still be living in this dump after so many years was only one reason the woman had proved to be unworthy of him. Like so many other things, she had simply refused to do anything to present that certain image that came with being a Boyd.

With gloved hands, ignoring Collin's nervousness behind him, he immediately began the attempt to jimmy the lock. As soon as he heard the lock pop, he pushed the door open and stepped inside.

He quickly realized she wasn't at home.

"Find a candle," Cade ordered his brother. "Any candle will work."

"Sure," Collin assured him, heading off in the direction of the bedroom.

Cade, on the other hand, headed to the kitchen where he found the tiny laundry room with a compact washer and dryer combination. He wedged himself into the smidgen of space and with the wrench began to unhook the gas connection to the dryer.

The deed took under five minutes. He knew he'd been successful when he smelled the odor of gas.

"Found one," Collin assured Cade when they met up in the kitchen.

"Good. Set it on that coffee table over there and light it."

"You gettin' romantic all of a sudden?" Collin remarked, laughing as he struck a match to the wick. The candle flicked to flame.

"Step on it, you fool. This place will be toast in less than nine minutes. Let's get out of here."

With that, Collin moved his ass toward the front door. "If this works, we could do the same thing to get rid of Boston and Kit. They're living in that big old Victorian on the outskirts of San Madrid. It's called Crandall House. I looked it up on the Internet. We could be there in under an hour, in and out of that place before anyone knew what hit them."

"Soon, Collin, but not tonight," Cade promised his brother, as they scurried down the darkened hallway like a couple of rats and out into the warm summer night.

&&&&&

For weeks, Trevor had kept the Boyd brothers under surveillance, mainly by the GPS tracking devices he'd put under their vehicles. And he'd listened to their plotting from a distance via the bugs he'd planted inside their houses. So when the cops had shown up with a warrant, he'd listened to that byplay as well. Even now they were still in the process of turning the Enclave upside down as they treated the place like a crime scene.

Since they'd found three bodies on the property, the police were busy going over every inch of the place, room by room, grid by grid. So he'd known the minute they had discovered each of the listening devices he'd planted.

Not a single one remained intact.

The cops had also confiscated the brothers' cars, which meant the GPS tracking devices were now useless.

He was down to tracking their cell phone usage.

It was because of that annoying development he had no idea where Cade and Collin had crawled off tonight since he'd had a previous engagement earlier in the day with their brother, Connor.

Leave it to the local cops to get in his way and screw everything up, he thought, mildly irritated. He shook his head, knowing it couldn't be helped. It was only a matter of time before the cops finally got around to getting a court order for their cell phones. It had taken months but it seemed the police finally had the Boyd brothers in their sights. He supposed he had to be grateful for that, even if the cops were two steps behind.

For now, though, he knew the brothers had a habit of spending money like drunken sailors on shore leave. They had expensive tastes in everything, frequenting all the upscale places within a fifty-mile radius of Malibu. They fancied quality-cut cocaine. Trevor had even located their supplier.

Because the cops were part of this now, it might take a little more work on his part, might be a little more difficult and time consuming, but he was determined to get to them first. Right now, he could do nothing less than keep up with their cell phone usage and their credit card purchases.

That's how he had known where Connor was, known he was stalking Baylee, and the rest could be chalked up to being in the right place at the right time. Trevor didn't particularly care how anyone sized up what had happened to Connor. Baylee's problem had been eliminated. End of story. Trevor was used to elimination, used to killing people, especially people like Connor. He'd already lived what felt like a lifetime of judging character.

He and Noah never accepted assignments they hadn't first checked out—in detail. It was a pact they had made and stuck to before they ever started in the business. Getting rid of people like Connor had been second nature to him for so long he didn't even think twice about it anymore, especially since he'd arrived in L.A.

There had been a time he'd lived a normal life with a wife and child, a life before the stars aligned and it had all been taken away from him in the blink of an eye. During the worst time of his life, Noah Parker had befriended him, befriended an angry, deeply enraged man and set his life on a different course altogether.

Not a better course, he thought now, just different, the elimination kind of different. He'd taken his rage and found a purpose again.

Who knew there were outlets willing to pay top dollar for a pissed-off widower where his fury could be put to good use?

Assassins were wanted the world over, needed by governments and private parties around the globe. Work had always been readily available. But he never took an assignment that he didn't feel was warranted, a job where elimination, in his view, would make the world a better place.

The philosopher inside him at work again, he mused.

At least that's what he had told himself. He had no grand illusions of what he was or what he wasn't. All he knew or cared about right now was ending the evil that had begun so long ago, evil that had put Noah's life on the same course as his.

In his mind, putting an end to Cade and Collin once and for all was the only thing that made any sense, no matter what price he had to pay.

From the info he'd gathered out of their own mouths and the personal accounts he'd hacked into over the last several months, he had a pretty good idea of the regular choices they made. That had led him to the Terrace Resort and its upscale bar, a favored place they liked to frequent where they could hook up with high class call girls.

If Trevor had any complaints about Los Angeles, it was the fact that available parking spaces were damned near impossible to find. Because of that, he pulled up near the Resort as close as he could get. The distance was far enough away so that no one would suspect he was there to keep an eye on the valet area and the front lobby.

His intent was to catch sight of Cade or Collin or both when they entered the hotel or handed off the keys to the valet. He couldn't cover all the doors to the hotel, of course, but knowing the brothers as he did, they would need to make an entrance. And that meant they would never use self-parking.

If by some chance they didn't show up here at the resort, he would be forced to go to Plan B.

☙☙☙☙☙

On the drive to her condo, Quinn had never felt more alone. In one short afternoon Cade had managed to pull the rug out from everything she'd worked so hard to get. What if this suspension became permanent? What if it prevented her from achieving her goal of becoming a pediatrician and opening up the clinic she'd planned? What if he managed to ruin everything she'd ever wanted?

She tamped down the urge to pick up her cell and call Kit or Baylee, pour out her feelings, get things off her chest. She didn't doubt for a minute either one of them wouldn't take the time to talk her down, talk her out of this pity party.

But after what Baylee been through today, the only thing she needed tonight was Dylan. And Kit, she had her own problems dealing with the upcoming hearing. Neither could let down their guards for a minute.

After all, they didn't even know she'd been suspended. She'd felt no need to add that layer to Baylee's distress while she was grilled by St. John earlier at the hospital.

Quinn wasn't stupid. She knew the dynamics had changed for both of her friends. Kit had Jake now. Things had changed for Baylee, too. Dylan wasn't going anywhere. She could see that tonight at the hospital.

While Quinn could be ecstatic for her friends, she seemed to be teetering on the edge of a precipice, ready to fall off. The suspension had her feeling as if she'd lost something very, very precious, something she'd wanted since—forever. She wasn't absolutely certain she could ever get it back, either.

It was that uncertainty that had her wondering what would happen to Mrs. Covington, a breast cancer patient she treated on occasion, or Mr. Sorenson, a man whose stomach cancer was in the final stages, or little Cassidy, a seven-year-old girl suffering from leukemia. The patients she cared about might be gone before she could set foot in the hospital again.

Three weeks for her would surely feel like an eternity.

She took a deep breath and tried to calm down. Could Reese really work some kind of legal magic and get her job back?

She wasn't used to relying on anyone but herself. She'd never been good at getting her hopes up. Too many of her early years had been mired in disappointment for that. She'd learned long ago promises were simply words strung together, usually made to placate a frightened, whimpering kid.

She had to admit now she'd spent plenty of those early years in fear mode. After all, a five-year-old never knew exactly what one of Ella's hyped-up, strung-out johns might do when they got fed up listening to a whiny, hungry child.

She'd made damn sure she didn't complain for long.

When she got to her building, a renovated, three-story rectangular strip of art deco limestone built in the '40s during the post-World War II era, she glanced in the rear view mirror to make sure Reese was still following her.

Spotting his sporty Lexus 600, a bolt of lust tingled in her belly that had her anticipating getting him out of that tailored suit. She rolled down the window and motioned for him to find a parking space on the street while she made the turn into a narrow drive-up that led to the underground parking garage. She pulled the Miata up to the card-reader and swiped her card. The gate went up.

She was about to press on the gas to pull forward, to go inside the garage a short ten feet away, when an explosion belched out debris onto the front windshield. The blast was so fierce it rocked her car.

This was no earthquake. Frantic, she threw the gear into Reverse and hit the gas.

About that time, she heard another boom that sent more fragments flying through the air. Fire and smoke engulfed the underground parking area and what was left of her beautiful old building.

Still shaking, she parked the car at the curb and threw open the door. Reese came running toward her. They met in the middle of the street and stood there watching orange flames climb into the night sky. At least they did for a stunned minute. Mesmerized by the fiery scene, they stood rooted to the spot as approaching sirens wailed in the distance.

But then, both Reese and Quinn, along with several neighbors who ran up to help, began to approach the inferno for any entrance into the burning apartments. As they got closer, though, another blast knocked them back.

Reluctantly, they had to give ground. Getting inside now would be a death trap.

Reese spotted a few stragglers, a few tenants, coughing and hacking their way through the wall of smoke and rubble. He grabbed Quinn's arm and pointed.

She let out a whoop of delight. "That's Mrs. Channing who lives on the first floor. She's got her three cats in her arms."

Reese and Quinn got to her about the time Mrs. Channing dropped to the ground, collapsing in a heap.

A fleeting look at her sixty-year-old neighbor had her instincts kicking in. Quinn went into doctor mode. By that time, the first ladder truck roared up. Firemen jumped off, swinging into action, grabbing and unrolling hoses to get water flowing onto the orange blaze. But in a matter of minutes the flames had already reached a staggering sixty feet in height.

Reese heard them radio for more units. And no wonder, he thought as he surveyed the damage. What had been a quiet tree-lined, residential neighborhood just minutes earlier, now looked like a bomb had detonated there.

With borrowed first aid supplies from the EMTs, Reese became Quinn's field assistant. They waded into the chaos like warriors on a mission. Whenever she said lift, Reese lifted. When she snapped out instructions about slings or compresses, Reese did his best to comply.

If Quinn had thought she'd seen everything in the ER, this was carnage beyond her comprehension. The street, the yard, any level surface became a triage.

Lawyer and first-year resident worked as a team, along with a dozen or so good-hearted bystanders, as they aided the paramedics with diagnoses and sorted out the severely injured and burned from the walking wounded.

For the next several hours, Quinn applied antiseptic cream to burned arms and legs, wrapped them in bandages, applied compresses, even treated head wounds and gaping cuts on arms and legs. She gave comfort to anyone who needed it. It didn't take long to realize neighbor children she'd watched grow up from toddlers to preschoolers were dealing with a combination of injuries from burns to broken limbs. Some of her neighbors were in shock at realizing they were now homeless.

Hours later, firefighters finally managed to get the fire to die down to a smoldering black searing mass. But the body count had risen: five verified dead so far, and investigators were still digging through the rubble.

Around four-fifteen, Reese took one final look around, surveyed the ruins of the building, the chaos in the street, and realized they had done all they could do.

Most of the seriously injured had long been transported to the hospital hours earlier. Those that remained had been bandaged at the scene and were now off to stay with relatives or friends. For those that didn't have anyone to stay with, the Red Cross had already shown up and provided them with hotel vouchers.

At the first good break, Reese tugged Quinn toward his car and announced, "You're done, exhausted. You need sleep. Come with me."

She didn't argue as he opened the car door and she all but fell into the passenger seat. "I should probably move my car."

"Done already."

She cocked her head his way and declared, "You know, Reese, you aren't nearly as obnoxious as most attorneys."

"Well, gosh, thanks. I'm moved."

She shot him a weary smile. "Do you think I could get sued for treating those people back there after getting suspended? It seemed like days ago Mendenhall gave me the boot."

"Nah, I think you're safe."

"Damn it, I really had my heart on getting you out of your clothes tonight."

"Now you tell me. Wait, I'm so tired I don't know what I'm saying. Getting you out of your clothes was supposed to be my mission for the night."

At this time of morning there wasn't much traffic and the drive to Westlake Village took no more than twenty minutes. The entire trip, though, Reese kept a vigil eye in the rear view mirror, wondering if Cade might be out there somewhere following them.

Not one to jump to conclusions, he'd already decided the person responsible for all the suffering he'd witnessed firsthand was Cade Boyd. Somehow the man had found a way to blow up that building and take five lives, maybe even more, in the process. And the realization that the woman sitting next to him could have been one of the dead had his gut tightening.

About halfway en route to his house, Quinn nodded off.

When he made the turn onto the street where he lived, he did two passes just in case they'd been followed. Deciding the coast was clear, he finally pulled the car into his garage. She didn't wake up when he shut off the engine, or when he picked her up and carried her inside to his bedroom. Her hair and clothes smelled like smoke. She had soot and grease and grime on her face and arms. But to him as he stared down at Quinn Tyler, the woman was still stunning.

The minute he put her down on the bed, she stirred a little and tried to sit up.

"You want a shower or sleep? Your choice."

Barely audible, she replied, "A shower would be great, but I'm so tired, Reese."

"Sleep it is then. But you need to get out of your clothes. They reek."

"'Kay." Without further prodding, she simply yanked off her shirt, leaving him to stare at the simple white cotton bra and all that smooth, creamy skin beneath. She unzipped her pants and Reese offered, "Let me take your shoes off first."

"'Kay."

He knelt down at her feet, slipped off simple, once-white Keds that were now filthy with remnants of ash residue. Without her shoes, she leaned back on the bed and shimmied out of her chinos. He pulled them off and tried not to stare at the stingy band of red silk underwear left, realizing these few articles of clothing might be the only ones she owned at the moment.

They'd have to do something about that, he thought, as he went into the bathroom, grabbed a washcloth out of the linen cabinet, and soaked it in warm water.

When he got back to the bedroom she was sprawled diagonally across the bed on her back, eyes closed. He took the washcloth and began to wipe dirt and grime from her face and arms as best he could.

She put up no resistance whatsoever as he slowly rubbed away the film of dirt from her skin. When he'd finished, he pulled the sheets down invitingly around her. Leaving on the bra and panties, he gently picked up her limp body and slipped it between the bedding, tucking her in.

Without another word between them, in a matter of minutes, she snored softly in slumber. Opening her handbag, Reese pulled out her cell phone, turned the thing off, put it back inside the purse, and backed out of the room, quietly shutting the door.

He headed into the shower in the guest room. He was pretty sure she was down for the count, but he didn't want to take the chance the running water might disturb her sleep.

∆∆∆∆∆

By six a.m. Trevor realized the Boyd brothers weren't coming back to their hotel room. And he desperately needed sleep. Even though he dozed in the car, he needed to get back to his own bed, back to his laptop, and find out where the hell the two brothers had decided to hide out.

He'd heard the news about an explosion over his police scanner. He'd looked up the address on his iPhone.

Quinn Tyler's building had been destroyed. There had been kids in that building.

He needed to find Collin and Cade Boyd and he needed to do it before they had a chance to hurt anyone else.

CHAPTER 5

It was her first memory.

One of those scenes from a normal childhood that had a tall, lanky man with kind brown eyes and shaggy blonde hair taking her small hand in his bigger one and showing her around his land, a farm with rolling green hills and plenty of fresh air filled with earthy smells of hay and horses.

That day, Quinn's perfect day, the sun had been warm on her hair and her face. The big man had given her a huge lime green stuffed frog with big purple spots on it and black and white buggy-eyes. She'd hugged it to her chest while he had played tour guide and showed her all the barn animals.

She remembered a bunch of fat lazy cows, along with a couple of beautiful, spirited horses that kept sneezing and braying for apples. At least that's what the leggy man had told her when he cut up several slices from a basket and fed the fruit to a big, black stallion that seemed happy to see him.

She peered into another stall where a giant mother pig lay on straw. The mommy pig had been surrounded by several hungry little piglets wedged into her side.

She'd held her first real cat that day, a black-and - white calico that had six lively babies trailing behind. Kittens. The tall man had given her one of her very own, a solid white one to pet and hold and cuddle. The furry little thing had purred when she held it up to rub her chin into its soft fur.

She'd called it Snowball.

After they'd spent time in the barn, the tall man had taken her into the house and given her tea and biscuits, which turned out to be homemade sugar cookies with pink frosting.

Quinn remembered a grandmother-type who talked funny, so much so she could hardly understand a word the woman said. The man had let her pour tea from a bright blue teapot and hadn't even yelled at her when she'd spilled some. The tea had looked strong and yucky but had tasted sweet and delicious because the man had poured enough milk in it to make it almost creamy-looking.

She had wanted to stay, to live in this clean, perfect house with these caring and generous people. She had wanted to keep the kitten and take it with her on the plane. But as soon as the car pulled up, as soon as she had spotted Ella getting out, she knew. The adults made her let go of the kitten. The moment she relinquished it to the giant of a man, she knew the adults would make her get in the car. She remembered crying because she had to leave with Ella.

Her perfect day gone, like so many other things she didn't understand.

Remembering that picture-perfect scene as it pulled away and faded to black, Quinn began to mumble in her sleep, trying to keep the memory from disappearing entirely.

She reached out and tried to grab at the tall man as Ella forced her to get into the backseat of the car. She called out, she screamed to keep from leaving the tall man behind and the beautiful farm.

But all her yelling and screaming did no good at all. As it always happened, the tall man grew fainter until soon he was gone from her vision completely.

⚜ ⚜ ⚜ ⚜ ⚜

Reese heard Quinn cry out, or at least he thought he did. He rolled over in bed, tried to shake off the dregs of sleep. Something moved next to him. He saw her body toss and turn. Once again, he heard her mumble in her sleep.

Half asleep himself and exhausted, it took him several minutes to differentiate the moaning from actual words. More awake now, he made out Quinn thrashing about on the other side of the mattress.

Obviously in distress, she seemed to be calling out to someone. Either she was saying goodbye, leaving something or someone she didn't want to leave. And Quinn didn't like it one bit.

Moving closer, he studied in fascination as she carried on a conversation as if she were a small child of about three or four years old. She wasn't even awake. And yet, she was clearly upset about something.

He leaned over. In the dark he saw her lips moving, made out the sadness in her voice. Talking in her sleep was one thing, but when he saw the tears spill out and trickle down her cheeks, it grabbed at his heart.

He picked up several strands of raven hair off her face, ran the silky texture through his fingers. "Oh, baby, what is it that causes you so much pain even when you sleep?"

But the tears dried on her face as she slept on, leaving him wondering what, or rather who had haunted her dreams enough to make her cry.

⚜ ⚜ ⚜ ⚜ ⚜

It wasn't until later that morning Reese learned the casualty count. Three more people had succumbed to their injuries and died at the hospital. Eight innocent people had lost their lives in the blast. Dozens more had been injured, including children.

This wasn't just a news story on the local news. He'd seen the pain on the faces of the kids and the heartache in the eyes of adults who realized everything they owned no longer existed.

And for what?

Because a pissed off, misguided rich boy didn't get his way, thought Reese bitterly.

Even though the television stations were reporting the fire department suspected a gas leak, he knew better. And when Kit called around ten, she reminded him what he already had been mulling over. "I think Cade did this."

"Yeah," had been Reese's weak response.

Ten minutes after he hung up the phone with Kit, he had virtually an identical conversation with Baylee. "Cade did this. I just know he did."

Okay, so it wasn't his paranoia fueling this gut feeling.

Logic be damned, it seemed to be a consensus. After all, Kit and Baylee knew the Boyd brothers much better than he did. But as a lawyer even in a city the size of L.A., he'd been well aware of the Boyd reputation long before he'd ever even heard about Kit Griffin.

It was widely known the founding partners were ruthless in court. Now it seemed their offspring had turned into merciless, cold-blooded killers.

Would the police be able to do anything about it though? That was the nagging question.

While Reese sat at his dining room table amid briefs and paperwork, his laptop open, waiting for Quinn to wake up, he realized he couldn't argue with recent history. It made sense to blame Cade because he'd heard the man with his own ears threaten Quinn.

Hell, the man had threatened all of them.

This morning, he'd already had another conversation with Max St. John about his suspicions. He could only hope the detective had taken him seriously. After all, Max had been right there in the ER when Cade had gone postal. That had to count for something.

His mind kept drifting back to last night. What if he hadn't asked her to dinner? What if Quinn had gone straight home from the hospital? The timeframe would have put her inside the condo. What if she had been there to confront Cade? What if she had been killed or injured?

He sucked in a breath and ran a hand over his face. It wouldn't do to dwell on the what-if scenarios. Better to concentrate on keeping her out of Cade's reach.

Funny how he'd thought the last couple of months Jake had acted a bit melodramatic trying to keep Kit safe. And Dylan tended to go over the top when it came to Baylee and Sarah. He'd misjudged his friends, he thought now. Hell, he had misjudged the entire situation from the beginning. No more, though.

Better to overcompensate and make sure Quinn stayed safe rather than ignore his gut feeling and have her suffer the consequences later.

When his cell phone buzzed, it brought him out of a daze. Caller ID told him it was Jake.

"Reese here."

"You okay?"

"I'm fine. It's Quinn who doesn't have a place to live."

Jake chuckled. His friend sounded like he'd already taken the fall. "Don't I know it? Look, Kit and I are down the street. Kit brought Quinn some clothes, some personal items she'll need for the immediate future."

"She isn't up yet."

"That's okay. We'll just drop off the stuff and let her sleep. But when Quinn wakes up, plan on heading over to Crandall House. We're meeting up there, all of us. And pack a bag, Reese, the dynamics have changed. This'll take some planning and sorting out."

"Strategy session?"

"For lack of a better description, yeah. And it's better if we're all in one place anyway. We need to think about the next forty-eight hours and come up with a viable plan of action."

⚠⚠⚠⚠⚠

Gradually, Quinn came awake. Light filtered through the curtains. Every muscle in her body burned. She stared at the bedside clock. It read one-fifty-six. She'd slept the day away. Then suddenly she remembered last night.

It all came back to her in crystal clarity. She'd lost everything she owned. Her apartment was gone. The only real home she'd known, the one she'd fixed up with thrift store finds and garage sale treasures since moving there at sixteen. Her life felt as if it were in ruins.

Her neighbors, people she'd known for almost ten years, were either dead or injured or homeless.

Well, she'd been down to nothing before hadn't she? When she'd moved out at sixteen, she'd started from scratch. But then so had Kit and Baylee.

She scrubbed both hands over her face. She could come back from this. At least she was alive.

Quinn crawled out of bed and went into the bathroom to take a shower, even though she didn't have a clue what she'd use for clothes afterward. Glancing at the rumpled bed, she decided to grab one of the blankets to use for a robe.

Reese waited until the shower shut off, waited for several long minutes before knocking on his own bedroom door. When it flew open, Quinn stood there wrapped in nothing but a towel.

He cocked his head. That caramel-colored skin looked damp and moist and good enough to eat. She held another towel in her hand trying to dry that long, silky black mane of hers. He managed to control the primal urge to taste and nibble. "Nice."

When she merely smirked at him, he held out several shopping bags. "Kit brought you some things to wear."

"Clothes," she cried, as she jerked the bags out of his hands. "Is she here?" she asked, as she immediately started going through the bags. Selecting one of the solid, rose-colored tops, which was a form-fitting tunic tee, and a pair of jeans, she moved into the bathroom out of Reese's view to begin to dress.

"No, she dropped them off a couple of hours ago, hung around for a while, but when you didn't wake up, she left. We're supposed to meet up with them whenever you feel like it."

"I feel like it. Got anything to eat around here? I'm starving."

Good thing he'd anticipated her appetite. "I made BLTs."

"Bless you. And coffee?"

"That, too. How do you feel?"

"Better, almost human."

"You needed the sleep."

She stepped into range, wearing her borrowed clothes. Her long mane of damp, straight-as-string hair fell well past her shoulders as she ran his comb through its thickness, getting out the tangles. He watched, a little disappointed, as she bundled the still-damp mass up and bound it back with a simple rubber band.

"I washed your shirt and pants from last night…but…laundry isn't my strong suit. Some of the stains didn't come out."

She laughed. And it was a nice laugh for a woman who had lost everything she owned the night before. "You did my laundry? Reese, you are a wonder. Thanks for trying. I should probably send them out to the cleaners though. I guess from here on out, I'll need every stitch of clothing I can lay my hands on."

"Kit assures me she has you covered in the clothes department, at least until the two of you can go shopping. And if you need a place to stay, Quinn, my guest room is an option with no strings attached. Although I prefer you sleep where you did last night."

She walked over to him then, put her fingers to his face, and brought it down to her level. She touched his lips in the faintest of kisses. "Hmm, thank you."

This man had tucked her in last night. He'd let her sleep like the dead without pressing any advantage. Not every man would have done that. After she gave him another chaste kiss, she said, "I may have to take you up on that since Baylee's got dibs on Kit's old place."

"I'm not sure Dylan plans on letting Baylee go anywhere at the moment without him, and that includes San Madrid. Besides, I think he's planning to tuck her into his little house in Palisades before long."

Her forehead crinkled. "You make it sound like Dylan is calling the shots. Baylee is pretty independent..." Not used to Baylee having anyone special in her life, she thumped her own head. "Oh hell, who am I kidding? You're probably right. I think she's head over heels in love with the guy."

She snapped her fingers. "I just thought of something. Gloria's guest house is empty."

"But Cade knows that place."

"True. But he'll find me here and that puts you in jeopardy. No matter where I go, he's bound to find me. It's silly to think he won't. For crying out loud, he broke into my locker at the hospital, all he had to do was bribe a security guard. And last night..."

Reese frowned. He didn't like the sound of that. Maybe he could persuade her to take a two-week vacation instead of trying to get her back on rotation so soon. With that, he decided to approach this thing from another angle entirely.

"Is there any family you want to call, Quinn? Let them know what happened." He was thinking of her father, Nick Tyler. Maybe he could locate her mother, Ella Canyon, too, let her know Quinn needed some help. Kit had mentioned the woman's last known address was in the San Francisco Bay area. But then she had also reminded him that Ella would be the last person in the world Quinn would want to contact.

When she didn't say anything, he prodded, "Don't you think it's time you got in touch with him? You could use this time to work out your…issues. You're an adult…"

In the act of going through the clothes Kit had brought, taking inventory of what she had on hand to wear, Quinn's body went rigid. Reese saw her jaw lock tight and knew he was in for a fight. "No. Don't even think about it."

"Quinn, don't be hard-headed about this. You have three weeks susp…"

She didn't let him finish. She whirled to face him. "And last night you said you'd try and help me fight that, make it shorter. Now, you want me to what? Contact a man who's never given me the time of day for no good reason? I'm not doing it. Things have been bad in my life before…I don't need him around now. Stay out of this, Reese. This is none of your concern, none whatsoever."

He held up a staying hand. "Just wait a minute. I wrote the injunction to fight the suspension this morning. I got an emergency protection order against Cade, too. It's good for five days, at which time I'll apply for a temporary restraining order before we're granted a hearing for the real deal. So, be reasonable here, Quinn. This is a time to turn to family. Cade blew up your fucking house! What if you'd been home?"

"And trying to contact a man who's never bothered to get to know me will change that how exactly? Why would I want to do that?"

"He's your father. After all this time, he might be interested in knowing your situation, concerned to learn you're in danger."

"Oh, for god's sake, spoken like a man who doesn't know a damned thing about my life." She gave him the onceover. "Don't tell me you used to listen to his music. Oh, my God, you're a fan of his music! News flash, the rock star isn't interested in me period. He never has been. Now drop it, will you?"

Recognizing the obstinate look in her eyes, this wasn't getting him where he wanted to go. He tried a different tack. "Look, if you won't make the call, we could all go over to Ireland, get out of L.A. for a while until this whole thing blows over. It would get us out of town, maybe let this thing with Cade cool off for a bit."

For a lawyer used to presenting his case, he was falling woefully short.

"And then what? I'd still have to come back and Cade would no doubt be waiting. And have you forgotten? Gloria and Kit are expecting Ben Griffin to step off a plane at the end of the week. I might add that whole brother-slash-son reunion has me curious. I want to be there when it happens. So I'm not going anywhere, let alone setting foot in Ireland to see a man who hasn't given me the time of day in twenty-five years."

"That's just it; in light of the situation, shouldn't you at least try to…"

"I'm not begging that asshole for five minutes of his precious time! Been there. Done that. He's never once taken the time to even see me. And that was when I was much younger, a kid. Why would a rock star care anything about meeting a grown woman now? I won't go begging for his attention at this late date as an adult."

Reese started to reply, but she bowled right on. "There's absolutely no reason he'd want anything to do with me now anyway. Don't you get that, Reese? You had a loving father. I had no father. Period. Accept the difference. We all can't be lucky enough to have Mike and Carol Brady for parents."

And with that, she pushed him back through the open doorway and slammed the door shut in his face.

Okay, he wouldn't tell her he'd already taken it upon himself to make contact via a phone call to Tyler's attorney, some guy named Baines. And he realized now what a mistake that had been.

Good intentions, he decided, was going to cause her to explode in his direction. Just when things were getting friendly between them, he'd taken a step on his own he had no business taking.

Ten minutes later, a strained silence hung between them as they ate the tomato soup Reese had heated from a can to go with the chunky BLTs.

Finally Quinn said quietly, "I know you mean well, Reese, but…"

"No, I was out of line. I had no right to interfere." He sat there looking out the dining room window. "It's just that if I had a chance to talk to my dad again, I'd take it in a heartbeat. I miss him, the talks we used to have. I even miss his reminiscing about the old days. Although to tell you the truth, at the time his stories bored me silly. But I'd give anything to hear him tell me one of his corny jokes."

She put a hand over his. "But Reese, it isn't the same thing. Don't you see that? You had a relationship with your father, a good one. I never had that. Surely a guy who had a four-point-seven grade point average all through law school would understand that."

"You asked about me."

"Once. Jake and I were having difficulty finding anything to talk about and your name slipped into the conversation. That's all. And wipe that smug look off your face."

For the first time that day, he smiled. The woman could be such a hard-ass when the opposite was true. "I admit the situation is different with your father. But that's inconceivable to me. My dad was always there for me, my mom too."

But thinking about her early years, anger bubbled up in him at Nick Tyler for not having the balls to check on the welfare of his own flesh and blood. In Reese's opinion, whether the child had been conceived out of wedlock or not, the man should have at least met with her before now. His financial responsibility certainly had not included a caring heart.

"My parents were a joke. Face it, Reese. You had that Norman Rockwell family we all wanted."

"I wouldn't go that far. But my childhood was pretty normal."

"Lucky you." As if to change the subject, Quinn stared at the half-eaten BLT on Reese's plate. "You gonna eat that?"

He shoved the plate her way, just as a hail of gunfire pierced through the front window, causing glass to shatter all around them.

He grabbed her as they hit the floor on the way down. Bullets flew past them as he lay sprawled on top of Quinn while the pings of metal hit every surface inside his house. Plaster and shards of glass rained down over both of them.

Just as suddenly as the gunfire began, it was over. Reese heard the squeal of tires and made a dash to the living room window in time to see an SUV peel down the street.

The walls were riddled with holes. His flat-screen TV hung at an angle. Glass shards from lamps and photographs were scattered all over the floor. Debris lay everywhere.

Pulling out his cell phone, he dialed nine-one-one, even though he could hear sirens already in the distance.

CHAPTER 6

In a drug-induced haze, Ella Canyon sat in her tiny room in East Oakland, wondering what had happened to the gravy train she'd once rode hard and fast. Somehow she'd fallen off and never managed to get back onboard.

Once upon a time she'd had it made—even lived in Beverly Hills for chrissakes, had a Mercedes parked in the driveway, diamonds on her fingers. She'd been able to shop on fucking Rodeo Drive, eat in the fancy-schmancy restaurants where celebs like Steve McQueen had once dined.

Those were the days when she'd worn the best clothes, lived in a mansion and had a roof over her head on a regular basis. During that time, she'd done her best to walk the straight and narrow. For about six months.

She'd walked away at the first opportunity.

She'd gotten used to another way of life long ago. Having to sell her body to survive came easy. Old habits were hard to break.

Because God knew she'd loved the smack. She could survive on snow and uppers in a pinch, but it was the smack she used for escape and that which had ultimately dragged her down to the gutter where she found herself now.

She rarely had a lucid day anymore. And when she did, she tended to ramble on to whoever would listen about that lap of luxury in which she had once lived.

"Shame the kid had to grow up," she mumbled now to the four walls as they closed in around her. So she'd left the kid to live the life she was meant to live. Little brat should be grateful for that.

It had been five years since she'd laid eyes on Quinn. That last time they'd had a good, old-fashioned catfight about her heroin addiction. Not just screaming and yelling either, but honest-to-God yanking hair and face-slapping.

Ella cackled at the memory with the laugh of the insane.

She licked her dry lips and began to shake, her body knowing full well it was time for the generous dose of methadone it craved on a daily basis. She took in her surroundings. She'd lived in worse.

Somehow she needed to make it to the pay phone downstairs, though. It was time to call the uppity little bitch and remind her to wire her some cash. After all, it had been six months since she'd heard from the kid, Christmas to be exact. At least she thought it had been Christmas. Maybe it had been some other goddamned holiday. It was hard to keep the days straight any more.

It didn't matter. It was past time to go to the well again. She could always count on Quinn for at least a grand to get her through the rough spots—like now.

As she wiped spittle from her mouth, the shaking grew worse. She crawled out of bed and padded into the bathroom for a drink of water.

Glancing at her reflection in the mirror, she saw an old woman looking back at her. For chrissakes she was only forty-seven but looked a good ten years older. Her bloated face sagged. Her eyelids dipped over rheumy eyes. Her teeth were brownish stumps, rotting from years of chasing the white dragon.

And that was on the outside. The crystal meth had done its own number burning the linings in her lungs. Her body itched with a constant, red splotchy rash she couldn't make go away no matter how much prescription cream doctors handed out.

She began clawing at her arms, where visible needle marks scarred the sallow skin.

When the four walls closed in even more, she muttered louder this time, "Damn shame the kid had to grow up."

&&&&&

By early afternoon, Dan Holloway's day had already passed hectic and was running down the fast lane to frenzied. He'd spent the better part of the morning hanging out with arson investigators, going through the site of the explosion the night before. So he'd been on the scene when they'd discovered additional bodies under the rubble.

That part of the job, staring at dead bodies, no matter how they'd met their deaths, had a tendency to make his stomach lurch.

That had been one of the reasons he'd missed lunch.

He'd been about to head back to his office to fill out paperwork when he'd gotten the call about a drive-by shooting in Westlake Village.

It seems Reese Brennan's house had taken a hit. Because he'd seen firsthand the destruction back at Quinn Tyler's apartment building, he might be tempted to jump to conclusions. So far, he couldn't prove Cade had been anywhere near Tyler's apartment building when it had exploded. Presumption wasn't his friend. As a third-year detective in Homicide, he knew better than to begin any investigation with a false premise. Not only was it unprofessional, it could lead a good investigator down the wrong path really quickly with no way to turn back.

The fact that he could keep an open mind was his best trait.

Having to maneuver in gridlock traffic, though, it took him forty minutes to reach Brennan's Mediterranean-style house. Wearing his suit coat and tie in the summer heat, the detective surveyed the busted glass scattered in the flower beds and on the lawn, even as the criminal lawyer, sporting a pair of jeans and T-shirt, hammered nails to board up his windows.

Holloway glanced up and down the trendy street and took in the tidy manicured lawns of the upscale neighborhood. "Never knew Westlake to have a drive-by—in broad daylight, no less. Seems too peaceful for something like this."

Reese shot him a steely-eyed look of disdain. "I've lived here ten years, first time anything like this has ever happened. You think this was random or a coincidence after last night? Think again."

The uniform cops were still on the scene, milling about, still bagging spent shells they'd dug out of the walls. The insurance adjuster had shown up an hour earlier but was still in the process of snapping photos of the damage to go with his claim forms.

"Did you see them do it?" Holloway asked pointblank. "Because right now I could really use an eyewitness account."

Still holding a hammer in his fist, Reese bobbed his head toward the uniforms. "They took my statement. It's all in the report. I saw a big-ass SUV peel out of here like a bat outta hell. The Boyds have a thing for big gas-guzzling SUVs. You know they do."

"Doesn't mean they did this, I need something concrete."

"Yeah, well, you heard Cade in the ER threaten Quinn. That's good enough for me."

"I'll look into it."

"You do that," Reese grumbled as he looked over at Quinn standing on the lawn holding the pot of coffee she had fixed for the officers and insurance agent.

While he fumed and worried, she had gone into cool, composed doctor-mode. It was either practiced, something a physician needed to convey in a crisis situation, or a side benefit as a result of how she'd grown up in chaotic disorder.

But fury still ran hot through the usual calm demeanor he had worked so hard to perfect over the years. He didn't like losing his composure. A defense attorney had to keep his cool under fire in and out of the courtroom. Usually he could contain his emotions; today not so much. He wasn't in a courtroom now. And this was personal.

Plus, he hadn't been around cops for ten years for nothing. They might need rock solid evidence to go after Cade Boyd, but he had all the proof he needed.

ॐ ॐ ॐ ॐ ॐ

By the time Reese and Quinn walked up to the wraparound porch at Crandall House, carrying two suitcases mostly packed with stuff belonging to him, it was almost six-thirty.

Kit opened the front door before they even had a chance to knock or ring the bell.

"Hey, what kept you guys?"

"Cade shot up Reese's house. What a mess! Reese's beautiful home is boarded up now, shot full of holes. It should be on the news," Quinn announced. "But I took photos with my phone. Wait till you see what Cade did to it."

"Oh. My. God. We didn't have the TV on at the store and we just now got home. Are you both all right?" She pulled them inside and began to give Quinn the once-over, like a mother hen.

"I'm fine. Don't worry, Mom," Quinn said as she stormed inside. "Even though it's my fault."

"We've been over that, Quinn," Reese scoffed.

Dragging them into the spacious front room, Kit automatically ran her hands over Quinn's shoulders. "Jake, get in here!"

Jake appeared in the doorway, followed by a still-limping Pepper, a result of injuries from the car accident

Collin had caused. "What's up? What took you guys so long? Did Quinn make you take her shopping?"

Reese shot Jake a withering stare. "No. Drive-by courtesy of Cade Boyd. I gave the cops a description of the SUV I saw speeding down the street, a black Yukon. I'm certain it was a rental, not the Escalade or Connor's Hummer, either. But we all know it was them."

"And the cops?"

"Need concrete evidence linking them. And I couldn't provide it. Maybe I should've made something up. Anyway, I wouldn't go putting any faith in finding this particular SUV any time soon. No doubt these guys have a string of vehicles at their disposal. A rental maybe, I don't know. Besides, the cops put out an APB, even set up roadblocks in and around my neighborhood, got zip."

"Reese thinks they'll go underground after this," Quinn proclaimed. "They do that and what chance will we have finding them?"

"We'll come up with something," Reese promised.

Stunned at the boldness of the daylight attack, Jake ran his hands through his hair. "They're ramping up, taking things up a notch. After the attack on Quinn's apartment building, I called Jordan. He's posting guards here beginning tonight. That's why we're all holing up here under one roof until we can think of some place better. Six people are easier to contain if they're in one spot."

Reese cocked a brow. "Contain? It's hard to believe these guys have gone this far off the deep end."

Jake shot Reese a searing glance. "Don't start that skeptic crap again."

"No skeptic crap. But I've gone up against Cade in court. Never thought one day he'd be blowing up a building, shooting up my house, and going on the lam as a fugitive."

"Killers," Kit corrected. "They're both killers now."

"Okay, killers. At this point, I'm wondering where they'll strike next. And it isn't sitting well with me not knowing. Show me where to stow our stuff, okay?" The question got the desired reaction. Jake motioned for Reese to follow him upstairs so they could talk in private.

On the way up, Jake asked, "You and Quinn sharing a room yet?"

Reese sent him a sidelong glance. "I'm not rushing her. You should've seen her last night taking care of all the injured. The woman is a natural. Not just with the doctor stuff either, but with people. She actually cares."

"And you'd like to sample that bedside manner, right?"

Reese grinned. "I'm working on it, but with people trying to kill her it's a little tough to get her into that frame of mind and keep her there."

Jake grinned back. "I know exactly how you feel. Baylee and Dylan will be here any minute. I say when they get here we all sit down and formulate a plan."

"That talk doesn't have to include the women, does it? I've already gotten into trouble, deep quicksand as a matter of fact, by putting my nose into Quinn's business when I shouldn't have. I tried to talk her into taking a trip to Ireland to see her estranged father."

With that, Reese dumped the gear onto a bed in one of the recently finished guest rooms designated as his and went into a detailed account of the other mistake he'd made.

"Wait, you called Nick Tyler's attorney without asking her first? Are you nuts?" Jake shook his head and slapped Reese on the back. "Quinn will kill you when she finds out. You should call this guy back on the QT and beg insanity."

"I thought I could reason with her."

"Not about that you can't. Look, I've known Quinn quite a bit longer than you have; Baylee, too, for that matter. I've known these women since they were teenagers when all three hung out regularly at Morty's law firm, ostensibly under the guise of lending a hand with the filing. At the time, I wondered why Morty would hire girls so young. Now I know. Had I paid more attention, I would have realized that, even then, they didn't want to spend any time at home. The job was merely an excuse to get them out of the house. Of course, I didn't put the pieces together until now, didn't focus on the red flags right there in front of me.

"Those three have been living under dark clouds their entire lives. The threat of constant instability must have been hell. I think that's what makes all three of them so incredibly independent. But Kit's stubborn streak pales in comparison to Quinn's. I've never met a woman more obstinate than Quinn Tyler."

Reese rubbed his chin. "Gee thanks for the heads up. You might have mentioned this before I stepped off the cliff."

"Who knew you'd take it upon yourself to contact Tyler, a man who's shown absolutely no interest in his own daughter for over a quarter of a century now? If it hadn't happened at this late date…"

"In that case, what am I worried about? The son of a bitch will probably ignore the call and the fact that she's in trouble like he has her entire life. By the way, you say you know Quinn. Did you know Ella Canyon was a hooker? Were you aware Quinn lived a hand-to-mouth existence before ever getting to Beverly Hills?"

"Hand-to-mouth, as in going hungry and stuff? No way. I had no idea. Kit never mentioned that."

"Maybe she doesn't know."

"Trust me. She knows. There isn't anything that happens between those three that they don't share in minute detail."

"I might agree with you if it wasn't for one thing. Baylee kept what happened with Connor Boyd from both of them. She didn't share the fact she'd been raped or that she was even pregnant. When there's trauma involved, when something hurts that badly, maybe they aren't as close as you think."

"Okay, there is that. Maybe Quinn did hold something back about her early years. But trust me, anything that happened to those three once they became a unit, every morsel got dissected."

But Reese wasn't so sure. He'd seen Quinn's eyes last night when she'd hinted at how rough those early years had really been. He could only wonder if she'd kept certain things to herself to keep from reliving it or for some other reason.

By the time they got downstairs, Dylan was in the process of unloading his boxy G500 crammed full of all Sarah's baby stuff.

"Well, don't just stand there, follow me and grab some gear. Believe me, there's enough to go around," Dylan admitted as he disappeared out the front door, going back for a second load.

Dutifully, Reese and Jake followed him out to the car.

In the kitchen Quinn helped herself to a can of soda out of the fridge. She leaned against the counter and tried to explain to her friends why she hadn't told them about the suspension. "Baylee had a lot going on last night...I..."

"Don't push this onto me," Baylee screeched through gritted teeth. "Don't you dare use me as your excuse. As soon as the cops took off, you had plenty of time to mention that Cade was the cause of your getting suspended. It would have taken what...four little words? But no, not Quinn Tyler, Quinn has to keep that to herself."

"She's right, Quinn. You do that martyr thing better than anyone I know. You've shut us down before."

"And you have the gall to get all bent out of shape knowing I kept stuff to myself about Connor," Baylee pointed out. "I don't think so."

"That's completely different and you know it."

"No, it isn't. The night I went to that charity benefit, you were focused on starting the last year of med school. And Kit here had just gotten the Bock & Bean out of the red into black for the first time. You guys didn't need my problems taking away from your efforts."

"Fine," Quinn threw out. "Okay, I should have said something. Happy now? But really, what was the point? By the time I got upstairs, I was sick of Cade Boyd and this whole damned thing. All I wanted was a soak in the tub and a good night's sleep. And look how that turned out. Eight of my neighbors are dead because of me. You should see Reese's neighborhood, talk about swanky. But not now, not after Quinn Tyler checks in for the night. Now, Reese's house is an eyesore. His neighbors didn't look too happy about that either."

"Oh, Quinn," Kit sighed as she put her arms around her friend's shoulders. "See, that martyr thing you've got down to a fine art. You had no way of knowing Cade's madness would touch Reese in such a dramatic way. The brothers are nuts. They've always been nuts. You know that. You shouldn't blame yourself for something you couldn't have predicted they'd do. And that includes them shooting up Reese's house."

"That's not exactly accurate, predicting what they'd do. When he lost it in the ER, he said he was coming for me; in fact he said he was coming for all of us. There were cops there who heard him."

"See? They didn't do a thing to prevent them from blowing up your building or shooting up Reese's house," Baylee pointed out. Black and bruised, Baylee jutted out her chin. "Yeah well, we're smarter than these guys. And we've got this mysterious stranger on our side, the one who keeps helping us. Between the seven of us we should be able to take down what's left of The Unholy Three."

Kit stretched her free arm out to include Baylee and little Sarah. They drew closer together like they were football players huddling on a field. Just as they had done this ritual a thousand times before, or at least since they were eight years old, Kit held out a curved pinky on each hand, the gesture, a symbol of their unity. Baylee held out hers and the baby's. Then on cue, Quinn did the same.

In a circle, in unison, the three women repeated the chant. "Together we let no one hurt us. We are most powerful when we are one. We draw strength from each other. One."

They fist-bumped each other as they always did before suddenly separating and breaking apart.

All at once they turned to see three pairs of male eyes gaping at them from the kitchen doorway. The three men stood still as statues watching the women go through the brief but touching ceremony.

Suddenly it all became clear.

Reese spoke first. Staring straight into Quinn's chocolate eyes, he stated, "This is what you were trying to tell me last night. This is your true family right here. For so many years, that's all the three of you had—each other. You were each other's sounding boards, each other's support system, each other's anchor through what had to be the most difficult of times growing up the way you did."

Quinn swallowed, overcome with emotion she'd never felt for another man. She stared into Reese's face and saw not ridicule but rather genuine admiration.

She went over where he stood. Without prelude, she kissed him deeply on the mouth. "You are the first man on the planet who has ever gotten that about me."

Dylan went to Baylee, even as Jake reached for Kit. "I think we all get it now."

There in the middle of the kitchen, arms stretched out resting on each other's shoulders, all six of them drew together in another impromptu huddle.

Dylan joked, "I've always wanted to do a pinky swear."

Baylee elbowed him in the ribs. "Then you're lucky we let you in to our very exclusive club, Surfer Boy."

It was Reese who took up the chant while the women stood a little stunned at having the men included in something they'd shared with no one else since childhood. But under the circumstances it seemed fitting. Soon they too repeated the words. "Together we let no one hurt us.

We are most powerful when we are one. We draw strength from each other. One."

When Reese looked down at Quinn, she was smearing away the tears on her face. She laid her head on his chest. "For what it's worth, I think I just got *you*."

He leaned down and placed a kiss on the top of her head. "It's worth more than you could possibly know."

Dylan broke the somber mood. "Look, I'm starving. I just lugged around enough baby stuff to stock an 'R us' store. Got anything to eat? I could've sworn when I opened the door I smelled Italian."

Baylee took his face between the fingers of her free hand, kissed him gently on the mouth. "Better feed this one before he has to set up the Pack 'N Play again and gets grumpy."

"Hey, that Pack 'N Play is a piece of cake. I've taken it down and put it back up so often now I could do it blindfolded."

He reached over and took the baby out of Baylee's arms. "Besides, Sarah's worth every minute of it, aren't you, Gidget?"

The baby cooed, "Daaaaaa," and grabbed Dylan's nose.

Quinn turned completely around from the fridge. "Did she just say Da? My God, she's only six months old."

"Exceptional, huh? I know, talking already. That's daddy's girl, aren't you, Sarah?"

The others eyed Dylan with disbelief. It was Reese who asked, "Is this the same guy who boasted three girls in one…"

Holding the baby, Dylan couldn't very well retaliate in the normal physical way by beating Reese into the ground, so he chose a verbal response instead, sure to shut up Reese's ribbing. "Five words, Brennan." He ticked them off with one hand. "Cancun. Jennifer. And. Janie. Dinkins."

The mention of Cancun and what had happened during a wild college week of spring break had Reese stopping in mid-sentence.

"I didn't think so," Dylan declared as he jostled Sarah in his arms.

Kit giggled at their banter. "This guy knows his food. I made lasagna and strawberry pasta salad."

"With that pesto stuff?" Dylan asked.

"With the pesto stuff," Kit repeated.

As they set out the food on the table, they tried to keep the conversation light and centered on upcoming events, like the anticipated arrival of Ben Griffin.

"When exactly does he get here?" Quinn asked Kit.

"Four days, seven hours, and..." Kit held up her right hand and looked at her watch. "Twenty-five minutes. Jake and I decided to send a car for him."

"More like, I'm not taking Kit and standing on a curb at LAX waiting for Collin and Cade to show up. Sending a car to pick him up makes the most sense," Jake explained.

"Did you talk to him yet on the phone, Kit?" Quinn asked.

Kit sighed, shooting a look of disdain at Jake. "No. Funny thing about that though. After Jordan Donovan found him, after that initial phone call, so far our only communication has been via e-mails."

"You don't find that a tad odd?"

Jake looked skeptical. "I find that a lot strange, but he did agree to make the trip. At this point, as long as it took to locate the guy, we have to be grateful for that."

"It's a step closer to getting him to meet his birth mother. At least Gloria will finally meet the son she's never seen. And I want all of you here to meet the brother I've never met, especially since I'll need your backup in case it gets weird."

Quinn put her arms around Kit. "Oh, honey, weird? This entire thing moved past weird a long time ago and sailed straight into the world of bizarro, that which we laughingly recognize as our lives."

Baylee laughed. "You know you've got our support without having to ask, Kit. You and Gloria deserve this."

"Okay, so now that we have that out of the way, any chance we could talk about where I'm going to live during my forced leave of absence? Hello? Reese offered his place but now it's all shot up."

Quinn looked around the table, all eyes on her. "Do I have to remind anyone here that my condo blew up? Plus, I have to spend some of this time going shopping and replacing everything I owned, especially every stitch of clothing I'd had since college."

Baylee picked up her glass of wine, toasted the air. "Which is the very reason you seriously needed to replace most of your wardrobe, some of it was so out of style… No one wears acid-washed jeans any more, Quinn. No one."

"Jeans never go out of style," Quinn reasoned, slightly insulted. "I read that somewhere."

Baylee shook her head. "They do, Quinn, and if you ever went anywhere other than the hospital you'd see it for yourself."

Kit placed a hand over Quinn's. "You'll stay here, of course. I thought you knew that. You both will until Reese gets his house back in working order. We were trying to dance around the topic, didn't think you were ready to talk about losing all your stuff yet."

"I guess there's no point in mentioning I could stay in Gloria's empty guest house then?"

In answer to that, in unison, five unanimous voices yelled out, "No!"

Quinn snickered. "Okay, okay. Just checking to make sure everyone's on the same page. As long as the Nutty Brothers are on the loose I guess it's all for one and sticking close together. We'll probably get sick of each other."

"This is a big house with plenty of room for everyone. If we start getting on each other's last nerve, we send whoever it is to their room for a timeout," Kit proposed.

Baylee chimed in, "Who wants to bet me Dylan will be the first one who ends up in time out?"

"Me? I'm laidback. I'm the good one, the peacemaker, the surfer dude who's full of witty repartee and all kinds of wise..."

"More like full of crap," Jake pointed out, tempering his words with Sarah not two feet away.

But Reese didn't get the attempt at humor. "Is anyone going to bring up the question, first and foremost on our minds? Or are we just planning to sit here and make jokes and wait for Cade and Collin to drive up and start opening fire on us again? I'm done with that. These guys aren't gonna stop until somebody's dead."

As they dug into the hearty pan of lasagna, Jake answered, "We're all ears. By all means enlighten us on what you have in mind to get the assholes out of our lives for good."

"Ben Griffin isn't due to show up for four more days." He slanted a glance in Quinn's direction. "In spite of the papers I've filed to fight Quinn's suspension, I doubt we get a hearing for at least a couple more days. I say we head to a destination the Boyds know nothing about..."

Dylan busted out laughing while Jake simply shook his head and waited for the women to explode.

Predictably, it was Quinn who shouted the others down first.

"Before we got here he wanted to take off for Ireland. Now, he wants to run for the hills. What is it with you Brennan? Until a few days ago you thought we were all crazy and you were the only voice of reason in the room. Now, you want to take off on a pilgrimage somewhere to protect us womenfolk."

"We tried that already, Reese. Dylan got Baylee to go as far away as Catalina before he had to bring her back," Jake pointed out.

"We aren't going anywhere," Kit reminded them. She sent a scornful look at Jake. "I have a business to run. That business requires me to be on the premises daily."

Baylee agreed. "And I need to stick around because my father might come out of his coma and be willing to tell me more of the story about what happened to my mother."

Dylan sent her a sympathetic look. "Let's hope he does. But…" He didn't want her expectations too high. "Look…"

"I know. Okay, maybe he's pretty far gone, but at this point I need to be there at his bedside, see if I can pry any more info out of him that might be useful the minute he becomes lucid. There's a chance, even if it's slim, he might come out of it. Besides, his days are running out, barring a miracle of some sort. And I'd like to go back over to his house on Bel Green and see if I can locate Sarah's last diary."

"Stubborn is one thing but need I remind all of you that Cade killed eight people in that blast. If Quinn and I hadn't gone out to dinner, she might not be sitting here at all."

"Aw, you're growing on me too, Brennan, even if it's taken a psycho like Cade to bring us closer. But hey, I suppose I'm game for a road trip. If you can talk these two into taking a couple of days off, that is, I'm in. I've got nothing else to do. Where'd you have in mind to go?"

"A cabin, up at Big Sur. My dad and I used to go there all the time. Jake and Dylan have been there."

Baylee laid her hand on top of his. "A trip sounds wonderful, Reese. But honestly I don't feel I could leave Dad in his condition. You and Quinn should go, though. Get Quinn away from all of this, even if it's just for a couple of days that would help."

Kit wrapped an arm around his shoulder. "It sounds lovely, Reese. But I'm not going off on a trip and splitting us up. I'm with Baylee, though; you should get Quinn out of here. You two go, get out of Dodge."

But understanding dawned suddenly. Quinn stood up and exclaimed, "Wait a minute, if they don't go, I'm not leaving them behind."

Dylan nodded. "Strength in numbers; we split our forces we weaken the team."

Reese sighed. "I had to try one more time, not that I thought anyone would go for it. If we all don't go as a unit, then forget it. We stay together, do this together."

Quinn smiled at him then. "Damn straight we do."

⚶ ⚶ ⚶ ⚶ ⚶

Dredging close to shore, ten miles south of San Madrid, the *Wild Goose* decided to head into port earlier than usual. It wasn't because the crew had reached its three-hundred-pound catch yet or because they'd had engine trouble. Today, Captain Ryland Phillips, the father of two young boys who both played little league, had promised his sons he'd make it to their game that night and it started at six o'clock sharp. His oldest, ten-year-old Kellan was starting pitcher and had a streak of five wins under his belt.

Ryland didn't want to miss the first pitch.

As the sixty-foot shrimp boat got closer to the jetty, though, Ryland's eye caught something hung up on the rocks. From where he stood on the deck, it looked like a bloated mass of something.

He took out his binoculars to get a closer look. Sure enough, the mass was a body.

Captain Phillips didn't know it yet, but he could attest firsthand that the Pacific Ocean had just given up Uri Jankovic to the land.

He reached to radio the Coast Guard.

He could only hope he wouldn't be late for his son's first pitch.

CHAPTER 7

When Trevor finally woke that afternoon, he turned on the telly and blinked at the screen. The local television anchors were reporting a drive-by shooting that had taken place earlier in the day at the house of local attorney, Reese Brennan.

Okay, it was official. Cade and Collin Boyd had gone bat-shit crazy.

He ordered a steak from room service before going over to his laptop, booting it up. It was time to face facts.

One person for this task was spread too thin.

Failing to locate the brothers at this point could result in more unnecessary deaths. Lives were at stake. It was time to enlist an army, people who also had a vested interest in the outcome, people with limited skills, maybe, but if he balanced the emotional investment, it might make up for a lack of skillset with a deadly weapon.

Even though he was a damned fine hired gun and a trained sniper, Trevor was also a decent hacker. But his resources told him he had at his disposal two who were even more talented in that area. If the skills were applied correctly, hackers could do some serious damage, enough to weaken the enemy.

It took him under five minutes to crack the network of Brennan's law firm. Once in, he sent Brennan an encrypted, untraceable e-mail, laying the groundwork for what he hoped would be a joining of forces.

☙☙☙☙☙

Inside Crandall House, Reese sat at the desk in the guest room designated as his. He had just polished off a brief and sent it to his paralegal with instructions for the next day's filings when an e-mail appeared in his inbox with the subject line that read:

Dossier on Boyd Boyd Geller & Gatz

Reese checked the sender and noticed it read anonymous. He also saw that it had a rather large attachment. Relying on his virus software and hoping it was up-to-date enough to ward off any malware or Trojan horses, he double-clicked the message.

For the next thirty minutes he read page after page of incriminating evidence against the Boyds, some he and his friends already knew. But as he flicked through document after document onscreen, it soon became apparent there was even more they didn't.

And knowing was about to change the game—yet again.

☙☙☙☙☙

Downstairs, Jake was locking up for the night when he heard a car pull into the driveway and saw headlights illuminate the living room wall. Immediately wary, he went to the front window, pulled back the drapes, and peered out into the dark. Because Crandall House was rather isolated, there were no streetlamps to provide lighting at night.

Even though he knew Donovan's men were out there guarding the perimeter, watching the house, knowing that didn't make him feel any safer when it came to keeping the Boyd brothers away from Kit, Baylee, and Quinn.

He went on alert as soon as he heard a car door slam shut. At that very moment his cell phone rang. By this time

Reese had come into the room, the nine-millimeter Luger clutched in his fist with Dylan tagging along behind holding his own M-nine Beretta.

Jake spared them both a glance and pushed the button to answer his phone. "Boston."

"Max St. John. I'm right outside your front door. I've got news."

Jake went over to the double set of doors filled with hope, keenly aware Max wouldn't be here this time of night if it weren't important. He squinted through the peep hole and sure enough spotted the detective in charge of Claire's murder standing on the porch.

A certain amount of expectation rose in his chest. Was it possible Max had already discovered who killed Claire? He turned the lock. "This better be good," he said with a grin.

"Funny how it always seems to be late at night when I get around to solving a puzzle. Why the hell do you guys have to live so far out here in the boonies anyway? What the hell's wrong with a nice neighborhood like Westlake Village? Holloway tells me it's got a nice view of a scenic lake."

Jake wasn't quite used to Max's sense of humor yet and traded glances with Reese, mostly because at one time the bulldog detective had been such a formidable adversary to both of them.

But now, hoping the man held the key to Claire Boston's murder, he slapped Max on the back. "Let me see, scenic lake versus the ocean? No contest here, Max. Strange how two short months ago I hated your guts. Now look, we're just one big happy family."

"Smartass," Max replied. For the first time he took in the handguns Reese and Dylan were clutching and added, "Jesus. I don't even want to know if you have permits for those."

Reese threw him a smirk. "Turns out, I'm legal. So is Surfer Boy here."

Jake didn't want to wade through small talk. "You got the results of the DNA already? How is that possible?"

"It pays to have a friend in the lab willing to work overtime." Max smacked a thin manila folder into Jake's chest. "Good work, Boston. We're closer and at least headed in the right direction this time to finding Claire's killer."

"Wait," Jake said as hope died. "Closer? What the hell does that mean?"

"Read the file," Max insisted. "DNA under your wife's fingernails is *similar* to Connor Boyd's DNA."

"But not a match," Jake finished as he tried to absorb the words on the single sheet of paper in the file.

"It's called familial DNA. See the short tandem repeats on the Y chromosome? That tells us that Claire's killer shares some of the same tandem repeats." When Max took in the confused faces around the room, including those of the women who now gathered as a unit around the bottom step of the stairs, he shook his head.

"A full sibling, a father, someone close to Connor killed Claire Boston. Cade, maybe Collin. Won't know for certain until we manage to finagle a DNA sample out of them."

Jake heard Kit let out a whoop for joy right before she launched her body into his.

"You did it!" Kit yelled. "How does it feel knowing who killed Claire? For the first time in two years you have peace of mind about this and can put it behind you once and for all."

"It isn't solved yet, Kit," a disappointed Jake uttered.

"I don't understand." She turned to stare at Max. "You said it's either Cade or Collin. You know who did this to Claire. So go—get him—arrest him."

"That's just it, Kit. They aren't in custody yet and until they are..." Jake sent a distressed look at Baylee, remembering what they'd talked about that night in Catalina. "I was sure it was Connor, Baylee. I'm sorry, I would've been wrong."

Finally Kit understood the implications of the DNA not matching Connor's. "Oh, God, if it hadn't been for Mr. X…" Her voice trailed off as she went over to Baylee, put her arms around her. "I'm so sorry, Baylee."

It was Dylan who asked, "You're certain about the results?"

Max nodded. "You bet. Plus, I have cause to obtain another search warrant, a search I hope results in finding something conclusive. The point is, I'm out to get a warrant for Collin and Cade Boyd based on the results. Once they're in custody, I get two more DNA samples to compare."

"But you have to find them first," Reese asserted.

Noting the somber mood of the group, Max added, "Hey, don't look so glum. I thought you'd sleep better tonight knowing the news. I want these guys too, you know."

Reese slapped Jake on the back. "He does have a point. At least you narrowed it down to one of the Boyds."

"I guess." Jake groused, still sounding a bit dejected. "A part of me does feel like a huge weight's been lifted off but still…I was so sure it was Connor."

Max stretched out his hand to Jake. "No hard feelings, I hope. Reese is right. You actually are the one who pointed us in this direction."

Jake had no intentions of telling him about the anonymous e-mail from their Mr. X he'd received pointing him to Connor. Not only would it complicate matters, he felt it would break a trust in some weird sort of way.

"Then my work here is done for tonight," Max declared, turning to Reese. "Although I can tell you what caused Quinn's apartment building to blow. You were right, Brennan. It wasn't a natural gas leak. Someone deliberately disconnected the gas dryer in one of the units, on purpose, set out a candle, lit the damned thing—and waited for the gas to reach the flame. Arson investigators assure me it's quite an effective way to achieve an explosion. Coincidentally, that unit just happens to belong to Quinn Tyler here."

"Cade."

"The only person of interest at this point," Max agreed flatly. "Turns out, one of those victims last night who died was a little five-year-old girl named Tara Evers."

Quinn's hand flew to her mouth. "Oh, God, Tara's the little girl who lives next door to me. Her mother, Connie, must be devastated. She's a single mom who only moved into the building eight months ago."

Reese slung his arm around her waist, drew her closer while Max went on, "The firemen didn't find Tara until this morning buried under a ton of rubble. She was alive but they lost her in surgery."

"I feel so responsible...if not for me..."

"Don't do that, Quinn," Reese cautioned. "You couldn't possibly have known they'd do anything like that."

"That's one of the reasons I'm on this. Cade Boyd's the number one suspect. Oh, and while I'm here, might as well tell you this afternoon cadaver dogs hit on a fourth body out at The Enclave about twenty yards from where the other remains were unearthed."

"Jesus, you're just full of news tonight, Max." Reese ran a free hand through his hair while Quinn rested her head on his shoulders, still clearly upset about Tara. "What happens now?"

"We wait. This one hasn't been in the ground all that long, certainly not as long as the others." He shot a look at Baylee. "I'm sorry, Ms. Scott."

"It's okay. I understand. In fact, the technician who swabbed me for DNA explained the whole mitochondrial thing to me. He even told me how they extract the stuff from the dental pulp and if they get enough and if it matches mine, I'll know it's my mother who was buried there all this time for the past twenty-two years. I wonder who the others are, though, some other poor souls who happened to piss off Jessica and Alana."

"And were expendable," Reese added.

"The first three sets of remains won't be yielding any fingerprints, that's for certain, been in the ground way too long. The forensics team is working overtime on this. We'll see if they can get you an answer, Ms. Scott—and soon. But the one they found this afternoon couldn't have been in the ground more than four years maybe. I'm told there's a slight possibility we could get enough of a fingerprint to ID the victim, especially if we get lucky and the prints are on file."

Max shook his head and went on, "Two months ago I was ready to retire. I'm staying on because this is turning out to be the damnedest case of my career. It just keeps spiraling outward from the core."

He turned to leave and stopped as if he'd just thought of something else. "I remember walking into the Stevens crime scene that morning, remember talking to Jessica, and feeling empathy for the victim and her best friend. But I have to tell you after finding out some of this stuff about her and the Boyd woman now, my sympathies are stretched to the limit. Those women were heartless."

After scouring the e-mail attachment upstairs, Reese could attest to that. But he had no intentions of sharing what he'd learned. He kept his mouth shut until after Max had said his goodbyes.

As soon as the front door closed, Reese turned to the group and announced, "I know it's late, but we need to huddle. There's been a development."

"What's up?" Dylan asked.

"I got an e-mail about an hour ago from Mr. X. It seems when it came to BBG&G, Noah Parker did his homework, went the extra mile to solve his own personal puzzle."

Jake and Dylan exchanged deliberate looks. It was Dylan who wisecracked, "If he warned you to take Quinn and go on the run, he's about twenty-four hours too late."

"But we already know about the Parker murders," Jake reasoned. "We figured that much out on our own."

"And it was Dylan who got us looking into my mother's disappearance before Dad ever got around to telling me the truth. What else do we need to know?"

Reese shook his head. "This isn't about the Parkers, at least not all of it. And I doubt anyone knew about the bodies buried on Boyd property, at least no one alive. It seems Noah Parker and our Mr. X uncovered more recent, very damaging information, stuff I doubt either one gained by legal means. There's at least fifty pages of documents to pore over, maybe more. I got through some of the stuff but..."

"If we split it up among us, it'll go faster," Quinn finished.

"Exactly."

Kit headed to the kitchen. "Then I'll get the coffee started."

After printing out the attachment from Reese's laptop on the wireless printer set up in the kitchen, Quinn divvied up the sets of documents and passed a stack to each one. "There has to be sixty-five pages here, Reese."

As they got comfortable around the table, Reese stated, "I know, but I think you'll find them informative. First off, let me paraphrase what the e-mail said. The man's obviously used to working on his own, but says it's past time we understand exactly what we're dealing with since we have the most to lose. He's willing to trust us with this because he can't be in two places at one time. It seems he had a GPS tracking device on the Boyd cars. But since the cops..."

"So that's how he knew their every move," Jake concluded.

"But why trust us now?" Dylan asked, clearly skeptical.

"Because I didn't tell the cops I know what he looks like," Kit admitted.

"What?" Baylee and Quinn said at the same time.

"He's the guy who came into the shop the afternoon Baylee moved into Gloria's guest house. He was fascinated with Ella Canyon's painting, thought he was going to have a heart attack right there in the Book & Bean because of it."

"*Woman Rising*? Mr. X is an art lover? You're joking?" Quinn cracked.

"He thought the blonde on the canvas resembled his late wife. You should have seen him that day. He acted like he was having some kind of seizure or something. I'm surprised he didn't faint."

"Get out. You were in the shop with this guy alone and never said a word to us. That's holding back," Baylee grumbled.

Jake tried to explain. "I was right there with you about her not saying anything to anyone about the man's odd behavior. But after he saved Kit and then kept the Book & Bean in one piece, Kit and I agreed to take a wait and see attitude about telling the cops anything at all about him. Then when he made it three for three with Baylee, we decided to keep what he looked like to ourselves."

"Why mention it to the cops when he did us a favor we'll never be able to repay?" Kit clarified.

Dylan agreed. "I suppose he could somehow realize how grateful we are and he's willing to trust us now to help him out."

"Actually, it's the other way around," Quinn said matter-of-factly.

When they all turned to stare at her, she added, "Consider it this way. Mr. X has already admitted he can't be in two places at one time. So if we don't manage to find a way to keep track of the Nutty Brothers ourselves it could cost one or more of us our lives. The next time they decide to blow something up or do a drive by, one of us sitting here at this table might not be so lucky. Our safety depends on not only figuring out a way to track down the two of them, but also to lure them out into the open."

Impressed with her acumen, Reese tamped down the jolt of lust to his system that was starting to become a habit. "Mr. X has some ideas on that."

He slanted a long look at Jake and Dylan. "And it involves a skill you two possess better than any two people I know. Apparently, he's a fan. But I should point out you'd be breaking several laws, because our hit man is suggesting we make their funds disappear."

Jake looked stunned for a moment before cocking his head to stare at Reese. "You want us to hack into their bank accounts and make their fortune go bye-bye."

"Not me, but I wish I'd thought of it. Mr. X figures if we cut off their non-exhaustible cash source, including all of their hidden overseas assets, which are considerable according to the documents you now hold in your hands, they'll get desperate and have to surface. And when they come up for air, our friend will be there to take them out."

"That's brilliant!" Dylan bellowed. "I'm in."

Jake rubbed his chin, considering. "It can be done. But it means we create a huge paper trail that leads nowhere, which means bouncing the money to all kinds of different offshore accounts before setting up several fake corporations," Jake reasoned. "And what does our mystery man want us to do with all this cash?"

"He leaves that up to us."

Kit chimed in, "Well, I know I don't want anything to do with Alana's estate, knowing where it came from. I say we find out if this Noah Parker has any heirs and give Alana's money to them, maybe even all this other cash. After all, it'll take months to liquidate Alana's assets while we could be giving away the Boyd family money instead."

Jake put his arm around Kit and kissed her squarely on the mouth. "And that is why I'm crazy in love with you. I vote to find Parker's family, too."

Quinn looked around the table, saw the nods of approval. "It's unanimous then. But what if there are none, what if this Noah has no heirs?"

"Then we give the money back to all the people BBG&G swindled and cheated over the years," Dylan suggested.

"That could be a very long list," Baylee pointed out. "They had to be scamming people right and left for years. How in the world are we going to know exactly who got ripped off?"

"True. Plus, that's a lot of power to wield," Quinn concluded.

Dylan nodded. "Okay. Then we'll pick a charity. Donate it to a better cause."

"It'll be like Robin Hood. We steal from the asshole Nutty Brothers and give it to the needy. I like it," Quinn weighed in. "We need to give our Op a name though. Any suggestions?"

"Operation Neuter," Baylee deadpanned.

They all stared at her for about five seconds before busting out with laughter.

"Perfect." Dylan planted a kiss on her mouth. "And that is the reason I've found the love of my life, people. The woman I plan to marry."

Reese stared at his friend. "You? Settle down with one woman?"

While everyone exchanged looks, Baylee's cheeks blushed. "I know we haven't known each other very long but...when you know, you just...*know*."

After taking a moment to absorb the shock, Kit went to Baylee first, then Dylan. "Congrats. I'll say one thing for both of you. I've never seen two people more suited to one another."

"Really?" Baylee beamed. "That's what I said about you and Jake. I was worried you'd think it was too fast..."

Quinn grabbed Baylee in a hug. "If you're sure, honey, I can get behind this, even if it is moving lightning-fast. No offense Surfer Boy, but Baylee's got a kid."

"None taken," Dylan replied jovially before getting serious. "You forget, Sarah's already *mine*. I've got a piece of paper that says so. But even if I didn't, I love that baby like she came from a part of me. And Baylee, well Baylee is the first woman I've ever truly loved, heart to heart..."

"And soul to soul," Baylee finished.

Quinn eyed the friend she'd known for more than seventeen years. Baylee looked as happy as she'd ever seen her. More moved by Dylan's declaration than she wanted to admit, Quinn said simply, "Then welcome to our humble little family, such as it is."

Upstairs, getting ready for bed, Quinn walked into the pristine guest bathroom to brush her teeth. She had to give it to Jake's determination to hire the best carpenters and plumbers to bring Crandall House into the twenty-first century.

In record time, he, or rather his contractors, had taken an old shell of a house and made it not just livable but a thing of beauty. She ran her hand along the sleek, tempered glass countertop that gave the room a clean, modern look and pulled open one of the drawers in the vanity.

She picked up a brand-new toothbrush along with a regular size tube of toothpaste. She shook her head. Leave it to Kit to provide all those necessary but forgotten small amenities she hadn't remembered to shop for and no longer owned.

So far she'd managed to keep the tears from flowing. But alone now, Quinn's eyes blurred. She took a minute to consider why she had absolutely nothing left of her very own. Cade Boyd had been trying for years to make her pay for that crappy, brief six weeks of bad judgment. And now, he'd finally committed the ultimate. He'd taken the lives of innocent people he didn't even know just to get back at her.

And for what?

Because he'd had a history of getting his own way for too long, a history of having never been denied anything in his irresponsible, miserable life, she thought now.

It certainly wasn't revenge for his brother's death. No, if that were the case he'd be going after the person responsible for killing Jessica and Sumner and now Connor. No, blowing up her apartment building was personal and meant to make a statement.

She finished washing her face and dried the tears away.

Crawling between the crispy clean sheets, she remembered those six short weeks of dating the man. She sighed with frustration. For years she'd carried around that pang of regret.

But now as she closed her eyes with fatigue left over from the grueling night before, it was long past time to put a stop to bemoaning her mistakes.

Together, all six of them would do their best to locate Cade and his stupid brother, Collin.

And put an end to this destruction for good.

CHAPTER 8

*T*he smells in dingy, dumpy motel rooms never varied.

Regurgitated beer pretty much smelled the same in the Valley as it did in Riverside. The same could be said for the stench from cheap perfume and cologne, ditto for how stale cigarette smoke managed to linger and foul up the already rank air no matter how much air freshener you sprayed out of the can.

Not that anyone ever thought to pick up a can of anything that might make the rooms smell better.

Because of that, five-year-old Quinn learned a long time ago not to complain about something so trivial. There were other, more essential things to deal with, like getting a decent meal on a regular basis.

She'd even gotten used to playing on all the threadbare carpeting, dirty from years of over-use, or sitting on the stained, shabby furnishings, out of date by decades. That never seemed to change either. It seemed seedy motel owners rarely set aside money to redecorate.

Then there were the constant piles of dirty laundry that seemed to follow them from place to place because Ella consistently reminded her daughter household chores were not her thing.

At least the cheap motel rooms were better than sleeping in Ella's beat-up old Monte Carlo, Quinn reasoned. She craned her neck to stare up at the television set which almost touched the ceiling because it was attached to a stand bolted high onto the grimy wall.

But Quinn wasn't tall enough to reach it even if she stood on a chair. Instead, she had to lie back on the bed or sit and hold her neck at a funny angle looking up at the thing where some soap opera diva held court to the masses and had for hours.

Because the TV stayed on practically twenty-four-seven she picked up the remote to lower the volume. Since this time of day yielded no cartoons, the soap didn't hold Quinn's attention for very long.

Besides, Ella was enough of a drama queen to deal with on a daily basis without watching more of it play out on the tube.

Left alone for almost five hours now and bored, Quinn picked up her tousled, dark-haired, Starlight Carousel Barbie and went over to the window. She climbed up on the slice of a ridge above the AC unit so she could keep an eye out on the parking lot.

Surely Ella would be coming back soon. She'd been gone since noon and Quinn's stomach was beginning to rumble with hunger. The dried corn flakes she'd eaten for breakfast that morning a mere memory now, Quinn absently stroked the tangled hair of the doll whose tattered blue dress had long since lost its sheen.

Not spotting any sign of Ella, she crawled off the sill and went to grab the only other toy she owned, a stuffed, bug-eyed, polka-dotted frog, she'd nicknamed Broggy. It too, like the doll, was a bit frayed around the edges. But Broggy's sad shape didn't deter Quinn from taking it wherever she went.

Out of habit, she crossed to the dresser and opened each drawer, going through the contents of one before moving on to the others, making sure there were no crackers left. But just as she already knew, the box was empty. She tossed the carton into the over-filled wastebasket and went back to the window—to wait.

Holding Broggy tucked under one arm while clutching Barbie in her other hand, Quinn kept a vigilant watch out for Ella. She could only hope that when Ella came back the woman would be alone and not dragging one of her male friends from wherever she'd found to spend the afternoon.

Quinn chewed on her thumbnail, little worry wart she was, and bit her lip. It was getting dark outside. How much longer would she have to wait for something to eat?

All at once she spotted Ella's familiar gait walking between the cars in the parking lot. It was hard to miss that drunken sway. But as soon as Quinn spied the white sack she carried in her hand, the one with a well-known fast food logo on it, she let out a whoop, almost tumbling off the window sill.

When the key fit into the lock and the door opened, Ella burst in. "Hi ya, kiddo. Look what I brought you, a burger and fries for supper."

Ella threw the sack in Quinn's direction. The little girl dropped Barbie and Broggy and made a dive for the food. She had already crammed her mouth with two bites when she looked up and realized Ella wasn't alone. A grubby looking guy with dark eyes and dark hair rubbed at a grease-stained shirt that barely covered his belly.

"Why don't you take your burger into the john for me, Quinn honey? Give me and Reuben a little alone time. How about it, baby doll?"

Quinn began to wrap her burger back up and put it into the sack.

"Hey, the kid can watch if she wants," Rueben suggested as he already began to strip off his clothes.

Ella giggled and told him, "That'd cost extra, now, wouldn't it? Go on Quinn, get a move on, I don't have all night. And thank Reuben here for the burger."

"Thanks," Quinn muttered as she dutifully moved toward the bathroom, taking her food with her. She pushed the door shut and turned the lock.

The sounds they started to make penetrated the thin door.

Quinn sat her sack down on the edge of the tub and took out her burger again, which by now was stone cold. As she did her best not to listen to the mattress sounds the adults were making in the other room, she wished she had thought to grab Broggy and Barbie so she'd have something to play with and wouldn't be alone.

Because there was no telling how long Ella would be going at it with dirty old Rueben.

⚭ ⚭ ⚭ ⚭ ⚭

Quinn rolled over in bed and groaned when she saw the time on the clock. Two-fifteen.

Usually when the hellish dreams from the past took hold this time of night, they never wanted to let go. She rolled her neck and shoulders a couple of times, hoping to get her tense body to relax, did her best to shake off the walk down memory lane.

Good thing she was used to going without much sleep. Out of habit, she swiped her hair back and bundled it into a ponytail before crawling out of bed. She reached for the robe she'd borrowed from Kit.

Maybe a two a.m. snack would get her mind off those miserable days of yesteryear with Ella the junkie.

As she made her way downstairs, resentment simmered along her nerves. How old did she have to get before those nasty memories stopped trying to weasel their way back in? Would it always be a battle to shed those years she'd spent with Ella doing without, going hungry? How long before she quit remembering the sounds and the smells?

Rounding the last of the stairs into the spotless kitchen she'd helped clean up only a couple of hours earlier, she spied Reese sitting at the table hunched over his laptop, fingers flying over the keyboard.

She went to the pantry, dug out a box of Cocoa Puffs, found a bowl and a spoon. "It's a little late to be sending out the bat signal in computer code to mystery man, don't you think?"

Reese visibly jumped at her voice. "No, he makes sure we can't reply to his e-mails. I'm working on…something else."

No way was he going to tell her he was sending an e-mail to Nick Tyler telling him not to bother showing up after all. He'd gotten the man's personal e-mail addy from Jordan Donovan, who'd gotten it from a musician friend who had asked a music industry insider for a favor.

He had to believe if he went to the source it would keep Tyler from getting curious and keep him the hell away from L.A. and the daughter he didn't know.

Reese took the time to look up and study Quinn's face, her eyes. Those deep chocolate pools said it all.

"How long have you been bothered by dreams, Quinn?"

She stopped in mid-pour as the cereal fell into the bowl in a heap before reaching in the fridge for the milk. "Who says I had a dream?"

Defensive, Reese decided as he got up and took down a bowl for his own cereal. "You tossed and turned in your sleep less than twenty-four hours earlier. Now here you are up in the middle of the night—restless."

"Look, I've got a lot on my mind, okay? I've been kicked out of the job I love, lost the only home I've known since I was sixteen. If you ask me, that's plenty cause for loss of sleep."

Reese wasn't buying it. He took a deep breath. "You don't want to talk about it? Fine, but don't stand there and evade the question or lie to my face."

Did the man always have to be so…damned know it all? She grumbled and took a seat at the kitchen table. "God, do you always have to sound like a lawyer, cross examine everyone? I don't want to talk about my fucking dreams, how's that?"

"Good enough, at least it's an honest answer. So you're up at two in the morning because you had a craving for Cocoa Puffs?"

"Geez, a woman can't get a bowl of cereal without getting grilled. Do you ever go off the clock and act normal?" Looking at the stubborn set to his jaw, two could play hardball, Quinn concluded. "Why are you on your laptop this time of night? Signs of a workaholic? Hiding something? Scratching your online porn itch? Stretching your billable hours to the limit maybe?"

They were butting heads again, Reese thought. "Who's the workaholic here, Quinn?" He put up the free hand that wasn't holding his bowl as if he wanted peace. "How about we head to neutral corners for two seconds, okay? Let's start this round over."

"Hey, I just wanted a lousy bowl of cereal. You're the one who went into lawyer-mode and started the twenty-questions routine."

"Out of concern," he added. "Jesus, hasn't anyone ever just worried about you, Quinn?"

"Nope, just Kit and Baylee. And I like it that way."

"Because you like shutting down anyone who tries. Oh, believe me, I get it, loud and clear."

She threw out both arms in gesture. "Maybe it's because I don't want to get hurt. How about that? I opened myself up once and look where that got me."

"Goddamn it! Do not compare me to that piece of shit Cade Boyd."

She'd hit a nerve with that little slip of the tongue. "No, no, I didn't mean to do that." She scrubbed a hand over her face. "Look, it's just that I've never been able to rely on a single soul except for Baylee and Kit. It's a habit. Opening up, you get hurt."

"Oh, baby, no one wants to get hurt. But you, you're like a cactus. Don't get too close to Quinn Tyler, or those spikes of hers are liable to cut deep and leave a gaping hole."

She huffed out a breath, getting madder by the minute. "What brought this on, because I won't talk about the past? I let you push me last night to open up, but this is... just back off! Maybe if I'd had a Hallmark moment growing up..." Her voice trailed off before picking up steam again. "Why do you have to poke at me about stupid old dreams, Reese? What makes you think I'd want to talk about them if I were having them?

"Because. Both Kit and Baylee were tormented for years by their dreams. Both ignored them until they couldn't. If it weren't for Kit's dream about Alana and Jessica we might still be wondering how this whole thing got started."

He wondered if he should even bring it up and then decided to hell with it. "Besides, you were crying in your sleep last night. Calling out for a kitten you couldn't have, forced to leave a place you didn't want to leave, people you didn't want saying goodbye."

It had broken his heart at the time, watching those big fat tears roll down her cheeks even while she slept.

She blinked in surprise. "What? That's..."

"You were tossing and turning and wanting the kitten. You were also saying something about Broggy, whatever that means. You sounded like a small child, Quinn, not more than two or three years old."

"But...it's just a dream I've had since I was a kid, that's all." She eyed his face, noticed he wasn't buying it.

"Okay, maybe it's my first memory or something. I don't know. It's stuck like glue to my brain though." She went into detail about the farm and the animals and the tall man. "I remember crying that I had to leave that beautiful, clean place. Even at such a young age, I knew for certain I did not want to crawl back in that car with Ella."

"And earlier, just now?"

"Boy, you won't let anything go, will you?"

He sent her a curvy grin. "I'm like a dog with a bone. Maybe talking about it will help you sleep."

"Oh, please. Therapy is something I tried…once…a long time ago. Talk, blah, blah, more talk, doesn't help a whit."

"So you shouldn't mind telling me then."

She hunched her shoulders, giving in, and murmured, "I dream about those years when Ella had it bad with the drugs—and men, back in those sleazy motel rooms around all kinds of other junkies. I've seen ugly things, Reese, things a normal child shouldn't see, or even know about."

He picked up her hand and brought it to his lips, placed a kiss on the palm. "You need a distraction."

She whooshed out a laugh. "Is that what you're calling it? Why allude to the deed? Why not just get down to it? "

"Because seduction, the buildup is, a diversion you'll thank me for later." With that, he lifted up her chin with one finger, leaned over, took her mouth, managed to tug out a low groan from somewhere inside.

Her blood heated. Juices spiked as she gave back every bit as good as she got. Layer by layer, lust built in her belly. She shimmied onto his lap, felt the hard lump in his jeans. "I want you. I've wanted you for weeks now."

"Ditto." He pulled her robe apart, took a moment to stare at the perfect breasts before cocking his head and taking a pebbled point into his mouth.

At that moment, Reese's cell phone rang.

"It's three in the morning!" Quinn grumbled. "Doesn't anyone sleep anymore?"

"Which means I better answer." He reached for the phone. "Reese here. What? When? Okay, but you handle it until we get there. Yeah, I'll let Jake know. He's probably got his cell turned off for the night."

Quinn grabbed his hand. "What?"

"Donovan says someone broke into the Book & Bean, went so far as to get inside and pour gasoline near the back door, even lit a match, took off though when something spooked them. He says there was a brief fizzle of a fire because the sprinklers kicked in, doused it. The place reeks of gasoline though. We'll have to clean the shop up before Kit opens in a couple of hours."

"This is ridiculous. We're in defensive mode here. We need to go on the offense, not just sit back and wait for those assholes to keep hitting us."

"Might be the second time in the last forty-eight we've agreed on anything. I'm done waiting for the phone to ring to find out what disaster they've planned for us next." He got to his feet, walked to the bottom of the back staircase before turning to tell her, "And we're going to finish what we started here, Quinn. Count on it."

"Damn right we are," she muttered when he left to go upstairs to get Jake.

🔺 🔺 🔺 🔺 🔺

When he got back to the hotel suite, Collin did his best to open the door and be as quiet as possible. But in his inebriated state, half high, half drunk, he knocked over a lamp trying to find the light switch.

His brother, who had been passed out himself only hours earlier, pounced. "Where the fuck have you been?"

Collin snorted the laugh of the very intoxicated. "Hey bro, had somethin' to take care of, took longer than I thought, that's all. You go back to bed now, get some sleep, it's late."

Cade picked up on the inflection of the lie, mainly because he knew his brother. "Where'd you go, Collin? I want to know. Now! Don't try to bullshit me."

"Scott and I took a little drive, that's all."

"Scott? The cops are crawling all over The Enclave and you go joyriding with Scott!"

"He's always up for an adventure, you know that. Besides, the cops have torn up our home, our cousins had to find other places to live, too. I dropped by his house in Santa Monica. We're family; family covers each other's asses. He covered mine tonight."

"Then tell me where you were."

He started fidgeting. "Look, I'm tired."

Cade took a step toward him. Fearing the worst, he caught the unmistakable whiff and narrowed his eyes. "You reek with the smell of gasoline. What did you do, Collin?"

"I made sure the Book & Bean is toast. Okay? You wouldn't do anything so... That left it up to me and Scotty."

"You and Scott set fire to the Book & Bean? You idiot! Boston put in a security system with surveillance. That's why I told you to wait." He slapped Collin across the face, hard. "Pack! Now! We have to get out of here in case anyone followed you back here."

Cade picked up his cell phone, dialed his cousin, Scott Geller. The minute Scott picked up, Cade went into a frenzied rant. "Since you let Collin talk you into insanity, you need to get your ass over here. Now! You've compromised this whole thing. You'll have to rent another car. Use a rental agency at LAX. And don't leave a paper trail either."

On the other end of the phone, Scott, the middle son of Frank Geller, did his best to explain. "Hey, I tried to talk him out of it, but you know Collin when he sets his head on something. He just won't be persuaded to listen to reason."

"Yeah, right, sure you did. Boston put in a security system with a camera. There's video out there now."

"I didn't get close enough for that. Collin is the one who went inside, set the fire. We took off right after."

"I don't care who did it, we've got to move just in case you guys were followed and Collin led them back here. Why do I have to do all the thinking?"

"I thought if I went with him, it would go faster."

"Just get over here with another car. You know the drill, make sure you aren't followed."

CHAPTER 9

"**S**tupid idiot obviously didn't see the security camera," Reese pointed out to Jake and Dylan as they watched the tape of Collin jimmying the back door lock in the dark of night, then stepping inside the bookstore. "What the hell does he keep looking around for anyway?"

The three men continued to stare at the computer screen while Collin made a big production of walking around behind the counter, bending down, searching right then left.

"It isn't matches. He dumps the gas right there in the back storage area and then takes out his own lighter. Good thing the sprinkler system kicked in."

"And the silent alarm alerted the fire department." Reese replayed the video for another scan to view it from the beginning when Collin had first appeared at the back door. "Look at that, he comes in and goes directly to the counter. And right here, he's still looking around for something…wait a minute, see that right there. What is that he takes out of his pocket?"

Dylan leaned over Reese and tapped in a few keys to enlarge the image. "Is that a candle?"

"There's no gas at the Book & Bean is there?"

Jake shook his head. "Nope. Kit does all the baking at the house, off-site. No oven here except for a microwave."

"Remember St. John said Quinn's apartment exploded because they unhooked the gas connection to the dryer."

"That's what he's looking for then, a gas source, stupid asshole."

"And look here. Something spooks him. He throws the candle down into the gasoline and takes off like a shot out the back door."

"Maybe Cade," Dylan surmised. "But then he's smart enough not to get within camera range. Waiting in the car, maybe?"

"I don't think it was Cade that spooked him. My guess is this was a rogue act by Collin and not sanctioned by his brother," Reese stated. "See right here, he gets flustered when he discovers there's no source of gas like at Quinn's, doesn't know what to do next. Check out the panicked look on his face, right here." Reese stopped the video. They all stared at the screen.

Clearly puzzled, Jake asked. "Why do you think he went rogue?"

"Because Cade isn't this stupid to hit where there's a surveillance camera at the back door. Collin, on the other hand, is stupid times two."

"No argument there but if Cade wasn't with him…who alerted him, scared him off?"

"Had to be Mr. X," Dylan surmised.

"I don't think so."

Jake eyed Reese. "If you know something, now would be a good time to spit it out."

"There was a part of that e-mail I didn't share with…everyone." He spared a quick glance over in Quinn's direction as she continued to help Kit and Baylee clean up the back area of the store where the fire had done most of the damage to the wooden oak flooring. At the moment, she was busy mopping up water from the floor from the sprinkler system.

He lowered his voice to a whisper. "He pointed us in the direction of Connor for Claire's murder, right?"

Jake nodded. "At the time I thought he was yanking my chain."

"He got it wrong. We know that now since Max has DNA pointing to either Collin or Cade."

"Go on."

"Before he ever got started on this whole process, he did considerable legwork on his own, checked out all of the people associated with Alana and Jessica—in detail." He studied Jake's face. "Yeah, that includes everything about Kit. But when he found out about the abuse after Alana was gone, he reevaluated things where she was concerned, considerably."

"You aren't making me feel warm and fuzzy about the guy, Reese."

"Hold on, hear me out. He might have moved on past Kit, but not so with Jessica's branch of the family tree or with Frank's or Eva's for that matter.

"It seems he came up with some interesting findings. He discovered the cousins share a weakness for cocaine and partying, along with a penchant for prostitutes. He suspects Cade of killing several call girls, strangling them. He sent me a list of women who worked as escorts and have since gone missing."

"Let me get this straight. Mr. X sent you a list of call girls Cade is supposed to have killed? Okay, I'm feeling a whole lot skeptical here, Reese. Not saying he isn't capable but..."

"He's capable. Cade tried to strangle Quinn. She told me about the incident that happened in college and said if it hadn't been for Adam Gatz showing up when he did, she's convinced Cade would have killed her that night."

"But what does that have to do with who spooked Collin?" Dylan posed.

"I'm getting to it. Cade's got a temper, right? I've seen it firsthand. And after talking to Quinn, knowing what he did to her in the heat of the moment, it's easy to see him going a step further and killing defenseless women. These call girls put themselves in a vulnerable position. A man like Cade's going to push his advantage. And there isn't a damn one of us that doesn't suspect he blew up Quinn's building, right?

"Let's consider Collin for a minute. He's not the brightest. The most you can say about Collin is he's a follower, a dipshit absolutely, but is he a serial killer?

"Which brings us to their cousins? What do we really know about Adam and Jacob Gatz, or Taylor, Scott, and Garrett Geller for that matter?"

A stupefied Jake asked, "Where are you going with this, Reese?"

"Mr. X was wrong about Connor killing Claire, right? What if Cade's good for killing these hookers but with a caveat? What if Cade had help?"

"That still doesn't tell me who you think spooked Collin," Dylan pointed out.

"Think outside the box. Don't focus on the obvious. Cade and Collin have gone off the deep end before and Collin is easy to manipulate. But Collin's the obvious accomplice, too obvious."

"You think Cade is getting help from a cousin, the cousin gets a pass because we're focused on Collin. That's a leap, even for a skeptic like you, Reese."

"There might be two killers involved, that's all I'm saying. Cade being one of them and the cousin, whichever one it is, either is part of the actually killings or simply helps dispose of the bodies. Either way, he covers it up for the Type A, more aggressive personality, which would be Cade. Think about it. Cade's already fingered as the guy who blew up Quinn's building. He's killed before, no question about that. What if this partner in crime is someone other than Collin? I think our Mr. X isn't infallible, brilliant in some areas, sure, but not without errors in logic."

"You think one of the cousins helped Cade kill these call girls and Claire?"

"Cade could have killed Claire by himself. But the hookers? Anyone of the cousins could have helped him with those. Since Cade doesn't like to get his own hands dirty he would most likely want help disposing of the bodies. I say we dig into the lives of the other cousins."

At that moment, Quinn meandered over to the monitor they were supposed to be watching. Reese deftly changed direction from serial killer back to the subject at hand. "Watch this, see; it looks like it was definitely Collin who started the fire."

Jake and Dylan exchanged knowing glances. But it was Jake who led the charge to conceal their previous discussion even further. "We'll turn the tape over to St. John, of course, give him more fuel for his case against Collin."

"Collin's such an idiot if he thinks he can waltz in here and do this to one of us." She placed a brief kiss on Reese's cheek before moving on to help Kit get set up for the morning rush.

Dylan wiggled his eyes up and down. "So, you and Quinn hooked up, huh?"

"Yeah, Surfer Boy, we'll pass you a note about it in study hall, how's that?"

"Wise ass," Dylan muttered. "Maybe I should mention to her how you suck at personal relationships."

"Yeah? Like you know so much about having anything but a one-night stand? At least I have a track record for going out multiple times with the same woman."

Jake ignored the same kind of banter he'd heard between these two for years. "Guys, could we focus here?" Once he was certain Quinn was out of earshot, he picked up the cousin theory again where they'd left off. "Let's say Cade's the killer of the call girls, how in the world does Mr. X know about these missing escorts?"

"Legwork maybe? Look, I don't know. He pointed you in the right direction in Claire's murder. He just pinpointed the wrong brother or cousin. And Cade's a bully, in personal relationships, in court, in all aspects of his life. I'm thinking our Mr. X dug around enough to find out some very disturbing things about the Boyd, Geller, and Gatz family tree."

Dylan agreed, "Connor was a bully, might be they all are. How do you know he isn't the one who murdered these call girls?"

"I don't. That's the point here, guys. Up to this point we've pretty much been led around by the nose, pointed in the direction people wanted us to go. I say it's time we did some digging of our own, get solid answers on our own. Get off our asses and get involved in this thing for real, put an end to it."

"I want Collin and Cade to do time, lots of time," Jake agreed.

"Same here. Go on the offensive. Then we need to find some evidence, turn it over to the cops," Dylan reasoned. "Now you're talking. We cut them off at the knees by taking away their funds, Operation Neuter, and then get down to finding out what these guys are really like on our own terms, hit 'em where they hurt."

Pleased that his friends were on board, Reese stated matter-of-factly, "Then what are we waiting for?"

🜋🜋🜋🜋🜋

Once the three men had a united goal, they set out to put the plan in motion.

It was decided someone needed to go undercover that very day.

For the rest of the morning, Dylan devised the best possible way to get inside BBG&G. At his laptop, it didn't take longer than fifteen minutes to breach the firm's simple firewall to their network.

Stupid amateurs, Dylan decided, used the most common passwords. Simple passwords were like wrapped Christmas presents sitting around under the tree, waiting for a determined hacker to discover and use them to his advantage.

Once in, he read individual emails, both personal and work-related, from most of the key employees and their staff.

Since he needed to pay a visit to the firm's computer room, see for himself the inner workings of the place, he looked for a reason that would get him inside the building without a lot of fanfare.

He found it when an administrative assistant mentioned to her boss that one of the copiers required maintenance. The company providing repairs was a major supplier who had long ago ordained uniforms obsolete and insisted their field personnel wear basic white dress shirts with ties and black dress pants.

It was a ridiculous notion to think repairing a copier required such formal attire, but then who was Dylan to argue? Those articles of clothing were readily available. Now, all he had to do was come up with an official-looking ID bearing the company logo.

By three-thirty that afternoon, Dylan had donned his disguise. His blond ponytail had been dyed a raven black and left loose, the locks feathering his shoulders. The horn-rimmed glasses he wore had him looking more like Johnny Depp's brother than a copier repairman.

But hey, if he could rebuild an engine in a '68 Camaro he ought to be able to fix a simple printer.

After presenting his fake ID with the name John Frazier to the security guard on the first floor, he stood at the downstairs reception area waiting to be led up to the tenth floor and the malfunctioning machine. When a cute, plump thirty-something brunette appeared named Donna Fontaine, Dylan put the innate Burke charm to the test.

On the ride up in the elevator Dylan flirted and discovered a bubbly Italian who liked to cook and go to the movies. He used his film buff knowledge to fluster the admin so much he had her laughing at his movie quotes and trivia. By the time they stepped off into another upscale, spacious reception area, he decided Donna seemed more than willing to hand over the key to the executive washroom. He had only to ask.

Good thing he didn't really need Donna's generosity.

He'd planned his foray into the camp of the enemy in late afternoon for a reason. It was a known fact most of L.A.'s work force began their mass exodus home between three-thirty and four o'clock to avoid the inevitable traffic jams.

He could only hope that was true for the dedicated workers here.

After Donna showed him to the copy room and somewhat reluctantly left him alone, it took him less than five minutes to locate the paper jam, another five to oil the drum, and the other time—to look busy.

Sure enough, in a matter of thirty minutes, employees started to abandon their cubicles and drift toward the elevators. After Donna's floor grew silent as a tomb, he found the break room, treated himself to a soft drink and candy bar before setting out to locate the computer room.

It took him forty minutes, but five floors down he breezed into the firm's version of his own beloved Command Central, courtesy of Donna's pilfered security card, which he intended to leave conveniently under her office chair as if she'd simply inadvertently dropped the piece of plastic before heading home.

Command Central stood blessedly deserted.

Sitting down at the nearest work station, Dylan, aka John Frazier, went to work. Priority one was finding a place to tap into the mainframe where his wireless device wouldn't get noticed.

It took him a few minutes to scout the area before he found the perfect place to conceal the existence of his router. The modem would relay all information to another designated remote server he'd already set up for just that purpose.

In less than an hour he was done with the installation.

Once he left the building, he found an ideal place to hide the repeater which amplified the signal from three blocks away, which in turn relayed the data to the remote server and would allow them twenty-four-seven access to anything on the firm's mainframe.

After he finished the work, he took out his cell to let Jake know everything from his end was a go.

Back at Crandall House, Jake went to work concentrating on everything the database had to offer. He discovered financial records he could readily tap into inside the vast Boyd, Geller, and Gatz personal portfolios, which included their bank accounts, stocks and bonds, and all of their property holdings, both foreign and domestic.

For now, any hidden assets he found he intended to keep separate from the so-called legitimate monies he discovered. Separating the illegal stream of money from the genuine clients became almost impossible. Almost. He had to give it to good ol' Jessica and Sumner's talent for evasion, though. They'd done a decent job of masking which was which.

While his friends took care of their part, Reese zeroed in on everything personal he could find about Cade, Collin and all the cousins, which included Garrett, Scott, and Taylor Geller as well as Adam and Jacob Gatz.

Since Trevor had been kind enough to supply every single one of their passwords to their social networking sites, it wasn't that difficult to ascertain what they were up to via the Internet.

He soon had an idea of what all seven men did in their downtime.

It wasn't a pretty picture.

☙☙☙☙☙

While Reese spent time searching Cade's online persona, Cade Boyd returned the favor by finding out everything he could about Reese. Like Reese, Cade might not have been a hacker, but he could utilize a search engine.

To Cade's way of thinking, just because the guy had graduated top of his class didn't mean shit. He couldn't stand the way the guy acted all Perry Mason in a courtroom anyway. And now that Quinn was with him he'd find a way to take them both down—down into the gutter where they both belonged.

For years revenge had stewed in his gut. For all the wrongs he'd put up with, he intended to make both of them pay—with their lives.

☮☮☮☮☮

It didn't take Quinn long to suspect something was up. As soon as Jake had returned with Kit from the Book & Bean, he'd closeted himself away in his study. From the other side of a closed door, she could hear his fingers furiously tapping computer keys.

Dylan had been gone for hours. He'd disappeared by claiming a work emergency had come up and he needed to handle it before things got thorny.

Quinn wasn't buying it.

Because Reese had taken refuge in his room as well, she headed that way, prepared to wage a war if necessary. When faced with another closed door, this time Quinn knocked once but didn't wait for an answer before she turned the knob and barreled inside.

Reese sat at yet another laptop, pounding away. She sauntered into the room, crossed her arms over her chest. "Hmm, isn't it interesting how you guys have all gone to ground at the same time?"

"Work," Reese grunted as he barely looked up from his screen.

"Uh huh. Where'd Dylan go then?"

"A work thing came up."

"Uh huh. Reese Brennan, what are you up to? What are you all up to? I saw the way you guys were huddled and whispering this morning at the bookstore, changed the subject whenever we members of the weaker sex got within five feet. You think you're so clever but you aren't fooling anyone."

He managed to grunt again before she made her way behind him and his laptop. At the last possible second, he snapped down the lid.

His eyes cruised up her long legs, the length of her body, until he got to her face.

He made a grab for her waist.

"You're here 'cause you want me. Admit it, Tyler. You want to finish what we started at three a.m. this morning and couldn't wait for night." He nibbled and grazed along her jaw before pulling her down to his lap. His hand rubbed a circle on her lower back before he started playing with a hard pebbled point under her top.

She itched to raise the lid up and see what he'd been doing. But his mouth and fingers made her consider other possibilities. "You're deep in thought there, distracted even. Are you sure you can bring your A game, Reese?"

"You're joking, right? You mean you can't feel my A game? I must not be doing it right then." He put some emphasis into rearranging her butt across his lower half, where he was stone hard. "I want inside you."

At that moment, Kit poked her head into the room, cleared her throat. "Oops, sorry to interrupt, but Dylan's back and there's some heated discussion downstairs about Operation Neuter." Kit narrowed her eyes in disgust. "Which apparently was put into motion without input from *all* of us."

Quinn exploded in his ear. "Ah ha! I knew you guys were up to something. What happened to letting us in on the game?"

"No need to yell," Reese managed. "We saw an opening and took it."

"This is our personal war and has been for a long time!" Quinn snarled.

"Was. It *was* your personal war," Reese corrected. "Now, it involves all of us."

"Oh please…"

But the kiss he planted on her lips shut her up. "This house is too damn crowded, never a moment to ourselves. Tonight, we either find some way to be alone or we're leaving this mad house and checking into the nearest hotel."

Quinn patted the side of his cheek. "Aw, that is so sweet, but I think I can manage to sneak you into my room tonight without creating a media sensation." She nipped his ear and snuggled against his neck. "I want you, Brennan."

"Yeah? Right backatcha, Tyler. I knew it was just a matter of time. Now let's go downstairs before I rip your clothes off and have my way tasting that body of yours."

CHAPTER 10

No one ever said communal living would be a walk in the park. With six adults and a baby living under the same roof there were bound to be disagreements eventually.

Even in a huge house like this one, living together meant there wasn't a lot of privacy for things like settling differences of opinion or keeping out of anyone's face when you were pissed.

At the moment, Baylee was pissed and waging her own war.

As she stood in the living room, furious, Reese saw another side to the diminutive blonde.

Who knew her five-three petite frame hid a fierce temper? And it was aimed in Dylan's direction.

Hands fisted on her hips, she stood like Xena, warrior princess, staring down the much taller man. "Look at your hair. Why on earth did you have to do that to your hair? What were you thinking? You deliberately didn't do that here…you deliberately snuck out of this house…"

"My house, my bathroom. I didn't want to get black dye all over Kit's brand-new sinks."

"So you admit you snuck out of here and drove all the way to Pacific Palisades…to do *that*? You deliberately went to that place without telling me, didn't tell me where you were going because you could have easily been arrested. But you're so thoughtful and considerate when it comes to *Kit's* bathroom fixtures, Kit's feelings and not mine. And what if you'd been caught, did you consider that?"

"But I wasn't."

"That's beside the point. They've got you on surveillance cameras now. That place is like Fort Knox. And you lied to me."

"I omitted, that's not the same as lying."

"Don't parse words with me, Dylan Burke. You told me you had a work thing to take care of; you lied."

"Geez woman, are you going to throw every word I said back to me?"

"If I have to, you bet I am."

"I didn't want you to worry, which you would have done if I'd told you what I planned to do."

"Of course I would've worried. I could be bailing you out of jail right now."

"But you aren't because I was brilliant."

"Don't you dare joke about this and try to get on my good side. You took an awful chance, Dylan. What if…"

He crushed his mouth to hers just as she was wavering. "I'm sorry. I should've said something. But I didn't want you spending the entire afternoon stewing about it."

Kit crossed her arms over her chest. "Yeah, well, you guys think you can cut us out of this, think again. The Boyds are our nemesis, always have been. From now on we do things as a group or that's it…Operation Neuter is ours, not yours. You start sharing everything because you aren't the only ones who can heat up the action."

"You seem to forget we've known these people most of our lives, fought with them, fought against them," Baylee pointed out.

Quinn simply stared at the men until finally she demanded, "Now, which one of you wants to come clean, catch us up on what you were whispering about this morning, besides this venture into the enemy camp done without our knowledge?"

All three males now faced a trio of pissed off females. Reese cleared his throat and started sharing, telling them about the missing call girls and his accomplice-slash-cousin theory.

Quinn's eyes went wide. "You think Cade killed these women with the help of one of his cousins? Wow, and I thought you were the skeptic from hell. Looks like you've been hiding a creative side."

"I think it's entirely possible."

"Wait, Mr. X put this on the table?"

"He had us looking in Connor's direction for Claire's murder, didn't he? He got that one wrong. I'm thinking Cade needs help disposing of the bodies so he enlists someone he knows he can control."

"But why would Cade need to turn to a cousin when he's got a built-in brother stooge named Collin?" Quinn asked, not buying his theory for a minute. "That makes no sense."

"Because no one has a bigger mouth than Collin, think about it. He'd go bragging about it first chance he got, you know he would, makes him a loose cannon. Even Cade would understand he couldn't be trusted."

Kit agreed, "He's got you there, Quinn. In a weird kind of way it does make sense when you take the time to consider it, truly consider the way Cade is and how he wouldn't want to get his own hands dirty getting rid of the bodies."

"How many, Reese, is he supposed to have killed?" Baylee asked, a little sick to her stomach at the thought.

"Five disappeared, two of which were eighteen. Their families have no idea what happened to them, either. Some of them have been missing for almost three years now without a word. These girls were part of the same escort service and haven't been seen since they left to go on their assignment to meet Cade Boyd."

"Then why don't the cops arrest him?"

Jake entered the fray. "They have to have bodies to get evidence. I'm the last person to defend that perspective but... I'd have to add, it's that same old lame excuse about who they know and how powerful the families are."

"Were. The family tree has thinned out quite a bit now," Kit added.

"Never underestimate the value of who you know and how powerful your friends are," Reese pointed out. "Especially when it comes to the system and getting justice."

"And no cop is gonna suspect a rich boy like Cade could be a serial killer unless he's got the goods to back it up," Dylan said.

Quinn mulled it over. "Sounds like Mr. X knew from the start the Nutty Brothers were bad news."

"I'd say that's a pretty good bet," Reese concurred. "At this point, we have to hope the cops nab him with the DNA that's a match in Claire's murder."

"I don't like it," Quinn said bluntly. "Thus far, the cops don't have Cade's DNA. Wait. Any chance we could get him to meet with us?"

Reese cocked a brow. "Who?"

"Mr. X."

"Why? The man's a professional killer. He has no allegiance to anyone and that includes us."

Kit disagreed. "But you can't have it both ways, Reese. We're either in or out here, on his side, or we're not. We either accept him as an ally…"

Jake shook his head. "You don't think making their money disappear shows him we're on his side after getting his e-mail?"

"I think we need to make sure he knows."

"That's nuts. We barely keep in touch via e-mail; it's all one-sided. He sends, we receive. That's the way it's been."

"Not good enough," Quinn said. "Kit's right. We need to make sure we're all on the same page. That includes him. To coordinate a successful strike against these guys we shouldn't take anything for granted."

"I agree," Baylee put in, eyeing Dylan with a stubborn jerk of her chin. "And anyone who thinks this shouldn't be an organized effort is just…wrong."

"There," Quinn said. "We have programming geniuses in this room. Surely, Mr. Software and Surfer Boy here can figure out a way to contact him."

"I guess we've been challenged, eh Mr. Software?" Dylan proffered. "Fine by me. Look, I'm thinking someone needs to go back to Catalina and sail the *Sea Warrior*, bring her back. Since I'm the one who got her there..."

"I'll go," Reese volunteered. "I'm getting antsy sitting around doing nothing. You and Jake know I'm not any good to you anyway at hacking all the financials you'll need to access."

He cast a glance at Quinn. Going to Catalina for the boat was a clever way to get her alone. "What do you say, Quinn? You up for an adventure or do you want to sit around and brood about getting suspended?"

"Brood, my ass. I'm worried about my damn career here, Brennan. If you can't see that..."

"I told you, there's nothing to worry about. I'll have you back doing rounds a good week ahead of schedule. Bet?"

"You're on. If I'm not back on rotation in a week, you lose, and I post an online message for all the world to see that says the great lawyer Brennan is nothing but a shyster."

"But if I win, you post that I'm the best damn lawyer in the entire state of California."

She shrugged. "Sure, why not? I can lie with the best of them."

Dylan glanced around the room. "If you really want to get to Catalina today, I'll call my buddy to fly you over there in his chopper, same way Baylee and I got back here."

"It's kind of late in the day. Once you get to Avalon, you might as well stay at Dad's house for the night. I'll go get the key," Baylee offered.

Reese slapped Dylan on the back. "Make the call. I'll go get my gear. Quinn, if you're coming with me, pack up. We leave in twenty minutes."

"Sure, how else am I going to bug the hell out of you to do what you promised?"

⚜ ⚜ ⚜ ⚜ ⚜

As it turned out, Dylan's friend couldn't fly them over to the island, so they went with a commercial helicopter charter out of San Pedro harbor for a hundred-and-seventy bucks a pop that promised to get them to the island in just over fifteen minutes.

For Quinn it had been a long time since she'd indulged in a trip—anywhere. Immersed in med school for the past several years, she couldn't remember the last time she'd packed a bag for an overnight stay.

As she crawled into the leather seats of the Eurocopter AS-350, she felt a little like a competitor on *Survivor*, off to an unknown adventure to some exotic place. Sure enough, once they lifted off and became airborne, she knew she'd definitely left her comfort zone as nerdy doctor. In minutes, they were out over the glistening, sapphire water.

The only other times she'd flown to Catalina, they'd made the excursion in William Scott's little plane.

The ride in the helicopter wasn't that much different, other than it was far noisier. The charter had promised a soundproof cabin, but there was no mistaking the whoop whoop whoop of chopper blades. Now, without thinking, she gripped Reese's hand in exhilaration.

Once out over the ocean, Reese leaned into her ear. "What are you thinking?"

She leaned back. "This was a good idea, to get away. After last night…"

He nibbled her ear and said, "Let's make the most of having the house to ourselves then."

Their eyes met. Quinn turned her mouth to meet his so she could kiss those sexy lips of his. They stayed hugged up against each other, like lovers, her head on his shoulder for most of the trip.

As they got closer to the Island, though, her sense of adventure kicked in. She sat up straighter to gaze out the window. The first thing she noticed was how green the hillsides were this time of year. She might not know a whole lot about blossoming plants, not like Kit or Baylee, but she could differentiate a daisy from a tulip. Thanks to spring rains, these slopes were bursting with an array of golden lotus, purple chia, and white mariposa lilies.

After all, she'd hiked these same trails and terrain as a kid, exploring its rocky slopes and climbing its peaks and valleys. She'd once made a point of studying the vegetation, the indigenous plants and wildlife, too.

She smiled at the memory of the teasing she'd endured from Kit and Baylee. They'd pretty much tagged her as a nerd even back then. But her friends couldn't possibly understand the freedom she'd felt at trekking those hills, getting outside, enjoying nature after spending so much of her early years confined to grungy surroundings.

Her mind deep in thought remembering those carefree days of summer, before she knew what was happening, they were touching down at the Avalon heliport.

As dusk fell, as the sun started its descent over the horizon, the summer sky became a burst of dazzling oranges and reds, a view Quinn often missed while inside the hospital on duty.

Crawling out of the cabin onto the asphalt tarmac, they both took the time to stand there a moment and marvel at the atmospheric conditions that would turn a simple setting of the sun into such a brilliant sight.

"We might have found something else we have in common," Quinn commented and nodded her head in the direction of the skyline. They watched, mesmerized, as the sun completed its drop below the horizon.

"Who knew the lawyer and the doctor could find common ground," Reese wisecracked.

"Yeah, I was starting to wonder if we might kill each other in our sleep," Quinn agreed.

Since the price of the charter flight included ground transportation, they jumped in a waiting taxi, one of the rare vehicles allowed on the Island, and headed off to their destination.

Twenty minutes later the cab pulled up in front of William Scott's Spanish-style villa, a place Quinn knew well since she'd spent several lazy, laidback weeks of blissful summer vacation here.

Standing there on the street looking up at the house, it didn't take long for a big dose of nostalgia to hit her.

The beach, the mountains, the house itself, reminded her how many hours she and her friends had whiled away at this very spot, either boogie-boarding, snorkeling in the pristine water, or exploring the surrounding hilly campgrounds, scavenging for all kinds of treasures campers had inadvertently left behind.

The Island had been a kid's outdoor paradise.

Somewhere between MCATs and surviving med school, she'd forgotten all about those special times.

A jolt of flashback took her to third grade and the very first time she'd seen this place.

⚮ ⚮ ⚮ ⚮ ⚮

Spring break that *year had finally arrived the third week of March, when she'd been shocked to learn her new friends, Baylee and Kit, wanted her to come with them to someplace called Catalina Island.*

All Quinn knew was it sounded tropical and a little bit like heaven to go away for a week anywhere without Ella or Ross bugging her.

The fact that Kit and Baylee had invited her to tag along with them to someplace called Avalon and to a beach house, no less, had been nothing short of a gift. No one had ever invited her anywhere. It hadn't required a great deal of persuasion on her part to get Ella or Ross to agree to the trip. They'd been as eager to get rid of an eight-year old as the eight-year-old was to get rid of them.

At the Santa Monica airport, with her two friends chatting the entire time, Quinn, a little awestruck to be included, had taken her first airplane ride. She'd climbed into a compact cabin crowded with enough stuff for ten people and listened as the occupants bubbled with more enthusiasm than she'd ever witnessed firsthand.

For a child who hadn't known much stability up to that point, to go from roach motels to the grandeur of Beverly Hills was a journey in itself.

Since August, she'd gone from eating store-brand peanut butter spread on stale crackers to devouring three healthy meals a day, some of which were now prepared by an expert, five-star personal chef. And now, to be included on a weeklong sojourn six months into the school year with two new friends was a lot to digest over a short period of time.

As compelling as that all was for Quinn, the icing on the cake seemed to be leaving behind that feeling of oneness forever and actually having friends, friends who seemed to experience their own challenges at home.

It hadn't taken more than that first month of September, when the school year was still brand-new, or a genius mentality for Quinn to recognize black and blue marks on both of her classmates.

To sit and listen as Mrs. O'Malley talked about math or spelling while Quinn did her best to acclimate to her new surroundings, she'd noticed things. Things like how terribly shy Kit was about raising her hand to answer questions—about any subject. The only activity the tall-for-her-age Kit seemed to like doing was when she got to use her crayons. Then there was Baylee, so much shorter than both of them but unwilling to contribute anything of her own to the conversation, especially whenever an adult was nearby.

Those little details tipped the scales for Quinn.

She could certainly tap into their mindset. All three girls seemed reluctant to pipe up and join the discussion.

After all, history had told Quinn adults could not be trusted.

⚜ ⚜ ⚜ ⚜ ⚜

When the grown woman thought back now to those first couple of weeks of a new school year as she struggled to adjust to getting up every morning and heading off to class on a regular basis, she could pity that little girl.

Finding a comfort zone in the exclusive Beverly Hills private school they had chosen for her had been anything but easy.

Back then Quinn Tyler hadn't just felt poles apart from the other kids. She'd even looked the part. Her Native looks had caused more than a few pushes and shoves in line. The insults and slurs she'd tried to mostly ignore were the main reason she'd had a couple of fights by the end of September.

So months later, when she'd found herself standing at this very spot as an eight-year-old guest…no one had been more surprised than reticent Quinn Tyler.

CHAPTER 11

"Let's go down to the beach, see if we can spot any fish," Kit suggested the minute they hit the front door to the beach house on the run.

"Okay, but let's grab towels to put under us so we don't get all sandy," Baylee proposed.

"Who cares if we get sandy? This is a vacation. I can get dirty if I want and not have to take a bath," Kit countered. "And I'm gonna do what I want. It took a lot to get Alana to let me come and I'm not spending it scrubbing my skin off in a stupid bathtub. I'm getting outside and I'm staying outside."

"You have to take a bath, otherwise you'll stink. Who wants to smell bad?" Baylee pointed out.

"I'll wash off when I go swimming. You just wait and see. I intend to stay in the water all day tomorrow," Kit emphasized. "That is, when I'm not looking for shells or rocks or fossils."

To Quinn, exploring the Island looking for shells and rocks and fossils sounded a lot better than getting in the water. Since Quinn didn't know how to swim it was the only downside to coming on the trip.

As the newest member of their trio, she listened while the other two did what they usually did. They bickered good-naturedly like best friends, like they were comfortable with each other because they'd already been together for years.

Quinn didn't want to admit it, but she was a tad jealous of their closeness.

"Hey, don't worry about it. I'll take a bath—eventually—if you don't rat me out beforehand."

Insulted, Baylee declared, "You know darn well I'm not going to rat you out."

"Good. Besides your dad won't stand over me with a hairbrush and whack me every time I don't scrub the right way. But it doesn't mean I'm taking one until your dad makes me."

Baylee nodded, knowing full well how awful Alana treated Kit. "But you better hope he doesn't pull out a bottle, otherwise we'll all get it for sure 'cause Tanya didn't make the trip this time. She isn't here to intervene and help us like usual."

Even though she was revved up, Kit took the time to lay her hand over Baylee's. "We'll be on our best behavior. We won't make him mad." She didn't want Baylee to start worrying about it.

"I'm just glad he let me come," Quinn admitted.

"Tanya put in a good word for both of you," Baylee confessed. "She sort of made him bring all of us."

"Remind me to hug her when we get back then. Hey, time's wasting. Hurry up, will you? I told you I wanted to go see if the treasure box we buried at the campground last summer is still there."

"Oh, good idea. I forgot about that," Baylee said. "Let's pack sandwiches and juice boxes and eat them on the trail. They'll tide us over to dinner."

"Now we're talking. Come on, Quinn." Kit dragged her along the long hallway into a sunny kitchen. "We need to remember to bring shovels so we can dig up the treasure box."

Kit ran into a laundry room as if she knew exactly where to look and came back with two garden spades. She sat them down by the back door and took off her backpack.

While Baylee started digging around in the pantry for peanut butter, Kit poked her head down into one of several sacks of groceries sitting out on the counter.

"Boy, you are so lucky, Baylee. Tanya thinks of everything. Look at all this food she had delivered already. Come on Quinn, don't just stand there. Find the fresh loaf of bread and anything else that looks good enough to take with us."

Kit emptied her backpack to make room for some of the supplies, including the garden trowels for digging. Quinn dutifully dug into the bags and began pulling out various items. When she got to the Oreos, Kit swooped in and jerked them out of her hand. "Good find," she yelled as she crammed them down into her own pack.

When Quinn pulled out a bag of M & M's, Kit did a little happy dance. "I'll carry these, too. See what else you can find in those sacks to snack on."

After throwing together peanut butter and jelly sandwiches and stuffing them into plastic baggies, Baylee stood at the counter going through an assortment of apples.

When Kit saw what she was doing, she grabbed Quinn's arm, yanking her through the back door and headed down to the water's edge all the while yelling at Baylee. "Leave the stupid fruit. We have a bag of M & M's so there's no more room in my pack for apples anyway."

Baylee shook her head. "But Tanya says we should eat fruit at least once a day."

"How many times do I have to tell you that's regular days? That's for when we're back at home. This is spring break, where you throw out all the rules and do what you want." Looking for an ally, she turned to Quinn. "Right?"

"Sounds good to me."

Baylee harrumphed out in frustration, took off after her friends, stuffing three apples down into her own backpack for good measure.

"Look at how clear that water is," Kit stressed to Quinn. "Where else can you see so many bright orange

fish swimming around in the ocean? Those are called garibaldi damselfish. The baby ones have blue spots. Wait until you get in the water, go snorkeling, get up on a board for the first time. We should go swimming," she announced after finally managing to take a breath.

For someone who didn't say a whole lot in class, Quinn thought Kit sure made up for it outside of school. When she wasn't around adults the girl became a chatty Cathy that refused to shut up.

"I told you before I came that I don't like the water," Quinn reminded her.

"We'll fix that," Kit gushed as she traipsed off in the direction of the campground. "Now let's go dig up our treasure."

She took off leaving Baylee to explain to the newcomer about their cache.

"It's an old metal box my dad used for fishing lures before he got a new one. It's full of stuff we found all over the campgrounds, stuff no one else wanted."

"Like what?" Quinn asked.

"Like a bracelet made out of plastic beads and a mood ring and one gold earring. We find a lot of jewelry. 'Course it's usually junk stuff. And last summer we found a couple of shark teeth and some fossils. Then there are all the cool shells we pick up."

From up ahead, Kit concluded, "Sure it's junk, but it's ours. We found it and no one knows about it but us. That makes it special. It used to belong to just me and Baylee, but we'll share our treasure with you, Quinn."

"Why?" Quinn wanted to know. No one had ever shared anything with her before. There had to be a catch.

"Because we're pals now," Kit revealed while she ran back toward Quinn and slung an arm companionably around her shorter friend's shoulder. She left it there while they hiked into the hillside away from the beach, pointing out each time she recognized a familiar shrub or flower along the way like a helpful tour guide.

Quinn didn't have the heart to tell her she got half the native shrubs wrong. Quinn might not have spent any real time in the wilds before today, certainly not enough to know the Island the way Kit and Baylee did, but she had asked Mrs. O'Malley all about Catalina. The teacher had picked out three books for Quinn to read before making the trip.

Kit didn't seem to have any idea what manzanita looked like. And it was all over the place. But just when she had decided to set her straight, Kit changed subjects entirely and started talking about an old shipwreck off Ballast Point.

By the time they passed a ranger station, tromped the length of the camping area before coming to a small clearing, they were all sweaty and the only one who still seemed excited about the trek was Kit.

But as if recognizing the glade, both Kit and Baylee dropped to their knees while Kit pulled out the trowels from her backpack.

The two began digging in the dirt near a grove of fern and lupine.

Woots and shouts went up the minute the spades connected with metal. After that, uncovering the infamous battered green tin box became a mission. Lifting it out of the hole, Kit unlatched the metal lock and flipped open the lid.

Like Indiana Jones showing off his loot, Kit proudly displayed a plethora of shells, a mismatched assortment of rhinestone jewelry, fossils that resembled seaweed imprints, and an array of oddly-shaped small pieces of driftwood they'd found washed up on the beach.

"It's still here. Now we just have to find a better place to bury it." With that, Quinn watched as they took off to scout the immediate campsites.

Quinn didn't understand why they had needed to dig up the box, let alone re-bury it, but she trudged after them anyway until Kit spotted an ancient ironwood tree about twenty feet in height laden down with new white blossoms and long, scalloped tooth-like leaves shooting out abundant with spring growth.

Kit took out her trowel again and dropped to her knees. At its narrow base, she began to brush away twigs along with the reddish cinnamon bark collected there so she could get her shovel in the dirt.

The three of them watched as a family of red squirrels scattered up the trunk of the tree in retreat. Kit took their flight in stride and announced, "See, this is a better spot. Come summer, we'll remember it here because by the time we make it back the babies will be a lot bigger. I bet they make their home in this tree year round. When we come back this summer, all we have to do is look for that same family of squirrels and this tree."

Baylee shook her head. "They won't still be at the same tree, Kit."

"Sure they will. Where else they gonna go?" Kit reasoned.

Instead of arguing the point, Baylee grumbled, "You sure get bossy when you get away from Alana."

"Shhh, do me a favor, for the next week, don't mention her name. I don't want to think about that woman again until we go back Sunday night. Okay?"

Leaving Sunday night? Quinn didn't want to spend her precious time thinking about going back to Ella or Ross. Not now when they'd only just arrived. From what little she knew about Kit's mother, the woman sounded too much like Ella, mean-spirited with a foul mouth.

Not as willing as Kit to get dirty, Baylee gingerly sat down on the ground. Then as if she'd just thought of something, she handed her trusty trowel off to Quinn. "Here, you can use mine to help Kit with the hole. I'll use that flat stick over there."

Feeling for the first time like she'd truly been included and given some way to contribute in sharing the treasure box, Quinn got into the spirit of the moment and did her part to dig.

But when she caught sight of a fat reddish, brown bird, she stopped long enough to point it out. "Look at that, a partridge! See it searching for twigs to eat."

"As in partridge and a pear tree?" Kit questioned, turning to study the squatty fowl as it pecked the ground for roots and whatever bark it could find.

"Yep. They're also known as grouse."

"It looks like a chicken," Baylee noted.

"It's in the chicken family," Quinn stated. "But it's an omnivore."

Kit rolled her eyes and hoped Baylee didn't ask what that was. It seemed as though everyone knew a lot more about stuff than she did. But this wasn't school and she wasn't in the mood to listen to a lecture about some stupid bird. She dug harder in the dirt.

After working the hole bigger, Kit adjusted the box down inside and the three of them got busy covering it back up again.

As soon as she was satisfied with the work, Kit stood up and announced, "Your dad should be back with the food by now. Anyone else hungry besides me?"

"You just ate a sandwich on the way here," Baylee declared. But realizing Kit didn't get all that much to eat at home because Alana usually kept her on a strict diet so she wouldn't get fat, she sighed. "Okay, fine, let's head back then."

"I could eat," Quinn offered amicably. With so much food around, she never seemed to get her fill, either.

Huffing out a breath, Baylee grumbled to Kit, "I thought you wanted to go swimming."

"Later," Kit muttered as she led the way, long legs striding back down the hill and out of the grove of trees and back to the house. "Maybe your dad ordered us a pizza."

But when they got back they learned Mr. Scott had brought them giant, juicy hamburgers and skinny French fries instead from a little take-out joint in downtown Avalon.

The man had also managed to remain stone-cold sober during the meal and had even carried on a conversation about what they'd done and seen in the few hours since they'd arrived.

After stuffing their faces, the three girls recovered from chowing down on the big supper by going back outside. The three of them got comfortable near the water, stretching out on the beach towels Baylee had insisted they bring.

Staring up at the night sky, gazing up at the sky full of stars overhead, the three girls were grubby and sweaty from the shortcut they'd taken earlier down the side of a hill on their way back, where they had come upon a herd of bison, live, honest-to-goodness buffalo.

Okay, so maybe the creatures had smelled really bad and the smell had almost made Baylee throw up, but they were still real animals, not just lame pictures in a book. To Quinn, who cared about how badly they smelled?

"You should be glad you're Native American, proud of it, you know. That's a heritage not everyone can brag about. And with all that black hair, you're really cool looking. You look kinda like Cher," Kit told her as she patted her stomach and stared out over the calm waters of Avalon Bay.

"Yeah, it's kind of boring to have stupid ol' blonde hair all the time. I wish mine was black and straight like yours," Baylee admitted. "Tanya says I should be grateful for having curls, but I hate them. They make me look dorky. I want straight hair like you and Kit."

Quinn blinked in astonishment. No one had ever thought she was particularly attractive, certainly not cool-looking. In fact, most places where Ella had dragged her, people had often stared at both of them like they were little more than trailer trash. Now, she not only had these two for friends, they thought her Native American heritage made her look like a celebrity.

While the boom box played a dreamy Michael Bolton tune in the background, Baylee confessed, "I love his voice."

"I love his hair." Kit admitted. "He's so good-looking."

"You want to marry him," Baylee accused.

"Sure, like he'd ever want to marry a kid."

"I'm never getting married," Quinn announced. "Adults are stupid for ever going all ape over each other anyway and for ever getting married in the first place."

"Yeah, I'm never doing that either. Ever," Baylee tossed in. She thought about her no-good mother who had up and left her so she could run off to be with her lover. The adults didn't think she listened to them, but that's what her dad kept crying about every time he got drunk, which was almost all of the time. "Adults are mean every time they open their mouths anyway."

When the song changed from Bolton to Bonnie Raitt's guitar riff for "Love's Sneakin' Up On You," Quinn confessed, "I'm going to play guitar like that when I grow up. She plays better than those stupid, male rock stars. She's talented and I bet nobody tells her what to do, either."

"Sure they do," Baylee declared. "She's got managers and producers, even a director for her videos and all sorts of other people in the background telling her what to do every single day."

That assessment made Quinn think of her father, who was supposed to be some stupid famous singer in a band. But since she had yet to lay eyes on the guy, she doubted the whole story was even true. More than likely, Ella had made the whole thing up. But then if that were the case how had she and Ella come to be living with his record producer in the biggest house she'd ever seen?

She sighed; sometimes she didn't know what to think about Ella's story. "But that's just part of having a successful singing career. I'm going to have a career when

I grow up and no one is telling me what to do or bossing me around."

That sounded pretty good to Kit, too. "Do you think we'll ever grow up and be like the boss of ourselves where no adult can...?" She'd almost said hurt us, but at the last minute changed it to, "...tell us what to do?"

"Sure. We could live together in our own house, not ever get married to anybody, and do whatever we wanted. Be independent women."

"Well, we'd have to get jobs. I'm going to be an actress and my dad will direct me in the movies. Quinn's going to sing and play guitar. What're you going to do, Kit?"

Kit thought long and hard to come up with something Alana didn't allow her to do. Because the list was really long it took her some time to come up with an answer. But sports seemed to upset Alana the most, so she went with that. "I'm going to play volleyball."

"You can't play volleyball for a living," Baylee stated flatly.

"Sure you can," Quinn reasoned. "Kit could be the best damned volleyball player in the history of volleyball."

Kit beamed at her. "That's right, I'll be legendary" She flexed her biceps. "I'm good at spiking the ball. People will talk about me all over the world wherever I go."

But Baylee didn't think Alana would be too happy about that career choice. "You could paint. I know you love that." It sounded better than volleyball to Baylee. Little worrywart she was, she thought on it for a bit and then cautioned, "If you play volleyball you'll be outside a lot. You could get skin cancer spending all that time in the sun."

"Geez, Baylee, you're just full of goodwill and cheer tonight."

"It's true. Tonya read about it in a magazine. Getting too much sun without wearing sunscreen causes something called mel-a-mo-ma. If you get too much, you could die."

"It's pronounced melanoma," Quinn corrected, risking the fact that these two might make fun of her for being so nerdy. Ella had always made fun of the fact that she liked to read, especially when the subject material was about something as adult as cancer. Plus, that very week, she'd watched a segment on the morning show on TV about that very topic.

"Well, whatever it's called, it's seriously bad news. We should always put on sunscreen when we go outside, even if it's just for a little while. We'll start tomorrow when we go surfing and swimming."

That was Quinn's cue to remind them how afraid she was of going into the ocean. "I told you guys when you asked me to come I don't like the water and because of that I don't know how to swim. You guys should go ahead though. I'll read a book or something while you guys do whatever it is you do in the water."

"Nope, that won't work," Kit reasoned. "You can't live in So Cal this close to the beach without learning how to swim. Baylee and I'll teach you."

"But I don't like the water," Quinn repeated. She wasn't about to admit no one had ever taken the time to show her how. Even with all the motels she'd stayed in, most of which the closest thing to water they'd had was the bathtub, there had been few opportunities to swim.

"You will by the time we're done with you," Kit stated. "We'll start you out on a paddle board first, get you used to the ocean. The water's not that deep right off shore, anyway. It isn't deep unless you go farther out. And you won't. We'll keep you in knee-deep water at first. And we'll be right there with you."

"You aren't gonna drown, if that's what you're worried about," Baylee reassured. "We won't let you."

Kit took in the scared look on Quinn's face. "Don't worry about it. It's easy. With us two teaching you, you'll be able to swim in no time."

ᚼ ᚼ ᚼ ᚼ ᚼ

And Kit had been right. It hadn't taken long for Quinn to learn how to swim.

Sometime during her first trip to Catalina Island, Baylee and Kit had become her family. That week they'd fought like sisters, fought over anything and everything from the last piece of pizza left in the box to which movies to watch. They'd fought over swimsuits, which shorts to wear with which top, which pair of flip-flops belonged to whom, although Kit's feet were a lot bigger than theirs. They'd traded jewelry, painted each other's fingernails. They'd even dabbled with trying on makeup. All the while Mr. Scott directed them in the fine art of presentation.

They'd laughed like hyenas at the stupid lines from the movie *Dumb and Dumber* they'd paid to see at the Avalon Theater, pantomimed vocals from *Smells Like Teen Spirit* horribly off-key, and laughed and giggled until Mr. Scott had yelled at the three of them to settle down for the night and go to sleep.

After spending most of the day outdoors, swimming, they'd invariably tumble into bed, exhausted.

Days were spent primarily at the beach, where Kit and Baylee did indeed teach a reluctant Quinn how to eventually do more than dog paddle.

And just as Kit had predicted, Quinn had fallen in love with the water.

No longer cooped up in dreary surroundings, Quinn had blossomed on a boogie board. At about that same time she'd envied Kit's and Baylee's ability and sheer will to teeter and balance themselves on a full blown surfboard.

No longer content to just dog paddle, determined to become a stronger swimmer so she could graduate to a surfboard, Quinn worked tirelessly that week to perfect her stroke.

Dedicated to their friend's goal, Kit and Baylee set out to do everything they could to help Quinn achieve Esther Williams Olympic gold-medal status.

From that point forward, they'd turned out to be each other's strongest advocates. It was during that first trip to Catalina they'd started sharing their fears, their old nightmares, and more importantly, their hopes and dreams for the future.

Somehow during that first trip, the three became sisters.

☮☮☮☮☮

Dropping her bags in the entryway, Quinn pulled herself back from another nostalgic glimmer from the past. "Wow, I haven't been here in years. This place brings back so many memories, good ones, times when things were a lot simpler."

Reese caught the wistful look on Quinn's face and realized for a while there she'd gone someplace else. At least he could be grateful there had been a few good times mixed in with the early painful, bad ones.

He glanced around at the spacious, open ranch style floor plan and recalled, "Jake and Dylan and I had our own special places growing up, too.

"Like what?"

"Jake's grandmother's place in Santa Cruz for one, my father's cabin in Big Sur, then there was the getaway at Dylan's aunt's place near Muir Woods, north of San Francisco."

"Oh, I love Muir Woods, one of the best places on the planet to hike among giant redwood and sequoia trees."

"You've been there?"

"Once. Kit and Baylee and I went up to explore Napa. Gosh, that must have been when Kit turned twenty-one and we decided on a road trip. You know she's the tallest one of us but the youngest because she has a fall birthdate. Anyway, it was beautiful there in October. We got bored with the wine tour and ended up spending the day outside trudging through Muir Woods."

"Just a day? To get the full experience you need to take the time and explore the trails, the winding roads, the wildlife, enjoy a sunset or two. You weren't there nearly long enough. You like to camp?"

"Are you kidding? Right here on this Island the three of us spent more time camping out than we did indoors. Haven't gone camping in ages," she said as she swiped her hand along the dusty table in the hall.

"No better place for pitching a tent and enjoying nature than Big Sur or hiking near Big Bear."

She shook her head. "A nature lover? Who knew? And here I thought you were mostly a desk jockey. Tell you what, I get my job back, we get all this mess behind us, and first chance we get, we'll explore some of the trails up and down the coast. But tonight, we get settled. Should we eat or unpack? I'm really hungry. I vote we eat."

"You're always hungry."

"True, so I guess I'll go rustle us up something for dinner first."

"You cook?"

"I'm an expert at utilizing the microwave. Hey, I'm no Kit in the kitchen but I get by. You'll have to take your chances and eat what's put in front of you." She eyed him curiously. "Unless…please tell me you're a legal eagle by day and a culinary genius by night."

"Afraid not. But I'm hungry, too. I use a can opener though and I'm excellent at nuking stuff in the microwave. Dylan said they stocked the kitchen when they were here before."

"Yep, that's what Baylee told me. Let's see what we've got to work with." They headed off to peruse the kitchen.

Opening the fridge, Quinn announced, "Eggs are still good. I can nuke eggs. Milk's still in date, too. Woot! See if there's a can of chili in the pantry?"

Reese wrinkled up his face at the idea of eating anything out of a can. "You're kidding? A can of chili?"

"Come on, Brennan, adventure isn't just a ride in the air or a bounce at sea. Live a little. What's the worst that can happen?"

"Indigestion from hell? Food poisoning?" He did his best not to watch her butt wiggle into the pantry as she bent down and sure enough brought out a can of chili. His lower belly lurched with a hunger that had nothing to do with canned food or eggs.

"Please tell me that can isn't left over from the '90s? Look, why don't I take you out to one of those cute little restaurants we passed on the way here?"

"Don't be ridiculous. Of course, the can is in date. Baylee said they had all manner of canned food delivered. Do you think I'd risk giving us a foodborne illness? And we don't need to eat out. I'm tired. After not sleeping much the last two nights, I just want to eat something, take a shower and hit the sack."

"Okay, but don't say I didn't try."

She shrugged. "I'm used to winging it with takeout and delivery."

He had to admit he wasn't used to watching a woman as appealing as Quinn work on preparing a meal. It might've been overtly chauvinistic, but Reese couldn't help it. Quinn looked so damned gorgeous standing at the counter cracking open eggs.

"Anything I can do?" he finally managed.

"Open the chili," she commanded as she scooped up butter, and dropped it into the egg mixture, and added a little milk. She stuck the bowl in the microwave, punched a few buttons and stood back to wait.

"Seriously. You're going to serve this with eggs?" he asked as he used the old-fashioned can opener to get into the disgusting contents inside the can, masquerading as meat.

"*Over* the eggs. You wait and see how delicious this is, trust me. You set the table."

He got down plates from a cabinet, opened a drawer for silverware.

When the timer dinged a couple of minutes later, she dug out the steaming bowl, replaced it with the one that held the glumpy concoction of chili, and covered it with a generous stream of paper towels to avoid the splatter. While that heated, she grated cheese over the steaming eggs.

"You've eaten this before."

"Lots of times; haven't died from indigestion yet."

"Cast iron stomach?"

"You could say that." When the microwave sounded, she scooped up several spoons full of chili and plopped it on top of the artery-clogging dish.

He scanned the contents of the fridge. "Beer, all is not lost."

"You're actually afraid to eat my cooking? Big chicken. I'll have you know I'm great at throwing together a meal with whatever's on hand, be it leftovers or out of a can. I'm great at stretching a food dollar, too. Ask Kit and Baylee next time you see them, about how great I am at the grocery store, finding stuff on sale. Give me three ingredients out of any pantry and I can make you a meal."

He shook his head. "I don't even want to know what you could do with a can of Spam."

"The wonder that is Spam should not be taken lightly. It's the kind of food you can eat for breakfast, lunch, or dinner, fried, or just out of the can."

"Spam has yet to be defined as food."

"Not when you're hungry."

That statement put a sobering end to the teasing. He realized now a starving kid might consider Spam a luxury. "It's just that I haven't eaten chili and eggs since college."

She cast him a long look. "*You* are a food snob."

He grinned. "I guess I am. Let's eat this before it gets stone cold."

Either he was extremely hungry or she did make the best scrambled eggs and chili concoction he'd ever tasted. Surprisingly, the meal turned out to be a tasty change of pace.

They ate in companionable silence until Quinn gushed, "See, lots of protein in one fell swoop." She picked up her beer. "You really think Cade Boyd is a serial killer?"

"Mr. X thinks so. Since Connor didn't kill Claire, I'd bet money she was one of Cade's victims."

She shuddered. "You have no idea how creepy that makes me feel. God, I wished I had listened to Kit way back when."

"Why didn't you?"

"Good question. Have you ever thought you knew more about yourself than anyone else did at the time but in the end you realized that maybe Mom was right about a few things all along? I didn't have the Mom thing going on. We were always willing to play that role for each other, though, get up in each other's face, give it our all, or tried to." She sighed. "Turns out, Mom was right."

"Mom being Kit or Baylee."

She laughed. "In the instance of Cade, yeah, that was Kit. But it just as easily could have been Baylee Diane, depending on the situation. You think you've put it behind you, but the man just isn't able to let it go. Eight of my neighbors are dead because Cade wanted to get back at me for something that happened when I was nineteen, might as well be ancient history."

"The Boyd brothers have a problem with women, Cade in particular."

"I know and it has me thinking about Baylee. If Mr. X hadn't taken out Connor, she'd still be dealing with the custody battle from hell."

"Don't think about it. There's no need. Connor's no longer left to hurt Sarah or Baylee. It's done."

"Thanks to…"

"Yeah." He took a pull on his beer. "Let's clean up these dishes and take a walk, stretch our legs." He cocked his head. "Yeah, I know you said you were exhausted but a walk on the beach will help you relax."

She eyed him, not buying that for a minute. "Sounds good but you just want to—relax me—and get me into bed. Besides, I cooked, so you get to do cleanup."

"But it'll go faster if we both load the dishwasher," he pointed out, grinning. "And we both want to—relax— eventually."

"Okay, but you're breaking the hard and fast rule of the kitchen."

"Another Mom thing?"

She chuckled. "Now that I think about it, it's Kit's steadfast rule, probably because she always did the cooking while Baylee and I got stuck doing the dishes."

"Smart woman."

"Oh yeah. Kit's no dummy, even though Alana did everything she could to make her feel like total crap."

"I'm glad I never knew the woman. Jake did, though. I remember how he described her back then. Of course I didn't realize she had a daughter she'd habitually abused. But Jake told me about Alana's—lewd conduct during a business meeting. She tried to coax him into bed."

"Please do not put that image in my head." She puffed out a breath. "But that sounds like something Alana would do. I saw her at her worst, so nothing you could tell me would surprise me."

"Yeah? How about knowing that on the night she died, she and Jessica were still out patrolling an upscale Beverly Hills bar for..."

"Companionship?" Quinn finished for him, cocking a brow in amusement.

"Okay, we'll call it that. It got me to thinking though. Why would old Sumner Boyd put up with such an arrangement from his very public figure of a wife?"

"Because the old goat was more than likely screwing anything and everything he could that got within ten feet himself."

"Probably. I don't think the word faithful ever entered into their long partnership. The cheating was more than likely a two-way street. But there were rumors at the courthouse..."

She tilted her head and waited. "Something tells me you're about to surprise me."

"Gossip around the courthouse said Jessica had a female lover."

"Alana? I thought she loved men."

"I'm pretty sure Alana loved Alana."

Quinn laughed and shook her head. "Okay, can't argue that logic."

CHAPTER 12

After they were done with kitchen duty, Reese grabbed her hand and tugged her out the back door. They immediately toed off their shoes and hit the wet sand.

Walking along the sandy beach under a brilliant starlit sky not twenty yards from the house, it felt like they were a world away from L.A. instead of fifteen minutes by air.

On the warm June night, the light breeze that blew in over the water stirred the air and felt good on the skin after they'd been inside the stuffy, closed-up house.

"I'd forgotten how peaceful it is here."

"Believe it or not, this is my first visit."

"Really? Lucky for you I know the Island like the back of my hand. It's a shame we'll only be here for one night."

Studying the relaxed calm on her face for the first time since her apartment blew up, he wanted to keep that stress-free look there for as long as possible. "Who says?"

"Shouldn't we get back to L.A.?"

"Sure. Eventually. But what's the hurry? We're here. Nothing's stopping us from enjoying the Island for a couple of days."

She laughed. "I wouldn't mind some downtime if I could spend it here. I'd forgotten how fond I am of this place."

"Taking an extra day won't matter in the grand scheme of things. Why here?"

"Because coming here was the first time I ever went anyplace—with friends."

"Aw, baby." With that, he reached and coaxed her into his arms. "I have to do this," he said as he tugged on the bright blue Scrunchie holding back all that black hair up in a tight ponytail. He watched as it fell down around her shoulders.

"I've seen you wear your hair pulled back ever since that night at the hospital, except for the other day standing in my guest room—after your shower. You were damn sexy standing there with wet hair. I've imagined it down for a while now, draped around your neck."

"It gets in my way if I don't pull it back."

"I guarantee it won't get in mine," he promised as he nibbled down her jaw, taking a good hold on all that hair.

She sucked in a breath right before his mouth came down full on hers. Hard. His arms locked her up.

"Let's go back inside," he whispered while he pulled her along toward the house.

Expecting him to immediately lead her upstairs to the bedroom, he surprised her by going over to his gear still sitting in the entryway and digging out a music CD.

"What're you doing?" She asked clearly perplexed.

He looked around for a CD player, spotted the one he recognized as Dylan's sitting on top of the old-fashioned stereo system that looked like it belonged in a'70s sitcom. "Setting the mood," he explained as he slid the silver disc into the slot.

A little embarrassed for some reason, she stuck her hands in the back pockets of her jeans and rocked on her heels. "Reese, I don't need ambiance."

"Sure you do. Ambiance is an essential part of seduction."

"It is? Since when?"

The lilting voice of Teddy Thompson singing *Tonight Will Be Fine* drifted from the speakers. "Since now. Dance with me, Tyler. Put everything out of your mind. It's just the two of us and no one else right now matters." He held out his hand.

She opened her mouth, fully intending to come back with something smartass until she met his eyes. Either those calm gray pools were tugging at her heartstrings or it was the dose of lust she recognized in their depths.

Unbelievably moved because she couldn't remember the last time anyone had seduced her into bed with music and a dance, she finally found her voice. "I bet this gets you laid a lot, huh, Mr. Smooth?"

"It certainly never hurts my chances. Come on, Quinn, where's your sense of adventure? Adventure isn't just a ride in the air or a bounce at sea."

Recognizing her own words, she lifted her arms, draped them around his neck.

He circled her waist in a liquid embrace. They swayed to the melody until soon she wasn't sure where he began and she ended.

Never known as light on her feet, she knew rhythm when she sensed it. The man knew what to do with his feet. She floated, dreamlike in a fog, caught up in the man, the tender way he held her, the way his body responded to the song and to her.

When the track switched to *In My Arms* a faster tempo, Reese never missed stride but kept her hugged up as they took another spin around the room, this time at a faster pace.

She wasn't sure when his tongue began to trace along the pulse in her neck or zero in on that sensitive spot next to her ear. All she knew was she didn't want him to ever stop this romantic gesture, so she tilted her head to give him better access.

His mouth covered hers briefly until he suddenly stepped back. His hands tugged up his own T-shirt and sent it flying in a basketball arch across the room. "Miss Tyler, you've bought into part of the package. Now it's time to check out the whole thing."

Quinn blinked in surprise as she stood watching the stuffy lawyer turn into one of the Chippendale dancers.

With the drum beat soaring, he slowly unzipped his jeans, all the while keeping time to the music. His hips gyrated while at the same time, leg by leg, he kicked out of the denim. By the time the song changed to *Looking for a Girl* Reese was down to his boxers.

Not to be outdone, Quinn returned the favor. She pulled her Tee up and over her head, tossing it in the air. Doing her best to keep the beat, she unhooked the front clasp of her bra, but kept it in place in a teasing fashion. Seductively, she moved first one shoulder, then the other.

Reese let out a low whistle of encouragement.

Striking a sexy pose, she let go of the bra and twirled it in time to the music. She unsnapped the top button of her jeans, slowly glided down the zipper.

Reese narrowed his eyes as he watched her slither out of the pants one long leg at a time. He sucked in a breath when he realized she wore no underwear.

They made a dive for each other.

She ran her hands along his back, worked his boxers down and off.

He tilted his head down and devoured.

Her breath hitched.

He felt her tremor right before he took the kiss lower. Adept fingers ran a line to her breast where they toyed with a nipple as he began a slow taste and lick along her neck.

He backed her up in the direction of the sofa.

Quinn grabbed his butt on the walk backwards until together they missed the couch entirely and slid down to the rug on the floor.

Between mouthy kisses, she murmured, "Now. Reese. Now."

Body to body, he covered hers.

She yanked his head down to her level, fed off his mouth.

He nibbled his way down her neck again, nipping and biting before coming to a stop at one rippled peak. His tongue savored the texture before toying with its hardened point.

He went after the other until it popped out firm and rigid.

His fingers sought out the heat. Stroking, probing, he felt every layer by rising layer as he watched her climb, watched her eyes glaze over with pleasure. She cried out when she came.

"Now, Reese, now—for God's sake!"

"Mmm, not yet. I need to taste you first." He moved lower, used his tongue until he tormented a couple of low moans out of her. First in, then out, until he felt her body quake and shudder to another climax.

With that, he rose over her, his mouth connected with hers again. He wrapped his hands around her hips and drove himself inside.

Under him, this time, Quinn launched her own beat to match his. Fast, slow, and then long, slick strokes.

The minute he felt her body quiver once again, he let himself go, flowing everything he had into her.

� ☗ ☗ ☗ ☗

Quinn breathed out a shaky breath. "God, how did you— hold out for that long? I came three times, that's—unusual for me."

"Superior intellect?"

She poked him in the ribs. "Show off. And what was that Chippendale routine? Work your way through law school as a dancer?"

"Hey, who says a lawyer shouldn't be able to take his best girl for a twirl on the dance floor every now and again?"

She giggled in spite of herself before meeting his eyes. They were staring into hers.

He leaned down, kissed her nose, then all at once reversed their positions until he was the one on the floor. "You have the most incredible body." He ran his hands along her rear end and up her back, twirled some of that black silk through his long fingers.

She gave him a mouthy, wet kiss. "You have a really nice ass."

He busted out laughing. "I get that a lot."

"You do not."

"You'll never know, will you?"

"You surprise me, Brennan."

"And you are way too serious, Tyler. You need to lighten up, get some spontaneity in your life."

She wasn't sure how to respond to that. "Like I've never heard that before," she tossed back.

Reluctantly, they started gathering up their clothes scattered all over the living room but they didn't bother getting dressed. Naked, they made their way to the foyer, where Reese picked up one bag and Quinn the other.

They lugged the stuff up the stairs. He watched her take point while he willingly followed her bare ass all the way up the steps.

"I need that shower. Me first," she declared.

"Uh-uh. We shower—together. The hot water heater in this place looks like it was around in the '40s."

Knowing it was true, she agreed, "Deal. If I remember correctly, the master bedroom is up here at the end of the hallway."

Sure enough they entered a large room with a hideous, ornate gold rococo bed taking up a good portion of the space. The two nightstands on either side had the same matching gold legs as the bed.

"Oh, my God, I forgot about this."

"You mean the ugly furniture."

"Yeah, another thing we might have in common. You recognize bad taste when you see it."

Reese dropped his gear on the floor. "All it needs is one of those red canopies and I'd swear we were in a brothel."

She raised an eyebrow. "And how many brothels have you seen up close and personal?"

He'd walked right into that one. "Well, whoever decorated this room I don't think it was wife material, as in Baylee's mom, Sarah Moreland."

"Like minds and all that because that's what I was thinking. Ick, you don't actually believe Alana and Jessica ever slept…" But all of a sudden another image popped into her brain, one she didn't want to think about, one where she remembered Ella and William Scott sharing this very bedroom for six weeks during one summer vacation when Ella had finagled an invite. William Scott hadn't declined the opportunity of having a willing partner for the duration of the trip either.

"I'm not sleeping in here," Quinn announced. "There's a perfectly good room down the hall, smaller maybe but…" She trotted off, peering into the other rooms.

She found the middle bedroom, one with mission-style furniture painted a pale but conservative yellow much more to her liking.

Reese trailed in and said, "Ah, much better. At least we won't wake up thinking we're in a cheap motel room in Vegas."

But Quinn took one look at the unmade bed where the sheets and covers were thrown back every which way as though someone had just crawled out of it and said, "We need to change the bedding. I'll go see if there are any clean sheets in the linen closet. You strip off what's on the bed."

"Typical. You get what you want out of me and turn bossy."

"Hmm, let me get my whip out then," she replied, rolling her eyes. She headed into the bathroom and soon came back with a mixed color assortment. "This is it, a pea green bottom sheet with bright purple for the top."

"Colorful," Reese said as he bundled up the used bedding. "This entire place looks like it was decorated in the '70s."

"Maybe even the '60s. I know for certain the house was built in the '40s." She unfolded the green sheet; let it drift down to the mattress before tucking it in and under. "You know, I bet Dylan and Baylee were the first ones who've actually stayed here for any length of time in probably five or six years. As far as I know Mr. Williams stopped coming after Baylee left home."

"That must be why everything's covered in several layers of dust. Why did you guys completely stop coming over here anyway?"

She shrugged. "Once we moved out, the three of us just never made it back."

"Why?"

"I don't know. It didn't seem right. Baylee's dad threw a fit when he found out she'd left home. There was about a year there when he blamed me. Of course, he was right. If I hadn't taken the leap..." She abruptly stopped in mid-sentence and got busy working on getting the bed ready.

Her reluctance didn't escape Reese. For some reason, she obviously did not want to revisit that time period when she'd left home. Instead of asking any more questions, though, out of the corner of his eye, he watched those lithe arms, her firm breasts, flat stomach, watched that nude body bend and twist over the bed.

The minute they got the last corner of sheet in place, Reese nipped her around the waist and backed her toward the bathroom.

She squealed like a kid, pumped a fist in the air. "Shower sex? Yessss!" She ran her hands up and over the muscles in his shoulders, and then latched on to his ass again. "You take pretty good care of yourself, Brennan—for a desk-jockey lawyer."

"Backatcha, Tyler, for a doctor." He reached around her to start the water. While it took the ancient hot water heater forever to warm up, he made use of the time.

His mouth ravaged hers.

Slanting a look down at those dark eyes, he lowered his head, slicking his tongue along her breasts. "Love these," he muttered. To prove it, he took a rosy peak into his mouth, savored it until it grew rigid.

Her nipples already throbbed from his sucking motion. By the time her head lolled back in a sated state, he picked her up, stepped into the tub under the spray.

Quinn already wanted him inside her.

Dropping her to her feet, he began an assault on her mouth again.

Between wet kisses, emphasizing each word, Quinn told him, "You're such a dirty boy, Brennan. Let me take care of that." She began to soap his rear end.

"Good. 'Cause I plan to get a lot dirtier."

They took turns soaping each other while hands and fingers massaged, kneaded, explored slick and wet skin.

"Now, Reese," And with that she reached down, started working him into her. She climbed aboard, rode him hard and fast. Her eyes glazed over with white hot light while blasts of silver burst through her.

He leaned her back against the tile, slipped his hands under her bottom and gripped her hips. With that, one deep thrust after another, he drove them drowning into bliss.

☙ ☙ ☙ ☙ ☙

Later, as they toweled off, Quinn told him, "Remind me not to do that with you standing up again. My legs are shaking. I think I saw stars."

He chuckled. "I'll take that as a compliment."

"You would," she mumbled, but returned his grin with one of her own.

She had no intentions of sharing any more than that. It had simply been sex, nothing more, she reminded herself as she crawled between clean, crisp sheets, and fell exhausted into slumber.

CHAPTER 13

Even though the slap stung, it had been well worth it.

Quinn hated her stepfather, Ross, with a passion that came from knowing how the man looked at her each and every time he got within ten feet.

It had been that way now for a couple of years.

She hated the looks he gave her almost as much as she hated the way he smelled. He had fat, chunky fingers that always seemed to be wet and sticky when he touched her.

Not that she let him get close enough to touch her very often.

But sometimes at meals it was difficult to avoid him passing her a dish where his fingers might invariably linger for a little too long.

Ever since she'd starting getting a chest, Ross Jennetti had become an even greater nemesis than he had been before. It got so bad at one point she'd taken to putting the chair from her desk in front of her bedroom door at night when she slept.

She also kept her ever-present, trusty softball bat at the side of her bed where she could get to it just in case Ross ever got past the first line of defense. A propped-up chair, after all, wasn't much of a deterrent to ward off the advances of a determined, six-foot-one inch man.

That's why there were nights she merely dozed, especially when Ella lit out for parts unknown and left her alone in the house with only Jennetti as her guardian.

During those times it was left up to her to see that she never ended up spending much time in the same room with him for very long.

It was even more important that she never let Jennetti get inside her bedroom.

Even if it meant taking a slap, a slap was better than the alternative.

That's when she got into the habit of using a sharp tongue as a weapon. Slinging insults at the guy seemed to keep him at arm's length. Even if it meant a slap across the face.

Most times it worked.

But tonight, she woke to find him standing over her, a hand to her mouth. She fought to reach the titanium bat, but felt the sting of another slap before his hands held her shoulders down, pinning her to the bed.

She could handle the slap, but his body on top of hers made it difficult to breathe. She bucked. She kicked because Ross wanted to…

♢ ♢ ♢ ♢ ♢

Reese came awake at the sound of Quinn flaying about in bed next to him. Once again she didn't seem to be awake but dreaming.

Or was it a nightmare?

Thrashing and turning her head to and fro, she was fighting an imaginary combatant. Her head bobbed and weaved as if she were in a fight for her life. Her body primed to take a blow.

"Baby, come on now, wake up. Quinn…"

He took a right jab to the jaw. Her ferocity and determination to land another punch had him capturing her arms. Not fully awake, he wasn't quick enough to dodge another shot to the chin.

Finally he straddled her. "Quinn, come out of it. You're dreaming, honey. Come on, wake up."

Her eyes popped open. "Reese. Reese. You aren't...get off of me! I can't breathe!"

"Not until you promise not to whack me again. You were dreaming."

"What? I... I..." She tried to erase the image of Ross on top of her and his sweaty hands gripping her legs. "Bad dream."

"No kidding. How often does it come back to you?"

"Too often," She breathed out and scooped hair out of her face, a face beaded now with perspiration. She hadn't yet realized what she'd admitted.

Still fog-brained, still shaky, she mumbled, "Water. I need some water."

He got up, went into the bathroom, turned the faucet to cold, and soaked a washcloth under the tap. On the way back to the bed, he dug into the gear they'd brought for a bottle of water.

By the time he handed off the cool compress for her face, Quinn was sitting upright, the sheet draped over her crossed legs.

As she wiped the sweat from her face, he uncapped the water.

"When did it happen?"

He did his best to sound calm even though he was anything but. He saw her swallow hard before chugging down half the bottle. She took several deep breaths as if buying time.

He waited what seemed like an hour, as an old-fashioned clock on the nightstand ticked off the loud, eternal minutes.

"This is one reason I never let guys spend the night."

"Never?"

"No. I'm careful no one is ever around to...see me like this."

"You've been reliving this for what...? Ten years? Longer? When did it happen?"

"First time, I was thirteen."

Reese sucked in a breath. A child, she'd been nothing more than a child. He wanted to hit something, preferably the bastard who'd touched her. But that wouldn't do either one of them any good tonight.

Instead, he gritted his teeth. "And you never told Kit and Baylee." It wasn't a question.

"No." She thought she saw disappointment on his face and tried to explain. "Look, the first time I was so ashamed. I thought they might no longer want to be friends if they found out." She swallowed hard. "I didn't want to take the chance."

"You know differently now though."

"Yes, but back then I was still awed by the fact that they were my friends. They were the only two people in the world that really mattered to me. I didn't want them to…to be disappointed in me or embarrassed for me."

Sitting on the edge of the bed, he was tempted to move closer, wrap her up, but judging by the look on her face, she needed some space and some room to breathe. Finally giving up the secret she'd been holding back for so long had to cost her dearly in terms of emotions.

It wasn't lost on Reese that to share what had happened showed a remarkable sign of trust on her part. Even if she wasn't fully aware of it now, he was.

"And the second time?"

"The second time, I was a little stronger, a little bigger, and bloodied his nose. I was three weeks shy of my sixteenth birthday. I got out of there that night, packed up some clothes and spent two weeks living in the cabana house over at Baylee's until I got a job in a coffee house and found my own place to live with some money I'd been squirreling away for emergencies."

"Baylee and Kit didn't ask a bunch of questions or want to know details of why you chose then to finally bolt and get out of there?" Knowing those two women, he couldn't imagine that they wouldn't want to know every aspect, every detail.

"As far as they were concerned, Ross had simply slapped me for the last time and fed up, I lit out on my own. He'd done it before. This time, I had bruises on my arms from his hands so they just assumed he'd pushed me around again, got more physical. I let them assume. It wasn't that difficult to pull it off."

"And it didn't come up during three years of therapy?"

"I talked about the slaps and the verbal arguments, sure, which were all true. I just left that part out. How did you know? Was there something I did when we...made love, when we had sex...?"

He gave her an incredulous stare. "Don't be ridiculous; you were perfect in every way."

"Then how...?"

"Honestly? Your passion for becoming a pediatrician clued me in, that's one. And you're so filled with drive and ambition enough to push yourself toward that goal. The fact you left home at sixteen, that's two. A lot of kids do that after something traumatic happens. Those two things were both big red giveaways for me."

"Come on, Reese, there has to be more. Tell me, I can take it."

This time he did move closer. In fact, he crawled back in bed, pulled her into his chest. He brought her chin up so that she could meet his eyes. "Now you listen to me, okay? There is nothing in you that told me. After hearing Kit's story that day at the hospital, I had my suspicions about all three of you. And when we went out to dinner the other night, I felt you were holding something back from Kit and Baylee, something that had to be major, something you were obviously ashamed about. It was a guy feeling. That's all."

He placed a kiss on her forehead. "You do realize you have absolutely nothing to be embarrassed about, don't you?"

She nodded. "Now, I do. But back then..."

"No buts. Quinn Tyler is an amazing woman. Look at all you've overcome, missing so much school in those early years, somehow managing to make it all up to graduate high school at sixteen. Then you go on to college, not just any school but picking a tough one like UCLA, finishing med school, getting into a residency program. There are people who had all the advantages, all the privileges, and haven't accomplished half of what you have, Quinn—and in record time."

"I was determined."

He laughed out loud. "Honey, you were a freaking superhero. My dad would've loved you."

"Parents tend to love doctors. It's just that I'm not in this for the money."

"I know, honey. You look exhausted." He stroked her back, kissed the top of her head. "Do me a favor."

"What?"

"Try not to think about it anymore tonight. My chin can't take it. You've got a helluva left jab."

For the first time since wakening, she laughed. "I'm sorry I belted you." Sensing he wanted to say something else, she cocked her head and asked, "What?"

He leaned his head back on the headboard. "You've been harboring this terrible secret all on your own. It's weighed you down for years. Now that it's out in the open…"

She grabbed his arm. "You aren't planning on telling Kit and Baylee, are you? You can't."

He shook his head. "It isn't my story to tell. If you decide to continue to keep it locked inside, promise me you'll think about talking to someone, professionally."

"Reese…"

"Hear me out. You've been carrying this around so long, somehow feeling guilty over something that wasn't your fault. Even after all these years, you're still blaming yourself."

When she started to object, he added, "Don't deny it, you are."

"Maybe."

"Think about it."

"Thanks for being here tonight. You made it better somehow."

"Good. Now get some sleep, unless of course you happen to want the hat trick portion of our evening's entertainment."

She flashed him a grin. "You read my mind. I guess one of the perks of letting someone hang around is access to the hat trick."

"Oh, yeah. Access isn't a problem."

She giggled. "Most men would be freaked out right about now and want to bolt for the door."

"It's time you realized, Tyler. I'm not most men."

$$\text{△ △ △ △ △}$$

After making love again, after he was certain she'd fallen asleep, Reese crawled out of bed as silently as he could without waking her. He grabbed his cell phone and snuck downstairs. Despite the fact the time on his phone read eleven-fifty, one-handed, he brought up his contact list. When he got to Jordan Donovan's number, he hit the call button and waited for an irritated voice to come on the line.

"Christ Jesus, this better be important. Do you know what time it is?"

"Sorry. I need you to find a man for me by the name of Jennetti, Ross." Reese spelled both names.

"What the hell did this Jennetti do that it couldn't wait eight hours until morning?"

"He hurt someone I care about. Look, on this matter, you don't share what you find with anyone, not Jake, not Dylan, got it?

"Yeah, yeah, I got it. How long have we known each other?"

"Just find the man."

"Do not do anything stupid, Reese Brennan."

"Me? I gave up doing stupid stuff after law school, remember? You know all my stupid stuff anyway."

"Yeah, well, I also know you. You don't call in the middle of the night unless it's—very—personal. What else can you tell me about this guy?"

"I know for a fact he's no longer living at his last known address in Beverly Hills." That little nugget he'd done on his own after learning Kit's story and that of Baylee's.

"Checked on your own, that tells me this is close to home. Okay, I'll take it from here."

Having passed the baton to Jordan, Reese headed back upstairs, confident he knew the consequences of an adult male who engaged in unlawful sex with a minor, even if it had occurred more than ten years earlier.

Every criminal lawyer in the State of California knew that Section 261.5 of the California Penal Code, otherwise known as California's Unlawful Sexual Intercourse Law, provided for prosecution in the event of statutory rape on a case by case basis, depending on the nature of the crime and the situation.

In other words, there was no statute of limitations on statutory rape per se. A good district attorney could weigh the seriousness of each violation, take into account the age of the victim in ratio to the age of the offender and make the determination whether or not to prosecute even after a decade had passed.

And that meant Ross Jennetti might still be held accountable under California law.

Unfortunately for Jennetti, Reese Brennan had no intentions of abiding by the law.

CHAPTER 14

Shortly after midnight, Nick Tyler's eighteen-passenger Gulfstream touched down at LAX without much fanfare. As pilot who had flown his own planes now for almost fifteen years, he taxied the sleek corporate jet to a private hangar at the end of a deserted stretch of tarmac and throttled back the engine.

The jet came to a stop.

Usually he didn't mind spending time in L.A. even if the place was so different from home. But this time, he wasn't looking forward to the stay. He had little choice in the matter though. This had nothing to do with music or recording or shooting a video.

This trip was personal.

He should have come to her years before now. Decisions he'd made a quarter of century ago had him cornered now and there was no way out. At this stage in his life, he was at a crossroads.

It was past time to do the right thing.

He'd known there would come a day, maybe a judgment day, when he had to face the daughter he'd never bothered getting to know. But he'd supported her all this time and that had to count for something; maybe a huge checkmark in someone's plus column.

She had to appreciate that, didn't she?

No one could say that Nick Tyler hadn't done the right thing, owned up to his responsibility. Hadn't he seen to it that Quinn had been financially provided for all these years? What could she possibly have against living in luxurious Beverly Hills anyway, with all the materialistic trappings that place had to offer?

His one lone passenger, his attorney and lifelong friend, Gerald Baines, stood up in the luxury cabin and stretched his back.

"Long flight, jetlag here we come," Nick remarked. "The body's not as young as it used to be, Gerry. Back when I made these long flights it was no big deal but now..."

In a nice, slow brogue, Gerald replied, "We're not as young as we once were, that's for sure. Insomnia is the least of our problems right now, Nicky boy. We're in it now, mate. We're out of Cork for sure, definitely out of our depths. They'll feed us to the wolves I bet. There's still time to turn tail and make it back home without anyone knowing we've been about."

Nick shrugged. "We've discussed it now for several thousand miles. I'd like nothing more than ignore her as you suggested, but I can't put this off any longer, Gerry. My conscience won't allow me to keep doing that. I'm surprised you didn't mention this Reese Brennan's earlier query—the e-mail he sent. If he hadn't e-mailed me direct..."

Gerry smiled broadly and explained, "I suppose I didn't want to bother you with the past. That includes this lawyer fellow, surely trying to come at us from another angle altogether, make us feel sorry for her for whatever reason. They all have one, you know, and it always centers on the pounds and pence. Mark my word, he has his eye on your money, as does she."

"According to the e-mail he sent, it's nothing like that."

Baines wasn't buying it. "History tells me this is no different. But as your barrister and best mate, I had to point out the loophole, didn't I? For once this is a part of your life I don't envy. You've no responsibility to do this, you know. But you're a good man for traveling so many miles to straighten the young lady out."

Emerging from the plane, the tall and lanky Nick Tyler walked down the steps and snorted. "Yeah, I'm a bloody saint. I'm here because this Brennan chap says she's in some sort of danger. I'll see what it's about and be better for it."

Out of habit from dealing with years of paparazzi, overzealous fans, and just plain stalkers bent on getting close to him, he took in the dark surroundings.

A poorly lit hangar beckoned.

The slightly built Gerald, a good foot shorter than Nick, was still skeptical. "Well, I wouldn't go that far, but if you sleep on it tonight and decide in the morning to make a break for it, head home to Ballybrack, I'm in your corner."

"If only we could, Ger," Nick said, slapping his friend on the back. "If only we could."

As the two men stood outside on the tarmac and watched as the ground crew pulled the jet into the hangar, there was no entourage, no media present, and no fans waiting for them in the luxury lounge.

And that was fine by Nick Tyler. He'd made this trip not for publicity's sake but because he needed to see her.

There had been a time in his life when he couldn't take ten steps outside his front door or go out for a bloody cup of tea without being hounded by someone or other who wanted a quote about this or that or wanted his bloody autograph.

Oh, he was still an icon, make no mistake. But over time and with age, his mega success had been replaced by the likes of other, younger bands that had put their own mark on the music business just as he once had.

But tonight, he carried his own suitcase.

Casually and with ease, he threw his laptop bag on his shoulder and walked through the lounge. Looking out through a huge plate-glass window, he spotted the waiting limo that would take them to their hotel.

Thanks to his personal assistant, he wouldn't be trying to maneuver around L.A. traffic on unfamiliar streets.

Even in the dark he could sense he was in a heavy populated area of L.A. The night sounds of summer so different here than his own quiet Ireland farm. As a commercial jet rumbled overhead, it briefly drowned out the hustle and bustle of traffic noise coming from somewhere in the distance.

The limo driver waited at the curb, holding the passenger door open. Nick headed that way, followed by Gerald.

An uneasy feeling hit his stomach. Surely his daughter would understand what he had wanted to achieve, what he had wanted to carve out of the music industry, what had infinitely been more important than she had been.

At least for once, he hoped he could explain it to her in person.

࿊ ࿊ ࿊ ࿊ ࿊

Quinn woke wrapped around Reese like a clinging vine. It was a first for her. She hadn't been kidding the night before. She never let men spend the night in her bed. She'd known for years what might happen if she did.

And the first time she had let a man stay over, the dream surfaced and ruined everything.

She'd been caught up in the moment, caught up in Reese. She'd let down her guard. Now, this man knew the darkest part of her past, a chunk she'd kept hidden away even from Baylee and Kit.

Looking back, when she'd been thirteen, she'd been so afraid they would take one look at her and guess what Ross had done to her. When that hadn't happened, she'd pretended it had never taken place. For two years it had worked. And then…it had happened again.

She shook her head, did her best to ward off those old feelings of anxiety. She rolled over to stretch and Reese snaked out an arm to bring her back into his body.

The first thing Reese saw was Quinn's black curtain of hair draped across his chest.

The bright morning sun filtering through the window fell on that long mane of hair just so, and for some reason, poetry popped into his brain. *"One shade the more, one ray the less· Had half impair'd the nameless grace Which waves in every raven tress· Or softly lightens o'er her face; Where thoughts serenely sweet express How pure, how dear their dwelling-place."*

Quinn's eyes bugged out. "What manner of man quotes Byron so early in the morning?" She planted a kiss on his mouth. "'*She Walks in Beauty*' no less?"

"It's your hair, all that black glistening in the light. I've had a thing for your hair since that first night I saw you swaggering down the corridor in your white doctor's coat looking so—hot. Yeah, it was the ponytail and how I imagined it draped over me in bed. Kind of like it is right now. You have incredibly sexy hair."

She whooped with laughter. "Whoever heard of sexy hair? I knew that you'd have to be eloquent for court, but where do you come up with this stuff? You're an absolute wonder, you know that, Reese Brennan?"

"I know. It's about time you came to your senses in that department, become a fan."

"And create more of a monster? No way. You're confident enough without me feeding your ego."

"Aw, you're such a hard ass."

She ran a hand down his body. When she got to his lower belly, she stated, "Mmm, something else is hard."

"The question is what do you intend to do about it?"

"Hmm, I guess I'll have to show you."

Later, standing in the kitchen, Reese had just poured his first cup of coffee waiting for Quinn to finish getting dressed and was about to take a sip when his cell phone rang. He sighed and stepped to the back door to take in the view. He let himself enjoy several more seconds of blissful solitude and took in the glistening, calm water of Avalon Bay. Maybe after all this was over they could take some time off and enjoy more of what the Island had to offer.

Reluctantly, he left the peaceful outdoor view and went over, picked up his ringing cell phone.

"Reese Brennan," he stated as he leaned over and automatically got out his laptop from the bag he'd brought.

"Mr. Brennan, is it? This is Nick Tyler. You e-mailed me about my daughter, Quinn, sent one e-mail to my attorney first and then sent another one to me. The last said there was no need for me to make the trip to America after all."

To Nick, it sounded funny saying those three little words, "my daughter Quinn," to a complete stranger, but what choice did he have? "Your last e-mail said to disregard the earlier one to Mr. Baines. Do I have that right?"

Taken aback by the caller, Reese had to think fast. "That's correct. It isn't necessary to come after all. We have the situation well in hand now and it was premature of me to alert you to any type of problem."

"But that's just it, Mr. Brennan. I have made the trip over to America to see my daughter. I'd like you to set up a meeting between us."

Reese stuttered at the knowledge the man was in L.A., especially when he looked up and saw the daughter in question, who still looked rumpled from their bout of morning sex, stroll into the kitchen.

She took the cup of coffee out of his fist and drank deeply. "Mmm, who are you talking to at this hour of the morning, Brennan? Sheesh, you *are* a workaholic, so dedicated you're on the clock, worse than me."

Reese did his best to ignore her and get rid of the father she didn't know he'd contacted behind her back. "Uh, uh, I'm not sure that's such a good idea. As I said, the situation is under control now."

Nick frowned. Maybe Gerald had been right. Maybe this was some kind of scam. "Look, do you know Quinn Tyler or not? If this is a ruse of some sort I'm in no mood to be played. My own attorney discouraged me from making the trip. But I'm here now and if you know Quinn I insist on seeing her."

"Could I get back to you on that?"

"For chrissakes, are you telling me this is a bad time or what?"

"That's exactly what I'm saying. This is a very bad time to talk right now."

"Fine. But if you're playing me..."

Reese cut him off. "I assure you my e-mail was genuine."

"So you can set up a meeting? Can you do that?"

"Yes. When would be a good time for you?"

"The sooner the better, this has been a long time coming. Would this afternoon work for you?"

"No, not this afternoon, tomorrow morning would be much better." And would give him an extra twenty-four hours to either explain things to Quinn or come up with some way to get her into his office. "Can I use this number to reach you?"

"Absolutely. Or you can contact me here at the hotel. I'm staying at the Bel Air Monaco. So we're on for tomorrow morning, then? Where and what time?"

Reese shot a glance at Quinn, sucked in a nervous breath. "Ten o'clock tomorrow morning, my office. My assistant will call you back with directions on how to get there."

Once the phone call ended, Reese weighed his options. He'd just spent a wonderful night with the woman he wanted. Just when they'd taken two steps toward firmer ground, could he rip that ground from under her feet by bringing her, like a lamb to slaughter, to the father who'd never given her the time of day?

He considered his own father and what a great relationship the two of them had shared growing up. What if he'd never known that? What if he harbored a lifetime of resentment over neglect? How would he handle a father who had never bothered to get in touch?

He zoned back to the present. Surely she would understand the importance of getting to know her father at long last.

He made his decision because there were simply too many unanswered questions from Quinn's past he didn't understand. He only hoped she would see the relevance of asking Nick Tyler for herself.

"I'm sorry, Quinn. I know I promised you a couple of days of downtime but something's come up. We have to head back to L.A."

After pouring another cup of coffee, she assumed that "something" had to do with the Nutty Brothers. Perusing the contents of the refrigerator for something to eat, she grumbled, "When's this Boyd thing going to end anyway? When do we get our lives back to normal?" She turned from the appliance and tilted her head to stare at him. "What's up with you anyway? You seem—preoccupied. Are you having regrets about us sleeping together?"

Time to run out the clock, he decided. He went to where she stood and took her mouth, a deep kiss that had him wanting to spread her out on top of the counter for breakfast.

But there were other more pressing matters to deal with at the moment. "Where is this sudden lack of self-confidence coming from? We've known each other two months. During which time you've managed to give off enough self-assured vibes to scale Mt. Everest in a single bound. If this is about…your nightmare from the past," he grabbed her arm. "Cut it out!"

She ran her fingers down his stubborn jaw. "You're right. It's just that I've never shared that with another soul and—you knowing—it's bothering me."

"I get that but...do you want a pinky swear or something that I won't say a word to anyone else?"

She giggled. "Okay. I'm being silly. Look, you made the coffee. I'll start breakfast. How's that? If we're leaving then we'll finish off all the eggs and the bread. Hmm, might as well cook the bacon, too, no sense letting it go to waste."

"How does a woman eat like a linebacker and stay so fit and trim? Do you even know what the inside of a gym looks like?"

"Metabolism," she muttered as she lined up strips of bacon on a paper towel to pop into the microwave. "And I'm on the go a lot. Now that I'm suspended, though, I'll probably gain ten pounds."

"Yeah, right," Reese said as he slid bread into the toaster. "Maybe we can come back here after all this is over, take some time to enjoy the area."

"That'd be nice but after I go back to the hospital I won't get a lot of days off."

"We'll work something out. As you pointed out last night, it's only fifteen minutes by air."

After breakfast, while they got the *Sea Warrior* ready to sail, Reese's phone rang again. This time, it was Jake. "When are you guys heading back?"

Fearing Nick Tyler had somehow managed to phone the others and the jig was already up, Reese demanded, "Why do you ask?"

"Jordan Donovan wants a meeting with us this afternoon at three."

"We're about to head out now. With sailing time around three hours, we should be back to Crandall House in plenty of time. " Fearing another one of his secrets might have been exposed, Reese asked, "Do you know what this meeting is about?"

"Yeah. Mr. X has a name."

CHAPTER 15

Reese had sailed the *Sea Warrior* on many occasions. Even though Jake was her registered owner, the prior year when he'd been busy in Japan, Reese and Dylan had gladly stepped in and kept the boat seaworthy by taking turns putting her out on the water.

There had been times during that year he'd sailed solo, while at other times he'd taken the boat out with a client or two or acquaintances from the courthouse.

Before that, since all three had roots in the Bay area, there had been those buddy times where he and Jake and Dylan had set sail north to see relatives or keep in touch with old school chums and then sail her back down the California Coast.

During those times together there might've been as many as twenty people on board, mostly family. They'd invited parents, or siblings and their spouses. They'd partied, drank, and always enjoyed spending whatever time they could manage on the water.

Anytime Reese could get away from the grind of work, away from filings and briefs, he tried to treasure getting out on the water.

But not today.

Today, he felt like the biggest jerk.

Setting up a meeting with Nick Tyler behind Quinn's back he'd no doubt have to pay a price, a huge one, one he wasn't sure he wanted to pay at all.

He already knew that when she found out, he'd have to make damned sure there were no cherished items sitting nearby that she could pick up and throw at his head.

He glanced over at the woman standing at the railing, looking down at the water, studying a school of fish. She looked exactly the same as that very first time he'd ever laid eyes on her.

And yet, something was different, something was off.

Since last night, she acted as though the disclosure of dark horrible events from her past, things that had been completely out of her control, might somehow alter his opinion of her.

And that pissed him off. If he could find Ross Jennetti, if he could bash in his face with his own two hands, it might make him feel better.

As he stood at the helm, he wondered what was running through her head. She'd been distracted since they'd boarded. Something was going on inside that head of hers she didn't intend to share, especially with him.

As much as he wanted to find out, he had a more pressing, bigger problem. How could he change her mind about meeting Nick Tyler in a short twenty-four-hour span? And how in the world did he intend to get out of this mess he'd created?

When she came around to the helm, and put her arms around his waist, rested her head on his shoulder, he decided he needed to work on getting her to talk to him. Because there was no way he could drag her into his office and then yell "surprise!"

"You okay? Got your sea legs yet? You look sleepy."

"The Dramamine helped."

He ran his hands up and down her back. "I'm worried about you."

She yawned and then kissed him soundly on the mouth. "Sorry, I'm not a very good sailor."

Uneasy, once again, he delved into the subject of the Rock Star. "Mind if I ask you something?"

She eyed him warily. "Okay."

"What if you could talk to Nick Tyler? What would you want to know?"

She glanced out at the blue water and frowned. "You mean if I could see him face to face?"

"Yeah."

"I'd ask him when his fans were going to wise up and realize his music sucks."

Reese busted out laughing. "Okay, that would definitely get his attention. But come on, Quinn, there has to be something you'd want to know? As a doctor there must be a medical history you'd be curious about, like his side of the family and all."

"Reese, give it a rest, okay? I'm not about to ask the asshole anything. Period. Since I have zero plans to ever hit him up for a kidney, why think like that?"

Reese sucked in a breath feeling like he was mired in quicksand up to his neck and sinking fast. If he didn't come up with something soon…he tried a different tack. "Don't you think he might be able to provide valuable info about your background, stuff you've never known before?"

"Like what? That I came from two people who had the parental instincts that make pythons look warm and fuzzy?"

She had him there.

How could he relate to having parents like hers? Truth was, he couldn't. Instead of pressing the point, for the time being, he gave up. He took her chin in his hand, brought her mouth up. "How about we stop talking and take advantage of our alone time, what's left of it?"

"Now you're talking."

"As long as you think you'll be okay for the next two hours until we get back to land…"

She gave him a long, hard look, her eyes moving slowly down his body from head to toe. "I'll be fine. Is there any way you could park this thing and we take a little siesta? I'd really like to get you out of those clothes."

He cocked a brow, perused up and down her lean figure. "By any chance, did you drink alcohol with those pills?"

"I assure you I took the proper dosage—without wine. I've never made love on a boat before and this might be my only chance." She wiggled her eyebrows up and down.

"That could definitely be arranged. How about I lower the sails?"

"Hmm, you talk like such an able-bodied seaman—*Captain Brennan*." She started pulling him down the steps to the stateroom. "How about some serious naptime with your first mate? Only…we aren't going to nap."

☙ ☙ ☙ ☙ ☙

As the boat rocked to the gentle sway of the sea, they lay in bed entwined in each other.

"Feeling okay now?"

She stretched catlike and purred, "Oh, Reese, surely an astute guy like you can tell I'm feeling much better than okay right now. You seem to have found all my—sensitive spots—several times over."

Chuckling, he tugged on her hair. "Always did strive for excellence in all the things I'm truly good at."

She rolled her yes. "Geez, you might be cockier than the surgeons at the hospital and that's going some."

"Hmm, gone out with many surgeons, have you?"

Wary, she looked for any hint of jealousy in his eyes. Relieved when he seemed only curious, she said, "No, I don't date doctors. You seem to forget I've only been on rotation for two months. The pressure's been on me up to my eyeballs to get Mendenhall's attention and approval. I was just getting comfortable with all of it when the wall known as Cade comes crashing down around me."

"Then I guess now would be an excellent time to reveal I got a text from Mendenhall when we were loading the boat."

She grabbed his arm. "And?"

"The man was—impressed, maybe a little intimidated to know his newly suspended resident went out and got herself a lawyer."

Her lips curved. "You just love being right, don't you? What else did he say?"

"He moved up your appearance before the review board."

She let out a whoop and grabbed him around the neck. "You did it! How soon?"

"Next week."

She gave him a long, mouthy kiss. "What happens next?"

"We make absolutely certain you're prepared for the Q & A and can explain this ridiculous situation with Cade as an annoyance and someone who has stalked you in the past."

Elation at the news had her leaning over him, hovering over his stellar rock-hard abs. "How are we doing on time?"

"Oh, I think we have time to fit in another appreciation round."

☙☙☙☙☙

Back on the mainland, success at locating Cade's cell phone relied on nothing more than a clever phone App already integrated into the platform.

Lucky for Trevor, Cade had purchased the latest technologically advanced cell phone on the market and with it had bought himself a little-known device that had been marketed to help you locate your phone in the event you misplaced it.

The phone App made tracking his phone incredibly accurate and easy.

Trevor finished the configuration in a matter of minutes.

He didn't intend to waste any more time.

CHAPTER 16

Later that afternoon, Reese and Quinn moored the *Sea Warrior* in the San Madrid harbor and walked up the hill hand in hand to Crandall House.

He figured he might as well enjoy the time he spent with Quinn since it might come to an abrupt end in less than twenty-four hours. Even though he still had time to convince her that meeting her father might offer an opportunity to get at answers she'd longed for, he didn't hold out much hope.

But despite her stubbornness, he refused to give up.

Once they got closer to the house, Reese spotted the three men on guard duty standing just inside the perimeter of the property. These guys had been tasked to protect them all. At least he hoped that's who they were. He noted they were dressed in khaki slacks and golf shirts but wore guns strapped to shoulder holsters.

He didn't recognize a single one of Jordan's men.

Sure enough, as he and Quinn approached, one of them held up a hand. "I need to see some ID."

Just as Reese reached in his back pocket for his wallet to take out his driver's license, all hell broke loose.

Gunfire erupted from a car moving north at a fast clip on the road in the direction of downtown. Reese pushed Quinn to the ground and fell on top of her. He looked around and saw all three of the guards pull their weapons to return fire. Shots whizzed by his head from every direction as the bodyguards took cover behind Jake's Benz sitting in the circular gravel driveway.

But in a matter of what seemed like five minutes, the hail of bullets suddenly stopped. Reese smelled burning rubber as he heard the squeal of tires on the road below the cliffs.

When Reese was sure they were in the clear, he got to his feet and pulled Quinn upright. "You okay?"

"I think so. This is getting to be a very annoying habit."

"Yeah. Anyone hurt?" Reese asked the three men who had risked their lives to keep them safe.

"Got Rob in the shoulder."

Reese reached in his pocket for his iPhone, called nine-one-one. "I'll get an ambulance here. Come on, Quinn, looks like you're getting more action in suspended-mode than working in the ER."

"I don't understand why the cops can't catch these guys. They seemed to have never left San Madrid." She mumbled some swearword before going over to the injured man, who by this time was down on the ground, holding his arm. She started ripping open his shirt to examine the wound. "Let's get you in the house. No sense bleeding out here on the lawn waiting for the EMTs to show up."

About that time, the front door opened and everyone streamed outside.

"That was Cade, wasn't it?" Jake shouted as he ran over to Rob to help Quinn get him up and onto the porch.

"Yep. Looks like Boyd won't give up until Quinn and I are both dead."

⚱ ⚱ ⚱ ⚱ ⚱

Cade Boyd gunned the blue Chevy Tahoe and sped through San Madrid going a good sixty miles an hour. He spun the vehicle into a turn, heading back the other way to meet up with the Coast Highway. At the corner of Main, he slid through a four-way stop sign and kept on going.

Sitting in the back seat, still gripping the semi-automatic AK47, Collin cackled like a crazy person. "Did you see that? Did you see them hit the dirt? I think I got that bastard," Collin shrieked. "Woohoo! We did it. We shot the bastards!"

Once on the PCH, Cade hit the gas as he accelerated to seventy-five. It was then he looked to his right and noticed, his cousin Scott Geller slumped in the passenger seat, his body leaning heavily against the door. The gun Scott had gripped during the shooting was now on the floorboard.

Cade reached over and shook his cousin. "Hey, Scott, what's wrong? Are you sick or something?"

That got Collin's attention. He crouched into the front seat and started trying to shake Scott awake. "Oh, man, he's bleeding, Cade. Bad. We need to get him to the ER."

"Are you nuts? We can't do that without explaining how he took a bullet."

"Then what're we going to do? We could take him to the same doctor who treated my shoulder."

"You mean the one who spilled his guts to the first cop who decided to question him? The one who will testify for the district attorney at your hearing? Is that the one you want to call? Forget it. Scott knew the risks."

Collin fretted over that. "Then pull over so I can take a look at him."

"Not now, Collin. We just shot at five fucking people. We have to get as far away from this bumfuck town and find a place to ditch this Tahoe."

"How about we take him to Grant's place? No one would look for us there."

"That's clear across town. Besides, the entire fucking LAPD has been crawling up our asses for days, checking out anyone who knows us. They've surely checked out all of our friends by this time."

Collin started crying. "Everyone's dying. They're all dead. I'm sick of this, man. I'm out of here, Cade. This could've been you or me. I'm done with this. I'm heading down to Mexico."

"No! Goddamn it! You're in this until I say you're done. Stop that crying shit! We owe it to Connor to get those bastards, to get all of them and finish this thing out for good."

"We got them today. That's enough. Now it's time to get out of here. We use the money in the offshore accounts no one knows about. We get new identities, start over in Tahiti or someplace warm."

"Stop it! I know a place to go where no one will ever find us. A place that ensures we get back at Kit once and for all. That's what you want, right?"

"I guess." It didn't seem so important now that Scott was bleeding to death. "He's stopped breathing, Cade. It looks like the bullet pierced a lung. There's blood everywhere."

Cade sighed. "Collateral damage, bro. Collateral damage is part of war. And this is fucking war!"

"Rob's lucky it's just a bullet graze to his shoulder. If they'd been better shots, I might be one man down and that would just piss me off even more right now," Jordan said as everyone gathered in the Crandall House living room.

Once they'd gotten the police out of their hair, they settled in for the meeting, hoping to put the shooting behind them, at least for the next hour or so until they could figure out the next step.

"I think I've found your Mr. X. I got my hands on a classified file from the State Department." Jordan glanced around the room. "Don't ask. Anyway, Noah Parker had an associate he trained. And let's be clear here, people.

According to the file, Noah Parker was the best at what he did. He'd been an Army Ranger in Vietnam, a sniper, a damned good one.

"But one day he gets captured by the Viet Cong, spends six years in captivity. Once the war's over, he sort of disappears, goes off the radar until he re-enlists in the Army. But at some point he becomes a private contractor for the CIA.

"Enter the associate. Together he and this guy took assignments all over the world, even worked under Presidents Reagan and the first Bush. It seems these two were a team and worked as such."

"Name?" Reese snapped out.

"Trevor Dane. Got his start early as a petty enforcer for the IRA. When they were told to lay down their arms, Dane wanted out, saw an opportunity to get out of the nasty business he'd lived in for years and leave it behind once and for all so he could live in peace and quiet with his wife and child. The IRA saw it differently. To make their point, they went after him. Instead of killing him, they made the mistake of taking out his wife and daughter."

"Ohmygod," Kit said. "That file didn't happen to come with any photos of his wife and daughter, did it?"

Jordan looked perplexed for about ten seconds and then replied, "As a matter of fact, there were no photos of either Parker or Dane. I have no idea what he looks like. That's the way the CIA rolls or so I'm told. Why?"

Kit glanced at Jake. "No reason. I was just curious."

"How did they kill the wife and daughter?" Quinn asked.

"It had been raining. Skid marks on the road showed the car had been forced off onto a narrow shoulder and then forced over a cliff. They think the car exploded though before it ever hit the water, which indicates it might've been the result of a car bomb. No one really knows for certain. The thing is they only recovered the wife's body. The little girl apparently drifted away in the water…" Jordan's voice trailed off.

"How horrible," Quinn commented, as she too, glanced around the room at her friends, but her gaze stopped at Reese. "I guess everyone has a story, something horrible that happened to them in their past they'd like to forget. Losing his family like that, what happened to this Trevor Dane is not much different than what happened to Noah Parker and his parents."

Reese eyed her curiously, trying to figure out what was still going on in that head of hers. She'd been acting weird since they'd gotten back, growing even more distant than she'd been that morning on the boat.

But for now, he forced himself to turn his attention back to Jordan. There was too much at stake to get distracted now.

"So at some point, Noah Parker must've come back to L.A., uncovered what Alana and Jessica had done, realized they'd capitalized on his parents' estate and decided payback was the only way," Reese ascertained.

"Ron Blake, the cold case detective at the sheriff's department, told me that about ten years back a man came in and pleaded with them to re-open the Parker case. He talked to another detective, someone who has since retired. But Blake made a point to locate the detective who worked the case. He remembered the guy's ridiculous theory though. The son accused the lawyers at BBG&G, his parent's own lawyers, of being mixed up in their murders." Jordan shook his head. "Nothing came of it. Of course, you know the detective didn't pursue it."

"Well, if we don't figure out how to get rid of the Nutty Brothers, eventually one or more of us will end up dead," Reese commented.

"Kit came close," Quinn reminded them.

Jake went white, remembering how scared he'd been the day Collin had taken Kit out of the house. "Dylan and I have already drained their numbered bank accounts, at least all that we could find," Jake told them. "And when they discover we've emptied the Icelandic accounts as well, you'll get more of a reaction than that drive-by earlier, which I'm certain was in retaliation for putting an end to their domestic cash flow."

"Imagine what they'll do when they realize we also got to the stash of Krugerrands they had hidden in South Africa in a vault that belonged solely to Jessica Boyd. Once we found that stockpile, Jake paid a courier to go in, pick up the bags, and transport them to another location. The bags are still in Cape Town but under a different name," Dylan added.

"We're making progress," Jake assured them all. "But we've hit a snag working on moving property holdings."

"That's a bit more complex and requires changing a slew of documents. Even online, we don't do it right, miss a step and we risk leaving a paper trail they can track," Dylan admitted. "But we'll get there eventually."

"In the meantime," Jordan stated. "I agree with Reese. If we don't figure out how to end this, it's only a matter of time before someone dies."

❧ ❧ ❧ ❧ ❧

No one was more surprised than Collin when his brother turned the SUV off the PCH and headed into a wooded area full of hiking trails and canyons, popular with local nature lovers.

Since they were less than ten miles from their own beloved Enclave, Collin remarked, "Is it smart to get this close to home?"

"We need a place to get rid of Scott's body. He's no good to us like this," Cade pointed out.

"You're going to dump him out here in the wilderness? I don't believe you. That's not right."

"Bury him. There's a difference. You want a damned funeral, we'll go that route on our own, have our own little private ceremony for him right here, perfect place, peaceful, nice. You know how he loved nature," Cade snorted as the vehicle bumped along moving farther into the rugged canyons, unmarked trails.

"What does that mean? Connor's still down at the coroner's in some cooler. We haven't even had his service yet. Scott said..."

"Look, I've been a little busy what with trying to get rid of Quinn and all to think about planning a memorial service for Connor. He's gone. We've had how many funerals in the last six weeks?"

"Too many."

"Exactly. I'm done with funerals for a while."

"We could pay a regular mortuary to deal with Scott. Pay 'em enough where they wouldn't ask questions."

"No, we can't."

"There has to be a funeral home in town that won't ask questions. This isn't right, Cade. He's our own blood, he's..."

"I know what he is. I don't have time to listen to your whining now, Collin. Grow a pair. Do you not understand they've taken our fucking money? All of it. I tried to withdraw two hundred dollars from an account no one knew about and there was no money, not a cent left."

"How is that possible?"

"Those assholes are hackers. Isn't it obvious? They've hacked into our accounts."

As Cade drove farther away from the main road and into remote terrain surrounded by rock formations and natural-forming gullies, Collin began to get even more creeped out than before. When he noticed the gate straight ahead padlocked with a heavy chain, he squeaked out a question. "What is this place, Cade?

"A little patch of land I like to call my own Eternal Gardens. He drew a key from his pocket. "Now do me a favor and unlock the gate so we can offer curb service."

Chill bumps ran along Collin's arms. "You're going to bury Scott out *here*?"

"That's the plan."

Once the gate opened, Cade gunned the vehicle over an incline and into a clearing. The minute Cade brought the SUV to a stop and put the gear into PARK; he hopped out of the car. Opening the passenger side door, Cade took hold of his cousin's shoulders, under the arms, and dragged his body out of the front seat.

With a bob of his head, he motioned to Collin. "See that underbrush over there? Bring me one of the shovels I have hidden there. Get the other one for you."

"You have shovels out here?" Collin surveyed his surroundings, realized for the first time how isolated the area was. "What for? Wh...what are you gonna do?"

"I'm taking care of Scott. Isn't that what you wanted?"

Collin swallowed hard, suddenly afraid of his own brother. The intense look on Cade's face was one he'd never seen before.

"Just get the goddamned shovels and help me." He walked backward, dragging Scott over another hilly incline and down into a narrow ten by ten foot trench-like section between a grove of trees.

After retrieving both shovels, Collin made his way into the thicker underbrush and met up with his brother in the neatly dugout furrow of ground. By this time Cade had let go of Scott and stood over what looked like a squared-off glade of freshly turned earth.

Collin watched as his brother began to remove scrub California privet along with dead branches of hawthorn covering what looked like an already freshly dug grave.

Before Collin could say a word, Cade mumbled, "Had this already dug for Quinn. It'll be okay. It's okay. Don't worry. I'll dig another one just for you, baby, because I'm coming for you real soon, Quinn, real soon."

He went on muttering as if to himself. "Shame, too, this is such a pretty place. Good thing I took to burying what belongs to me. Wouldn't do to leave them dead in a bedroom where they can take all kinds of DNA evidence. If they can't find the body there's no DNA. If you leave them, someone else will come along and find them. Not a good idea. Boston should've been arrested, should've been charged, prosecuted." He puffed out a huge sigh. "Just can't trust the cops to do their fucking job anymore."

The hairs on the back of Collin's neck stood up. "So it was you who killed Claire Boston?"

The question caused Cade to snap out of his rambling. "Another slut who made the mistake of laughing at me." He found that incredible funny. "Last thing the bitch ever did, too. But God did she put up a fight. I didn't think she'd ever quit clawing at me. Had her damn scratch marks on my face for days afterward."

He glanced up at Collin who stood staring. "What? You didn't really think Boston killed her did you? Nah, he's such a pussy. Help me get Scott into the hole, will you?" he asked as he stuffed Scott's body into his makeshift grave and began scooping up loose soil to go on top.

Collin hesitated, but only briefly. He didn't want to piss off his brother, especially not in this mood. Soon both men began their task of tossing dirt back in to fill up the hole. "You seem pretty goddamned comfortable putting someone in the ground," Collin grumbled as he sweated in the June heat.

Cade said nothing, seeming intent on his chore, as if reliving a better, more gratifying episode.

"What is that smell, anyway?" Collin asked a little sick at his stomach.

But Cade went on as if not hearing anyone. "Here you go, ladies. This time, I brought you a man to keep you company since I'm going to be a little busy for a while. It'll be just like old times," Cade finally said, and took to muttering incoherently all over again.

CHAPTER 17

That night as they were moving what few things Quinn had brought with her into Reese's bedroom, he decided to dangle his toe into perilous water. Because he was running out of time, he needed to take a few risks. "Quinn, were you ever told anything about your Native heritage?"

"No. Why?"

"Never got curious enough to ask Ella? I mean, don't you want to know more about the circumstances surrounding your birth?"

She rolled her eyes. "Reese, even if I had bothered to ask, which I didn't, what makes you think Ella would have told me the truth? She didn't exactly have a history of sticking with the facts and since she never saw the need to mention it, I sure never asked." She shrugged. "More like, she'd have made something up for sure, so what was the point in making a big deal out of it?"

"Okay. Good point."

She finished hanging up her clothes in his closet, turned around to meet his eyes. "Now that we're involved, is that something you're interested in knowing more about, my Native American roots? You're interested in my Irish ancestry? You knew before we headed into this thing I had a difficult childhood. If my history bothers you that much, if I don't have the proper lineage for a high profile attorney…"

"Will you stop it? Just stop it. Did I say or do anything that has you thinking I want to dig around in your past for any other reason than simply trying to get to know you better?" He threw up his hands in exasperation. "Who the hell gives a damn about your lineage? Geez, you were a prickly pear before but..."

"You mean before you knew about my stepfather, before you knew what he did to me?" she accused.

"For God's sakes, you're the exact same person I took to bed." Frustrated, he ran a hand through his hair. "See, this is why I think you need to talk to a professional. That chip on your shoulder you've been carrying around for too long by yourself is starting to get pretty damned heavy and is starting to piss me off." With that, he stormed out of the bedroom. leaving her with her mouth hung open.

"Arrogant bastard!" she shouted at his back. She most certainly did not have a chip on her shoulder. Did she?

At other times in her life plenty of people had looked down on her for no other reason than the fact she'd looked Native. Oh, God.

What was happening to her anyway?

She plopped down on the bed so she could sulk. Reese of all people did not look down on her. But she'd acted that way all day, ever since last night, ever since he had discovered her secret.

And she resented him for knowing.

About that time, Baylee came into the room carrying Sarah. "I just passed Reese in the hallway. Did something happen between you two? He looked upset." She tilted her head and studied her friend. "You don't look so good yourself."

"Can I ask you something?"

"If it's advice about men, you're out of luck. They're a strange breed, grubby, farting little boys, the lot of them. But then...no man on the planet understands why our breed feels the need to travel to the bathroom in a pack, either."

It made Quinn's lips curve but only briefly. "If you found out something bad about someone you cared about, something horrible, something they did, would it change your opinion of them?"

"Did they kill somebody?"

Quinn shook her head.

Baylee's maternal instincts kicked in then, ever wary of anyone passing judgment on Quinn, she asked, "Did Reese pick at you about something? Because if he did, I'll speak to him…"

That did make her smile. "No, Mom, it isn't that."

"Did you pick at him about something?"

"I guess I did."

"Did he deserve it?"

"That's just it, I don't think he did. In fact…"

"Looks like you've got a big, fat, ol' I'm sorry in your immediate future then."

"Yeah, I guess I do. Here, give me the baby. I need to borrow your daughter. It'll go better if I have a cute, adorable bundle in my arms."

Baylee relinquished Sarah into Quinn's waiting hands. "Wow, it must be bad if you need a prop."

"I guess I have been acting like a jerk."

"You? But Quinn Tyler is always so objective, so willing to listen to reason, so sweet-natured."

"Oh, shut up. I said it was my fault, didn't I?"

"Boy, you must really like him to admit that."

She sighed. "I fell into that trap. He wore me down. When you stop and think about it, this is really his fault. He knew I was a prickly pear. He called me a prickly pear, Baylee."

Baylee smirked at that. "Why that bastard! How dare he say such things to you? Why the next thing he'll call you is hard-headed."

"I guess, I—care about him." When exactly had that happened? She wondered.

Baylee could see that plain as day. It wasn't like Quinn to show vulnerability to anyone, especially to a man. Not since a young Quinn made a mistake and let Cade in, albeit briefly, had she seen her friend so raw. "You spent time on Catalina. It's the Island. That's where it happened for me with Dylan. He wore me down, too."

"I'm not used to…"

Baylee laid her hand gently on top of Quinn's. "I know, but sometimes there's no rhyme or reason to love."

"I never said anything about love."

"Hmm, that's right you didn't. My mistake. Now bring back my kid in ten minutes or less, okay? It's nearly bedtime and I guarantee your prop will get cranky if she doesn't get her bedtime snack soon. Get it?"

"Got it, Mom."

Quinn found Reese outside on the back deck with his laptop open and his iPod buds in his ears, his fingers tapping to music. She laid a hand on his leg to get his attention.

He glanced up, saw she had Sarah sitting on her hip. His heart did that little two-step and then went straight into a West Coast Swing. He removed the buds from his ears.

Quinn sank down next to him in her own chair, settled the baby on her lap, or tried to. Little traitor that she was, Sarah immediately stretched out her arms for Reese to hold her.

He accommodated the baby by setting his laptop on the table and then scooping Sarah up out of Quinn's arms.

"Little flirt, she didn't waste any time going after my guy."

He cocked a brow. "Am I your guy, Quinn?"

"I guess you are. Wow, maybe I should pass you a note in chemistry class. Look, I came out here to apologize. I've been acting like an ass all day. It's just…I guess knowing you knew, I thought maybe you wouldn't want to, you know, be with me. I thought you'd somehow think you were better than me or you'd judge me or—something."

The self-assured Quinn Tyler suddenly insecure, took some getting used to. He didn't like it. He wanted the smartass back. "Let me write this day down on my…"

"Oh, shut up. What more do you want me to say?"

"I want you to stop all this insecurity that's surfaced the last twenty-four. Self-doubt and Quinn Tyler don't exactly go together. I want the smug Quinn back."

She put a fist under her chin, leaned in on the arm of the chair. "Smug? I'm as down-to-earth as you could get."

He bounced the baby on his knee, shifted in his seat to meet her halfway. "Not snobby, smug as in major smartass."

She let out a sigh. "Oh. Well. Hmm, I guess I am a smartass. But in a good way."

Sitting there holding the baby Reese thought this might be the perfect time to mention the reason he was so edgy. "When you're working on a patient in the ER, you don't always have time to stop and ask that patient what treatment he or she wants, what's best for them? Correct? You do whatever it takes in the heat of the moment to make a gut decision to save his life no matter what, right?

"Sure, what's your point?"

"Over the course of working on someone you choose what's best for them in the long run, even if it might upset the patient later, right?"

She eyed him suspiciously. Believing he was making his case for therapy again she said, "Absolutely. But therapy isn't the answer for everyone, Reese. Where are you going with this?"

"Sometimes the only way to deal with an issue is meet it head-to-head. Before you can move on with your future you have to resolve the issues rooted in your past."

"Stop using that bullshit psycho analogy on me, will you? You don't know a thing about it. I'm not going back into therapy and talking about this with another living soul. That's the end of it."

"You don't even plan to tell Kit and Baylee, do you?"

"No. Don't you understand how mortifying it is? I feel like I let them down."

He gaped at her. "That's ridiculous. You've shared so much with them already. You know they won't judge you."

"I won't do it. You know, and that's enough. I don't want to hear any more about therapy or talking about it or baring my soul to Baylee and Kit either. I would never have told you…except…"

"And here I thought it was because you trusted me enough. I guess not."

She sighed. "Reese…it isn't that." She squeezed his hand.

When Sarah started to fuss like she was sleepy, Quinn reached over and snatched the baby out of his lap.

He ran his hands through his hair and watched her walk back into the house, knowing he'd have to meet her wrath straight-on when the time came.

Because in less than twenty-four hours she'd have to deal with yet another traumatic event—and come face to face—with the father she hated.

CHAPTER 18

In Agoura Hills, fifty-year old Gloria Gandis pulled her car into the garage, her mind anticipating the arrival of her son, Ben, a son she had yet to lay eyes on.

Two days. In two short days she'd get to look into his eyes, gaze upon his face for the very first time in her life.

She was so nervous about meeting him she'd gone shopping for a new outfit. She'd already gotten her hair styled in a new 'do, a sassy cut that spiked just below her chin. The hairdresser had told her it made her look ten years younger. Even though she doubted that, she did feel energized. She'd had her nails done in a French manicure that made her feel better about herself, better than she had in years.

She might not be the twenty-five-year old that had given birth to him, but she could damn well put forth the effort to look her best the very first time she saw him.

Her tall, statuesque frame had dropped six anxious pounds waiting for him to finally get to L.A., a fact she would admit to no one, even though it had precipitated the shopping spree.

She unsnapped her seat belt and crawled out of the car wearing a pair of brand-new, low-riding Capri jeans and a snazzy purple button-down shirt.

Once out of the garage, she set Morty down to wander off and hopefully take a pee on the grass while she headed to the mailbox at the curb to get her mail.

With her hands full, she walked up to her front door. Doing her best to balance her purse along with the mail without dropping anything, she took out the key and stuck it into the lock.

She had just taken a step inside when Morty set up a din of barking in warning. A noise behind the door had her turning around.

Envelopes fluttered to the floor.

She backed up, made a dig for her cell phone lodged somewhere in the bottom of her purse. But she never got the chance to make a call. She was still digging when a man hit her on the head with the butt of his gun, knocking her to the floor.

Her head came back hard on the sandstone tile. For a minute she saw nothing but stars.

Brandishing a handgun, Cade Boyd went to her, pulled her upright by her hair. "Come here, you old bat. You're going to do what we say, you got that?"

Through the pain, Gloria recognized the voice before she saw that Collin too held a gun in a nervous fist. She watched as Cade went over to the phone in the living room, jerked the cord out of the wall. He stripped the cable and used it to bind her hands, tight.

Meanwhile Morty kept up a steady yip-yip-yip.

"Collin, shut that fucking dog up. He's getting on my nerves."

"Nooooo! Don't hurt my Morty!"

Collin picked up the little Chihuahua and started to hurl it against the wall, but Morty bit down, clamped his teeth into the man's hand, and held on for dear life, taking out a chunk of skin in the process.

Collin dropped the dog to the floor. "That little bastard bit me."

"Shake it off, will you? It'll be okay. We'll put something on it later. Take care of that mangy mutt. Do it now! This'll be home base for the next couple of hours until we figure out what to do from here. They've cut off our fucking money and this old bat is going to be our key to getting it back."

Cade turned to Gloria. "You do what we tell you, when we tell you, and we might let you live. You understand?"

When she said nothing, Cade approached her, delivered an open hand slap across her face. "Nod your head if you understand me." When she still said nothing and made no move to respond, this time he backhanded her. "Look, I can kill you right now, it doesn't matter to me. But you're going to answer me, show me some respect."

He held his hand around her throat.

Still hurting from the dog bite, Collin grabbed a hunk of Gloria's hair and made a production of nodding her head up and down. "See, she does understand. This was fucking genius, Cade. No one is going to be looking for us here. We hide out here until we get ready to make the call. And we can use Gloria to get Kit to come to us. All we have to do is sit back and wait."

Cade bumped Collin on the back of the head. "How many times do I have to tell you to keep that mouth of yours shut about the plan? This is about taking them all down by surprise and getting them to give us the money back. Get that through your thick skull now. Gloria's gonna help us, though, no question about that. Aren't you, old woman?"

Eyeing the sandwich makings the two of them had already set out on the kitchen counter before Gloria got there, Collin announced, "Hey, she can cook us up a real meal. No need to eat this crap when she's a terrific cook. Aren't you, old woman? You need to get your ass over here and fix us a decent meal. From now on when I say move, you move."

🔗 🔗 🔗 🔗 🔗

Trevor Dane did a double-take when he zoomed in on the address that had already changed twice since he'd plotted their course. He punched in the location again on his phone just to make sure. It couldn't be. Could it? The only person he knew connected to this mess who lived in Agoura Hills was Gloria Gandis, Kit Griffin's biological mother.

Why would Cade and Collin be at Gloria's house? Unless...

He threw the Chevy into gear, made a U-turn in the middle of the Coast Highway and headed southeast to where he knew Gloria lived.

Thirty minutes later, he parked his car several streets over. He grabbed his weapon and crawled out of the vehicle, quickly making his way through the back alleys, approaching Gloria's house from the rear.

Knowing she had a yappy little dog, he had to be careful not to set him off. He struck around through shadowy patches of shrubs and bushes, felt spider webs cling to his face and even had to vault over a fence until he got to the backyard.

Carefully, Trevor crept along the house peering in window after window looking for any sign of Gloria. Knowing these two men as he did, he feared the woman might already be dead.

The only light source inside flickered from the living room as though someone might be watching TV there. As quietly as he could, he headed that way. Watching through a set of half-closed blinds, he spotted the Boyd brothers lounging on the sofa, staring at the telly, deep in conversation.

While they were occupied in that part of the house, he moved to his right and to another window. He saw Gloria sitting in a kitchen chair, her wrists bound, her blonde hair matted. Blood trickled down the side of her head. She had a gash to her skull.

She was either asleep or unconscious.

"They'll pay for this, I promise you that," he murmured to himself as he pulled his Beretta Cheetah from his waist and screwed on the silencer. Retracing his steps, he made his way back around to the front of the house.

Trevor had already decided to kick in the door when he noticed the brothers were no longer sitting on the couch. The TV screen black, the room now dark, Trevor realized they were in another part of the house, hopefully going to bed.

Okay, he decided, he could do more damage if they were asleep. But just when that idea started to have merit, he heard voices coming from the garage.

He ducked behind a row of hedges just in time to see the garage door rumble its way up.

Trevor watched as a blue Chevy Tahoe with Cade and Collin inside sped out of the garage and down the driveway.

Fearing the worst, Trevor raced to the front door and kicked it in, sprinted inside the house. On his way to the kitchen, his shoes skidded on the floor in a sizeable pool of blood.

"Fuck no, not again!"

Expecting to see Gloria dead, his eyes focused on her little dog. Someone had cut the animal's throat. A bloody kitchen knife lay on the floor.

He made a quick search of the rest of the house but found no one there.

They'd obviously taken Gloria with them. That had to mean they'd kept her alive.

Trevor rushed out the back door, heading to his car on a dead run.

Tossing his gun on the front seat, he put the car in gear and roared off. Remembering to turn on the tracking App on his phone, he raced down the street after the Tahoe.

Minutes later he caught sight of the SUV and fell back as far as he could without losing them. He went over all the ways he intended to make the assholes pay if they put any more bruises on the woman. He hadn't picked up a few tricks from his journeys for nothing. He could make their deaths slow and very painful. He would make them pay for this, and pay dearly.

☙ ☙ ☙ ☙ ☙

Inside the Tahoe, Cade looked at Collin and smiled. "I gave your suggestion some thought. It just so happens I have a key to Grant's cabin in the canyons. It isn't big, but it's out of the way. And it'll be vacant this time of year."

Collin grinned. "Told you it would be a great place to lay low until we can trade this crazy bitch in for our money."

"Who says we're going to trade her in?"

Cade took the Las Virgenes Road south until it dumped into County Road N1 weaving farther back into a stretch of winding canyons off the main road.

They were so busy patting themselves on the back at a job well done they never noticed the car that had been following them for the last thirty miles.

When they got to an unmarked turnoff, Cade took a right onto a gravel road.

Several hundred yards behind them, Trevor cut his lights. He slowed his vehicle to let them continue on before waiting a few minutes, then shooting a U on the narrow road. Circling back, he moved at a snail's pace along the unlit roadway until he spotted the Tahoe parked in front of a small A-frame.

Leaving his car a good hundred yards down the road off the shoulder, he got out and made his way up to the house. In the shadows, one of the brothers, it looked like Collin, struggled to get Gloria out of the backseat and up onto his shoulders.

"Come on, dumb ass! Get the fucking door open, this bitch is heavy."

Cade jiggled the key in the lock and Trevor watched as both brothers stepped inside a dark cabin.

Once they got into the small interior, Collin dumped Gloria onto the nearest piece of furniture, which happened to be a futon without much padding. Like a sack of potatoes, she landed hard, her head hitting the wooden arm with a crack.

"How long do you think she'll be out?" Cade asked.

"Another hour or so. Why?"

"'Cause it's time to call Reese Brennan and demand our money back. We go out, make the phone call from a public phone booth, that way they won't be able to trace the call."

"Good, because I could use some food. What about that convenience store we passed near the State Park?"

"That'll work. You stay here."

"No way, you'll pick out all the junk food. I want to get my own stuff. I'm sick of the crap you choose."

"Bitch, bitch, bitch. Fine, ditch her in the closet in the bedroom and lock the door."

Collin picked up Gloria and headed to the only bedroom the cabin had.

Outside, Trevor studied the house for the best way in. Suddenly, the front door flew open. He leaned back into the shadows sticking to the side of the house until he watched Cade and Collin climb back into the Tahoe without the woman.

⚭ ⚭ ⚭ ⚭ ⚭

At Crandall House, Reese and Quinn were snuggled in bed.

Still doing his best to find a way to work tomorrow's meeting with Nick Tyler into the conversation, Reese toyed with a couple of strands of her hair. "You feel better about things now, right? We're okay?"

"We're better than okay."

His stomach flip-flopped with nerves. "I have to go into the office tomorrow for a meeting."

"That thing you were setting up this morning? Okay."

He swallowed hard. The deceit wanted to lodge in his throat. "I want you to come with me."

Her brow furrowed, she narrowed her eyes. "Why?"

"Because Kit goes into the Book & Bean around six-thirty and Jake goes with her. Dylan's taking Baylee to the hospital to visit her father. Afterward, they plan to make a stop at the house on Bel Green Drive, see if they can come up with Sarah's diary. That leaves you here alone unless, of course, you want to go with Baylee, put in an unofficial appearance at the hospital, and get a good look at your co-workers hard at work while you're still on suspension."

No one could accuse him of not knowing the right buttons to push.

She wrinkled her nose. "That isn't an option. I want to go back and see Mendenhall on his knees begging for my return, telling me how he made the worst mistake of his career by letting me go and how he's removing the entire incident from my personnel file like it never even happened." She grinned. "I know. I know. But it's my fantasy and I'm sticking to it."

"Nothing wrong with a good fantasy as long as Mendenhall suffers, right?"

"Absolutely."

Plugged into its charger on the nightstand, his cell phone rang.

"That can't be good news at this hour," Quinn moaned.

He picked it up. "Brennan."

"Now you listen to me, asshole, I've got Gloria and I want our fucking money back in our accounts by tomorrow morning. You don't make it happen, Gloria's dead. You got that?"

"Calm down. I want to talk to Gloria. How do I know you haven't already done something to her?"

"I guess you'll just have to take my word for it. I want to talk to Quinn."

"I'm afraid that isn't possible."

"You put Quinn on now or so help me God I'll put a bullet in Gloria's head right now."

Reese decided to play hardball. "Call back in an hour and she should be back home by then."

"You better not be lying to me. You assholes give us our goddamned money back."

"I have no idea what you're talking about, but I'm sure we can work something out, okay? There's no reason to hurt Gloria."

"You just have our money back by tomorrow morning or she's a dead woman. And I'm calling back in another hour. Have Quinn waiting by the phone."

Cade disconnected the call.

Reese crawled out of bed and started pulling on his jeans.

"Ohmygod, that was Cade," Quinn breathed. "They have Gloria."

Reese nodded. "We need to let Kit know."

☧ ☧ ☧ ☧ ☧

As soon as Trevor was certain they were gone, he went around to the back of the house and to the door leading into what looked like a tiny kitchen. The cabin was rather small, a simple A-frame design with only two ways inside. But it did have a back door with panes of glass running down to the halfway mark.

In the dark, he took out his penlight, ran his hands around the rim of the doorframe to check for contact strips indicating an alarm system.

Confident there wasn't one; he punched in one of the square panes of glass on the door with his elbow.

Reaching past the knob, he turned the deadbolt lock. Stepping into the kitchen, not knowing if there was anyone else in the house, he drew his Beretta. His eyes scanned the room, quickly deciding Gloria wasn't in this one.

The little bungalow had no more than nine-hundred square feet of total space, so he moved on to the living room, where he found it empty. He headed into the bedroom; no one there either. He quickly checked the bathroom and came up with nothing.

He was on the verge of looking around for a cellar door when he snapped his fingers, remembering he hadn't looked in the bedroom closet.

He shook his head. He must be getting sloppy in his old age. Finding the closet door locked, he put his shoulder into the cheap wood and cracked it open.

A bound Gloria tumbled out at his feet in a heap.

Trevor holstered his weapon and bent down to feel for a pulse. Her eyes were closed, but she was alive.

He removed her blindfold, took the knife out of his boot to cut the cord binding her wrists together, as well as the one at her feet.

He tapped her gently on the face, trying to get her to come around. "Gloria, can you hear me? Come on, sweetheart."

As soon as she showed signs of life, she groaned. "My head hurts."

"Don't be afraid, I'm here to help you. Can you stand?"

"They tied my feet."

"I know, but I untied them. Come on; try to stand up for me."

"Who are you?"

"We need to get out of here. They'll be back—soon. Can you walk?"

"I'll do anything to get out of here. Collin killed Morty right in front of me. He…he…"

"Don't think about it." He started prodding her toward the kitchen and the back door, going out the way he'd come in. But once they got to the side of the house, without shoes, barefoot, Gloria started to falter.

Realizing they would never make it to the car unless he carried her, he scooped her up and threw her over his shoulder.

But at the midway point, Gloria started to squirm. Since he felt winded, and a little more than out of shape carrying her, he stopped to catch his breath.

He dropped her feet back on the ground.

"I can walk now. You don't have to lug me all the way to the car."

"Are you sure?"

"No, but do you have another one of those?" She pointed to the gun in his holster.

"What? You want a gun?"

"Yes, I'd feel better having one in case they come back."

Trevor eyed her curiously and reached around his back, pulled out what he called his suicide gun, a .22 caliber Smith and Wesson, from his waist. "Do you know how to fire a weapon?"

"You point it and pull the trigger?"

He chuckled, but flicked off the safety, pulled back the slide and released it, handed it off. "It's ready to point and shoot. Make sure you aim for the bad guys, okay?"

That got her moving again and she tentatively started walking to the car.

"I'm so grateful you came along when you did. Cade had already decided to kill me. They talked about it all the way out here. They thought I was out of it. I've just now gotten to know Kit as my daughter. I'm getting ready to meet my son—from Ireland. He probably talks the way you do. They were about to take all that away from me until you saved me! Thank you!"

Nothing like a chatty blonde to make the blood pump, Trevor thought. And this one looked ready to burst with babble. With his fingers, he scooted a few strands of stray hair behind her ear. "I always did have a weakness for blondes."

That got a laugh out of her.

And it was a great thing to be able to laugh, Gloria decided. Because he stood so close to her, she leaned over and planted a kiss squarely on his mouth. "That's for saving me. Will you take me home?" She laughed again. And it felt glorious to be able to kiss and laugh and act silly.

Pushing her toward the car, he explained, "We'll call Kit to pick you up, how's that?"

"No, I want you to take me back to Crandall House, okay? They'll want to see you, meet you. They have so much to tell you. Don't you know that?"

He shook his head. "I wish I could but…"

"You think they'll call the police? Don't be absurd. They won't do that. We all have to work at getting rid of these scummy bastards once and for all or they'll just keep trying to hurt us."

Trevor grinned. "That's why I'm calling someone to pick you up. The less you know the better. I'll take care of Cade and Collin."

"That's what I'm telling you. You don't have to do it on your own."

"I work alone," he pointed out and watched her blush before she spontaneously hugged him again. They stood there like that in a brief embrace until he had to nudge her along again.

They'd almost made it to the car when Trevor noticed headlights approaching fast from the other end of the gravel road. Quickly he opened the door, pushed Gloria down into the passenger seat of the Chevy.

Reaching in the glove box, he grabbed his backup pistol, a Glock 17 and crawled over Gloria into the driver's seat. He started the engine, shoved the car in gear, and took off down the dark lane, never bothering to turn on the headlights.

With any luck maybe they could fake out the two stooges.

Behind the wheel of the SUV, though, Cade yelled, "Did you see that? It looked like movement, someone running down the side of the road from the house."

Cramming his mouth with a protein bar, Collin said, "I don't see a thing."

"Son of a bitch, I bet Gloria's escaped. I thought you said she'd be out for another hour."

"Just get her, run her down if you have to."

"Wait, there's a car heading right for us with its lights off."

"I see it!" Collin pulled out his Luger and hit the button to roll down the glass. He opened fire from the passenger window.

Trevor returned fire as he floored the gas. "Stay down!" he yelled as the Chevy tore off down the road, skidding on the gravel.

As they drove past the Tahoe, though, Gloria hit the button to roll down the glass. She steadied the barrel of the gun on the rim as best she could and took aim. She fired off several quick shots in rapid succession. She heard bullets hitting metal but couldn't see much else as gunfire continued to erupt around them.

All of a sudden, Trevor felt a burn in his shoulder blade. He winced but took the time to cast a quick glance in the rearview mirror. "I don't know how you managed, but it looks like you punctured their tires. Nice shooting for an amateur."

"The tires? Damn it, I was aiming for Collin's head." Gloria turned back around in her seat to stare at the man who had saved her. "Oh, my God, you've been shot. There's blood on your shirt."

"It isn't the first time."

"Pull over, let me help you."

"Are you crazy? We're not stopping."

She laughed. "Some say I am, crazy that is. I like to think I march to my own drum."

In spite of the pain in his shoulder, he threw her a wicked grin.

They drove in anxious silence until they got back to the 101. Gunning the car up the ramp, Trevor merged onto the heavily trafficked highway with the other stream of vehicles. They hadn't gone very far though when the car abruptly began to weave.

Gloria looked over, heard him began to wheeze as if having difficulty breathing. "Your shirt is already soaked. You've lost a lot of blood. Pull over. I can take the wheel."

He did feel lightheaded, but he shook it off. "I'm fine. It's probably just a scratch anyway."

"You aren't fine. Where are you taking me?"

"Someplace safe," he muttered between clenched teeth. His right shoulder felt like someone had taken a fire poker and jabbed him a couple of times with it.

"Where, though? I deserve to know."

The car veered to the right again, this time almost clipping a call box. She glanced over and saw his head drop back onto the headrest.

"For God's sakes, brake!" Gloria shouted. "Pull over! Now!"

The car drifted completely off the roadway. When it finally slowed to a stop, Gloria went around to the driver's side. It took some time to coax Trevor, one leg at a time, to climb over the console into the passenger seat.

Blood spurted out onto his shirt now more than it had before.

And once she crawled behind the wheel, she realized just how badly Trevor had been hurt. Sticky blood residue clung to the steering wheel, as well as the upholstery. Knowing he needed a doctor, she had a decision to make. If she took him to the nearest ER there would be countless questions. Even she knew this man would not want to answer any of them.

She wasn't about to put him in harm's way after he'd saved her life.

There was only one place to go.

She reached into his jacket pocket, pulled out his cell phone, and punched in a number. She angled her head in the side mirror to check traffic before accelerating back into the steady line of cars.

Cade filled the night air with a string of blue obscenities as he realized the SUV wasn't going anywhere. "Now we're stuck out in this godforsaken area with two fucking flat tires."

"I'm telling you we need to head south to Mexico. This whole thing is falling apart. It's more than we bargained for. We need to get out of here."

"Shut the fuck up and let me think! I want my goddamn money and I'm not going anywhere until those bastards give it back. They aren't going to outsmart me. I'm going to kill every single one of those bastards just like I killed those goddamn cunts."

"Wh…what did you say? What're you talking about, Cade?"

"Forget it." Scott was dead and buried now and no other living soul needed to know what they'd done together. Cade took out his cell phone. "I'll call Adam and tell him we need some help out here."

"What did you mean, Cade? You and Scott killed those hookers, didn't you?"

"What do you know about it?"

"I know some of them went missing. That platinum blonde one, the one who looked like Kit, never got back together with me. I liked her but she never showed up again even when I called and requested her. They told me she disappeared, left without a word and didn't come back."

"Shut up, Collin."

"No, no I won't, not this time. That's why you weren't upset Scott took a bullet, isn't it? Scott knew because Scott helped you. That's why we buried him with those other rotting bodies."

Cade narrowed his eyes at his brother. "And that's the same spot where I intend to bury all three of those bitches. I plan to put Quinn, Baylee, and Kit in the ground right alongside those whores if it's the last thing I ever do."

When Cade moved toward him, Collin flinched and aimed his Luger at Cade's chest. "Don't you ever hit me again; I'm tired of taking your crap. I'm in this just as deep as you; have just as much to lose, too. You want to stay and finish this, fine. But after we get Kit and that Boston prick, I'm heading out of here. I'm done with all of this."

"Fine. Let's just get tires on the damn truck so we can get out of here."

"How do we get back our money now that Gloria's gone? She was our bargaining chip, our insurance."

"I believe in spreading around the insurance. There's another way we can take care of all of them once and for all."

"What time did Cade say he'd call back? It's been well over an hour," Kit pointed out as she paced the living room, back and forth, back and forth, all the while chewing on her thumbnail. "I knew I should have insisted she come stay with us until this was over."

"Kit, you tried and she said she had too much to do before Ben got here."

"Obviously, I didn't try hard enough. She was vulnerable and I...I let her stay at home by herself."

"You did try, honey."

"Then I should've made her."

Jake ran his hand through his hair. "There's no point in beating yourself up. If it's anyone's fault, it's mine. Some of Donovan's men should've been there with her. I should've thought of it."

About that time, Kit's cell phone rang. She looked at the display and grunted, "It's a blocked number. Hello," she said impatiently.

"Hi, Kit."

"Mom, are you okay?" Kit asked, her voice breaking with relief welling inside her chest. "We'll get you back, no matter what we have to do, I promise we will."

"It's okay, honey. I'm okay, thanks to my avenging angel who showed up out of the blue and got me away from them."

"What? What are you talking about? What do you mean you got away? She got away," Kit revealed.

"He saved me. But he's shot, honey. He's losing a lot of blood. I'm bringing him back to Crandall House right now. We're on our way. Tell Quinn I need her in doctor-mode ASAP."

"How close are you? Is there any chance you were followed?"

"I don't think so. We're humming along the 101 now, not yet at the Ventura County line."

But twenty long minutes later, the Chevy pulled into the driveway at Crandall House and six anxious adults poured out of its double doors. Kit ran around to where Gloria was getting out of the car and made sure she was all right while Reese, Jake, and Dylan headed straight for the passenger side door where they found an unconscious man with black hair but graying at the temples passed out on the front seat.

The three men gingerly picked him up while Quinn led the way into the dining area where she had already set up a makeshift trauma room.

Quinn sized up the situation as Baylee stood by prepared to assist in the role of impromptu nurse. As soon as the men stretched him out on the table, the two women began to cut away his shirt so Quinn could examine the wound.

"Before we do anything, let me see what we've got first. Looks like the bullet entered through his right shoulder and traveled up to the clavicle. Missed the subclavian artery, though, at least I think it did. But he's bleeding badly from somewhere. Without an x-ray I can't tell if it nicked rib bone, though. Baylee, try to keep the pressure on the wound, right here." She showed her what she meant near his right shoulder blade.

"I'm going to try and turn him over to see if there's an entrance wound."

"Should I get the alcohol?" Baylee asked.

"No," Quinn answered absently. She examined the underside of his shoulder blade and then found the pierced flesh near his armpit.

"Anything we can do, Quinn, just let us know," Dylan offered from the doorway, a little nauseous from looking at the red stains on the man's clothing. "Do you think he'll need blood?"

"Probably, but right now, I need supplies before I need anything else."

Baylee chimed in, "I brought everything I could find from the bathroom medicine cabinet already. There isn't a lot. Jake and Kit haven't lived here long enough to accumulate much of what you'd call first aid staples. Alcohol is all I found."

"That's fine. What time is it?"

"Almost midnight," Reese answered. "Why?"

"Perfect. There's a pharmacist supply clerk at the hospital who is having an affair with one of the nurses. Every night he's on duty, they manage to sneak off and leave the supply room door unlocked *and* unmanned. Reese, start making out a list of supplies. First on the list is a blood type kit, then Betadine, lots of it, gauze, all the bandages you can carry. And grab plenty of antibiotics.

"Baylee, go get Kit. I need the two of you to make a midnight run to the hospital pharmacy. I'll make due with Surfer Boy here as my stand-in nurse while you two go get the supplies I'll need."

Jake spoke up. "Now wait a minute, Kit isn't going anywhere...I want her here, safe and sound. Whatever you need, I'll go get."

"Damn right. Baylee's not going anywhere either. Jake and I'll both go instead," Dylan agreed. "I don't want Baylee leaving this house without me."

"Don't be ridiculous," Kit argued. "I'm a grown woman. If I can help…I wouldn't be here if it weren't for this man. Tell me what you want me to do, Quinn."

"Dylan Burke, after what you did, sneaking out of this house behind my back, you have the nerve to try and tell me what to do? Just back off," Baylee snapped. "Quinn has a plan, let's hear it."

"No need for anyone to get pissy. A man won't get the job done. It's that simple," Quinn stated emphatically. "The supply clerk *adores* blondes, considers himself a bit of a lady killer when it comes to the fairer sex. Either Kit or Baylee will distract him long enough to raid the place for what we need. I'd say the job falls to Baylee since he loves little petite women. Kit will only intimidate him. While you're at it please feel free to pay him back for being such a horn dog, horse's ass."

Kit snickered. "Oh, he's gonna love Baylee."

Baylee shook her hair back. "Damn straight. I haven't lost my touch either."

Dylan grinned at her. "I can attest to that."

"And if you drive like a bat out of hell, you should be there by the time he goes on break at one o'clock. Surfer Boy, get over here and keep pressure on this wound. Let the women handle this one."

Quinn grabbed a piece of paper out of Reese's hand and started drawing the map of the storeroom and the path to take to get there. "Most everything I need will be here. If you enter through the loading dock, say right here, take a right down the first hallway, there will be no one around to challenge you, or ask questions."

"I'll drive," Kit volunteered. "Baylee drives like an old woman."

"I do not. Will he be okay till we get back, though?" Baylee asked.

"He'll be fine. No way am I going to lose this guy after everything he's done for us."

☙☙☙☙☙

Four hours and one surgery later, they had transferred Trevor to an upstairs bedroom where Dylan sat on a chair next to his bed giving him blood. With his arm outstretched, Dylan supplied him with a new source of A positive, which happened to be a perfect match to Trevor's.

"How's he doing?" Baylee asked.

"Still out of it, but then Quinn gave him enough morphine to dull the pain after she got out the bullet."

"Quinn says he'll make it."

With his free hand, Dylan squeezed Baylee's. "Of course he will. He's getting my life force, some of my awesomeness thrown in there, too. He'll have super powers for sure now."

Baylee laughed and shook her head. "How is it there's so much ego stored up inside that little brain of yours? You'd think it would explode."

"That supply clerk didn't flirt with you too much, did he?"

"We have a date Saturday night."

"Like hell."

She grinned. "You're too easy, Surfer Boy. You think I'd two-time you with a sleazy supply clerk. No way. You should have seen this guy. He looked like something out of *Saturday Night Fever*. What's up with Reese, though? He's been quiet all night."

"Says he has a lot on his mind but I'm thinking he's fallen hard for the doc here and can't wrap his mind around it."

"Really? Quinn says he's a really good dancer."

Dylan shook his head. "Women. Why is it a guy who can dance gets you women all hot and bothered? Never knew Reese to turn down the opportunity to show off, though, that's for sure." He caught the twinkle in her eyes.

"Why? What gives? Did Quinn share some kinky thing he did that I should know about?"

Just then, Dylan looked up as the doc came strolling back into the room. Quinn handed him a glass of orange juice and immediately snapped on latex gloves, started removing the IV. "I think you're about done here, Surfer Boy. Drink that juice and get some sleep. And Baylee should not be sharing certain points of gossip when I know the most amazing deets..."

"Okay, okay," Baylee interrupted. "No sharing of deets."

Quinn leaned over Trevor, took his pulse for the tenth time since they'd brought him up to his room. "He's got a fever but that's normal for what his body's been through."

"At least you got the bullet out. Remind me if I ever get shot to let you dig around in the wound."

"You ever get shot, Dylan Burke, you go straight to the ER, do not pass go. Oh look, he's coming around," Quinn said.

"I'm telling you it's all that Burke awesome life force flowing through his veins now, works every time."

Trevor's eyes fluttered open. He tried to get up and blanched in pain. Weakly his head dropped back on the bed. "Fuck. Where am I? How long have I been out?"

"The Quinn Tyler Medicine Show and Traveling Circus at your service. Any pain?"

His eyes tried to focus on Quinn. "Some. How long have I been out?" he repeated.

"About six hours total. I'll give you more morphine." In one fluid motion, she reached over, filled a syringe with liquid and began to pull back the sheets to give him the injection in his butt.

"Six hours?" Trevor groaned and gripped the covers like a nun holding on to her skirt. "I don't want it if it knocks me out again."

"Tough guy, huh? We'll see how you feel about that when the morphine completely wears off and the pain comes back for real, especially after I dug around your upper chest for bullet fragments. There were several. That's why you lost so much blood."

"I've been shot before. This one felt—different."

"Hollow points," Dylan surmised.

"Probably," Quinn agreed. "All I know is they did some damage to the surrounding tissue."

Trevor zeroed in on Dylan. "The Boyd brothers last I saw were holed up in a cabin near Malibu Creek State Park. I could draw you a map but after six hours, I doubt they'd still be there."

"Gloria wasn't sure where they took her. She didn't see much of the cabin except the closet." Dylan shifted his feet. "By the way, that thing with Connor…"

"He said he wanted to kiss you on the mouth to thank you if he ever got the chance," Quinn tattled. "Come on, Surfer Boy, I'll stand aside while you give him a big smack on the lips and tongue. I'll even grab my camera phone."

Dylan looked dumbfounded for half a second before he moved closer. "I…we're… Baylee and I…thank you for what you did."

Baylee took pity on him and leaned over Trevor, kissed him on the cheek. "What he wants to say to you is how very grateful we both are for what you did. As her mother," she glanced back at Dylan. "As her parents, bringing Sarah back to us was nothing short of a miracle in our book."

Flustered now, Trevor looked like he wanted to change the subject.

Then Reese came into the room. "Awake and talking, that's always a good sign."

"Jesus." Trevor swiped his free hand down his face. "How's Gloria? She had a nasty bash to the head when I found her."

It was Quinn who answered. "Took three stitches to close, but she's fine now. She's in the kitchen. She's pissed they killed Morty and upset about them messing up her new 'do. But she and Kit are doing their thing in the kitchen and whipping you up some breakfast."

"Not sure I can eat."

"We'll force it down you then." She winked and picked up a bottle of water off the nightstand. "Drink some water. The bullet did some damage to your scapula." With her hand she waved it over her own shoulder. "I removed some bits of bone, too. Nothing you can't live without. And you had some internal bleeding, which I believe I managed to stop. Of course an x-ray would tell me more, but something tells me I couldn't talk you into heading to your nearest health care provider right about now if I tried."

His lips curved slightly. "Not if I can help it."

"Then I'm glad our little facility here could provide all your medical needs. We're a twenty-four-seven operation. Baylee here is standing by to take your insurance information." She gave him another wink.

About that time Gloria appeared in the doorway holding a tray. "Quinn said you could try to eat something if it's light."

Kit came into the room followed by Jake.

"Looks like the gang's all here. I believe you know most of the players," Quinn announced.

Kit went around to the bed to fluff up his pillows so he could sit up. "I hear we have matching bullet wounds in our shoulders." She knuckle-bumped him playfully on his left hand. At the astounded look on his face, she explained, "War wound from my time spent with Alana, mother of the year. Mine was clean, went straight through. Looks like yours is a bit more of a challenge. Are you right- or left-handed?

"Right," he answered, cautiously looking around at the crowd now gathered at the foot of his bed. Clearly uncomfortable with the attention, he wanted to be anywhere else at the moment.

"Since your right arm is at a major disadvantage, we'll spoon-feed you, how's that?" Kit offered.

"Look, if I could just have my clothes, I'll get out of your way."

"Oh, really?" To prove a point, one-handed, Kit pushed him back down into the stack of pillows.

"I don't think so. You're in no shape to try to make a run for it. Good thing we're an all-inclusive hospice. Besides providing excellent medical care we also run a nice little quiet B & B here in the boonies where no one will think to look for you."

With a bandage covering the side of her patched-up head, Gloria set the tray down on the nightstand and took a seat in a chair beside the bed.

In an upbeat voice, she wanted to know, "How's my avenging angel, the one who goes around saving everyone?"

Trevor's voice grew brusque as he screeched out, "More like avenger from hell. I'm certainly no angel."

Gloria patted his hand. "You are to us. And we have no intentions of letting anyone find you either. We're keeping you to ourselves and safe until you feel like traveling."

An amazed expression came into his eyes. "No cops?"

"No anyone. Whether you like it or not, you're one of us now. You'll just have to get used to it. Now, stop being such a pain in the butt and eat some of this chicken soup Kit made."

"Soup?" He made a face. "I thought I smelled cinnamon and apples when I woke up."

"Ah, good thing I consider a picky eater a challenge. What you smell is Kit's apple tarts. But you aren't getting any of those until you can keep down—the basics."

She spooned up some liquid with noodles, brought it to his lips. "Now, why don't all of you find something better to do like go get ready for your workday while Trevor and I get to know one another better?"

He stilled her hand, lopping some of the soup onto the bedding. "What did you call me?"

"Trevor. That is your name, isn't it? Yes, we know who you are. Now be a good boy and open your mouth."

CHAPTER 19

"So you should probably get dressed. With traffic we'll be cutting it close getting to the office on time," Reese suggested.

"Are you nuts? I'm not going now. I have a patient. And besides, Gloria's here so I won't be alone. Plus, Kit decided to hire a high school kid to open up the shop, run the counter. After what happened last night, she's sticking as close to Gloria as possible. And you heard Jake; he isn't letting Kit out of his sight. I'm not even sure Dylan and Baylee plan to head out now to the hospital, either. This place is like grand central station now."

Great, thought Reese, now what was he supposed to do?

"I'd really like you to come with me."

"Okay, let's have it. What is this all about? What are you *not* telling me?"

"Gloria can take care of Trevor. I want you with me, okay? I'd feel better."

"Aw, that's sweet." She patted his cheek. "Okay, I suppose he'll be fine until I get back."

He breathed a sigh of relief, but wondered what condition he'd be in ninety minutes from now conducting a meeting between an estranged father and his very pissed off daughter.

Once they got to his office, Reese whisked Quinn into the first vacant conference room and left her while he went down the hall to deal with Nick Tyler, the rock legend that *Rolling Stone* magazine had once called the best lyricist of his time.

Knowing how the man had ignored his own daughter, though, Reese wasn't particularly taken with the rock icon. But when Reese noticed him staring at something behind him, he glanced over his shoulder to see Quinn standing in the doorway.

She looked ready to explode in full rage-mode.

And when she opened her mouth to speak, what came out was loud enough for all the people on the eighth floor of his office building to hear and then some. "What the hell is *he* doing here? You went ahead and did it, didn't you, without asking me, without consulting me? You begged this asshole to come over here! How dare you go behind my back like this! How could you do this to me, Reese?"

"You wouldn't go to him, so I brought him to you. After I explained what a dangerous situation you were in, he was concerned enough about your safety, your wellbeing, to make the trip."

"Why? I asked you to butt out. I trusted you. God, when will I learn you can't trust a man to keep his word, let alone a *lawyer*?" She spat out the last word like nasty venom sucked from a poisonous snake bite.

"Whether you want to admit it or not the man's your father, Quinn. He's traveled eight thousand miles to answer your questions; questions you assured me had always been nagging at you since childhood. You need answers, answers to why you were an afterthought to him. I, for one, intend to find out. And speculating about things now with him here is a waste of time. It's better to get answers from the source. Now take a seat and see if you can be quiet for five damn minutes while I ask him where the hell he's been for the past twenty-five years while you were practically living on the streets."

"Be quiet, my ass. Do not talk to me like I'm a child! Just because we're hitting the sheets doesn't give you permission to interfere in my life like this. It's my life, Reese Brennan! What about that do you *not* understand?"

"Your life is connected to his. You want answers, now is the time to shut up and listen to what he has to say. And if you want me to stop treating you like a child then I suggest you stop acting like one!"

"I knew something was up. I knew it!" She glared at him, then at the other two men in the room, sitting wide-eyed watching the exchange between man and woman. "Fucking lawyers, you're all exactly alike. None of you show any regard for anyone but yourselves," she grumbled, but reluctantly took a seat at the other end of the table, the chair closest to the door.

Grateful she finally sat down, Reese wasted no time getting down to business. "First, Mr. Tyler, Mr. Baines, thank you for coming. As I just pointed out to my client, we have a few questions, so let's get to it."

"I see the Rock Star didn't leave Ireland without his fucking lawyer in tow. Figures."

"Quinn…" Reese warned.

Quinn sat there, arms crossed like a defiant three-year-old and fumed. But she shut up secretly hoping Reese could ply some answers out of the asshole who had fathered her.

Nick opened a briefcase and took out a three-inch, well-worn file folder and shuffled through the stack of papers. In an unmistakable Irish brogue, he offered, "Maybe this will help fill up some of the holes for both of you."

He slid the file folder across the conference table in Reese's direction. He slanted a look at Quinn, trying to gauge the depths of the woman's ire. He'd never seen anyone glare at him with such cold-hearted fury like the young, beautiful woman sitting at the end of the table. His daughter had turned into a stunning but consummate professional. Who would have thought his little girl would grow up to be a doctor? No doubt the life in Beverly Hills had been good to her, which only made the lawyer's earlier comments a bit perplexing at the moment.

Reese picked up the file folder, began thumbing through the papers.

With her arms crossed, Quinn simply glowered in the direction of all three men, fuming, waiting.

After several long minutes, Reese said, "I don't understand. There's no mention here of Ella Canyon."

Nick shook his head, obviously confused. "I'm sorry, who exactly is Ella Canyon?"

Quinn's furious glower turned into pure rage. "God, you are an asshole, you know that?" To emphasize the point to Reese, she ranted, "Rock Star here can't even remember all the women he's knocked up over the years."

She looked accusingly back at Nick. "How many were there for God's sakes that you can't keep them all straight? Lost count, Rock Star? You must be so proud of the life you've lived. How many others were there where you acted as nothing but a sperm donor? Oh, and by the way, I want you to know right here, right now, I can't stand to listen to your music. It's utter…garbage!"

Nick knew she'd be angry, this daughter of his. He'd come here knowing this day was an eventuality; someday, one day, he'd have to face her. But finding such an angry adult, he was in over his head.

But there was only so much a man could take. "I always heard Beverly Hills produced snotty, spoiled women, now I know for certain it's true."

Quinn snarled back, "Snotty? Spoiled? I'll show you snotty." She stood up and took a couple of steps toward Nick just as Reese snatched her around the waist and plopped her back down in the chair.

"Take your hands off me," Quinn shouted. "Don't you touch me like that ever again!"

Coolly, Nick looked at Reese. "Obviously I'm at a disadvantage. I came here under the impression this was a meeting between me and my daughter, the daughter who was the product of my relationship with Lisa Redfield."

Quinn shot back, "Who the hell is Lisa Redfield? My mother's goddamned name is Ella Canyon!"

Nick lost it then and shot back, "Like hell. Your mother's name is Lisa Redfield. I ought to bloody well know."

"Then I'll ask again, who the hell is Lisa Redfield? Another woman you obviously knocked up during the band's heyday?"

Warm, brown eyes met cold furious deeper brown. Nick shot a quick glance at Gerald Baines. "Lisa Redfield is the underage girl I had sex with in a San Francisco hotel room when she was fifteen years old. Though, I might point out, she didn't look fifteen. But you, Quinn, look just like her. You have her coloring, her Native American blood shows straight through you."

"Jesus! Under-aged? Are you kidding me? You're even more of a sleazebag than I thought! And believe me, I consider you scum." Even though an image of Ella at around twenty-four popped into Quinn's head, she had to admit during all their years together her mother had never once mentioned the liaison that had taken place at such a young age.

And fifteen? Something didn't add up. She knew Ella's birthdate as well as her own. Quinn also knew firsthand how her mother had looked dragging her from pillar to post. Even if she added three or four years to that, Ella certainly seemed infinitely older than eighteen or nineteen. Back then she'd been strung out. Even then Ella had been a hardcore addict.

Didn't druggies have a tendency to age faster than most people, though, especially if they were hooked on meth? That had to account for the age difference.

Nick ignored Quinn's outburst and turned to the cooler head in the room. "Mr. Brennan, Lisa's family hired a lawyer, a woman by the name of Jessica Boyd. It's all there in the file, if you'll bother to read it."

Hearing the name Jessica Boyd, Reese visibly winced.

When Quinn started to speak, Reese stilled her with one wave of his hand. "Maybe you should start at the beginning, Mr. Tyler. It might be easier than reading the entire file while we conduct our meeting. My playing catch up is going to take some time we don't necessarily have at the moment. What exactly happened after you got this fifteen-year-old girl pregnant and Jessica Boyd got involved?"

Gerald Baines spoke for the first time. "This lawyer Boyd came after Mr. Tyler with money in mind, not child support, mind you, but rather blackmail. Nick's team of lawyers, led by a man named Portman at the time, knew from that first contact it was all about the money.

"Ms. Boyd offered us a settlement of a million pounds, American dollars if you will, upfront and ten-thousand-dollars a month child support thereafter and she would keep it out of the papers, keep Nick from getting arrested, from spending time in jail for statutory rape."

Nick interrupted him. "I went along with it because I was twenty fucking years old by the time I learned she was pregnant. Our first album had just gone platinum. I let the lawyers handle it. All of it."

He turned his attention to Quinn then. Matter-of-factly, he offered an excuse. "I was young, Quinn. Twenty is too young no matter who you are or what your dreams happen to be at the time. Mine was my music back then. I had no need of being tied down to a kid, or a teenage bride for that matter. The way I saw it, why should I be punished for one bloody night in the sack, one night of a drunken stupor, to be tied down like that when I had the money to make it all go away?

"And from that point on, the whole thing skyrocketed out of my control. The music became a business for me and mine. I was on tour nonstop for almost three bloody years after that."

Reading through the file, Reese announced, "There was a paternity test."

Nick nodded. "My lawyers demanded one. And after the baby was born, turns out, I was Quinn's father. Lisa's lawyer even let her fly over to Dublin to have the baby there. Lisa knew my mother's family name was Quinn so she chose that for the baby's name. I was touched by the gesture… I want to make it clear Lisa was a wonder, a talented…"

"Touched, my ass," Quinn tossed in just in case anyone had forgotten she was in the room.

Once again, Nick tried to overlook the angry tone. "As I was saying, I gladly ponied up the million, agreed to the ten grand, and signed some papers to make the lawyers happy. About four months after the baby was born, Lisa eventually flew back to America, and took Quinn there with her."

He breathed out a sigh, staring directly at her now, taking the wrath aimed at him with the full force he deserved. "I'm sorry, Quinn. I was raised better. But I had my career to think about; my music was everything to me back then. At the time, that's all I wanted."

"Un-fucking-believable," Quinn said flatly, unmoved. "There's just one little problem here, Rock Star. My mother's name is Ella, Ella Canyon. Think real hard and do your damnedest to try and remember her. I have no idea who this Lisa Redfield is that had your other out-of-wedlock baby and who *touched* you so." She snorted at that. "Whoever Lisa is I'm sure she touched you a lot at the time, but she doesn't have a damned thing to do with me."

Quinn thumbed her hand at Nick and said to Reese, "These are the answers you thought you'd get? What a joke! I tried to tell you. Rock Star here never even laid eyes on me until today, twenty five years after the fact. He's a fucking sperm donor to me, nothing more."

Before Reese could say anything, Nick said quietly, "Uh, that isn't exactly true. I saw you twice. In hospital, of course, the day after you were born and when you were perhaps three-and-a-half-years-old. I was at home in Dublin, taking a break from touring, my first break in a long time. I had inquired about you when I had some downtime. Someone made a call to the lawyers, set up a meeting, so I could get a look at you again.

"Your nanny brought you to Ireland and out to the farm. We visited for maybe three hours. I gave you a big stuffed frog; you called it Broggy, because you couldn't say Froggy."

Reese shot a glance at Quinn, instantly recognizing her dream, the one she'd described as her perfect day.

Quinn had a look on her face that resembled a deer caught in the headlights. Nick had obviously hit a nerve.

"I took you on a tour of the barn that day. There you found a cat you fancied, a solid white one you called Snowball, and cried when you had to leave it behind." At the memory, sadness engulfed him, remembering a little doe-eyed girl who had wanted nothing more from him on that spring day than a tiny kitten.

He swallowed hard. "And then your nanny said it was time to go and you left. You were a pretty little thing. I remember being disappointed because Lisa hadn't accompanied you on the trip."

Quinn ignored the brief perfect-day scenario she'd dreamed about her entire life. Instead, she shook her head in disbelief. "My nanny? You remember my nanny? Get real." With derision in her tone, she informed him, "I got news for you Rock Star, I never ever had a nanny."

She stood up, pushing away from the table. She leaned over to where Nick sat. "I've heard enough of this bullshit. And if you sent ten grand a month across the sea those first few years, it goddamn for sure never made its way to me.

"For the first eight years of my life, I never even had a stable place to live or enough to eat or proper clothes to wear."

Or love, she thought now, from anyone.

"Sometimes I didn't even go to school regularly because I wasn't enrolled anywhere. As it turns out, it seems Ella had a problem staying in one place, and more than a passing fancy for the nose candy…and booze, the woman loved her morning vodka and orange juice. Naturally, in the evening she'd turn to the really hard stuff and mix the booze with a little of the candy so she'd be in the mood for her regulars."

She paused to take a breath. "I went hungry, Rock Star. It wasn't until Ella married Ross Jennetti and we moved to Beverly Hills that things turned around for me. I got to go to school on a consistent basis. So what if I took a knock or two once a week by a stepfather who never wanted a kid around? It was so much better than the way things were before I didn't dare complain. So if you want to sit there and believe you were so goddamn magnanimous with your fucking money, go ahead. But face it, Rock Star, you never cared shit about me and never wanted to.

"Your record producer had more involvement in my life than you did. But that was before he got a little too friendly with his hands. Those were my teen years when I started filling out, which obviously caught the man's attention, another sleazebag excuse for a man.

"And then of course let's not forget your slew of fucking barristers. They'd send me money whenever Jennetti happened to bring some special need to their radar. You never even bothered to sign those checks personally, did you? Some underling lawyer did it for you. So, go fuck yourself, Rock Star."

She stormed toward the door, muttering, "I'm done here. Thanks for nothing, Reese Brennan. Go to hell the lot of you!"

When the door slammed shut behind her hard enough for the walls to shake, no one quite knew what to say.

Reese had the urge to run after her, to soothe what he could of her temper. But the questions from two decades back nagged at him like a giant pesky fly.

Jessica's involvement sent up a huge red flag the size of Orange County.

And because of that, Reese was the first to recover from the outburst. "Mr. Baines, how were the payments handled?"

But Nick held out a shaky hand. "Wait! Wait a damn minute. Did she just infer that this Ross Jennetti molested her as a teen?"

Even though Gerald acted like he wanted to change the subject, Reese tightened his jaw. "Yes," he finally managed to answer quietly. "Still think she's a snotty, spoiled woman from Beverly Hills, Mr. Tyler?"

Gerald took advantage of the sudden silence and got them back on track. "The settlement went to the lawyer, Jessica Boyd, a check made out to Lisa Redfield for a million American dollars. There's a copy in the file you have in front of you. After that, each monthly check in the amount of ten-thousand-dollars was wired to her attention in care of the law firm. Our accountants will verify the information."

"I just bet they will," Reese murmured as he caught the stunned look on Nick Tyler's face.

But Gerald went on, "Whenever the child needed anything extra for school or whatnot, anything above that, she had to put it in writing, or rather, her representative did." Baines nervously mopped at sweat popping out on his forehead, before adding, "That eventually turned out to be the stepfather, Ross Jennetti."

Nick eyed Gerald Baines. "Please tell me you're joking."

"That was the arrangement. The details, the fine print so to speak, were that everything the girl needed had to be checked out and verified first. Look, Nick, if we hadn't done it that way, the chances were the girl's mother and her lawyer would have bled you..."

But Nick didn't let him finish. "Well for God's sakes, I can see why she feels the way she does. The thing is...this Jennetti...who the fuck is this stepfather? Jennetti was never my record producer. My producer is and always has been Austin Dempsey. We were schoolmates. Check it out if you don't believe me."

But no sooner were the words out of his mouth than Nick looked directly across the table at the friend he'd met in Catholic school at the age of six. He suddenly got a sick feeling in his gut. "Gerald Patrick Baines, you knew this Jennetti personally, didn't you? You handpicked him; put him in place here in Los Angeles as the representative?"

Nick didn't wait for an answer but stood up, braced his hands on the table, and leaned over to where his friend sat stoic. "Tell me now you, asshole, come clean this very minute or I swear to fucking God I'll reach across this table and pull your lying tongue out of your lying head!"

Visibly shaken, Gerald began to perspire even more. "I was looking out for you, Nick. I was right out of College Cork, the ink not yet dry on my law degree. I was going through the files. It was so obvious this Boyd woman kept nickel and diming Portman for every little thing. You remember Portman, don't you? That pot-bellied swine you had for a barrister who gave the Boyd woman the settlement she asked for without any attempt at bargaining her down? I had to get someone on the inside who could keep things in check, watch out for the bottom line."

"I'm not a bloody corporation! Quinn's not a bottom line. She's my own blood." Nick swayed with sheer rage coursing through his veins. He ran his hands through his hair and began to pace. He shook his head in Reese's direction. "You must think the worst of me. But I swear I knew nothing about this."

Reese took a controlled deep breath of his own to calm down. "That might be, Mr. Tyler. But your neglecting Quinn all those years is on you. Had you bothered to visit her even once a year, you'd have known about this entire scam. You'd have been aware of her early years, known what she had to deal with, what she was up against for yourself. That little girl sent you Father's Day cards."

He shot a look at Gerald Baines before turning to Nick. "Did you know that? She waited for a phone call from you, or as she put it, a one-line note that never came, any sign that you might possibly have taken an interest in her from one year to the next. Nothing ever came, Mr. Tyler. And that's on you. You can blame your lawyer all you want, but one visit in twenty-five years hardly rates a plus when you acted as though she didn't exist the other twenty-two."

Nick briefly hung his head but then snapped back like he'd just thought of something. "Go over the file. You have my permission to dig as deep as you need to, find out what the hell is happening here. Why does my own daughter believe this Ella Canyon is her mother?"

"Believe me, I intend to find out. I'll need copies of everything in the file. I'll give the originals back to you. And gentlemen, I'm hoping you're here in L.A. to enjoy all the sights and sounds our city has to offer until we get this thing figured out."

Nick nodded. "I'm staying put…" He eyed Baines with open disgust before adding, "until I know exactly what went on here, I'm not leaving."

"Good." Reese intended to make another point. "And one more thing, our side would like a new DNA test, just to be sure."

Gerald Baines took one look at his client and without hesitation agreed, "I think that's a good idea. What do you think happened here, Mr. Brennan?"

"You're asking me? You need to tell me everything you know about this Ross Jennetti and I want the truth. Where and when did you get him involved with Ella Canyon?"

Gerald glanced at his longtime mate, Nick. "You mean Lisa Redfield. Ross Jennetti married Lisa Redfield. At least that's what I was told. Jennetti came recommended to me through another client. The man was to keep an eye on both the child as well as the mother, keep the expenses down, the amount of extra money needed to a bare minimum."

Nick let out a groan. "That's it, Gerald. We're done. We get this mess straightened out and I don't want you anywhere near my family ever again. Is that clear? You work with Brennan here, cooperate fully with him until this thing has a solution, then fly back to Dublin, clean out your offices so there's nothing to ever remind me of you. Because I never want to see your sorry lying face again."

"Nick, you can't mean that? We've known each other for almost forty years."

"That's right. Funny how you think you know someone like a brother and then find out what a lying bastard he is." With that, Nick turned and left the room.

In all Reese's years of practicing law, he'd been involved with some strange cases. He'd had his share of odd clients, a few eccentric shady characters even. But this, this thing with the Boyd Boyd Geller & Gatz law firm was turning out to be the topper on the cake, one for the record books.

Gerald took out a handkerchief, wiped beaded sweat off his forehead again. "I thought I was looking out for him."

Reese wasn't interested. Instead, he got the focus back on details. "Okay. Start at the beginning. Tell me what you know about Jennetti."

When Nick Tyler left the conference room he went to the men's room and then walked back out to a plush waiting area where a middle-aged receptionist sat behind a computer.

"Did you happen to see where the woman with the long black hair went earlier when she stormed out of the conference room?"

"You mean the Native American girl? She's in Mr. Brennan's office. Would you like me to tell her you're out here?"

Did he? What would he say to her? Good God, no wonder she hated him. How had twenty-two years gone by without him getting in touch with his own flesh and blood? And what the hell had happened to Lisa Redfield? Were Lisa and Ella Canyon one and the same woman? They had to be. It was the only thing that made sense.

And what had his inattentiveness over the years done to an innocent child who now obviously hated his very existence? If he ever got his hands on this Jennetti character, he'd beat the man senseless.

When the receptionist kept eyeing him strangely, waiting for an answer, Nick simply shook his head, walked to the door, threw it open, and trudged outside, overcome with an emotion he didn't care to share with anyone.

☙☙☙☙☙

Later, to Reese's amazement, Quinn hadn't gone far.

When he opened the door to his office, Quinn stood behind his desk, back steel-straight, looking out of his office window at the traffic below down on Westlake Boulevard.

When she turned around he saw big, fat tears rolling down her cheeks. It was then Reese's heart rolled over in his chest. "I'm sorry. I owe you an apology."

She took a deep breath, exhaled shakily. "Yes, you do. Bringing him here without telling me was—wrong on so many levels. Coming here expecting…it doesn't matter. You lied. But your meddling brought me to a confrontation I've wanted to have for years. I want so badly to blame you for bringing him here but… I can't. I've needed this for more years than I know what to do about. I've said all of those things to him in my head, or acted them out in front of a mirror, countless times. It needed to be said no matter how badly I might have embarrassed myself or you."

"You didn't. Not me," he said, incredibly grateful she wasn't still furious with him.

"In fact, you exploded with the rage I wanted to show. You have every right to be upset, angry. But honey, there are things you need to know because as this thing moves forward, you need to keep one thing in mind. If Jessica Boyd was involved in this whole mess, you probably need to expect some kind of fraud occurred. It seems good ol' Jess was in charge of the money. What have we learned these past two months about Jessica and money?"

"She and Alana always found a way to plot and scheme for more."

"Exactly. The minute Jessica's name came up in there, the second I saw her signature on the paperwork in the file, I smelled scam and still do."

But he needed proof, hence the file he intended to examine in its entirety as soon as he had the chance. And he would take advantage of having Tyler and Baines here to walk him through the question that still lingered. Were Lisa Redfield and Ella Canyon one and the same person? And if so, why the name change? Why become a prostitute when she had a ready-made income of ten grand a month? Addiction aside, had she gone through a million dollars during the first years of Quinn's life?

"Do you want me to tell you what I learned about Ross Jennetti?"

She surprised him by laughing. "How about if I tell you what I know about the man? After all, I lived with the sleazebag for eight years."

"During any one of those years did you know Ella Canyon or rather Lisa Redfield was set up? Baines put Jennetti in place here in Beverly Hills for the sole purpose of being Gerald's gatekeeper, to keep an eagle eye on Tyler's money."

Eyeing the look on her face, he suggested, "Maybe you should take a seat, honey."

"That bad, huh?"

He repeated what Baines had told him and then when she started to protest, he added, "That wasn't Nick's idea by the way, it was Gerald's."

"How do you know?"

"Because you weren't in the room and didn't witness for yourself Nick's reaction. He was so upset he fired Baines on the spot. He's either a very good actor or he didn't know about Jennetti's involvement until today. Look, the ten grand a month was a lot coming in, and Baines wanted someone on the inside to keep an eye on Jessica, mainly because he thought she was milking the attorney in charge at the time, some guy named Portman. When Baines took over for an aging Portman, he slipped Jennetti into the picture."

"You're saying Ross was never his record producer? Ever?"

"I'm not saying it. That's what Nick claims. It's easy enough to verify."

"But you have another theory."

How was she always able to peg him so fast? "Yeah, I do. My guess is Jennetti was working both sides of the deal. While keeping a tight fist on the ten grand every month he also must have been working Jessica Boyd for some reason."

"You mean blackmail?"

"That's exactly what I'm thinking. But we need answers before we make that leap."

"Yeah, Brennan couldn't possibly take a leap in logic." She shot him a disgusting look before adding, "Maybe Nick's lying about Jennetti being his record producer. Maybe he knew the entire time."

"Why would he lie about that, Quinn?"

"Because he's a scumbag who can't remember the underage girl he knocked up when she was fifteen years old!"

Seeing the dubious look on Reese's face, she took a breath. "I don't know. But I still don't understand, Reese. If it's true that Rock Star sent all that money, then why did we live such a meager existence for so many years, destitute? Why did Ella have to hook?"

"Good question and one I'm sure Jessica could clear up for us—if she were alive. But without her, we do what we did with Alana. We dig into Ella Canyon's past. By hacking into the firm's database, Jake and Dylan got us access to their records. Until now we had no need to look up anything other than the obvious financial records we were interested in getting. But now…this is an entire other avenue we have yet to explore. We'll go through everything until we get to the bottom of this, Quinn. I promise you that."

For some reason, she believed him.

But when Reese looked into Quinn's moist eyes and his heart did a lurch he decided Tyler was also here for one other important purpose. This woman needed tangible family, flesh and blood, a connection to her past no matter how much she denied wanting it.

She also needed this time to resolve her issues with the Rock Star, if indeed he turned out to be her father. This would be a perfect time to do that. But he needed to know proof of paternity as a starting point.

"Honey, you're going to need to take another DNA test, the sooner the better. I can arrange that right now…"

She sighed heavily again. "I know." When his arms went around her, she laid her head on his shoulder. "How is it the asshole can't even remember my mother?"

It was Reese's turn to puff out a breath. "I don't know but keep an open mind, okay, Quinn? Now, let's go take care of that DNA test."

While Quinn got her mouth swabbed at a nearby lab, Reese phoned Jordan Donovan.

"I need you to find me everything you can on a Lisa Redfield. And while you're at it, get me everything on Ella Canyon. They might be one and the same person. But something tells me they are two different people entirely. I'll e-mail you the two supposed date of births for both women when I get back to the office. But remember, they, too, may not be real. You'll need to think outside the box.

Clearly finding out this info takes precedence over anything else."

"Good, because that other matter you wanted me to take care of is coming up a big, fat zero. No one has seen or heard from Ross Jennetti in more than three years. And the house in Beverly Hills was sold around that same time."

"Let me guess, Alana Stevens handled the real estate sale."

"The one and only. And Jessica Boyd acted as notary and witness. Her name appears on the papers for the sale of the house."

"Interesting," Reese agreed. "Make sure you keep digging. Something tells me if Jessica Boyd was Lisa Redfield's attorney, it didn't end well."

"Really? Well, here's something else to consider. Public records say Ross Jennetti and Ella Canyon were never married. I'll do a felony search as well as a background check, see if I get any hits."

"See, that's exactly what I'm talking about. These lies are built on top of lies. Jennetti was no stepfather to Quinn. Dig deep, Jordan. There's bound to be more we haven't uncovered."

CHAPTER 20

With a fever of a one-hundred-and-two degrees, Trevor drifted in and out of a state of consciousness. Dreaming about a happier time always brought him back to a cozy little house he shared with his wife, Nelia, and their little daughter, Annie.

He'd brought Nelia there to the cottage in Dalkey, a small seaside village outside Dublin as a newlywed where she could settle in and give birth to his child.

He hadn't realized until he'd held that tiny fragile bundle in his own arms how Annie would change his outlook on life and ultimately how he made his living.

But that's exactly what that tiny thing had done. Annie had made him want to be a better man.

He remembered every minute of walking the floor with her, her little face scrunched up red and fussy, how he'd quieted her with the Irish lullabies from his gran.

Memories of sitting outside on a sun-dappled front porch holding his Nelia next to him all the while little Annie dozed in her crib felt like a lifetime ago. Or maybe it had all happened to someone else.

There were times he could still smell the fresh, spring flowers Nelia had cut and arranged in fat jars she lined up along the edge of the veranda, flowers Nelia had clipped from her own beautiful sunny garden. She'd loved growing her own things, had loved growing herbs and spices and vegetables of all kinds.

Had a knack for it she did.

He used to tease her about her ability to grow anything. And how her green thumb hadn't extended into the kitchen, for his Nelia had been the worst cook he'd ever known. Could barely boil water and prepare a decent cup of tea.

But his Nelia had been a wonderful mother.

He remembered his beautiful blonde Nelia standing at the stove, laughing, and how her smile had been as wide as the Shannon River. Annie had her mother's smile and her silver blonde hair, locks that had glistened in the sunshine, sunshine that always drifted in from the bank of windows in their little kitchen.

Nelia would often take Annie out to sit under the wild cherry tree in the backyard of the little house, especially in the spring when the branches burst full of pinkish blossoms.

Nelia had loved that tree and the way it had budded out with fragrant buds destined to become the wild cherries they would pick and give away to the neighbors.

Those fading snapshots of his life back then were all he had now. He'd been clinging to those snapshots for decades.

That and the smell of cherry blossoms took him back to a happier day, a day of picnicking spread out on a blanket, on grass so green he could still smell clover. They had a favorite place, a sunny patch of hillside where the baby could run around after butterflies to catch while he and Nelia made out under the brilliant blue sky.

But there had been no blue sky the day they'd both died.

That day, torrential rains had poured out of the black clouds as if the gods themselves had known what was about to happen.

If it had been a mere accident, it might have gone down better for him. But he had known the minute he'd heard what had happened. They'd taken their revenge on his wife and child.

Three days after the car had exploded in a fiery heap and crashed over a cliff into the sea, he'd gone after the people responsible, hunted them down, one by bloody one.

☙ ☙ ☙ ☙ ☙

Trevor woke in a sweat in Gloria's arms.

"You were tossing and turning," she said as she grabbed a wet washcloth from the nightstand. She began to dab his face.

When he'd fallen asleep, she'd been sitting by the side of his bed. He needed to put a stop to this and tell her to get the hell away from him.

He stilled her hand. "Must you do that?" Annoyed that she'd watched him in sleep, he added, "Do you intend to sit with me all bloody day? What happens if I need to take a piss?"

"You're still running a fever. You were talking in your sleep, talking about Nelia and Annie. I'm sorry you lost them."

"I didn't fucking lose them." He shot her a scornful look.

"I know. I lost my Morty. He had a heart attack. I'm sorry you're so unhappy."

Trevor rolled his eyes. "Unhappy? I exterminate people—for a living—and I'm bloody happy about it, too."

Just as derisive, Gloria remarked, "Nasty will only get you more days in bed. If you want to sulk and be moody and let your fever get higher, just say so and I'll leave you to taking care of yourself. And if you need to take a piss, I'll get one of the men to help you to the bathroom. You've only to risk finding a few decent words and ask."

"Fine. I take care of myself and have for quite some time now."

"And doing such a good job of it, too," she snapped.

"I was…until I got involved in this mess."

"Anyone who got near Alana Stevens and Jessica Boyd was subject to...their wrath and all manner of bad things happening." She huffed out a breath. "Why are you being so difficult anyway?"

"Me?"

"Look, if it weren't for you, Kit would already be dead by now. Sarah wouldn't be snuggled in her crib at the moment asleep like a little angel, and look at me; I might yet live to see grandchildren."

At the prospect of that she did a little happy dance standing right next to his bed. "Because of *you* I'll get to meet my son for the first time tomorrow. Tomorrow's the big day."

His cheeks colored as if he'd been smacked.

She reached over and took his face between both of her hands. "Well, look at that, I'm embarrassing you. Imagine that, such a tough guy shows he's softhearted."

"Woman, listen to me. Not now, nor have I ever been, softhearted."

She touched her lips to his again, this time softer, for longer. "Oh, I think you're not so tough after all. You've had a hard life. Losing the ones you love tends to do that to a person."

Jake cleared his throat from the doorway while Dylan simply grinned at the bickering he'd overheard and it seemed at their growing attraction to each other.

Who would have thought Mr. X and Gloria had a chance at common ground?

"Are we interrupting anything?" Jake asked with a huge grin on his face.

"No," was Trevor's gruff response.

"Good, because there are a few things we need to discuss."

"For starters, like how the bloody hell you know my name."

Jake grinned. "I wish I could take credit for that. We only know the name that was listed in a CIA file. We don't know *you*. If you're more comfortable with us not knowing, that's okay, too."

"Your name isn't important to us anyway—or your sordid past," Dylan cracked.

"We have more pressing matters to discuss."

"But with you sidelined at the moment and out of the game so to speak, ending this comes down to Jake, Reese, and me," Dylan said, turning serious.

Reese came through the door about that time. "Which means you'll need to share what you know, a little more in depth than the e-mail you sent."

Quinn walked in and went straight to her patient. "How are we doing?"

"His fever dropped to one-hundred-and-two about an hour ago," Gloria explained. "But before that it had been as high as one-oh-four just as you predicted. He's also been talking out of his head and—irritable."

Quinn nodded, took his pulse, and started checking his wound by lifting up the bandage.

"I redressed it while he slept. But he was restless." Gloria related the patient's medical condition like any good shift nurse.

"I'm right here for God's sakes. You're talking about me as though I'm not capable of speaking for myself," Trevor growled.

"Cranky, too," Gloria pointed out. "But I think that's a good sign."

"Ever notice how bloody cheery doctors and nurses are when the patient is flat on his back? I detest that."

Quinn grinned. "Beyond cranky, not a good patient, I'll make sure to note that down in the chart so the other nurses are aware of your bad-tempered mood."

Reese came closer. "Quinn says that right shoulder is going to keep you out of action for at least another week. We don't have another week."

Trevor sized up all three men. "So? You guys are two computer nerds and one geeky lawyer. What the hell do you intend to do about putting an end to a cold-blooded psychopath? You're all amateurs when it comes to pulling a trigger. Ending Cade will take a little more than playing patty cake or putting a bullet in a tin can.

"And if you don't end Cade, this will go on and on. Because Cade is bloody well nuts, that's what I know—in detail. He'll keep coming after Quinn until she's dead. Is that what you want?"

Reese paled at the thought. "We're a little tougher than you think we are."

"Really? Then let's hear your dossier on how many men you've ended. Go ahead, because there's a helluva big difference in talking about killing a man and actually being able to do it. You never forget the first person you kill either, looking into his eyes as the breath leaves him for good. You'll be haunted in dreams for the rest of your lives. At least decent men usually are, no matter how pure the reason or how much the bastard deserved to die."

Trevor let his head fall back for a few seconds before lifting it enough to stare at the three men again. Good, he'd gotten their attention. "With a psycho like Cade, you hesitate pulling that trigger for a second and you'll be the one left bleeding out on the ground. Is that what you want?"

Dylan took offense. "I'll do anything to keep Baylee and Sarah safe."

"Will you? Will you really end a person's life to protect those you love?"

Reese turned to look at Jake, then Dylan before staring at Quinn long and hard. "I don't know about these two, but if I'm the only thing left between Cade and Quinn, I'll take Cade out in a heartbeat to keep him from hurting her."

Quinn's hand flew to her mouth. She met those calm, brilliant eyes. Those gray pools pulled her under. When had that happened? In the midst of all this she'd fallen hopelessly in love with the man. She wondered if he could tell, if he could see the love and the pride she had for him in her eyes?

She loved him.

She didn't like the idea of falling in love with anyone, least of all a...wait. She had to get over the fact that she hated his profession. Wasn't he trying to get answers to things she'd wondered about her entire life?

And now he was willing to risk his to keep her safe.

Quinn was big on loyalty. She had to take a step back and admit how much she respected him because he always took a stand. It might not be the stand she agreed with, but the fact he was more than willing to do so were big points in his favor. And look how he had acted after finding out about her stepfather. No other man knew that dark nugget she'd buried deep in the past for so long.

And yet, he did.

He'd reminded her there was nothing to be ashamed about.

Quinn did her best to zone back into the moment and found it difficult to concentrate on anything anyone said. But this was too important. She needed to know what their little group could do to end this thing with Cade and more importantly how to go about it.

Trevor was still in the process of giving them his take. "Collin's nothing more than a follower. Take down Cade, and Collin will beg for his life. And being amateurs, you'll fall for it."

Trevor stared long and hard at Jake. "But you let Collin live, send him to prison for let's say, ten years or so for kidnapping, and that's if you're lucky, especially if he cops a plea. You let him live and he'll come back after Kit. Guaranteed. Maybe not for a year, maybe not even in two. He might even hire someone from his jail cell to do it for him. How would that be? By this time you and Kit might have a couple of kids to worry about. But you'll never quite be sure when or how Collin will come back after her or your children. Because trust me, he's obsessed. He will come after her first chance he gets."

He thought of his Nelia and little Annie.

His mistake had been thinking it was over when he had testified against Paddy Murphy, sent him off to sit in a jail cell for a ten-year sentence, only to learn the man had directed his underlings from prison to go after his wife and child in retribution.

He remembered hunting every one of the bastards down, remembered how he'd slit their throats in the process.

The past for him had ended then, but his hell on earth had only begun.

He'd never been able to fully let go of memories both good and bad since.

"Then we're of a like mind there," Jake said matter-of-factly. "Their money is gone. Great idea by the way to make them poor, wished I had thought of it. But right now we need to know the best way to lure them out into the open. The promise of giving their money back is the obvious one, but then what?"

Trevor nodded. "That'll work but only if you realize even after you give them the money back, they still will come after the women. Cade would've still killed Gloria *after* you gave him proof of a wire transfer. You understand that, right?"

All three men nodded in agreement. It was Reese who pointed out, "We have no intentions of giving them back a dime. Their funds are gone and they aren't coming back. While we're on the subject of money, though, did Noah Parker have any children, relatives of any kind still living?"

Trevor narrowed his eyes, sent him a dubious look. "Why?"

Jake explained, "Because Kit wants his family to have every penny of Alana's estate. It rightly belongs to them anyway."

The look on Trevor's face said he clearly did not believe what he was hearing. "But that amounts to—millions."

"Around forty, give or take," Jake concluded. "It would be more but looks like Jessica got her greedy hands on Alana's bank accounts after she died. Of course, we have that lump sum too sitting idle in an offshore account. If you want it, say the word, it's yours."

"That's insane."

"No, it's fair. Alana and Jessica made millions on the backs of murdering the Parkers. Besides, it's what Kit wants—what we all want."

Unbelievably moved, Trevor managed to croak out, "Noah has a daughter who lives on a farm in Northern California. She has a fifteen-year-old son. He could certainly use money for university."

Reese made it official. "Then I'll draw up the papers, transfer the money to her and the boy as soon as we can make the arrangements."

"I don't know what to say."

Jake spoke up. "Say you were right when you figured out that Kit is nothing like the murdering bitch of a monster that beat the crap out of her growing up on a regular basis."

"I had no idea Alana wasn't her mother. Somehow that nugget got past me. Although I do know Jessica, the lawyer, had a nice little side business selling kids to people who were desperate to adopt. It's in the file I sent you."

"I read it. By any chance is there anything you know you didn't send us, something that would indicate Lisa Redfield and Ella Canyon, Quinn's mother, are one and the same person?"

"Lisa Redfield? The woman who painted *Woman Rising*? That Lisa Redfield?"

A stunned Quinn asked, "Lisa Redfield painted *Woman Rising*? That's…that would mean…it can't be? You must be wrong."

"The woman in the painting is my wife. When exactly Nelia posed for it, I haven't any idea. But it is her. After I took it from the Book & Bean, I got curious. The signature of the artist wasn't visible so I removed some of the paint covering up that area. Whoever painted over it used acrylic paint while the painting itself was done in oils. Even though I know nothing about art, the clumsy attempt to mask the artist was poor at best but effective."

"Ella didn't paint *Woman Rising*?"

"She did not. After chipping off a layer of acrylic, I discovered the artist's name scrawled underneath. Someone named Lisa Redfield signed the painting."

Quinn sat down on the bed. "Are you certain?"

"Which part? That the woman in the painting is my wife? Yes. That someone did a very poor job of covering up the artist's signature? Yes to that as well."

Quinn stared up at Reese. "Then that means it *is* possible Nick Tyler might be telling us the truth."

"It's more than a possibility. Nick Tyler admitted this morning Lisa went to Ireland to have her baby, which is Quinn, we think. We're getting another DNA test done. But let's say this Lisa liked to paint. Pregnant and bored, she decides to do a few canvases while she's there. Is it possible your wife was one of the people she could've met?"

"Depends. Do you know where in Ireland exactly? That day at the shop, I questioned Kit; Kit said to ask Quinn."

But Quinn shook her head. "I was never curious enough to ask much about it." She saw the skeptical faces around the room and said, "Look, every time I tried to find out more, I hit a brick wall. Ella gave me the same spiel and I let it drop especially, when Tyler never bothered to get in touch. At one time I even considered the possibility that the entire story of Ella getting together with Nick might've been just another made-up lie."

But Reese had no intentions of letting the conversation die down. "Tyler owns a farm near Dublin. After what he told us this morning, I looked it up on the Internet. It's near a place called Ballybrack. So Lisa probably stayed somewhere nearby."

"In County Dŭn Laoghaire?" Trevor blanched. He thought back to that time of his life, realized there were many instances he'd spent on the road for the cause. In those days the IRA had come first, not his wife, nor his child. "My wife…we lived…that's less than twenty miles from where I lived with my family."

He'd been so stupid back then to waste precious time away from the people he loved.

He stared at Quinn, recognized her despair. "There's something else. Kit mentioned Ella Canyon was at one time a renowned artist but I couldn't find a single other example of her work. I don't think she ever painted."

Quinn blinked. "I knew it. Something inside me has always known she was lying. If Lisa Redfield existed and painted *Woman Rising* then where does Ella Canyon fit into all of this? Ella's always run fast and loose with the truth but…"

"This Ella, this is the woman you think is your mother?" Trevor wanted to know.

"I'm beginning to have my doubts," Quinn decided.

"So am I," Reese muttered.

But Jake had his own point to make. "And Connor didn't kill Claire. Although I appreciate you pointing me in that direction, DNA's close but no match, something called familial DNA makes the killer a brother or a cousin."

Trevor cocked a brow. "They're sure? Cade then," he muttered. "Somehow you need to get his DNA for comparison."

"That's what we're thinking," Reese stated. "Plus, we think he's good for all the women missing from the escort service."

"Now that I am one-hundred percent sure about because the women went missing after making a service call to Cade, every single one of them. And he more than likely had help in that regard. But I don't think it was Collin because when a few of the women went missing he was on an extended vacation in Cancun."

Reese smiled. "Then we're of a like mind there, too."

Downstairs, Quinn couldn't wait to tell Baylee and Kit about the confrontation with Nick Tyler and relay what she'd found out about Lisa Redfield.

She found them in the kitchen with Gloria making a yummy chicken and cheese casserole for dinner. But before she got into the scene at Reese's office, she wanted to know one thing. "Did any of you know about Reese's plan to bring Nick Tyler over here?"

Kit turned completely around from the counter. Her jaw dropped. "No way. Without letting you know?"

"Wait a minute. Nick Tyler showed up at Reese's office? What was Reese thinking?" Baylee gasped. "You saw Nick Tyler, talked to him?"

Reese came into the kitchen about that time, went straight to the fridge for a beer. "I knew you were talking about me. My ears weren't just burning, they were on fire. Come on, Quinn, be fair. Tell them how it turned out."

Quinn sighed and went over the entire story. After she'd finished, Kit and Baylee exchanged looks. It was Kit who said, "If Jessica was involved that means Alana was, and up to her eyeballs in it too. Both women probably tried to scam for more money, milk the situation for all they could get."

"Exactly," Reese said raising his beer in a salute.

Kit wrinkled her brow. "But how does this Lisa Redfield connect to Ella Canyon? Nick Tyler needs to provide more answers. We should invite him out here to stay with us, get him out of his hotel room and into a friendlier atmosphere, pry more info out of him, get him to talk."

Quinn resisted that notion. "He actually called me snotty and spoiled."

Baylee's mouth gaped open. "He did not. That bastard!"

Still stinging from the insult, Quinn hung on to her resentment. "So sure, go ahead and invite him. In fact, get Reese here to make the call since the two of them are so *chummy*, e-mailing back and forth behind my back like they were."

Coming into the kitchen, Jake shot Reese a glance and Quinn immediately picked up on the exchange. "You knew about this thing with Tyler and let him drag me there without a heads up, didn't you?"

Kit glared at Jake. "You knew and said nothing, let her walk in there unprepared. How could you do that?"

Sheepish, Jake got out his own beer, twisted off the cap. "I told him it was a bad idea."

"He did," Reese admitted. "And I tried to follow his advice by sending Tyler an e-mail to say don't bother coming. Sue me because the guy didn't listen. I think he cares for you, Quinn. It might be two decades late, but the man cares."

Quinn shook her head. "He comes to see me once in twenty years and you're ready to hand out father of the year awards."

Reese gave her a withering look. "I'm not. But carrying around that chip for another twenty years will get you nowhere fast except another chunk of bitterness. You want to go through life like that, be my guest. Sooner or later, it will eat you alive."

"Screw you. What do you know about it anyway? Rock Star's story doesn't even make any sense about this Lisa person. Even if Trevor says she's the artist who painted *Woman Rising*. What the hell does all that have to do with me?

Kit held up a hand. "Wait, Ella didn't paint *Woman Rising*? This Lisa Redfield did?"

Reese explained Trevor's discovery.

"Then Lisa and Ella are not the same person," Kit concluded. "No wonder Ella always resisted picking up a brush to show us her brushstrokes and techniques." She turned to Baylee. "Remember that time when we were thirteen or so and tried to get her to help us with our art project? She went nuts."

"Sure. She liked to run her mouth about how she'd had all this talent once as an artist but never would actually *show* us?"

Quinn eyed her friends. "So? Maybe she was another Georgia O'Keefe but the drugs affected her talent."

Baylee and Kit both gaped at her. It was Baylee who said, "You're actually defending Ella Canyon. Wow!" She looked around the kitchen. "Where's a calendar so I can circle this day in red?"

Quinn blew out a breath. "Look, until Nick starts coming clean with a few more facts, I'm not ready to give him the benefit of the doubt yet. But I see all of you are."

Kit and Baylee traded knowing looks.

Reese picked up on some kind of female vibe, some sort of friend code passing between them. Good, he thought, maybe the women could get her to see reason where he could not.

It was Baylee who said, "You sound a lot like I did the first time Dylan mentioned he suspected Dad was hiding something about my mother. So believe me, I know exactly how you feel right about now."

"But Nick's story doesn't make any sense."

"We're all aware of that. But neither does the fact that you and Ella lived a nomadic existence out in the Valley for the first years of your life. The money wasn't trickling down to you two, not even enough to feed Ella's habit. Why did the two of you fall off the radar for so long?"

Dylan came into the kitchen, sensed tension, and immediately tried to lighten the mood. "Who knew we'd all have to make junior grade detectives to figure all this stuff out? When you think about it, it's like a minefield, twisting and turning with all kinds of obstacles to keep us from learning the truth."

"An Alana and Jessica minefield," Gloria repeated as she entered the fray. "How typical. But why aren't you coming up with more in the financial records? I always thought following the money trail led to the truth."

"We're making progress," Jake added. "But Jessica and Sumner were no dummies. As fast as the illegal money streamed in, it went through several offshore accounts so the IRS wouldn't find it. Like Dylan said, it's a maze we have to follow to get to where the most money is."

Reese couldn't get past one detail though. "My point is the ten grand a month wasn't going to Quinn for at least seven or eight years, not until she got to Beverly Hills. The money was sent. I saw the bank records for the wire transfers."

"Simple." Kit shrugged. "Jessica and Alana."

Then Baylee spoke up, "Look Quinn, I didn't want to believe Dylan's premise about what happened to my mother or Kit's version of what she saw in that vision she had. But I eventually had to realize my father had lied to me—for years. If Jessica and Alana were involved in this in any way you can bet nothing about it was aboveboard. Just keep an open mind, okay?"

"That's what I told her," Reese said. "Those two women more than likely put the screws to Jennetti, too."

Baylee watched Gloria putter around the kitchen, seemingly distracted and suddenly thought of something. "By any chance did you know Ella Canyon back then, Gloria?"

As Gloria took the casserole out of the oven, she sighed. "I knew you would eventually get around to asking me about that timeframe. Yes, I knew the entire family before that—through Alana. I knew both women were thick as thieves, into all kinds of little schemes. You have to remember I'd been shipped off to Maine to live, locked up myself after Kit and Ben were taken away from me. I didn't get involved in Alana's affairs again until Kit turned twelve. By that time, all I knew was Quinn's mother had a major drug problem. I used to worry quite a bit about Quinn in that environment. That's why I let you girls sleep over at my house so often, insisted on it really."

With that, Gloria walked over and put her arms around Quinn. "But this one had such a good head on her shoulders, an old soul to be sure, wiser than most adults I've ever known. Once I realized Ella wasn't much of an influence on her, I stopped worrying so much, even though to tell you the truth, that stepfather of hers gave me more than a few sleepless nights."

Kit and Baylee exchanged another long stare.

And suddenly Reese realized something else. Quinn might not have unburdened her secret to her friends. But somehow Baylee and Kit knew or at least had suspected Ross had done more than slapped Quinn at fifteen to get her to move out.

"He wasn't her stepfather, not officially," Reese stated. "Jennetti and Ella were never married."

Jake shook his head. "Where have I heard this before? Another set of layered lies."

"They were very good at it," Dylan added.

Reese turned then to gaze into Quinn's dark, unsettling eyes. All his years of singlehood came crashing down around him. He couldn't imagine sharing his life with any other woman. He wasn't sure when it had happened. But damn it, he was in love with the prickly pear, Quinn Tyler.

CHAPTER 21

*R*unning out the back door of the house, Quinn didn't bother with a jacket or an umbrella even though the rain beat down in sheets.

Her face hurt.

Ten-year-old Quinn could still feel the stinging slap of a heavy hand from her stepfather. Though it had happened a good two hours earlier, she still felt angry and upset and wanted out of the house so bad she could taste it.

Through bleary-eyed tears she made her way to the garage at the back of the house where she kept her bike. Even in the rain, she intended to get out of this house, get as far away as she could. She'd bike over to Baylee's house, where Tanya would surely let her hang out in her kitchen for a few hours.

But as she got closer to the garage, angry voices stopped her.

She paused to listen before taking another step.

Quinn's attention was riveted to the irate vocal outcry up ahead, not because of the miserable cursing words but because of who was doing the cursing. They hadn't yet spotted her. First lucky thing that had happened to her all day, she thought, as she scurried behind a tree trunk before they heard the rustle of leaves beneath her feet.

She needn't have bothered. The two adults were in a snit, which wasn't that unusual. It had been Quinn's experience that if adults weren't irritated about something they'd find a reason to get there.

Cautiously, Quinn peered around her hiding place, her favorite ancient oak.

Alana Stevens stood no more than twenty feet away going toe to toe in an argument with Ross Jennetti, her stepfather.

"You keep your damned mouth shut. You're here to do exactly what you're told. Don't try to get around me either because I'll nail you to the cross. I don't like people who underestimate me."

"You just take care of your end of the deal and keep the money coming. You're late with the money again and I'll take it up with Jessica."

"Don't you threaten me, you miserable piece of shit. I'll see you in jail first."

At the mention of jail, Ross seemed to back down. "Okay, okay. Just calm down. Maybe I overreacted. After all, I know you're good for the money. It's just that I have obligations too, bills to pay, responsibilities."

"Bullshit. You're a goddamned snitch playing both sides. You know it and I know it. You cause me any more trouble and I'll see to it that this sweet deal of yours comes to an end. You got that?"

Ross meekly nodded. "I got it. You know you're really hot when you're upset."

"Don't think you can get around me like that. I'm the one who got you this gig." Alana pointed a finger at him then looked him up and down and started twirling her hair. "But I could use your dick right about now."

With that, she watched Alana grab Ross's shirt and pull him into her for a kiss. She pulled him in the direction of the house, making Quinn very glad she was on her way out the door even if the rain were coming down in sheets.

Getting soaking wet was infinitely better than staying anywhere near Ross and Alana.

⟁ ⟁ ⟁ ⟁ ⟁

Quinn woke slowly, her brain on overload. The dreams about childhood had always been tough to keep at bay but now it seemed all this time off was making her crazy. She scrubbed a hand down her face and looked over at Reese, still sleeping handily beside her. She lifted his arm, which draped around her waist like a vise grip, and got up out of bed.

Grabbing her borrowed robe, she crept down the hall and into Trevor's room to check on him.

She was surprised to find him awake and the grimace on his face said he was in pain. Quinn glanced around the room. "Finally managed to run off Gloria, did you?"

"She went to bed about an hour ago. The woman needs to sleep. She gets to meet her son tomorrow."

"Today," Quinn corrected. Instincts had her touching her hand to his forehead. "You still have fever." She picked up a pair of latex gloves, filled a syringe with penicillin. To get his mind off the injection, she started talking. "Gloria is so excited I doubt she closes her eyes for five minutes. Kit's like that too, must run in the family."

Trevor grunted. "What are you doing making rounds this time of night anyway? Shouldn't you be cozied up to the barrister?"

She grinned. "Couldn't sleep. How are you feeling? Any pain?"

"You're quick to hand out the drugs."

"I hate to see anyone in pain." She got out another syringe for the painkiller, tilted her head. "Yes or no?"

"Yes. Thanks. The shoulder's troubling me some."

She plunged the needle into the morphine bottle, drew up the liquid into the barrel.

"I have a question though."

"Yes, I have to give it to you in the butt. The muscle is much larger there than the arm for this dosage."

He grinned and rolled over. "That wasn't the question, although I often wondered why it was the case."

She dabbed a cotton ball to his hip and stuck in the needle. "Now you know. What's the question?"

"How long will I be unable to use the shoulder? Is it true I'll be out of action for a week?"

"Ah. You could start PT in a week. There's a difference." When he just stared at her, she added, "Physical therapy. But since your insurance is— questionable." She smiled and went on, "As soon as the pain subsides, we'll start working on movement."

"We?"

"Yes, we. There are enough people here that will make sure you can move that shoulder properly before you take off on your own. Now, it's my turn."

"A question? Sure. As long as it isn't too personal."

"Please. Do I look like I'd intrude into your personal life?" Her lips curved. "Hey, I'm not the one who went all CIA on your ass. Anyway, here's the question. Do you really think none of us are capable of ending this thing with Cade and Collin, that we don't have what it takes to…pull the trigger, so to speak?"

He slanted his head. "Depends on how bad you want it to end."

"That isn't fair. I don't want Reese jeopardizing his career to break the law for me, or Dylan or Jake for that matter."

"Then there's your answer. But you'll always be looking over your shoulder, wondering if and when Cade will strike."

She sucked in a knowing breath. "Yeah, I will, and so will Kit and Baylee. Okay, here's the deal. After Cade knocked me around, I bought a gun."

Shock crossed his face. That was the last thing he expected her to say. "What kind?"

She laughed. "Is that a guy thing or what? A nifty little nine millimeter. I took a course in gun safety, too. I know how to shoot. I'm fairly accurate."

"Are you now?" He wasn't certain where she was going with this. "A gun-toting doctor, I'm impressed."

"Don't be. I learned because I didn't want to give Cade the chance to ever hurt me again. I don't want him hurting any of my friends, either. I don't want him hurting Reese."

"But he'll try."

"I know, and I'm telling you I'm prepared to pull the trigger if I have to. I made that decision when I bought the gun."

He gazed into her eyes, saw the steely determination there. "I believe you. And the others don't know, do they?"

"No. I went to the shooting range by myself. I've taken plenty of crap from that family since…for a long time, especially from Cade. I'm not letting him do this anymore, not to me, not to my friends or anyone I…care about."

"And you're willing to give up your promising career to make sure they stay safe."

"My career's in the early stages. Reese has practiced law for years. He's established his practice. But yeah, that's about the size of it. I don't have a long lost brother that's about to show up in about six hours for a big reunion. I don't have a six-month-old baby to think about raising over the next eighteen years or so. Kit and Baylee have their futures…ahead of them."

"And you don't?"

"That isn't the point. You asked the question. What are we willing to do for the people we love? I know what I'm willing to do, that's all I'm saying."

"What do you want from me?"

With that, she leaned over and told him.

☙ ☙ ☙ ☙ ☙

Quinn sat with him until the morphine kicked in. Once he'd fallen asleep, she crept down to the kitchen like a thief and was surprised to see Reese already sitting at the kitchen table eating a bowl of cereal.

"How's the patient?"

"Asleep. Worried he won't be able to use his shoulder any time soon." She bit her lip, wondering if he'd overheard her conversation with Trevor. She hoped not. "What're you doing up?"

"Today's the big day. Ben Griffin makes his grand entrance in…" He glanced at his wrist watch. "Less than five hours from now the long lost brother shows up. The countdown started a couple of hours ago."

"It's all Kit and Gloria can do to contain their excitement. Trevor said Gloria finally went to bed about an hour ago."

"Those two are giving off vibes." He wiggled his eyebrows up and down.

She gave out a genuine belly laugh. "I know. Just goes to show you, you're never too old for the love bug to jump out and bite you in the ass."

"That love bug is a sneaky little devil." He reached for her hand, entwined her fingers with his. "I woke up in bed and you weren't there. I heard you in with Trevor." Their eyes locked. But after several seconds he merely said, "I knew you'd eventually head to the kitchen. You had another bad dream."

She took down a box of Kix and a bowl from the cabinet, poured a generous portion of the cereal. "Alana and Ross were fuck buddies," she announced.

He lifted a brow. "Really? You dreamed about Ross and Alana fu…?"

"No. Yes. I guess I'd forgotten, put it out of my mind. I mean who would want to have that image in their psyche for very long?" She replayed the dream for him.

"So, Alana claims to have been the one who got him the gig. I think it's time I had a little talk with Gerald Baines, one on one. I felt he was holding something back this morning. I didn't pursue it because I didn't want him heading back to Ireland on the first plane. I wonder if Jessica knew Alana was taking a cut from Ross."

"Probably not," Quinn surmised. "Think about it, if these two women were used to double-crossing each other every time the wind changed direction, why was there never any retaliation on their part toward each other?"

"The Parker murders had to be the glue that kept them connected unless, of course, they were in love with each other."

Quinn rolled her eyes. "Alana had to hold the gun over Jessica's head for blackmail material. She got miles out of that and it worked until they both got rid of Baylee's mother and Luc Delaine."

"Which meant another connection and more material for further blackmail on both sides. So they hold something over Ella Canyon to get her to raise a kid that wasn't actually hers?"

"Stands to reason. But what?"

"Lisa Redfield."

"Bingo. Whoever she is…?"

"Or was. She was a meal ticket."

"She's more than likely dead, isn't she Reese? Whoever she was, wherever she came from, we have to find out."

"We don't know that for certain, Quinn, at least not yet." He coaxed her into his lap. "Just so you know, when it comes to protecting you from Cade, I can pull the trigger."

"You *were* listening."

He didn't answer her. Instead, he explained, "There's something primal in me I'm not even sure I knew was there before all this started. Whatever it is, wherever it came from, it wants to hurt Cade for hurting you."

"But that's just it. I don't want you to feel like that, responsible. It happened a long time ago."

"He wants you dead, Quinn. That isn't ancient history but a present-day fact. He fired a gun at us not twelve hours ago and wounded another man. He could have easily killed Rob, who happens to be married with two kids. That's three times now he's tried to kill you. I won't let him win this thing."

She patted his jaw before giving him a kiss. "On that we agree then."

CHAPTER 22

From the living room Kit heard the car make the turn into the driveway. She bolted out the front door with Jake on her heels. But when she reached the front porch, she stopped so suddenly that Jake rammed into the back of her as she stood still as a statue.

Kit watched in amazement as John Griffin, all six feet of him, unwound himself from the backseat of the white limo parked in the circular driveway. On instinct, she reached behind her for Jake's hand to steady herself before her knees buckled and she tumbled down the steps of the porch.

From the side of the luxury sedan, sixty-seven-year-old, John Griffin eyed the daughter he had abandoned some ten years earlier when she was fourteen.

A younger man stood behind him and gave him a little shove in the back to get his feet to move forward.

Jake felt Kit's death grip on his hand and couldn't blame her. He eyed John Griffin with open disdain. For ten years, this man had led her to believe he'd died on location shooting a film in Spain.

Hell, he had even confirmed that fact to her simply because a database had given him the wrong information, which he'd repeated. It was all Jake could do to keep from running toward the elder man and taking aim at his chin.

John Griffin finally began to close the distance. When he got to the bottom steps he stopped and looked up. With a slight twinge of a brogue, he said, "Hello, Angel. I guess you'll be wanting an explanation right about now."

Kit simply stood rooted to the wooden planks of the porch and stared at the man who had fathered her, the jubilation at meeting her twin brother a dwindling priority.

Instead, she suddenly let go of Jake's hand and turned on her heels to go back inside the house. "Jake, would you please tell Mr. Griffin and his son to come inside? After their long trip, I'll be serving coffee and sandwiches in the living room."

Jake nodded and turned to face John Griffin, who held out his hand in introduction. Jake ignored the handshake and brushed past him to greet Ben Griffin.

"You're a hard man to find. Was that on purpose?" Jake asked.

Ben Griffin spoke in a heavier Irish brogue than his father. "I never knew I had a sister, never knew anyone was trying to find me until two weeks ago. I think my father has a great deal of explaining to do. I'm reluctant to admit I'm more than a bit confused myself at this point."

"Your father had a few thousand miles to explain the situation to you before the plane touched down. But just like so long ago he had a chance to do a lot of things and passed on every last one of them," Jake divulged.

With that, he turned his attention to the limo driver. Reaching into his pocket he handed, him several large bills. "You might want to hang around. I'd give it at least an hour, okay? If you happened to overhear a great deal of yelling and screaming, maybe you could ignore it, okay?"

☖ ☖ ☖ ☖ ☖

Inside the house, the living room filled with people and tension. Kit's support system, Gloria, Dylan and Baylee, Quinn and Reese, along with Jake, crowded around her as if showing the enemy there was strength in numbers.

Because at this point, John Griffin was considered the enemy by everyone in the room.

From across the span of space, Gloria blinked twice at the stunning realization that John Griffin wasn't dead but alive.

She did her best to ignore the man who had stabbed her in the heart by being part of the plot to steal her children. Instead of giving him the satisfaction of showing surprise on her face or anything else for that matter, she concentrated on looking at her son, long and hard. Her hand flew to her mouth as a tall, handsome man stepped into the room behind his father.

For the first time in twenty-five years she laid eyes on the baby boy she'd given birth to and never got to hold.

Kit saw the struggle in her mother's eyes and took Gloria's hand. "Come on, Mom, let's go meet Ben. He's come a long way to see us."

Kit and Gloria moved toward Ben as a unit. Kit reached out her hand but at the last minute changed her mind and grabbed him around the neck. "Oh, hell," she said before her eyes filled with tears.

Ben shot them both a wide grin, a curve of lips so like Kit's.

With her hands on her son's face, Gloria exclaimed, "My god, you both look so much alike it's uncanny."

Kit elbowed Ben in the ribs. "Hmm, it'd be a shame if she couldn't tell us apart."

Ben snickered, and when Gloria tightened her grip, he reached down to wrap her up in his long arms.

The three stood locked in an embrace for several lengthy minutes before Gloria commented, "Such a tall handsome man you are with your white blond hair, your green eyes, so like your sister in looks. You both have my coloring."

She dabbed at her eyes as the tears came for real. "You have no idea what it means to me to have you here today, to be able to touch you, hug you, for the very first time."

A bit awkward, Ben replied, "I'm pleased to meet you. I've seen pictures. Pop here showed me plenty of pictures over the years but they aren't the same thing as finally getting to see you in person. I was told you were dead."

Her jaw dropped. She shot a furious glare at John. "Well, as you can see, I'm alive and well. Of course, I used to be a lot prettier."

Ben relaxed a little more and smiled broadly. "You look pretty enough to me."

Kit introduced Ben to Jake, "This is the man I plan to marry."

Even though they'd spoken at the car, the two men exchanged handshakes before Kit added, "And these people are the rest of my family. Baylee and Quinn are my sisters, not by blood of course, but in every other way possible."

She introduced Dylan and Reese, and then dragged Ben over to sit beside her on the sofa telling him, "Ben, you understand we're all a little surprised to see John here today. Because it just so happens I've spent the last ten years believing he was dead."

Ben sent a look of horror over at their father. "Pop, you let everyone think you were dead? Why? You told me you finally decided to retire from the movies because you got tired of all the travel. He told me my birth mum couldn't keep me so he brought me to live with my grandmother in Ireland. Then when I was maybe five or so, he told me you'd died in a car accident."

Kit put a hand to her mouth, took a deep controlled breath. "Such lies. Are you telling me you don't know that we were stolen from our mother? Two women, evil to the core, stole both of us. One kept me, raised me, beat me. Our father here was part of the plot."

"Stolen?" Ben looked horrified. He shot a look at his father. "Pop?"

But Kit went on, "Gloria had no idea she'd even had a son. You and I were snatched from her, stolen mere hours after she gave birth, by two women who had no regard for anyone but themselves. Up until a few weeks ago, I thought the woman who raised me was my mother. It's only been that brief time that I've known the truth."

Sensing a complete slide into turmoil, Jake decided it was time to address the entire sham. Having never taken a seat, he stood jingling the change in his pocket and stared down at John Griffin, who sat stoically on the couch.

Jake wanted answers, enough of this polite stall. "We'll catch Ben up on the circumstances of his birth after Mr. Griffin here tells us what precipitated him to fake his own death ten years ago in Spain."

John Griffin licked his lips and swallowed hard. "I had to do it to break the hold Alana had over me. It was the only way. I'd tried so many times in the past to get her to relinquish her iron-fisted control, but I just never could get her to back off."

"Bullshit," Jake challenged. "You have the nerve to fly seven thousand miles, get here only to hand us another layer to the lie? We want the truth and we want it now. After what you put Kit through over the years, she deserves to know everything."

John nervously licked his lips again and scrubbed his fingers over his mouth. "Do you have anything stronger than the coffee? Maybe a little whiskey would give me the courage to tell you the story."

Reese got up and strolled to the bar, took out a bottle of Jameson's, poured him a generous glass, and handed it off to Griffin. Without a word he sat back down next to Quinn on the love seat—and waited for the whiskey to loosen the older man's tongue.

As if more comfortable with a glass in his hand, it didn't take long for John to start talking. "Alana was good at blackmail. She and Jessica both were. There was an incident in my past that would have been the end of me as a working actor, put an end to my career for certain, if it had come to light. Alana and Jessica knew about it because they were there when it happened.

"I'd been drinking one night after a party. It was a little after seven the next morning. I was hung over and driving down Benedict Canyon arguing with Alana, who sat in the front seat while Jessica sat in the back. The women were flapping their gums about the meat at the party the night before. And I'm not talking about steak here, people."

He stopped long enough to glance at everyone sitting around the room. "Don't look so shocked. We're all adults here. Anyway, I took my eyes off the road for a second and hit something on the narrow shoulder of the roadway. I stopped the car, got out, and discovered I'd hit a little boy on his bicycle." This time he paused to take a long stiff drink of the liquid before going on.

"There was some discussion about what we should do, but in the end…" He wiped his mouth and took another drink before admitting, "We did nothing. The boy was already gone and… we left him there on the side of the road."

He swallowed hard and went on. "When we got back to Alana's, I telephoned the police, made an anonymous call, told them there was a little boy…those were the days before cell phones. A couple days later I found out his name. David Foster. He was nine years old. He'd had a morning paper route. That's what he was doing on the road so early, delivering his papers."

Kit stared at the man she had so loved once upon a time when she had believed he was the best thing that had ever happened in her life.

All she felt now was revulsion, a sickness in her stomach, watching him drink like a fish knowing what he'd done to a little boy.

"From that moment on, Alana and Jessica blackmailed me into every goddamn scheme they cooked up."

He stared up at Gloria. "And yes, that includes taking away your babies, Gloria. I knew what they planned to do all along. For two months before they did it. I wasn't on location making a film when you went into labor but rather five miles down the road holed up in a beach bungalow waiting for you to give birth. The surprise came when you had not one baby but two.

"Alana certainly wasn't willing to take both of them and Jessica had just that past May given birth to her third boy. That would be Collin. So when it was decided that Alana would keep the girl that left the boy to deal with. Since no one wanted him, Jessica planned to put him up for adoption. But I put my foot down, said no way. I wouldn't sign the papers for that. So, I took the boy here, got on a plane and took him to my mother in Ireland so she could raise him there same as she did me."

"And left Kit in the capable hands of a psychopath," Jake finished.

"I swear I didn't know…"

"Save it," Jake practically shouted at him. "Any time during those first five years when you saw the bruises on Kit and the list of broken bones a mile long, you could have snatched her up and taken her to Ireland just like you did Ben here. But you didn't do that, Griffin. How does a father leave a defenseless child with a habitual abuser like Alana?

"Not to mention by this time you had to wonder about Alana and Jessica. Just what exactly were these two women capable of doing?"

For the first time since coming into the house, John's eyes got misty. But Jake ignored the tears. "How does a father leave his own little girl with a woman he knows isn't her mother, a woman who is so into porn that we found reels of the stuff in her attic?"

John's face went white. "Now wait a minute, most of that stuff was done long before Kit ever came along."

Realizing what he'd said, he started to backtrack. "Okay, I know. I'm sorry, Kit. I'm so sorry I left you there time and time again with that monster. You need to understand I tried to talk sense into her. She'd promise the abuse would stop and that it would never happen again. But of course it always did."

Jake shook his head. "I'm not sure you know the depths of Alana's depravity over the years, Griffin. Or do you? These schemes you were dragged into, did they also include murdering the Parkers?"

John's face showed confusion whether forced or genuine, Jake couldn't tell.

"Who are the Parkers?"

Jake went through the details about their deaths, the gun, and how they had tied the crime to Alana and Jessica. He studied the man's face to gauge his reaction and looked around the room at the expressive watchful eyes of his friends. He'd have to ask them later if they bought into the guy's performance.

Because John was adamant, he shook his head. "If I'd known they committed cold-blooded murder, don't you think I would've blackmailed both of them to get them off my back? That's how desperate I was back then. You have to understand I would have used any means, done anything to get out from under Alana's control. She was driving me nuts."

"So you couldn't use the porn as leverage but decided to fake your own death instead, is that it?" Jake wasn't sure who the man thought he was kidding. In his opinion, Griffin had lost every ounce of his ability to act.

"Yes. I gave up my acting career such as it was back then. I found people that would help me. The key was to make the story so convincing Alana and Jessica would have to believe it and never look for me."

For the first time since John's performance began for the crowd sitting around her, Kit spoke up. "I didn't believe it, not for a long time. As a matter of fact, I didn't believe it until two months ago. Tell him, Jake. Tell him how I wanted you to check out the story I'd been told."

He nodded. "She did. In fact, she was convinced you were alive and that Alana had told her that to simply get back at her for some infraction she'd committed."

John looked at Kit then straight on. "I'm sorry, Angel. I tried to come up with a way out but I just couldn't think of anything else other than to disappear."

Reese walked over to stand by Jake. "Are you telling us the truth, Mr. Griffin? You didn't even suspect that Alana and Jessica had murdered the Parkers for their money, to get full and complete access to their trust?"

"Look, I'm telling you, the only thing I knew for certain was both women held a ton of secrets. They had their hands in a lot of pies back then, if you know what I mean. I suspected Jessica was doing something illegal, using her law practice to do all kinds of underhanded things. After all, I'd been a party to stealing Gloria's babies. I knew she was into handling adoptions all over the state. The only things I ever suspected them of doing like murder was when..." He looked over at Baylee. "When Sarah Moreland disappeared. Something was a little off with their story. It crossed my mind back then that they'd done something to Sarah, Baylee's mother."

"What? Why?" Baylee asked the man she used to have such respect for. "Why did you suspect them? They did murder her, Mr. Griffin. And no one, not even my own father did a single thing to find out where she'd gone. They pushed her down the stairs, Mr. Griffin. They found Sarah's body not a week ago buried on the grounds of The Enclave next to the reflecting pool."

John looked as though he'd stepped off a cliff and were falling about a hundred miles an hour in a downward drop. "Uh... I don't know what to say to that."

"You might consider getting an attorney, Mr. Griffin," Reese suggested. "You've just confessed to a hit-and-run, a felony. As an officer of the court, I'd say the sooner you retain one and come clean, the sooner you'll get this behind you. I know this much. You're lucky. The statute of limitations for vehicular manslaughter is three to six years so you may not even be prosecuted after such a long time. But you left the state for some time and went to live in another country. Believe me, that will count against you and will negate the statute of limitations. By how much, I have no idea. The clock started ticking the minute you left California and faked your own death, which, I might add, is prosecutable if fraud was involved. After so long, the most you may get is a fine and two to three years of jail time."

"Three years? Is that all?" Kit asked. She stared at her father. "Reese is right, you are lucky. David Foster's family deserves to know what happened to their son."

"And look what you put your own daughter through," Ben pointed out. "All this time she thought you were dead."

John looked confused again. "You'd both throw me to the wolves, my own children? But I'm here to catch up, spend some time with Kit after such a long time away. Surely you won't be a party to turning me in for something that happened so long ago."

Disgusted, Kit searched her father's eyes for some semblance of right and wrong. She shook her head. "To think I used to worship the ground you walked on. How pathetic you are now. I'm going to say this once, John. You were responsible for a little nine-year-old boy's death. Don't you think it is past time you did the right thing just once in your miserable life? Instead of thinking of yourself, at least make some attempt at doing the right thing for that little boy's family."

She glanced over at Ben, the brother she'd known for less than an hour. "What do you say, brother of mine? How do you feel about what your father's confessed here today?"

"Ashamed. Surprised. A lot disgusted." He turned to John. "I'd want the father I've known all these years to 'fess up to what he's done. Kit's right. That boy's family deserves to know the truth even after all these years have gone by. The boy might have had brothers or sisters who still, even today, need some closure."

Proud to have a man like Ben for a brother, Kit leaned over and hugged him. "Welcome to our little family such as it is. How about we take a walk and get to know each other better?"

She put her other arm around Gloria. "Come on, Mom, you come with us. It'll be the best family reunion I've ever had."

❦ ❦ ❦ ❦ ❦

After the intense scene with John Griffin died down, Baylee and Quinn did their best to make sense out of things. Back in the kitchen they sat at the table with Dylan and Reese, going over everything John had told them.

"Why didn't he just stay in Ireland?" Dylan asked.

"He couldn't very well send his son, Ben, and remain out of the picture. Sorry for the pun: actor, picture. Anyway it was sad to watch Kit's face while he went over everything. You could tell she was devastated at learning how he lied."

Quinn sighed. "Yeah, that was the worst, watching the disappointment on her face, seeing how crestfallen she was that everything she'd believed about him had been a lie. She trusted him."

Baylee stared at Quinn. "All three of us did. We thought he was—the good guy. Sad to know there doesn't seem to have been any good guys in our little world back then."

"True. At least now she knows the truth and out of his own mouth. She deserves to know that much."

"We all do," Baylee said as she linked fingers with Dylan.

"Of course she does. It's just that Jake's feeling a little raw right now because he's the one who verified the man was dead from the fall in Spain. He taps into a database listing that info on the site, trusts it enough to verify he's gone. Bam, she's upset all over again, has to face the fact Alana didn't lie. Then he walks in here, big as life."

Quinn looked sympathetic for about two seconds. "Jake wasn't to blame for John Griffin setting out to lie and deceive his own daughter. What kind of men become fathers only to walk away from establishing that bond with their own blood?"

All four knew she wasn't talking about John Griffin at that point, but Nick Tyler.

"Just remember, Quinn, my own father kept such horrible secrets after doing despicable things."

"Will you be able to forgive him?"

She shook her head. "I don't think so. But watching him suffer, go downhill a little more each day is…heartbreaking."

Quinn squeezed her free hand. "You've such a good heart. I wish I could say I'd forgive but I'm not sure I have that in me. We were so young. We were supposed to be able to trust the adults around us. And now…"

"Quinn, we were caught up in the overindulgences of adults, in their narcissistic pursuits, their selfishness. Don't you think it's time to put all that away, put it behind us once and for all and move on with our own lives?"

"You're right. It's just that…I don't like Ella, let alone love her. I never did. That's my burden to bear. Growing up, she was…always so…uncaring, even mean. Not like Alana mean but…a child deserves to have caring people around them."

Baylee reached over and scooped Quinn into her chest for a hug. "Yes, they do. I know Kit and I were poor substitutes but we did our best." She grinned. "The minute I looked over and saw you sitting next to me in Mrs. O'Malley's third grade class I knew we were going to be besties."

"That's only because I had all the answers to the math quizzes."

"There was that. How'd you get to be so smart anyway if you didn't go to school regularly until you came here?"

She shrugged. "The answers just came to me."

"Ah. Genuis. Kit and I were always proud of how smart you were."

At that moment, Kit and Jake came through the back door holding hands while Gloria and Ben lagged behind. "Where's John?" Kit asked.

Quinn waved a hand. "He's…somewhere. I think he went outside on the front porch to smoke a cigarette."

"As long as he didn't decide to steal the silver and take off," Kit grumbled as she took a seat at the table.

"I know you're upset," Baylee said. "But at least he finally came clean."

Kit sighed. "Yeah, there's that. He gets points for plotting to steal his own kids right from the get-go, not being able to take a stand with Alana, and faking his own death, letting me believe he was gone from my life for good. Yeah, he's a prize all right."

Baylee laughed. "Ah. Well. I don't think any of us won prizes in the parent department, except maybe Quinn here."

Taken aback, Quinn stared at her friend. "What? Why would you say such a thing? Two decades of neglect is hardly a reason to hand out father of the year awards."

"True. But at least he's here now trying to…"

"So what if he is?" Quinn exploded. "Twenty years went by and nothing. Now Nick Tyler gets points for showing up? I don't think so."

Kit exchanged looks with Baylee. "What she's saying, Quinn, is that Nick Tyler might warrant a second chance. From what you say happened at Reese's office, he thought you were being well-cared for, living a typical rich kid, Beverly Hills kind of life."

"And if he'd bothered contacting me just once, he'd have known better, discovered the truth instead of finding out after the fact, after it no longer matters."

Baylee shook her head. "It matters, Quinn. No one's saying it doesn't. But he believed the lies, lies we all grew up believing. We were surrounded by such evil and deceit and grew up with lies built on top of lies. It's got to end at some point. It might as well end with us. The three of us deserve better. We've got to put an end to this, end this evil that's haunted our past, put this crap behind us once and for all, and move forward."

Kit reached for her hand. "We aren't saying it'll be easy, Quinn. But you have a chance with Nick, your father, to make a fresh start. Don't let all the negative stuff from the past cloud the fact he's here now, willing to establish a relationship."

Baylee clasped hands with her friends, then pointed out, "Quinn, look at the love around this table, what we've meant to each other over the years. Don't let *his* mistake not getting to know you affect you for the rest of your life. Try to forgive and forget or you'll be letting it ruin the future, your future.

"And if all that still means nothing to you, then think of it this way. You'll only get the one chance at having a father, one chance, Quinn, that's it," Baylee reasoned.

She met Reese's eyes. "Reese said the same thing. I'm just not sure I can get past his never being there for me. It hurt, damn it. All those years it hurt."

"Of course it did. We were there with you. But trust me on this," Kit said. "You can and you should find a way. The anger and hate will only eat you up inside. Is that what you want? You have a brilliant career ahead of you. Why hold on to all that negative energy."

Baylee picked up the chorus. "Haven't we lived in the shadow of all of this too long as it is? Isn't it time to let go of the pain? I don't want to waste a single minute of my precious time with Dylan and Sarah fixated on the lousy way my father treated me any more. I want to let it go and look forward to my future, the future I have with Dylan."

"I guess I'll try, but I need you guys with me tomorrow when we get the DNA results. Just like Kit needed us here today, I want you there with me, all of you." She looked around the table and into the eyes of each of them. "I can't do this alone. In fact, I don't want to do it alone."

"And so we will be."

CHAPTER 23

By the time she'd reached twenty-one, the smack had hold of Ella Canyon so bad she'd have done anything for a fix. Anything. That included selling out a member of her own family. A small price to pay really to make certain the steady stream of heroin kept coming.

She didn't like thinking about that time, so long ago now, it seemed it might have happened to someone else.

It hadn't been her fault, she reminded herself. Just because she hadn't stood up for her cousin didn't mean what had happened had been her fault. No one dared confront Jessica Boyd and Alana Stevens, even she had known that.

Oh, but Lisa had. That had been her undoing. Lisa. She'd been so young, so naïve. If only Lisa had kept her mouth shut that day. If only she hadn't upset Jessica and Alana. If only Lisa had listened to her.

In her short *seventeen years Lisa Redfield had made two huge mistakes. Her first one had been to get pregnant at fifteen, to let a hunky Irish rock singer take her virginity. Her second was to put blind faith and trust in an attorney, especially, it seemed, this one.*

Lisa swallowed hard and glanced up into the cold, hard stare of Jessica Boyd. When she'd first met Jessica she had thought the woman walked on water. After all, Jessica had promised to get money out of the rock star. At the time Lisa had believed the attorney was a godsend, one who had her best interests at heart.

And why wouldn't she think that? After all, Ella Canyon, her own cousin, had recommended Jessica personally, family looking out for family.

She glanced over at Ella, who stood off to the side like a vulture.

What a poor excuse for family, Lisa thought now. Ella had been looking out for herself and had been since day one.

Lisa had to wonder if she would ever get out of this mess.

And how in the world had she not seen Jessica's dark side that first day? Because she'd been bubbly and upbeat and so sure she could handle all Lisa's problems.

If things weren't bad enough, Lisa hated it when she had to meet with Jessica while Alana Stevens was in the room. Jessica always insisted Lisa bend to do what she wanted. But Alana liked to threaten her with physical violence. The woman flat-out gave her the willies.

Up to now, Lisa had relented and done everything they'd wanted her to do. She'd met Jessica's demands and then some.

But now, as she sat in Jessica's office, there was another lecture coming, another threat of some kind, she could feel it—building to a crescendo. She could tell by the way the two women exchanged sidelong glances.

Lisa hated these two women with a passion. And she was getting tired of this whole scam. She wanted to take her baby girl, Quinn, and leave L.A. for good, go back to Santa Barbara and the way things were before she'd ever taken that trip to San Francisco to see Shatter in concert, before she'd ever gone to Nick Tyler's hotel room that warm April night.

She wanted to get as far away from these two women as she could get.

Lisa had it all planned out. She would let her mother's sister take care of Quinn while she got a job, a regular job. She could waitress. She was good with people. Or her mother could help her get a job at the bakery where she worked, just a way to earn a living until she got her artwork to payoff.

She'd been told she had talent. After all, when she'd been pregnant she'd spent hours and hours drawing and painting, something she loved doing with all her heart. Kind of like Nick Tyler had loved his music—certainly he had loved his music career infinitely more than he'd ever loved her.

How could she have been so stupid?

But if she got a regular job she could go back to school and get her GED. She knew that would make her mother happy. All she knew at the moment was that she should never have gotten mixed up with Jessica Boyd or the law firm or, for that matter, Alana Stevens. Unfortunately the two women seemed to go together like two matching halves of one personality. She knew that now with certainty.

Lisa shook her head and thought about how much she'd grown up in the last two years. That had a lot to do with being a mother, being totally responsible for a thirteen-month-old baby was a lot of hard work.

She stared into Jessica's cold, dark eyes.

"You will do as I tell you, do you understand? If you want the money to keep coming in every month, stop fighting me every step of the way and listen to me. I know what I'm doing."

"I know, but it's just that Nick was so sweet to me when Quinn was born. He even showed up at the hospital and held her for the first time. I know he was moved by the fact that I named her after his mother. I hate to…"

Jessica's tone changed. "Lisa, have you forgotten? The man took your virginity. And the law says if a man has sex with an underage teen, he does jail time. Period. Don't you know by now Nick doesn't care a whit about you or the baby? He never did.

"He hasn't spent another moment thinking of you or the time you spent at his disposal. He used you and nothing more. If you won't think of yourself, at least think of your baby, who has needs as all children do. And she won't be a baby forever. As a mother you have to think about a decent place to live, food and clothing, and then there's college for little Quinn down the road. Surely a girl like you, with your blue collar background, wants a good education for your daughter.

"The man's raking in millions and Quinn is entitled to her fair share, as are you." And didn't Jessica know the amount of Tyler's assets to the penny since she'd had to sleep with that old fart Portman to get him to send her Tyler's account statements every month? The doting little man had been putty in her hands.

"Quinn's entitled," Lisa corrected. She might be young, but she wasn't stupid. And if she was supposed to be getting so much money, where was it? It was taking a long time to trickle down to her and Quinn.

"Babies have needs, Jessica. By now I thought I'd be back in school. I thought I'd get the money and, you know, it would be mine to do with what I wanted. But every time Quinn needs something the money has to come through you. And I'm getting tired of my living arrangements, sharing an apartment with Ella Canyon wasn't part of the deal."

Even from across the room, Lisa noticed Ella go rigid with anger.

"You ungrateful, little bitch. I'm the one who has to babysit this one. Make sure she does what she's told."

Not to be intimidated, Lisa continued, *"She uses drugs and she brings men around at all hours of the day and night. I don't like it. I want my own place to live where Quinn and I can feel safe."*

Jessica didn't handle whiny children very well and Lisa was no exception. "Are you saying I don't take care of you and the child? Is that what you're implying? Because how dare you question me! I get you everything you need. You have a nice apartment, food in the pantry, a car. Didn't I fly you to Ireland where the little brat could be born just as you requested, the place where you wanted her to be born just like her father? Aren't I looking out for you?"

"Yes but, sharing the place with Ella is...unnecessary. She's constantly smoking weed, and I found a bag of cocaine in the kitchen."

"What are you, a nark? How dare you rat me out!" Ella fumed.

Right then, how she wished Ella, her distant cousin, had never ever introduced her to Jessica Boyd. It seemed Ella was already hooked on the hard stuff and headed for the gutter.

"You couldn't go to Ireland alone, now could you, a young, pregnant girl? Ella acted as your birthing coach and..."

"Babysitter," Lisa finished. "I don't need a druggie babysitting me."

Up to now Alana hadn't said a word, but she'd heard enough. "You'd better listen to Jess, Lisa. She's helped others out just like you and they're in better circumstances for it. Stop being an ungrateful pain in the butt. You have a small child and don't have to work. Money comes in whenever you need anything. What more do you want?"

Lisa stood up defiantly. "You think because I'm young I don't know what you're doing. What's going on here? I'll tell everyone what you're doing, I swear I will."

Jessica's eyes met Alana's. "After all I've done for you, you threaten me?"

Staring into those cold, black eyes, Lisa swallowed hard. Maybe she'd gone too far this time. "I wouldn't really."

"Don't think we'll put up with threats from an ungrateful little tramp like you," Alana warned. "You get

knocked up, your mother kicks you out, and you don't know where your next meal is coming from. Unless you want to go on the dole for good then you'd better let Jess here continue working things out her way. And if I were you, I'd keep my goddamned mouth shut with threats of any kind."

With that, Alana walked over and calmly backhanded Lisa hard across the mouth.

The sting of the slap caused tears to form in Lisa's eyes. She rubbed her throbbing cheek and glared at Ella, who stood shaking her head.

"That'll teach the nark in you to keep your pie hole shut," Ella shouted.

Oh God, thought Lisa, there had to be a way to get these three people out of her life for good.

If only Ella didn't hover around her so much, she might be able to sneak out, take Quinn away from these horrible people, maybe buy a bus ticket back to Santa Barbara and get out of this mess she'd found herself in ever since she'd first walked through the door.

But as she looked around the room, her face still burning from Alana's hand, she feared she might have waited too late.

⚘⚘⚘⚘⚘

Trembling from the memory, Ella looked over at the tall man who'd busted her out of the loony bin, wondering if she might be hallucinating.

Was it time for her pills? She really needed her medicine.

She stared at the big man with kind eyes and wondered if he'd brought her medication. Who was he anyway? This visit he kept asking her a lot of questions about Lisa. Lisa Redfield, her cousin. He kept after her to talk about what happened to Lisa, that's all he wanted to know. Why was it always about Lisa?

Her name always brought back memories, both good and bad, along with jealousy, envy.

Bad times spent around Alana and Jessica when they spiraled out of control meant you never quite knew what to expect. She remembered being afraid. But this big man kept telling her she didn't have to be scared any more.

Ella wondered if it was true.

Because the big man was taking her away from this dump, somewhere she didn't have to be afraid. He'd told her so. She looked over at the other man, the one who was supposed to be a cop. He looked like one. Cops were bad news, everyone knew that. She would avoid talking to that one, she decided.

She liked the big guy with the Irish name. He hadn't been the first Irishmen she'd talked to, but he was certainly the nicest one. As he took her by the arm and led her out into the sunshine and to a waiting car, Ella resolved that maybe she'd see a glimmer of that life of luxury she once had, the one she'd had before the kid grew up and took off.

ᚼ ᚼ ᚼ ᚼ ᚼ

Quinn nervously looked around the conference room at her support system. There was Kit and Jake, Baylee and Dylan, and Reese. Her friends and family were here to offer support and love. Nothing she found out now could hurt her, Quinn decided.

She spared a quick glance at Nick Tyler. She might not even be his. It would be so like Ella to have lied to her all these years.

Didn't matter, she thought.

But oh, it did.

No matter how many times she reminded herself that she was a grown woman, an adult, not a needy child looking for validation or attention, she wanted—to know, once and for all, where she came from and from whom.

For some reason, it mattered.

She looked over at Reese, taking command of the room. So like him to orchestrate this to its conclusion. When their eyes met, he smiled. And her heart simply stuttered in her chest.

After everyone settled in, Reese eyed father and daughter sitting across from each other. He took out the piece of paper with the DNA results, passed a copy to each one of them.

"Mr. Tyler, Quinn, as you can see by the results, you two are definitely related, father and daughter."

"I know that already. I never doubted it for a second. I knew the moment I walked in here because she's the image of her mother, the image of that little girl who came to the farm that day so long ago." He stared at Quinn. "I never forgot about you. I forgot about doing the right thing, being a father."

Quinn started to open her mouth to speak but Reese sent her a look. "Do you have a photo of Ella Canyon, Quinn?"

She gaped at him. "You know I don't. We weren't exactly the type of people to get out the camera and celebrate a Hallmark moment for posterity's sake."

He turned to Nick Tyler. "And do you have a photograph of Lisa Redfield?"

Nick shook his head. "I don't believe we ever took one together, no." But as Reese was about to go on, Nick changed his mind. "Wait. My mother took one at hospital the day Quinn was born. But that photo is back in Dublin, probably packed away along with a thousand other photographs. If I'd known I'd need it...I'd've gladly brought it with me."

"Convenient isn't it that no one is around today who can positively identify either Ella Canyon or Lisa Redfield." He picked up two photos from the file folder Jordan Donovan had managed to provide. "Mr. Tyler, would you be able to recognize a photo of Lisa?"

Nick acted insulted at the question. "Of course I would."

Reese handed off the picture. "Is that Lisa Redfield?"

"No. Same Native American features, but Lisa was younger, much younger, at least five years younger than the woman here. This is the nanny who brought her out to the farm that day for a visit, though."

"Are you absolutely certain of that?"

"I am."

Reese handed the same photo to Quinn. "Who is that, Quinn?"

"It's Ella. My *mother*," she emphasized.

"That woman is not your mother," Nick insisted with some heat.

"What am I supposed to say to that? This is the woman who raised me."

"The drug addict, you mean," Nick shot back.

"Raging," Quinn added.

"Lisa did not do drugs. Believe me, I know. Look, for the last time, I ought to bloody well know the girl who had you. She was like a ray of sunshine, a breath of fresh air. Good, decent. She was a talented artist, a painter. While in Ireland she painted several canvasses. One of which I still have—of me. Lisa drew portraits like no one I've seen before or since, with a skill anyone with an eye for such things would envy. Anyone could see she had talent, even one so very young."

Quinn thought of *Woman Rising*. Instead of saying anything about what Trevor had told her, she eyed Reese with a confused look. "I don't understand any of this, Reese."

"I know. But you're about to." Reese handed Nick another photo, this one old, worn, the color faded. "Is that Lisa?"

Looking at that photo took him back to a time and place he wasn't exactly proud to own as his. Tears filled Nick's eyes. He nodded. "It is." After studying it for several minutes, it was he who handed the picture off to Quinn. "This is your mother, so without malice, so idealistic, so young."

Quinn took the photograph, stared at a young, Native American girl who looked radiant and shared her own facial features right down to her eyes. She might have been staring at a high school snapshot of herself. Reese heard her intake of breath. "She's so beautiful."

"Aye, she was."

Reese went to the phone and dialed his assistant. "Audrey, could you please tell our guests we're ready for them now? Thanks."

Reese turned to Nick and Quinn. "What happened is a rather complicated story but you both deserve some long overdue answers about a great many things. Somewhere along the way, Lisa Redfield vanished off the face of the earth and Ella Canyon stepped in to fill her role in every way that mattered, except, of course, as mother of the year."

When the door opened and Max walked into the conference room followed by Jordan Donovan, who held the arm of a very weak-looking Ella Canyon, Quinn looked as though she wanted the floor to open up and swallow her.

Despite the confusion Reese saw locked in her eyes, she remained seated, stoic at the prospect of getting her questions finally answered.

Max eyed Nick Tyler with a certain amount of admiration in his eyes. But one tour around the somber faces sitting at the conference table told him this wasn't the time to wax poetic or request an autograph.

He was here to clear up a long overdue mystery.

Reese broke the silence. "*This* is Ella Canyon. Jordan found her locked up in a mental hospital in Oakland, a dump where Jessica committed her almost three years ago, ostensibly to help her kick a very nasty heroin addiction. My guess is Jessica and Alana needed her someplace locked up where she couldn't tell anyone what she knew."

Reese nodded his head at Jordan.

The private investigator cleared his throat. "It took a court order to spring her. But since the attorney of record,

Jessica Boyd, is now deceased, the judge agreed to at least move her closer to L.A. Our flight got in about an hour ago. We came straight here from the airport. She's here because she's already gone on record with Max, given her official statement as to what happened. I brought her here to give us a firsthand account of what she says happened to Lisa Redfield, Quinn's *mother*. "I'm not guaranteeing Ella will make much sense. Between my digging and her account I think we've got a better idea of that timeframe. She seems to like me, so I'll prompt her by asking the questions."

With that, Jordan turned to the woman with blank eyes. "Ella, you remember Quinn here, don't you?"

"Quinn." Ella chuckled, the low laugh of a druggie that hadn't seen sobriety for too many years to count. "We pulled a fast one there, we did. Back then, I wanted to be like Jessica, like Alana, in every way. They had money. I wanted money, fame, to live in a big house. But they used me. They used everyone, sooner or later."

"I know," Jordan agreed. "Everyone here wants to know what happened to Lisa Redfield, though, and you're the only one alive who can tell us."

"She got knocked up by Nick Tyler. Everyone knows that. Should've been me. But Nick took a liking to Lisa that night at the concert. Hell, she wasn't even old enough to drink legally. But his roadie picked her out of the crowd to go backstage and meet Nick. Backstage, that should've been me instead of Lisa. Who knew she'd get invited back to his hotel room?"

"And once she got pregnant, you pointed her in the direction of Jessica because after all, Lisa needed an attorney to look out for her and the baby, right?"

"I knew Jessica. She'd helped out another friend of mine when she got pregnant, helped put the baby up for adoption. So when Lisa found herself knocked up, I called Jess."

"And Jess handled everything from there.

"Sure she did. Jess was good at handling the details, making problems go away."

"You had to wait for Lisa to have the baby of course, but after a paternity test…"

"Are you kidding? After that, it was a piece of cake. Jess got a million upfront and monthly child support. I thought we were in for a lengthy fight but…"

Quinn tired of listening to Ella's voice, spared a quick glance at Nick to see how he was handling this, but Nick didn't seem to be listening. He was staring at Quinn, equally curious how she was dealing with Ella's narrative.

Father and daughter locked eyes. For once, Quinn saw the emotion in those pools of deep brown. The resentment she'd harbored for so long cracked a little.

But since Ella never stopped talking, she did her best to focus on the drug addict she'd thought all this time was her mother.

Ella seemed to be relishing the attention. It was so like her, thought Quinn. Disgusted, but curious, she listened to the tale.

"Tyler's career was hot back then. He didn't want to risk the scandal over a roll in the hay with an underage fifteen-year-old. Jess convinced Lisa that the rock star just wanted all this to go away. Jess and Alana made it happen."

Ella lost focus remembering that day, the day everything had changed.

Ella heard Alana's laugh along with the woman's voice. Her rheumy eyes searched the room for Alana's face or maybe Jessica's. Unable to locate either woman, she began imitating the voice. "We're his fucking fairy godmothers now. Heeheeheehee! We make the baby and the scandal go away, problem solved. We're his fairy godmothers. We could get rid of the baby. We could, we could."

Ella started shaking her head. "But Jess says no. No, we need the baby to keep going to the well."

For a brief time Ella was in her own drug-induced world, taken back to a time when Jess and Alana were forever arguing, Jessica making demands, Alana acting like the enforcer.

Ella remembered the verbal war of words in detail.

☙☙☙☙☙

"Why is it you always react way too quickly to everything?" Jessica accused. "Getting rid of the baby is problematic."

"Too bad, she's a squalling little brat, just like Kit."

"I told you motherhood wasn't for you. But you wouldn't listen. You just had to get back at Gloria for taking John away from you."

"She pissed me off. And so did John. But John certainly has made it up to me lately. He keeps me updated. I can't imagine Gloria working as a maid. Can you imagine a maid of all things?"

"It's all those shock treatments they gave her. Look, could we focus here? You're always getting off-track. The baby we need, the mother not so much."

"She's a bitchy seventeen-year-old with a big mouth," Alana offered. "But if we get rid of Lisa, what will we do with the brat? I'm not taking her. Kit's enough of a handful. And I'm being magnanimous when I say she's a spiteful little thing."

"I hate to say I told you so but... motherhood isn't what it's cracked up to be, now is it?"

Alana ignored her friend, changed the focus yet again to Ella, who'd been sitting stoned on the sofa. She pointed a finger at the younger woman. "What about this one? Ella would be ideal. And she'd be easy to control. Look at her. She's drugged out. Besides, she owes us."

"As much as I'd like to get rid of Lisa, do you think a druggie is really the way to go?"

"Lisa is going to keep making trouble. If we don't do something she might end up going to the cops. Then where would we be?"

That got Jess's attention. "Okay. But I want it done neat and tidy. I hate cleaning up your fuckups."

☙ ☙ ☙ ☙ ☙

By the time Ella came back to them, she sat there dazed, spent.

Jordan had one more question. "Ella, is Lisa Redfield alive?"

The woman snorted. "Nobody takes a beating like that and survives. I was there. Alana beat the crap out of her. When she was done, Lisa wasn't breathing."

Jordan turned to Reese. "That's basically the same story she told Max." He looked over at Ella and said to everyone, "I'm sorry, but I honestly think that's about all we'll get out of her today."

"We got more than I thought we would." Reese turned to Quinn; saw the tears streaming down her face. He knelt down in front of her chair. "I'm sorry, honey. But Lisa Redfield was your mother, not this pitiful excuse of a person sitting here."

Quinn looked up at Nick. "I didn't believe you. I didn't think you remembered Ella, and now…"

Nick picked up her hand. "It's my fault. If I'd bothered coming to visit regularly like I should have done, I would've known what you were going through. I'm so very sorry, Quinn. I had no idea. I should have known something was up when Lisa didn't show up with you that day at the farm. It wasn't like her. She was a good person. I should've done something…"

Max spoke up. "Look, I hate to interrupt. I know this is a painful discovery for all of you but with everyone here, there's more I need to get out on the table. As you already know, about a week ago we found four sets of remains on the grounds of The Enclave.

"With help from Donovan here, we've positively ID'd all of them, two through dental records." Max turned to look at Baylee. "One is definitely Sarah Moreland, your mother. She was buried alongside a Luc Delaine, a man who went missing about the same time she did. His remains have been positively identified as well, through dental records.

"The third body was that of a young female, between the ages of fourteen and eighteen years old. Reese sent me over a sample of Quinn's DNA. This morning the lab confirmed the body is…was Lisa Redfield, a seventeen-year-old Chumash Indian girl from the Santa Ynez, who went missing, according to her mother, around the same time she and a cousin by the name of Ella Canyon drove down to Los Angeles from Santa Barbara to speak to Lisa's attorney, an attorney by the name of Jessica Boyd."

A sick feeling hit Quinn's stomach. She sent a panicked look toward Nick Tyler. My God, this couldn't be happening.

Kit and Baylee went over to her and put their arms around her in a massive embrace. "I'm so sorry, honey."

Reese filled in the rest. "Lisa Redfield's family never saw her again after she left for that fateful trip to L.A. By this time Quinn was about thirteen months old, according to Lisa's mother, who did not I might add, kick her daughter to the curb after she got pregnant. Sylvia Redfield wasn't happy about her fifteen-year-old getting pregnant, but she did not kick her out. In fact, as your grandmother, Quinn, she's very interested in meeting her granddaughter."

Quinn's hand flew to her mouth as it gaped open. She swallowed hard. "My mother, my real mother is dead because Alana Stevens and Jessica Boyd murdered her just like they killed Baylee's mother?"

"My God," Kit said. "I lived with that monster, suffered at her hands in that house all those years never knowing she'd killed so readily. Quinn and Baylee were often there. Who could have possibly imagined those two women plotted and killed whoever crossed them? All those years we had no idea we shared space with people who were so evil."

Max stared at Kit, blinked. This woman had suffered massive abuse for years at the hands of Alana Stevens. No one knew Alana better than Kit Griffin. "Well, I wouldn't discount what role the rest of the founding partners had in all of it. But we'll probably never know for certain. Burying bodies near their own reflecting pool took some muscle. I can't see Jessica or Alana digging a grave. They'd be too afraid they might chip a nail. I'd have to say someone knew what the two women were doing and why. Without giving you specifics there's reason to believe both women were certainly involved in a great many murders and over a long period of time."

Max took the time to glance around the room. "But there's more. The fourth body is that of Ross Jennetti. We know that for certain because, as I'd hoped, the lab was able to get prints. His fingerprints were already in the system from an arrest back in the late '80s for breaking and entering. At the time, he had a long rap sheet for burglaries and theft to support a nasty drug habit of us own."

"Son of a bitch," Nick fumed as he stood up and marched to the window. "You're telling us that Lisa Redfield, Quinn's mother, that beautiful young girl, was murdered not long after giving birth to my child and I've sat around on my ass while my daughter lived in squalor with this drug-addled Ella person and this bitch of an attorney, that this Alana Stevens and Jessica Boyd beat Lisa to death?"

Reese put his hand on his shoulder. "I'm afraid that about sums it up."

"What happened to the million dollars? Or the money I sent every month?" Nick asked, almost afraid he already knew the answer. "It never reached Quinn, did it?"

"From what we've managed to learn from a database on Jessica's hard drive at work, she kept the million and told Lisa you were playing hardball. In the meantime she was nickel and diming Portman for all she could get out of him, too," Jake explained. "During that thirteen months, I doubt Lisa or Quinn ever saw anything more than ten grand from the million, certainly never enough to live on until Gerald Baines slipped Jennetti into the picture. Now, that was a complication Jessica didn't see coming."

Reese picked up the story from there. "Baines admitted Alana approached him with the idea of keeping a tighter rein on the cash flow. Baines bit hook, line, and sinker. Alana had a friend named Jennetti, who needed a steady job. What better job than to oversee ten grand a month?

"But to pull it off, Quinn had to change addresses. Up to that time, Ella and the baby had been living hand to mouth out in the Valley. Because after all Jessica had made it clear Nick's attorneys were not cooperating with the settlement. How she managed to stretch out the story for eight years is due to the fact that Lisa was no longer in the picture, no longer a threat.

"We all know Nick's attorney Portman met Jessica's demand, so there was no hardball on Nick's part, no fighting the settlement. Jessica and Alana played on Ella's drug habit, her weakness, and kept stringing her along. Ella at that point would do just about anything to make sure her supply of drugs never ended.

"Then for some reason Alana changes the dynamics. We'll probably never know the exact reason. But it might have something to do with the fact that she has this house in Beverly Hills she owns and needs to liquidate at the time. As a real estate agent, she sees an opportunity. She negotiates the sale of the house to Baines, who in turn, sets Jennetti up in the house to keep an eye on Ella Canyon and Jessica Boyd.

"All the while Alana is playing both sides, as is Ross. They stick to the story that Jennetti is Nick's record producer. The title gave him some clout because record producer sounds a helluva lot more impressive than a two-bit, ex-con, drug addict."

Nick turned to Quinn. "Words will never be able to express how sorry I am about this whole mess. If I'd only taken the time to check on you myself, not leave it up to so many other people. My own daughter… I'm so sorry, Quinn. I'm so very sorry for everything, for not visiting you, for not bringing you over to Ireland when I could have. My mother could have raised you. Try to understand, I thought you were being taken care of properly, seen to, fed regularly, sheltered, that I was fucking father of the year because I ponied up the goddamn money…and went on with my music."

Reese expected Quinn to explode.

Instead, he watched, a little stunned, as she simply got up from her chair and crossed over to where her father still stood by the window.

With tears still spilling out of her eyes, she told him, "It isn't your fault. Not entirely. Oh, the fact that you let the lawyers handle everything, well, you have to live with that. But if Jessica Boyd hadn't gotten involved from the start, things might have turned out differently."

"Who is this Jessica, this Alana person I keep hearing about?"

"They're both dead now, no longer important. But I'll tell you all I know. They were conniving, thieving, murdering women who killed at will for their own greed." She put her hand on Nick's cheek. "I want to know everything you can remember about Lisa, about my mother. Try really hard to think of all the things she said to you. The things she did. I want to know my mother."

"Sure, I remember things. I'll tell you everything I can think of."

"She painted. There's a painting I used to have in my apartment. I almost tossed it into the trash once. Thank God I gave it to Kit when she moved out. Of course, at the time, I was trying to get rid of it because I thought it belonged to Ella. Now, it seems it's the only thing I had of hers that was real."

As if Kit read her mind, she leaned over and whispered, "Maybe you could talk Trevor into sharing custody of the painting."

Quinn chuckled and wrapped her arm around Kit. "Thanks, I needed that." She wiped back tears and turned to Max. "How did you find out about all of this?"

Max nodded in Reese's direction. "His man Donovan found Ella Canyon locked up and tucked away where no one could get to her. I'm sure that was on purpose. She's been there for several years. For some reason she took to Donovan. He gets the credit for finding this much out and for bringing her back to L.A."

Nick lifted a hand to Quinn's face. "You really do look like her. You have her energy, her enthusiasm, her boundless joy. My mother wanted to come. Did I mention that? She'll be wanting to have a sit-down visit with her only granddaughter as soon as you can manage it."

She smiled. "I'd like that. I'm sorry I said your music was garbage."

He laughed and brought her into his chest for a hug. "Ah, I've always heard children make the worst of our critics."

He kissed the top of her head. "We have some catching up to do, girl. I hope you're up to having a father because I intend to be a part of your life, look out for you from here on out. Say no, and I'll just keep after you until you give in."

Quinn looked up into his deep, brown eyes. All of a sudden she needed to believe those eyes were part of her. "It'll take some getting used to but…" She looked over at Baylee and smiled.

She turned back to Nick and admitted, "A very wise woman once told me I'd have only the one chance in life at having a father. I think she might have been right. I'd certainly like to give a father-daughter relationship a try."

She tilted her head. "How comfortable are you at your hotel?"

He shrugged. "Hotels aren't really the same thing as home, never have been. No amount of amenities can ever take the place of what you have in your own home."

She glanced over at Kit. "You wouldn't happen to have room for another guest, would you?"

Kit grinned. "Sure, there's always room at the inn for one more member of our growing family."

CHAPTER 24

Out in the hallway, Reese found Max St. John.

Pulling him aside where no one else could hear, he asked, "I need to know what evidence you actually have against Cade and Collin that points to them blowing up Quinn's building. Fingerprints, DNA, anything at all enough to go to a judge and get an arrest warrant?"

Surprised, Max replied, "Looking for more clients, Brennan?"

He threw him a disgusted glance. "Don't even start that crap. I ask because I checked this morning and there is only one warrant out for Cade Boyd and it's for Claire's murder. There's nothing out for Collin. And I'm really wondering at this point, why you can't find this guy?"

"We're coming up empty regarding evidence pointing to them for Quinn's building. And just recently both brothers changed out their cell phones on us. We know Collin more than likely will not show up for the July hearing on the kidnapping charge. But our hands are tied until he is actually a no-show. We're doing our best, Brennan. Show a little faith, a little patience, let the system work in your favor."

"That's what I thought. And you have to wait until the preliminary hearing in July to see if he's a no-show before you issue another warrant? Got it. I just want to make sure you have nothing tying them to the arson and the eight deaths at Quinn's building. You have no actual evidence pointing to them."

"We know they did it, we just haven't found that link to them yet. But we will. Hey, you know how the system works as well as I do." He eyed Reese warily. "Don't even think about doing anything where I'll have to arrest your ass, Brennan. Got that?"

"Me? What would I do? I'm just a geeky lawyer. It's also come to my attention that your department is investigating several missing prostitutes from the same escort service. Is that info correct?" He saw cop-interest flicker in Max's eyes and knew he had him hooked.

"It isn't my case." But Max gave him a curious look. "You have information about that? It's your duty to share it."

"Come into my office. Let's call the detective in charge of the case, see if he's interested in looking into a tip from a concerned citizen."

Later, after Max had taken off, Reese explained what he'd learned to Jake and Dylan. "Just like we thought it looks like Cade and Collin could walk away from all of this, except maybe for Claire's murder. Which means Cade could leave the country."

"How did Max feel about the call girl theory?" Dylan asked.

"Interested. But that's a far cry from having anything concrete. DNA is the answer. He's going to follow that route. But first they have to find Cade in order to get it on the sly."

"So, are we talking about going the typical route here, take them down via warrant and an arrest where they might just make bail and leave the country, or are we moving forward with ending this thing for real?" Jake asked.

"Look, handing Max the call girl theory was simple backup for me. As far as I'm concerned, we end this thing, the three of us." He glanced at Dylan who seemed to be wavering. "Doubts? Second thoughts? Concerns? Now would be the time."

Jake narrowed his eyes, took the time to glare in Dylan's direction. "Nothing's changed for me. You?"

"It's just that, how long have we known each other? Thirty years? We've been in some dicey situations together and managed to get out of all of them."

Reese nodded. "Go on."

"Remember the time we went down to Tijuana when we were in high school, got into a fight with those German tourists, tore the place up?"

"You feel like walking down memory lane now?"

Jake didn't like where this was going. "Yeah, we were real bad asses back then. So? You want to back out? Is that what you're saying? Because it's convenient for you that Trevor took care of your Connor problem, isn't it? Reese and I aren't that lucky. If we don't end them here and now, we'll both still be dealing with Cade and Collin long after Kit and I get married."

"That's not what I'm saying at all. We've always had each other's backs no matter what. And now is no exception." Dylan held out his hand. "There's no one else I'd rather stand beside in a fight than you two guys."

"Aw, we like you too," Reese said as he reached to grab his outstretched hand. "Want a hug, too?"

"Kiss ass."

"Okay, but I'm really more of a leg man and the thing is I've always had this thing for your legs, Surfer Boy. You have the nicest legs, all tanned and strong and..."

Dylan shot him his middle finger. "You're sick, Brennan. You know that?" He turned to glare at Jake. "Now you want to tell me what that was all about because I'm for ending this thing, too."

Jake nodded. "Okay. Sorry, I'm a little edgy."

"We all are. Then as long as we're in agreement, I'll put the wheels in motion," Reese added.

⚜⚜⚜⚜⚜

Back inside the penthouse at the Bel-Air Monaco, Nick Tyler began gathering up his clothes and personal belongings from the dresser drawers and bathroom, stuffing them down into his bags.

His daughter had invited him to stay at some place called Crandall House in a small fishing village north of Los Angeles known as San Madrid.

He was so excited about the offer he'd already called his mother back in Ireland to let her know the granddaughter she hadn't seen in more than twenty years had decided to give him a second chance.

At the knock on the door, he hesitated to answer it. He already knew before opening it Gerald was more than likely standing on the other side. He didn't want to deal with the man right now.

"Come on, Nick, I just want to talk to you, explain things."

"Go away, Gerald. There's nothing to talk about. I told you I'd pay for your way back to Dublin on a commercial flight. I left the ticket info downstairs at the front desk."

"No, I want you to face me."

"That's just it, Gerald, I don't want to see your fucking face ever again," Nick shouted through the wood.

"After forty bloody years the least you can do is hear me out."

Nick threw open the door. "Make it fast. I have a car waiting." That's when Nick saw the gun Gerald waved in his right hand. "What the fuck are you doing with that?"

"If you don't listen to reason, I'll bloody well kill myself. I swear I will and I'll take the famous Nick Tyler with me. I thought I was looking out for you, looking out for your best interests, like a brother. You know I'd do anything for you. You know that."

"Gerald, give me the gun."

"No, I want you to listen to me. I didn't know about Lisa. I swear to you I didn't know she was dead. Ella looked like the Indian girl even though I was fairly certain she was nothing but a druggie. How was I supposed to know about the switch they made? I didn't know Jessica kept the million. I didn't know Alana killed Lisa. How could I have known something like that? Back then Portman was your barrister, not me. If you're looking to blame someone, blame him. Me? I was only looking out for you."

Nick realized then his friend had gone slightly mad. "Okay. You were looking out for my money. And this Alana woman, how is it she was able to talk you into this whole scheme, Gerry? You bought her fucking house. Answer me that and put down the gun."

"The woman was incredible-looking, a fucking goddess. She would do things in bed no other woman would do. But despite all that you should be grateful I intervened. If not for me the little bitch would surely have continued to live on the dole."

Nick glared at his lifelong friend. How could he have not seen this side to Gerald a long time ago?

Nick waited for his opportunity, realizing he had to keep Gerry talking. "So you knew? You knew what kind of life my daughter was living and did nothing about it."

In the meantime Gerald kept waving the gun carelessly back and forth. "You didn't seem to give a shit, so why would I?"

Nick didn't like hearing the truth. "Face it, Ger, the only fucking reason you got involved when you did is because you saw an opportunity to screw this Alana and make a couple of extra pounds out of the situation."

Gerald started laughing. "If you could have seen Alana, what a body she had, she looked like a goddess and fucked like a whore."

One too many times the gun went back and forth until finally Nick tackled Gerald body to body, sending the man flying back against the plate-glass terrace doors.

The gun came out of his hand then and hit the window with a thud.

Nick overpowered the much shorter man as he landed punch after punch, blow after blow into Gerald's face. "That's for calling my daughter a bitch." When he landed several more hits, he muttered, "And that's for the part you played in letting that son of a bitch Ross Jennetti get anywhere near my daughter."

☙ ☙ ☙ ☙ ☙

Several hours later, charged with disorderly conduct, specifically disturbing the peace, Nick looked up from his holding cell to see Quinn gesturing a piece of paper in his direction from the other side of lockup.

He grinned. His daughter had made bail and in record time.

He held up his hand to let her know he'd seen her and watched as the burly, uniformed guard meandered across the hallway to unlock the door and let him out.

As soon as the barrel-chested man turned the key, Nick pushed the metal back and stepped into the corridor.

The guy immediately shoved a piece of paper in his face. It wasn't his release papers. "How about an autograph? My wife's a huge Nick Tyler fan. You should've heard her when I called her and told her you were in my lockup, said if I didn't get your autograph I shouldn't even bother coming home tonight. Her name's Betty."

"Okay," Nick grunted, more than a little embarrassed about his incarceration. He just wanted out of this place. He signed what was put in front of him, something about best of luck, Betty, and made the short walk with his head down until he got to where Quinn stood.

She had a big grin on her face and then he saw she was actually laughing at him.

"Geez, I can't let you out of my sight for an hour without you embarrassing the family." She snickered again. "I thought parents were supposed to bail their kids out of jail, not the other way around."

"I can explain. Thanks for coming, by the way. You were the only other person I knew to call."

She let out another belly laugh. "The cops said you beat the crap out of Gerald Baines. Is that true?"

"I'm not proud of it. But yes. He deserved every punch and then some."

It didn't take long before they were outside on the sidewalk.

Reese waited at the curb where he took the time to peruse Nick's face up and down and remarked, "You don't even look like you've been in a fight. The cops said you went after Baines, had a brawl right there in your hotel room, tore the place up."

"Nah, Gerald always was a lightweight. He never even landed a blow."

"But they said he threatened you," Quinn added. "He had a gun."

"That he did. A big one." He blew out a frustrated breath. "He knew, Quinn, all this time. Gerald knew about your early living conditions as a child. The only reason he did anything is because he wanted to sleep with this Alana woman and somehow benefit from the ten grand a month. I'm sorry."

She put her arm through his as they walked around to the car. "It's history now, Nick. Let it go. I think I have. But I need to ask you one thing."

A fear gurgled up in his throat. "What's that?"

"You didn't decide to get back in touch with me after all this time because you have only six months to live or something like that, did you?"

He scratched his head and grinned. "Not that I know of. Besides, you're in luck; we Tylers' have a history of living a long and prosperous life."

With that, she put her arm around his waist. Then there's one more thing I need to ask. "Did they feed you in there? Because Kit and Gloria are terrific cooks and they're making this huge pot roast with those little baby carrots and plenty of potatoes and gravy."

Reese let out a laugh. "Better get used to it, Tyler. Your daughter genuinely *loves* her food."

⚜ ⚜ ⚜ ⚜ ⚜

Back at Crandall House, Nick found himself surrounded by a close, tightknit group of Quinn's friends. These same friends had been there with her at the law office to show their support. Some had even been there for her during those tough years of living with Ross Jennetti and Ella Canyon.

There were enough people milling about the place to remind him of the family he'd left behind at his farm. He'd already taken the time to walk to the cliffs and back, to gaze out over the harbor at the setting sun as it dropped into blue ocean and had to admit he was a bit homesick for Ireland.

But nothing could make him leave Quinn now, no matter how he pined for home. How incredibly lucky could one man get in his lifetime, he wondered. While he stood there looking out at the little fishing village below, not so unlike his Ballybrack, he thought of how his daughter had turned into an incredible young woman. And he had absolutely nothing to do with getting her to this point in her life. He turned to go back inside with the unwavering determination to change that.

While waiting for his hostess to get dinner on the table, Nick took a tour of the downstairs. When he spotted the baby grand piano sitting by the window in the massive living room, he went over to the instrument like a moth drawn to flame. As it had since the age of ten, the keyboard pulled at the musician in him like a habit that refused to let go.

He sat down on the bench and started fingering the keys.

At the touch, notes lilted the air. Soon he had an audience. Nick glanced up, saw his daughter staring at him. He'd have to get used to that face, he supposed, so like Lisa's, just as Quinn would his.

His hands dropped to his sides as if he'd been caught doing something wrong.

"Don't stop," Quinn suggested. "I recognize the song you were playing, *Girl by the Sea.*"

He studied her expression, trying to gauge if he should tell her. "I wrote it for you. I don't expect you to believe me, but it was right after your visit."

"I still dream about that day. I never truly believed it actually happened."

"I wanted you to stay with me, Quinn. I didn't want you to leave that day. I simply didn't act on it. My parents gave me grief about it for a bit of time afterward, especially my Da. He died this past Easter."

Quinn wasn't sure what to say. "I'm sorry." But then realization dawned. "So you made this pilgrimage because of him?"

He decided he'd gone this far, he might as well go the distance and tell her everything. "I promised him as he lay dying in hospital I'd finally get in touch with you. He had cancer. During his treatments we'd sit and talk about—the past." He picked up her hand. "Try to understand, I thought you were better off with your mother. Lisa truly was a beacon of light."

"You mentioned that in Reese's office. It's pretty fancy words for a simple roll in the hay, a one-night stand that meant nothing," Quinn commented.

"She wasn't. A one-night stand, that is."

Quinn's eyes widened. "Excuse me? What are you saying?" But then the light came on for real. "You knowingly had a relationship with a fifteen-year-old girl." It wasn't a question.

"I met her in April. I was nineteen. She followed the band for several months afterward, especially that summer. At first, I really believed she was eighteen."

Quinn slanted him a disbelieving look.

"Okay. Even after I found out her true age, I still took her to bed. She got pregnant in July, found out about it in September. You were born the following April." He took a shaky breath. "By that time, the band had taken off. We were getting gigs other places besides California. I was on tour in New York playing Madison Square Garden when this attorney showed up."

"Jessica Boyd."

"No. It was a man, Sumner Boyd I believe. I put him in touch with Portman and cut a deal to stay out of jail. You already know about the money."

"Thanks for telling me. I guess."

"I want to make amends, Quinn. I want you in my life. I want you to get to know your brothers."

"Brothers?" Her mouth dropped open.

"Jack turned eighteen last week. Sean will be fifteen this fall. Their mother and I are divorced, but we're still very much friends. Usually I get the boys during the summer. Right now, they're back at home, anxious to meet their only sister."

"So, you left them alone to come take care of this little problem that occurred a quarter of a century earlier?"

"Spending time with you," he corrected. "I've had other summers with them. Not a single one with you. They know that, Quinn. They know I've been a shitty father to you. I want that to change."

She sighed. "Then I guess I have another family reunion in my immediate future."

☖ ☖ ☖ ☖ ☖

Upstairs, Trevor felt better but still couldn't seem to shake the fever and with it the delirium. Because the fever meant infection, people kept hovering over him, especially Gloria.

***Through a mindless** fog in which he could only guess what was happening around him, Trevor weaved a tapestry of images, both real and imagined. Part of him wasn't sure he cared any more about either one.*

But he knew she did, somehow she kept waiting for him to wake up. He wasn't even sure why. He wasn't even sure he liked having her here. He wasn't even sure he wanted to wake up.

He dreamed of green eyes, not brown like his Nelia's had been. but deep green pools, as green as Irish heather.

The face that kept coming to him might have been older but it was just as striking with golden skin, a wide smile, a stubborn chin, and those kind eyes of jade.

She was mostly leg. Not like his petite Nelia at all.

When his own eyes popped open, he saw the platinum blonde hair first, bluntly cut, angled down her chin. The word cute hung on the tip of his tongue. For some reason, he didn't think she'd be too impressed with it.

"You were dreaming again," she said matter-of-factly. Once again, she mopped his brow.

"Why don't you look more like Alana?"

The question must have come out a little too harsh because he saw her flinch.

"Ten year age difference for one. Believe me we had nothing in common either. I was naïve, she was worldly."

"She was a heartless bitch."

Gloria laughed and the sound soothed him for some reason.

"That too. She took my twins away from me. But you know all about that already. You know about loss, too. I

like that about you, that you know how awful it feels to lose people you truly loved."

"Since it was my fault my wife and child died, I thought I might as well kill other people for a living. For a while afterward, I went on my own personal crusade against evil and if people wanted to pay to get rid of the evil, so much the better. I got so good at my job I didn't think twice about it either."

"But your eyes have so much tenderness in them."

⚵ ⚵ ⚵ ⚵ ⚵

He felt Gloria's lips on his, her mouth full and wet. His body responded even before fully awake. If this were a dream he didn't want to wake up. With his one good arm he brought his hand behind her neck, finally getting a good hold on her golden tresses. The kiss went on until his eyes fluttered open. There she sat next to him on the bed.

"What was that for?"

"You were dreaming about me."

He locked onto those jade pools to keep from drifting away again and saw how they twinkled with mischief. "I was?"

"You were tossing and turning and talking in your sleep. Rambling."

And she had made out the gist of his angst. "You mentioned my name, and you looked like you needed kissing."

He chuckled at that. "Am I awake now?"

"Uh huh, that was some kiss." She narrowed her eyes. "You didn't feel that?"

"Aye, I felt that just fine, although I thought it might be an earthquake. Maybe we could do it again."

She covered his mouth until she drew a low moan out of him. When she started to get up to wet another washcloth to cool his face, he reached to pull her back down on the bed. "Don't go."

Since he was naked underneath the sheets, she ran her hand along the planes of muscles in his arm before running her fingers through his chest hair. "Let me lock the door first."

"Okay."

The minute she sat down on the bed, she asked, "Are you sure you're up for this?'

He took her hand and brought it under the cover. "Does that answer your question?"

"Mmm, I believe it does." She began to unbutton her shirt.

With his one good hand, he tried to help her get out of her top. "I am slightly at a disadvantage, though."

"That's okay," Gloria muttered. "I don't mind doing all the work." And with that, she straddled him.

����� ����� ����� ����� �����

The minute Gloria walked back into the kitchen, Kit asked, "How's Trevor doing?"

Gloria looked around the room, realizing all eyes were on her. They were all about to sit down to the table for supper. She wondered if her face indicated to everyone that she'd just had amazing sex. "Uh, he's fine."

"Still hot?"

Her mind went blank until she remembered he'd been burning up with fever. She could attest to the fact that it certainly hadn't affected his performance. Like a schoolgirl caught in the backseat of a muscle car, she sputtered out, "Uh, the fever is still there if that's what you mean. For a while he was delirious."

That got Kit's attention. "What was he saying?"

Gloria wasn't about to share that with anyone. To take the focus off her, she suggested to Quinn, "Maybe you should increase his antibiotics."

"He isn't septic, so I think it's the usual signs of the body healing. We'll give it until the morning, see if he's gaining his strength back. He isn't lethargic, is he?"

Gloria stifled a chuckle. "He seems to be right on schedule then."

⚜ ⚜ ⚜ ⚜ ⚜

After supper, inside Trevor's room, the men gathered with the intentions of going over the plan.

From his bed, Trevor acted as tactician. "Remember, you're dealing with men who have a distorted view of reality, a sense of entitlement; the laws don't apply to them. It'll be easy to draw them into the illusion. But once they realize they've been tricked, they'll have nothing to lose."

"That's why we need to be ready for anything."

"There's a house in Palos Verdes with all the weapons you'll need." He threw Dylan a look. "You remember the one I mentioned where you could take Baylee for safekeeping."

Dylan nodded. "I remember. But that night I couldn't trust anyone I'd never met."

"Understandable. How about now?"

Dylan cocked his head. "Do you want a pinky swear? The women are big on it."

When Dylan looked up and saw the women standing in the doorway, he abruptly stopped talking.

"You aren't making fun of our pinky swear are you, Surfer Boy?" Quinn asked as she came farther into the room, crossed her arms over her chest, and announced, "I thought we agreed no more secret meetings. You guys aren't very good at covert. You disappear all at once, you raise our suspicions."

"I believe this constitutes a clandestine meeting," Kit accused as she stared over at Jake.

"Sneaky is the way I see it," Baylee concurred.

"What gives, guys?" Quinn asked innocently.

"We were just talking about the lousy Dodger season this year," Reese lied.

"Is that your official story? Because if it is…" Quinn took out her cell phone. "I'm two seconds away from dialing Cade Boyd's number. I'm telling him to meet me at the *Sea Warrior* at ten o'clock tonight."

Kit took out her cell phone as well. "And I'm calling Collin with the story that I've finally come to my senses. I'm dumping Jake and desperately want to run off with him to Mexico to spend the rest of my life there. We'll steal Jake's boat while we're at it and sail off into the sunset. And you know what? Collin will buy it because he's two bricks shy of a full load."

"Now what's it going to be?" Quinn eyed Reese. "We're part of this whether you guys understand that or not. We have a surefire way to lure the Nutty Brothers out to the boat. Anyone interested in hearing a real plan?

"You wouldn't?" Reese accused.

"Oh yeah, we would."

Just then Nick Tyler and Ben Griffin trailed into the room. "We're in this, too. And we're with them." Nick nodded his head toward the women. "My daughter isn't going anywhere without my backup."

"Or my twin sister either," Ben said with a certain amount of pride in his voice. "I've only just now found her and I'm for keeping her safe."

"That's just it. I'm trying to keep your daughter and your twin sister completely out of this so they'll both be safe." Reese glared at Tyler. "Neither one of you understand how dangerous these men are."

"Quinn and Kit filled us in. Besides, I'm done sitting around while these spawn of the devil try to kill my daughter."

Quinn cleared her throat. "As delighted as I am to have my father and my lover arguing about my participation, I'm fairly certain this is my decision. Kit, Baylee, and I are in this whether any of you agree or for that matter like it or not."

"What am I, chopped liver?" Gloria railed. "I got kidnapped. I had my chance at shooting one of them but I missed. I want another chance."

"See. We're a united front. You either accept that or we find a way ourselves to take down Cade and Collin—without you."

Reese ran a hand through his hair. "You are without doubt the most stubborn, hard-headed woman on the planet. I'm trying to…"

Jake grabbed his arm. "I strongly suggest you shut up while you're ahead."

"That's probably what got her through med school, don't you think?" Nick pointed out. "And probably what you like the most about her."

Reese didn't want to burst his bubble, but her hard head wasn't it. On the other hand those deep almond eyes of hers could do a number on him.

Reese gritted his teeth. "Fine. The plan is simple. We make it look like we're all headed to Catalina in fear, with our tails between our legs. We load the boat with supplies, make sure they know when we're scheduled to leave, draw them out in the open and finish it, one way or the other."

"We're hoping once they see they're outnumbered, they'll give up," Jake added.

"But we aren't counting on it," Dylan finished.

"That's actually not bad," Quinn muttered.

"Of course we're dangling the fact that they're getting their money back as insurance that they'll actually show," Dylan said as he draped his arm around Baylee.

"But we need weapons. What about it, Trevor?" Baylee asked.

Dylan was not impressed. "Now, wait just a minute. Has it escaped your memory that you are the mother of a six-month-old baby? You will not…"

Baylee stepped away from him, let his arm dangle in midair. Her eyes turned to slits. "Do *not* remind me I'm a mother, Dylan Burke. It's because I am that..."

Trevor shook his head. "Hey kids, maybe you could take this argument out of my very crowded room and downstairs until you figure these all important details out."

'Now see what you've done, you've upset Trevor," Baylee said, crossing her arms over her chest.

"Me? I'm not the one inconsiderate enough to bring up guns when he's the one lying in bed shot up."

"Like you didn't already think about weapons. Wait, you did consider how we'll all be armed, right?" Baylee asked. "Please tell me you've planned for the guns."

"Good point," Quinn said. "Only a mother could think ahead like that, think on her feet, do that kind of planning, even if it is about—guns." With that Quinn cracked up. "Baylee and guns, it's official, we have definitely entered the Twilight Zone, people."

"Time out," Kit shouted over the din. "What happened to the conventional method of dealing with the bad guys? You know, locking them away from decent members of society because they've committed numerous felonies and heinous crimes against said society. Why haven't the cops already arrested the Nutty Brothers for blowing up Quinn's building? And what about all those missing call girls? And what about Cade killing Claire?"

"Turns out they have no actual evidence, no fingerprints, no DNA to link them to the arson and they're just getting started on the call girl theory," Reese said. "Although there's a warrant out for Cade about Claire's murder, they have to find him first."

Quinn blew out a breath. "And that falls to us."

"For chrissakes, how long does it take for them to do their jobs?" Baylee sighed, reality sinking in. "So it really is up to us?"

"Looks like."

"Then I say we better make it count," Quinn reasoned.

CHAPTER 25

Cade didn't trust Collin enough to leave him alone for five damn minutes.

For the past forty-eight hours since they'd allowed Gloria to escape things had gone from bad to worse. Not only were their bank accounts at zero, including their overseas accounts, but the financial institutions so far had been unable to trace each wire transfer. The money hadn't stayed long enough in one account before it had jumped to another.

The banks told him it might take weeks, even months to unravel the trail, if indeed it could be done at all.

The people he'd talked to had assured him of one thing though. Whoever had transferred the money had been in possession of the correct codes, every last one of them.

So how the hell had they gotten access to the numbered accounts?

It didn't matter. The money was gone and it wasn't coming back unless he could get Reese Brennan and those bastards at Billing-Pro Software to hand it over.

If that hadn't been bad enough, Cade had finally talked his cousins, Adam and Jacob, into arranging a funeral for Connor, only to drive up to the service and realize the chapel had been crawling with cops.

Because of that, he hadn't been able to muster up the balls to crawl out of the vehicle.

It might've had something to do with the fact he had five dead women buried in a grave near the nature preserve. In trying to put an end to Quinn, he'd taken the lives of eight people. He'd gotten his own cousin Scott killed in a drive-by in which he had yet to own up. And from what Adam told him there was an arrest warrant out for him.

He had discovered just that morning Adam and Jacob had filed a missing persons report about Scott. The report meant it was only a matter of time before authorities went searching for the cousin he'd already put in the ground. And one more reason for the cops to shove a probe up his ass.

Inside the motel room they'd rented, Cade looked over at Collin sitting on the bed. The seedy place sat back from the 101 as it met up with State Route 23 in what Cade thought of as a dump. It certainly wasn't the kind of place he was used to staying. A steady hub of traffic noise coming from outside pissed him off, knowing he couldn't afford a better place at the moment.

He watched his sibling fidget and drum his fingers annoyingly on the built-in nightstand.

At this point, Cade couldn't be sure Collin wouldn't spill his guts at the first opportunity and tell Adam and Jacob they'd already put their cousin in the ground, an unmarked four-foot hole next to a bunch of sluts.

He didn't think his cousins would appreciate Scott Geller's final resting place.

Even though he doubted anyone would discover the bodies on their own, the only other person alive who knew they were there was Collin.

Since the scene with his brother at the burial site, for some reason that bothered him. He didn't like the idea of Collin knowing so much because it meant he couldn't leave him alone for five damn minutes.

That meant he'd have to make the call to Reese, demand his money back within earshot of his brother. Very much afraid Collin loomed above some precipice and was about to fall off, Cade pointed out, "It's time to phone Brennan. Are you okay backing me up? Because I need to know if I can count on you no matter what."

"I said I'd see this to the finish," he returned in short, clipped tones. "I keep my word."

"I don't have time to coddle you, nor do I have the patience. Pull out of this sulky mood or so help me..."

"What? You'll kill me too? Yeah, I got that already. You don't like my mood, fine. I don't like the fact you pulled me into this fucking mess."

Cade narrowed his eyes. "Me? You seem to forget a lot of things, little brother, like who was the first one of us to sic Auslo and Taft on Kit and Boston in the first place. You did. If those two clowns had been better at blowing things up, your precious Kit would already be out of the picture and that would be on your head, not mine. Maybe if you'd had the guts to do it yourself..."

Collin stood up, balled his fists, ready to fight. "Kit was my problem."

"That's right, one you let hang around way too long."

"What about Quinn? You did the same thing with her."

"My mistake, one I'm trying to correct. I know that now. Like Quinn, those hookers laughed at me one time too many, defied me after I'd paid them. I couldn't let them get away with it. One said I tried to rape her. Imagine that, I gave her five-hundred dollars and she still wouldn't do what I wanted."

Collin took a step back, fearing the brother he loved had come unhinged. "Let's just get our money back. Once we get this behind us I want as far away from L.A. as I can get. Without Gloria, what's the plan?"

"We find a way to get one of the women alone."

"That's it? That's your plan? How the hell do we do that with cops crawling up our ass? You saw those rent-a-cops they hired. There are probably ten of them now guarding that place."

"Trust me, they won't be looking for us in San Madrid right under their noses."

"Says you, I don't like it."

"I'm not asking you to like it. I'm telling you this is the only way. Now, let's go. We'll need to make a stop at the warehouse, pick up more weapons and explosives."

⚜ ⚜ ⚜ ⚜ ⚜

Inside the kitchen at Crandall House, Reese roamed the room like a caged animal. Uneasy, jittery, he jangled the keys in his pockets and stalked back and forth. His movements bordered on annoying. But the rest of the people gathered there seemed oblivious, everyone that is except Quinn.

"Will you please stop that? He'll call when he calls," Quinn reasoned.

"He'll want to talk to you. He did last time. I don't like it."

"I know you don't. But we've been over this. I've got my part down to the verb. I know what I'm supposed to say, Reese. Damn it, stop that—pacing. You're making *me* nervous."

Quinn scanned the room, unwilling to own up to being just as edgy as Reese.

While Nick and Ben sat at the table playing a game of gin rummy with John Griffin, Dylan and Jake sat at the counter, perched on barstools, meticulously poring through database after database. At this point, it wasn't simply more financial data to untangle but they had to make certain they'd covered their tracks as well.

Gloria was somewhere upstairs sitting with Trevor because she couldn't stand to be in the same room with John for longer than five minutes at a time.

She'd even taken to sharing her meals with the hit man.

Everyone seemed to be trying to carry on as normal as possible—while they waited.

Kit did what she always did. She baked. She stood at the counter putting the finishing touches on the cherry tarts she'd made for that night's dessert while Baylee sat on the other side of Dylan trying to coax Sarah into eating some of Kit's homemade applesauce.

"Maybe I should take attendance. Our growing family seems to be swelling like a gigantic balloon," Quinn muttered to Reese, who tried to settle down by fidgeting with a game on his iPhone.

John, who had been downcast of late, spoke up. "I want to help out. It pains me to think that all of you consider me the enemy, that I had a part in all of this way back when."

Kit rolled her eyes, but it was Jake who looked up from his laptop long enough to enlighten him. "How many times do I have to tell you, every time you didn't act and get Kit out of that environment you risked her safety, her life. My feelings toward you have nothing to do with anything but your poor behavior as a father."

Quinn studied John's reaction, saw him hang his head. Sympathy wasn't an option. "You know, Baylee and I used to look up to you. We believed you were one of the good guys. Finding out you played a role in taking Gloria's babies away from her was like a stab to the heart. I don't even want to imagine what it was like for Kit figuring that part out."

"But I explained how Alana forced me into it."

Quinn lifted her chin. Kit might be reluctant to have this out with the man but she wasn't. "Come on, no one forced you to go along with anything, Mr. Griffin. Free will is a powerful tool. Any time during those months *before* Gloria went into labor you could have whisked her off to parts unknown, let her in on what was about to happen. You didn't. How could you have been so cruel to the mother of your children? "

"Haven't you ever been so afraid of someone you felt ill whenever you had to confront them about anything, knowing no matter what you did it was never enough to get them to leave you alone?" John asked, clearly battling for even a morsel of his former self-respect.

Kit had heard enough. "Look, I'm trying to get past all that happened with Alana. I have been for years. Discovering you didn't really want me with you, though, hurt. But again, I'm trying to get past it. If Quinn can forgive Nick Tyler, then I ought to be able to forgive you. At least you were there part of the time."

With that, she went over and put her arms around his shoulders.

The hug caught him off guard, causing tears to fill his eyes. "I'm sorry."

"I know. But just because I forgive you don't expect the same from Gloria. Did you know Jessica and Alana had her locked up? Were you aware of what they planned to do?"

When he dropped his eyes, she huffed out a breath. "Well, for God's sake. You knew about that, too. That might be the last straw. I'm trying to understand how someone does that to another human being, I really am but…"

Kit threw her hands up in frustration. "Is there a reason you did everything Alana wanted you to do other than getting her to produce several of your films?"

When he merely sat there staring at the cards in his hands, she went on, "Yes, it's fairly easy to check the credits, something I never bothered to do before now. Did any of you ever grow a conscience about any of the evil things you did?"

John threw his cards on the table and stood up. "What do you want from me? I've apologized. I've brought Ben to your doorstep so you two will have the chance to get to know each other. I've come clean about everything. What more do you want me to do?"

At that moment Reese's cell phone buzzed. He knew by the blocked ID who it was, which had him pressing his advantage from the get-go. When he answered he went into his act. "Look, we get that you're pissed. But we want you to leave us alone." He let his voice tremble slightly to show his fear.

"Pissed doesn't cover it. We want the money back you and the assholes stole. And if I don't get it…"

But Reese didn't let him complete his threat. "You'll do what? Try and kill us. Hey Einstein, you've already tried several times—and failed. By the way, you're a lousy shot, Boyd. So far all you've managed to kill is a lot of innocent people that never did a single thing to you and we're still here. Admit it; you've lost the upper hand here, Boyd. The money your family stole forty years ago and used to build the most corrupt law firm I've seen in years is crumbling. I suggest you learn how to live without the silver spoon in your mouth, learn how to live life on the run, because I'm calling every major newspaper in California, airing all your dirty laundry in the press."

"I want to speak to Quinn Tyler. Now!" Cade bellowed into Reese's ear.

Reluctantly Reese handed off the cell to Quinn, who swallowed hard, prepared to take her cue and run with it.

"Why hello, darling. Shouldn't you be somewhere attacking helpless females? Or maybe creating a new identity and packing for Mexico since you're on the run for killing all those prostitutes?"

"What? How did you…? You bitch. You've been spying on me."

"And what if I have? What are you going to do about it, Cade darling? Mommy and Daddy aren't around to protect your ass anymore and we've taken all your precious money away from you. Without your fat bank account you have no money to buy anyone off. It's so sad, really. What will you do without money or Mommy to protect you?"

On the other end of the phone, Cade let out a string of obscenities so loud Quinn had to hold the phone away from her ear. She let him rant before she whistled into the phone. "Now you listen to me, jerkoff, I want you to crawl back into your hole and never stick your head out again. You won't come after me, you don't have the guts. Go crawl off to Mexico and take that witless little brother of yours with you."

She handed the phone back to Reese, who promptly disconnected the call. Quinn wiped her hands together in a gesture that said, 'I'm done with him for good' all the while taking several deep cleansing breaths to calm down.

Reese put his arms around her shoulders, kissed her on the mouth. "Baby, if that doesn't have him crawling out of the woodwork, nothing will."

"I believe that will do the trick. He sounded absolutely foaming at the mouth."

☨ ☨ ☨ ☨ ☨

Less than two miles north of little San Madrid's downtown, Cade was indeed foaming.

His blood boiled so hot he didn't even bother hiding his anger when a fist punched the wall inside the tiny motel room, putting a sizeable hole in the sheetrock.

"I'll get that bitch! So help me god, I'll bury her with the rest of those... She thinks I won't come after her... She's wrong..."

"I take it we aren't getting a dime of our money back," Collin surmised, watching his brother seethe with rage.

"Maybe not but it's time to go to plan B. And by the time I'm finished with Reese and Quinn they'll both be worm food."

☨ ☨ ☨ ☨ ☨

By late that afternoon, Cade and Collin realized it was a little tougher to get to the women than they had judged. They'd already driven by the Book & Bean four times. They'd gone up to the door once and found the place locked up tight for the night.

But on the fifth pass as they circled the fountain in the square, Collin spotted a contingent of vans heading down to the harbor with Reese at the wheel of the lead truck.

Cade waited several minutes before taking a side street and heading to the waterfront. From several hundred feet away, using binoculars, Cade watched Reese and Quinn, Dylan and Baylee, Jake and Kit unload supplies from three trucks onto the *Sea Warrior*.

So that was it. They planned to use the boat to sail off into the sunset, probably tonight, Cade mused.

Good thing that would work into plan B.

"I think our luck just changed, little brother," Cade sneered. "After those bastards finish loading, we board the boat."

"A surprise attack?"

"You got it, dumbass. And the good news is we only need one of them left alive to get our fucking money back."

⚭ ⚭ ⚭ ⚭ ⚭

As darkness fell, the lights of the San Madrid harbor glittered to life.

Located at the base of the cliffs, the port might have been tiny compared to its counterparts to the south in San Pedro and Marina Del Rey but it didn't lack for its share of boats moored there.

For a small fishing village, the old-fashioned wooden pier that jutted out into the water divided the waterfront into two major sections where a mix of moneyed yachts and sailboats bobbed in the water alongside the working man's fishing trawlers and sloops.

One of the more affluent fixtures, the *Sea Warrior* sat anchored closest to the wharf, making loading and boarding her easier and more accessible.

Reese stood back from the glare of an old-fashioned streetlamp, hiding in the shadows, waiting.

He knew they'd done everything possible to set the scene and make the ruse look as real as possible. Now all they had to do was wait for their antsy prey to come to them.

Reese scanned the paved lot once more through Trevor's night vision goggles until he made out the SUV Trevor had described to him.

If the car were here, it meant they had taken the bait. God knows, the six of them had made enough of a show to alert half of San Madrid to the fact they were taking the boat and leaving town.

Standing guard nearest the first piling, he was calculating how poorly lit the parking lot was and how long it would take the Nutty Brothers to get out of the car when the car doors flew open.

Adrenalin shot through his veins in waves as he watched both of them crawl out of the vehicle. They started walking toward the *Sea Warrior*. But about halfway there, inexplicably, Cade stopped and turned to say something to his brother.

Fearing they already realized they'd been had, Reese checked his Luger, gathered up another magazine, and crept closer to his position near the second piling.

He hunkered down behind the largest post, not more than three feet high, trying to hide his large frame in the dark. He breathed a sigh of relief when he saw the two men continue strolling through the lot then walk farther down the landing.

Reese spotted Jake crouched down behind another sailboat a good twenty yards away, holding a desert eagle automatic pistol clutched in his hand, while Dylan did the same at the opposite end of the dock, armed with his trusty Beretta.

Knowing the three of them hadn't fired a weapon since they'd shot at tin cans in middle school, Reese was more than a little nervous about the outcome.

He did his best to steady his breathing, tried to focus on the reason they'd had to take this route in the first place. But it was too late to back out now.

He reminded himself for the twentieth time this was the real deal.

"Rock and roll," he mumbled, balancing the barrel of the weapon on the surface of the wooden post, prepared to take aim. He had to wait though, one beat, then two, wait until Cade made the leap from wooden dock and onto the *Sea Warrior*.

The moment Collin took his first step onto the boat right behind his brother, Reese yelled, "Give it up, Collin, Cade. It's over. You might as well throw down your weapons."

But with no intentions of giving up, Cade turned and fired his weapon in the direction of Reese's voice.

Reese, Jake, and Dylan returned fire. Shots rang out, pinging from several different angles. About that time, from the other side of the parking lot, Quinn emerged. Hunkering down behind one of the other pilings, she fired off several rounds from the nine millimeter.

On board the *Sea Warrior*, Collin screamed, "You stupid son of a bitch! You dragged me right into their trap."

"You idiot, this boat has everything we need to set sail, all we have to do is get it out of the harbor. Keep shooting at the bastards while I cast off."

While his brother made his way to unfasten the moorings, Collin did as he was told. Round after round exploded from the AK-47 he held in his hand. The hail of bullets made certain the enemy stayed well away from the yacht.

Back on shore the steady rat-a-tat-tat of gunfire had Reese biding his time stuck behind a stingy slice of wood. He squinted in the poor lighting, trying to determine if Quinn was all right. When he saw her still firing away, in the few seconds he'd focused on her, he heard the engine kick in aboard the *Sea Warrior*.

By that time, he realized they'd been out-gunned, maybe out-maneuvered.

Cade nervously fumbled with the mooring as several bullets flew past him. Collin had done his job for once, giving him just enough time to untie the ropes, so they could get the hell out of the harbor.

The minute Cade turned the engine over, the yacht rocked and swayed and started to move away from the dock. He didn't bother with the sails as he gunned the motor, clipping one of the other boats in the process as he motored his way out of the tiny marina.

From the other side of the waterfront Kit and Baylee stood on the deck of the *Emerald Isle*, a hundred-foot, gaff-rigged schooner anchored in the second row of boats farthest from the wharf, waiting for Quinn. Fisted in their hands they held matching nickel-plated Berettas.

But when they saw Quinn jump from the shadows onto the boat that looked a good deal like a pirate ship, they stopped firing momentarily and ran to her. Now as a unit, from another angle entirely, the three women had the *Sea Warrior* and the two brothers in a crossfire. They kept up a steady stream of firepower while Reese and Dylan and Jake still dodged the spray of bullets coming from Collin's AK-47.

At that moment, leaning heavily on Gloria, the injured Trevor managed to make it down the ramp that led to the pier onto the refurbished antique clipper. All at once, he slipped the detonator from his pocket and glanced around, taking the time to meet the eyes of each woman.

As the *Sea Warrior* maneuvered further out to sea, Trevor announced, "Ladies, it's now or never. What's it to be?"

As police sirens grew closer to the pier with every precious second, the gunfire from the escaping men became fainter.

Kit eyed Baylee. Baylee in turn, met Quinn's eyes before Quinn made certain they were all in agreement. When they each nodded their heads at the other and stuck out their hands in a show of unity, it was Kit who stated, "Good riddance then. We hate to pollute the ocean with such worthless trash, but a girl's gotta do what a girl's gotta do."

With that, Quinn yanked the device out of Trevor's hands.

"For the Parkers," Kit said as she continued to clasp fingers with Baylee, who held on to Quinn's hand.

"For Sarah Moreland," Baylee uttered.

"For Lisa Redfield," Quinn finished.

And with that, together the three women pressed the button.

The *Sea Warrior* had almost made it out of the harbor when suddenly, the fifty-foot French-built sloop lifted out of the water in a gigantic fiery ball of orange flames.

Not two seconds later another explosion shredded the pieces that remained into nothing more than loose debris.

At the sound of the explosion on the bay, Reese uncurled his frame, searching for Quinn's position near the pylon. But she was no longer there.

He squinted into the night, scanning the dimly lit marina for any sign of her. When he located the *Emerald Isle* at the other end, he made out Quinn standing on the deck, clutching something in her hand.

He took off at a fast clip.

With Jake and Dylan on his heels, he hurried up the ramp to the sloop, vaulting onto the starboard bow.

"You knew about this?" Reese said as he glared over at Trevor. "You might have shared this bit of information with the rest of us."

"Sorry mate, when I give my word to a lady, I try to keep it." Trevor nodded his head in the direction of Quinn. "She made me promise not to say anything."

Quinn locked eyes with Reese. "I'm sorry I didn't tell you but I didn't want you risking your law career on something like this. I didn't count on Cade opening fire on all of you, though. I know the plan was to have the Nutty Brothers give up and I thought they might do the right thing for once, throw down their weapons and surrender without a fight. That's what you planned, right? But I should've known better. It needed ending and I'm fully prepared to accept the consequences."

Before Kit and Baylee could point out that they had all three been a party to pressing the detonator, Reese grabbed Quinn and pulled her into his chest. "From now on, we do everything as a team, you got that? And if there are any consequences to this then we share and share alike."

"I told you I was prepared to pull the trigger and end this. My career's just getting started while yours is…"

But he didn't let her finish. "And I told you I'd do anything to keep you safe. I meant that."

"You did, Reese. You kept me safer than anyone ever has in my entire life."

He crushed his mouth to hers. "And my career means nothing to me if you aren't in my life. In fact, yours is more important than mine."

She lifted her hand to his cheek. "That's exactly what I thought you'd say."

Jake came up behind Kit, draped his arms around her shoulders, and stared hard at the device Quinn still held in her hand before turning to Trevor. "How'd you manage that?"

"You might want to ask the ladies that question," he answered, gripping Gloria's hand.

But when they all heard the first police cars screech to a halt in the parking lot, Trevor looked out to the fireball still burning in the water. "If I were you, though, I'd do that later after we explain to the cops how Cade and Collin snuck on board the *Sea Warrior* to steal her, carrying enough explosives to blow up the entire town. But novices that they were blew themselves to kingdom come in the process instead."

Reese eyed Jake and Dylan. "I believe they were trying to kidnap either Quinn or Kit or Baylee, don't you?"

Jake nodded. "After we prevented that from happening, we did our best to stop them from getting on the boat."

"And when we were fired upon, we were forced to defend ourselves," Dylan added.

"Damn straight we were," Baylee said to Dylan, who in turn whispered, "I just want to know one thing, who is watching our daughter?"

She elbowed him in the ribs. "Mr. Tyler agreed to stay behind for diaper duty."

Baylee glanced over at Reese and Quinn, who were wrapped up in each other. "I think his plan is to try and nudge those two toward grandchildren as soon as Quinn starts her clinic."

"He's taking a lot for granted."

"I don't think so. From what he tells me, Tyler's agreed to foot the bill for the clinic."

🜍 🜍 🜍 🜍 🜍

Several hours later after dealing with the contingent of police officers and detectives and crime scene investigators, they gathered back at Crandall House.

In the kitchen around the table, eating sub sandwiches, Reese explained what their plan had covered. "Part of the idea was to have Dylan provide the cops with altered surveillance video showing the Boyd brothers boarding the *Sea Warrior*."

"The Nutty Brothers didn't let us down there. If I do say so myself, I think it's some of my best work," Dylan bragged. "I had to set the camera up to focus on the *Sea Warrior*. That was two days ago. Now I hand over a doctored tape that clearly shows their attempt to escape by jumping on the boat. We hit the bonus round when Collin took out his illegal assault weapon, which we knew he had from the two earlier drive-by shootings, and opened fire in the direction of shore, where we were conveniently out of camera range."

"As long as it looks like they stole the boat and took off under their own power, and the boat explodes, which it did, that's all we're concerned with," Trevor pointed out. "The cops already suspect they're responsible for blowing up Quinn's building. This way, it simply looks like they got sloppy with explosives."

Reese turned to Quinn. "When did you put the bomb on board?"

"Once I found out what you guys were planning, to lure them onto the boat, hoping they'd give up, I asked Trevor what exactly to do if it didn't go down like we thought. Kit, Baylee, and I talked it over and decided if you guys got them on the boat, we couldn't just stand by and allow them to escape. They'd come back. They'd always come back."

Kit picked up the story. "So we snuck out of the house last night, planted the C4. With a walkie-talkie Trevor led us through the steps as to exactly what we needed to do."

Baylee finished up. "We put the C4 next to the fuel tanks. Set up a remote detonator. While you guys kept them busy under fire, we slipped onboard Trevor's boat, hoping one of us could get lucky and take at least one of them down, maybe lower the odds."

"It might've worked if we'd been better shots, but I'm not sure any of us ever hit either one of them."

Reese rubbed the side of his chin and looked at Trevor. "I guess that's what you were trying to tell us. We aren't expert marksmen."

"Your hearts were in the right place for all the right reasons, but your aim was off. You did more damage than I thought you'd do."

Kit turned to Jake, put her arms around him. "Sorry about your beautiful boat."

"Hey, if it got rid of scum, it was for a good cause."

From there, Reese went on to spell out the other facets of the plan. "What makes the story pop even better is the fact that Jake sent a ton of files to the DEA showing BBG&G laundered money for a Mexican drug cartel over a period of several years beginning as far back as the '80s."

"Icing on the cake," Jake concluded.

"In turn, the DEA will assure the cops the info came from an agent deep undercover, and that during his stint undercover he learned the drug cartel put out a hit on the firm's entire top tier because, let's face it, old Jessica and Sumner, Frank and Eva, too, for that matter, were known far and wide for their greed."

"So when the top tier burned the drug cartel, bang-bang, unknown hit man takes them all out," Jake finished.

Trevor smiled. "I like it."

Dylan added, "And I tipped off the IRS to the fact that the firm filed false tax returns. Actually, it was more like pretty Donna Fontaine did. She'll also get credit and the reward that goes with it for blowing the whistle on corporate tax cheaters. I discovered she could use the money, single mom with two kids who works her ass off sixty hours a week for that damn place. She deserves the reward money."

"You've got a soft heart, Dylan Burke," Baylee said.

Jake went on to describe the rest. "Then we completed the hat trick by sending files to the FBI and the SEC to let them know all about the insider trading the firm managed to do over the last two decades. I don't think we missed an agency or a detail."

But Dylan's brow creased with interest. "Well, there is something I've been curious about, though." He turned to Trevor. "How did you do it? How did you leave Jessica's car in the middle of Cross Creek Road and Eva Geller Gatz's car in the middle of a shopping center? How did you leave the scene?"

Trevor shook his head. "Come on, guys, a professional never reveals his tricks of the trade." He glanced over at Gloria, picked up her hand, kissed the palm. "Besides, I think those days are behind me. I've decided it's time to retire."

Kit blinked in surprise. "Wait, the two of you?" Her brow furrowed. "That's why you've been spending so much time in his room."

"You aren't upset, are you, honey?" Gloria asked, still gripping Trevor's good hand.

"Of course not, but...for God's sake...uh, my own mother is having...having..."

Quinn laughed at her attempt to find the right word and finished for her. "Is having a mutually satisfying consensual adult relationship."

Kit huffed out a breath. "Right. It's just that..."

Feeling sorry for her, Ben walked up and put a hand on her shoulder. "She looks happy to me. I think I approve."

Kit sent a sideways glance his way. "She does, doesn't she? If Ben approves, then I guess I do, too."

Dylan grumbled at the change of subject but stared at Trevor as if he were still trying to figure something out. "Okay, just tell us the significance of those gold cowboys then."

"Now that I can do," Trevor said, picking up his empty glass with his good hand and holding it out. "But first you break out the good Irish whiskey. It's for medicinal purposes. My shoulder's killing me and I'm tired of relying on anymore of the doc's drugs."

Dylan rose from the table, went to the cabinet, brought out a vintage, dated bottle of Knappogue Castle.

Trevor's eyes widened. "Now that's a drink, mate." He handed Dylan his glass.

"I'll pour all night, but I'm still trying to figure out how you left the scene. You had to have been inside the cars of both women. Before that, you must've left your vehicle near Cross Creek, doubled back some way using either mass transit or took a cab, blending into the crowd near the scene of where the two women had their cars parked."

Trevor grunted as he took his first swig of the whiskey. "This one thinks he's a criminalist."

"I nailed it, didn't I?" Dylan prompted, pumping his fist in the air. "I knew it!"

Trevor snorted and said, "You want to hear the story about the gold cowboys or not?"

"By all means."

"They belonged to Pete Parker, a minted set of twenty-four solid gold miniatures of himself sitting on his favorite horse that the studio gave him as a parting gift when he retired from acting. The set, one for each year Pete spent at the studio, was the only thing his son, Noah, had left that belonged to his father. It seems the old man gave him the set still in the box before he left for basic training. Noah locked it away in a safety deposit box. Good thing, too, since Jessica and Alana got every single thing the Parkers owned and then either sold it at auction or kept whatever they wanted for themselves."

Kit shook her head. "Alana keep anything around that came from a western-style ranch? No way. She and Jessica would have disposed of everything like garbage."

Trevor nodded. "I'm sure that's true. Did you know that after they sold the ranch off to a developer, Jessica had the house bulldozed down to the ground and sold off the livestock to a slaughterhouse? Noah found out the information buried in public records."

John Griffin shook his head. "I met Pete Parker a couple of times, nice guy. I remember he and his wife had a little boy, must be the Noah you mentioned. Even after old Pete stopped acting, he used to come around the back lot, bring the boy with him. Now that I think about it, the boy was a good rider, loved horses and seemed to worship his dad.

"You know I've had a couple of days to digest all of this. There were a few times I remember Alana and Jessica talked openly about how they'd like to have the Parker ranch and the land. I knew those two women were evil personified but I had no idea they'd actually go out there and murder that nice old couple."

"Yeah, well, they did," Trevor said matter-of-factly. "And I'm fairly certain the entire law firm was in on it from day one. But because Alana is the one who bought the gun, Noah was fairly certain she was there that night and in on the planning."

"Oh, she was more than there that night. She's the one who pulled the trigger," Kit said.

It was Quinn who went on to explain. "Our Kit here had a—dream, for lack of a better word, about that particular night."

He took in the look on Kit's face. "Really? Gloria said you were a bit psychic. I didn't believe it, though." He couldn't wrap his mind around that sort of thing. "Anyway, after Noah found out all the partners had shared the millions from the trust and the sale of the land…he was convinced they'd murdered his parents."

Jake nodded. "I can indeed confirm the money trail. It must have been what he discovered in county tax records because once Dylan got us inside the network we found evidence in databases where they all took a share from the sale of the Sundown Ranch. With the money, the partners purchased more land adjacent to what they had already started building on in Malibu, some additional twenty acres at a cost of about five-point-seven million. It later became known as The Enclave. From there, they added another series of homes until the compound itself consisted of ten in all, along with the guest cottages."

Nick Tyler put his arms around his daughter's shoulders. "Years later after I became somewhat well known, I remember being invited to that place for a party they called the Boyd Bash. My manager gave me a hard time because I turned down the invite. Think about it, celebrities stayed there from all over the world that weekend, right there on the grounds, sleeping near the bones of those that were sacrificed on their personal altar of greed. Your mother one of those entombed there, Quinn."

"Unfortunately I can top that. Kit, Baylee, and I were dragged there on numerous occasions for birthday or graduation parties."

Kit raised her hand. "My fault," she admitted. "I did the dragging because I didn't want to end up there by myself with those people. Alana allowed it because I refused to go otherwise. And sometimes Baylee's father didn't even know we'd gone there because we lied and told him we were going somewhere else."

"How could we have possibly known what was there on the grounds," Baylee pointed out. "We were naïve kids, who might have nicknamed the brothers, The Unholy Three, but had no idea how depraved they would eventually turn out to be. And we stopped attending events there when we were sixteen. All the while, the remains of my mother and that of Quinn's were a short walk away, down by the pool, a pool I might add we all personally swam in at some point. Makes you wonder if the authorities turned up all the bodies."

"That's a creepy thought," Dylan said. "Maybe after the cops get done doing their thing, we could hire a private company using ground penetrating sonar, more cadaver dogs, go in and do another sweep, maybe take a look at any other property they own within let's say a fifty mile radius."

"It'll take some time, but it would probably make us all feel better," Jake reasoned.

"Good idea," Reese stated. "Hard to believe Alana and Jessica stopped killing at, what's the last count? Six, or is it seven? They got away with all of these murders for a very long time. That has to increase the chance that there are more bodies out there they might not have pinpointed yet."

"And don't forget Cade's missing hookers. With Cade gone, you do realize we'll probably never know for certain what happened to all those women, don't you?" Quinn threw in.

"Not unless someone stumbles across the bodies, we won't. We don't even know for a fact they're dead."

"They're dead," Kit stressed, fighting that feeling she always got now that she could "see" things that had happened in the past. It didn't happen with everything. After all, she hadn't expected her father to show up. That had come out of the blue. But she had staunchly held on to the belief over the years that he'd never died. Scanning all those eyes directed at her she quickly added, "Don't ask."

While Jake kept his arms around Kit, Gloria stood up, went to her daughter. "You and I both know those girls are in the woods, buried somewhere on property Cade owns."

Kit simply nodded.

Trevor cocked his head, stared at both women. "You're kidding? You said Kit was the psychic one, you didn't say a thing about you."

But Ben suddenly hugged Gloria and revealed, "Make it three. I've always had an intuitive side to me, saw things I didn't understand at the time. All my life it felt like a part of me was missing. Now, I'm thinking that ability might run in the family—through my mother." He leaned in and kissed Gloria's cheek.

"Some psychic I turned out to be, though. I didn't know about my own beautiful boy here." Gloria dabbed at a few tears that wanted to spill over and run down her cheeks. She laid her head on Ben's shoulders. "I hope you stay on for a while and let me get to know you better before heading back home to Ireland. This little bit of time we've had, isn't nearly enough for me."

Gloria wrestled with something else. "It's sad that Jake won't get a resolution to Claire's murder. It will remain open on the books, unsolved, without knowing it was Cade."

Reese frowned. "Even though he's dead, we could still try to find something with his DNA on it. Submit it for a comparison with what St. John has."

"That's an idea," Jake said. "I'd like to go that route. I want it solved to Max's satisfaction and off the books for good."

Trevor shook his head, and stared at Gloria. "You really are psychic?"

"Intuitive might be a better word for it. Kit's ability is much stronger than mine ever was. It was Kit who had the vivid dream about the Parkers, the dream Quinn mentioned." She tilted her head to study him. "That dream about the Parkers led us to know for certain Alana and Jessica were involved."

"At the time we didn't have much to go on, not even a name," Jake disclosed. "It's fair to say, we were all more than a little skeptical in Kit's ability."

"Imagine, from one reprehensible deed that night, an empire was born that nurtured and condoned murder whenever it suited their purposes simply because two evil women wanted it that way," Trevor philosophized.

"And it took all of us to bring the evil to its knees," Reese acknowledged, raising his glass of whiskey in salute. "Here's to a job well done."

CHAPTER 26

The marine layer and notorious June gloom disappeared only to turn into a simmering, hot July.

The lure of a cookout, the promise of a stellar Fourth of July fireworks display over the San Madrid harbor had brought everyone out to Crandall House once again.

They had a lot to celebrate.

This time, the fear and unease that had dominated the past two months had dissipated. A slew of childhood nightmares had eased. Not altogether, maybe, but enough so that Kit, Baylee and Quinn could began to look forward to a different kind of future, a future minus so much pain and anger.

By ending the evil that began on that hot August night so long ago before they'd ever been born, the three women had turned a corner of sorts.

They could finally take that first step to putting their self-doubts to rest, as well as all those deep-rooted nightmares. Old habits might be difficult to break, but that didn't mean it couldn't be done—eventually.

On the last day of June, Baylee said her final goodbye to William Scott. The man had slipped peacefully away without ever getting another chance to say anything more about Sarah Moreland's death or what part he played in keeping it secret.

Dylan had watched as Baylee stood at his bedside in agony wanting so much for the father she loved to wake up and explain more. But in the end, William kept whatever secrets he held about Jessica and Alana to himself.

Even though she wasn't sure it was the right thing to do, Baylee decided to bury him next to Sarah, the woman whose memory had haunted him for over two decades. Maybe if there were a resolution in death her father would find it for himself.

At the urging of both Kit and Ben, the next day, John Griffin had turned himself in to the authorities. Later that afternoon, it had been his children who accompanied him to the home of David Foster's family.

There, John had finally admitted to the boy's mother and her other children that he had been the one responsible for taking the life of her youngest son that day on Benedict Canyon, a day that had forever sealed John's commitment to Alana and Jessica. Because after that day, the three of them had entered into a series of evil schemes and wicked acts, each of which, had altered a number of lives thereafter. Their bond had certainly unleashed the chain of events that led to Kit's growing up tormented by the likes of Alana.

John Griffin's hearing had been scheduled for August. He was looking at either a year in county lockup or six years in state prison. Either way, he'd have to pay for what he did. Any defense attorney worth his salt though would suggest he plead guilty in exchange for the sentence in county.

Together Kit and Ben stood by their father, but whenever he grumbled, his children would simply remind him he got off light.

Even though the police were skeptical of their story of how exactly the boat blew up, they could find nothing to contradict that version. The Boyd brothers had brought explosives onboard the *Sea Warrior* from another warehouse they owned and the police later discovered its existence in Thousand Oaks, filled with weapons and all kinds of explosives.

Days later, they officially closed the investigation and went on to other, more pressing, cases.

During that time, Quinn made plans to visit Lisa Redfield's mother in Santa Barbara and get to know a grandmother she'd last seen at the age of thirteen months. Even though she definitely didn't remember the woman, she wanted that connection to a part of herself she had never before experienced.

Something about knowing she'd had family less than a hundred miles away made her angry and wanting resolution. It hadn't been necessary for Quinn to spend all those early years in dirty motel rooms with a heroin addict for a mother. It was all just one more lie to add to a growing list, a list Alana and Jessica personally put together.

Consequently Quinn desperately wanted to get to know Lisa's mother, sample a small taste of what real family ties might be like, tangible enough to reach out and touch another person who had known Lisa Redfield.

Thanks to numerous long-distance telephone calls she had also assured Nick's mother in Dublin, a grandmother she remembered only slightly from dreams that she would gladly take the trip over to Ireland for a long visit just as soon as she could manage taking time off.

While Reese, Jake, and Dylan appreciated the fact Trevor had helped put an end to a nagging problem that had spiraled out of control from the beginning and put the women they loved in harm's way, they also learned something new about themselves.

If they were forced to do it all over again, they could and would cross the line in order to protect the people they loved.

It wasn't until the first fireworks speared into the night sky and reverberated with pops and blasts that Reese was able to pull Quinn aside and get her alone. "I not only got you back on rotation, I got the hospital to agree there would be nothing noted about what happened in your personnel file."

"I know and I don't even have to go before the review board. I already got my notice from Mendenhall I'm back on rotation starting tomorrow, my last free night before insanity."

"But you wouldn't have it any other way."

She grinned. "No, I guess I wouldn't." She glanced over at Nick Tyler sitting in a circle of lawn chairs, deep in conversation with her friends. "Would you look at him? I can't seem to get him to leave." She laughed. "He might be here a while. He's even making plans to go on rounds with me as soon as I give him the go ahead, especially to visit the pediatric cancer ward and visit those who are going through chemo."

"I heard he agreed to donate a substantial amount to the brand-new children's wing at the hospital. Besides, I don't think you really want him to go anywhere."

Her smile grew wider. "No. It really is nothing short of amazing to have him in my life now. My father, who knew? I didn't think it was possible to stop hating him, to let go of all that anger. I owe that to you for pushing me, for making me take that step."

"You'd have gotten there one day."

"No, Reese, I don't think I would have. And to know my mother had this incredible talent as an artist is— inconceivable. She wasn't a drug addict, but a sweet-natured artistic type that happened to trust the wrong people. It's amazing, isn't it? After all these years, Kit gets a mother and has her father back in her life." She glanced over at Gloria and Trevor. "She might even have a new stepfather soon. It seems the only one of us who loses is Baylee. She lost her father and her mother all over again."

"She held up well at the service for both of them. With you and Kit for support, she'll do just fine."

"She will. And let's not forget Dylan. He really is this remarkable source of energy for her. We all need that."

Reese toyed with a few strands of her hair as he brought her closer. Picking up her hand, he kissed the palm. "We make a pretty good team, too, Tyler, or haven't you noticed?"

Wary, she inched back to look up into those gray eyes, so cool, so calm. "I've noticed. It scares me. The only team I've ever been a part of for any length of time is what I've had with Kit and Baylee. We both know that isn't the same thing, Reese. I don't do well in relationships. I've never had one."

"So you want to go on like we have been? Nothing serious, just hitting the sheets."

She tightened her jaw. "I don't see why not."

"I would agree with that, except for one little thing."

"What's that?" She was afraid she already knew. In spite of the fear tightening her stomach muscles she really wanted to hear him say it, hoped like a kid at Christmas he'd use the L word first.

"I'm in love with you." His arm snatched her around the waist, bringing her up to eye level. "I want you to marry me, Tyler. I want the whole package."

She whooshed out a breath. "Good, because I'm in love with you right back." She grabbed him by his shirt. "The question first and foremost on my mind, though, is that little striptease you did just a one-time deal, or do I get that anytime I want?"

He nibbled her ear. "Why don't you come with me and find out?"

"Hmm." She nipped his lower lip, breathed in the night air. It was time to risk even more. "Okay, but what would you say to a couple of kids down the road, once I get my clinic up and going, that is?"

"I'd say I'm a very lucky man."

Dear Reader:

If you enjoyed Ending Evil, please take the time to leave a
review. A review shows others you've liked my work.
By recommending it to your friends and family it helps
spread the word.
Please Tweet/share that you've finished Ending Evil.

If you do write a review, by all means let me know via
Facebook or my website. I'd love to hear from you!!

*For a complete list of the author's other books visit her
website.*
http://www.vickiemckeehan.com/

Want to connect with the author to leave a comment?
www.vickiemckeehan.wordpress.com/ blog
www.facebook.com/VickieMcKeehan

Go to the next page for a preview of
Promise Cove
The first book in the Pelican Pointe Series

Promise Cove
Prologue

One year earlier
Twenty miles southeast of Baghdad

The combat post was rural, more like a farming community stuck out in the boonies. The roads were primarily unpaved, dusty twenty-four / seven, and at the moment littered with burned-out equipment. The convoy they were riding in was going a sluggish twenty-five miles an hour in a hundred-twenty-degree heat. There was no AC, no hope of grabbing an artery-clogging, delicious-tasting, fast food burger with a pile of over-salty fries, or even indulging in an after-duty dip in a cool, sparkling blue swimming pool.

Because this particular stretch of road had seen its fair share of hostile action the past couple of days the entire unit had to be extra vigilant.

As they made their way up a rise, a grove of palm trees came into view. The wind picked up causing the fronds of the trees to bend and sway. The hot, arid breeze kicked up the loose grit, causing the tiny grains of sand to become airborne and burrow in and under any exposed pore and crevice of skin it could find. A thick layer of sand stuck to their faces, to their uniforms, and their weapons. Homemade masks made from scarves and bandanas hid their sweaty faces and did little to protect them from the elements.

Dressed in full combat gear, the stifling heat inside the Hummer caused perspiration to pool down their backs. The prospect of a hot shower, a mere dream in the back of everyone's mind, was as far off at the moment as the idea of ever getting to go home.

But even in a war zone confined in the cramped space of the Humvee, the soldiers did their best to make light of their predicament by laughing and cracking jokes. Sitting in the back seat, two officers kept up a steady stream of chatter. At least one did. Glancing up briefly when another new barrage of sand hit the windshield, Captain Scott Phillips barely noticed as he yanked the bandana from around his mouth so he could talk. And the Captain loved to talk, especially any bit of conversation that crept into his head that had anything to do with his wife, Jordan, and their baby daughter, Hutton, a daughter he had yet to lay eyes on firsthand or even hold.

As had become his habit, 1st Lt. Nick Harris listened as patiently as he could. What else was he going to do in such close quarters but listen to the Captain's long-winded stories about home? Nick indulged him, not only because he was a captive audience but because, like most everyone in the unit, he genuinely liked Scott. The men who served under Phillips liked the no-nonsense way he ran his unit, liked the man who could routinely go from all-business to light-hearted in the blink of an eye.

And light-hearted usually meant Scott kept up a non-stop dialogue about his family back home. After spending a year of active duty with the guy, Nick felt certain he knew every nuance about the man's personal life. There wasn't much info Scott held back or didn't share. When it came to his wife and newborn daughter, the man simply refused to shut up.

On the surface the two men had little in common. Scott was blissfully married while Nick, unattached, single and happy about it had a bevy of women waiting for him back in Los Angeles. But despite their differences, Nick's affection for the guy overrode any annoyance over knowing every detail Scott chose to share. It seemed to Nick, Scott's family life back home in California was an open book, which made him long ago accept the fact that Scott just liked to talk. Period.

Nick watched as Scott tapped his flak jacket and reminded, "I promised Jordan I'd wear this thing 24/7 as long as I'm over here. I didn't have the heart to tell her it won't do a damn thing to stop an IED."

"There's no stopping an IED," Nick agreed amicably.

"When we get out of this mess promise me you'll come to Pelican Pointe for a visit, meet Jordan and the baby."

Here it comes, thought Nick as he shook his head, Scott crowing once again about his hometown and the people in it. Nick responded the way he always did whenever Scott mentioned Pelican Pointe, he made some smart-ass comment, making sure to insult the Captain's small town in a good-natured, guy kind of way. "Now why would I want to spend time in a Podunk town that sounds like a bird sanctuary? I'm a big city kind of guy, Captain. I'd go nuts in a small town. Besides, small towns are cliquish."

"Pelican Pointe's different."

"I doubt that. Everybody knows your business in a small town."

"When we get out of this mess, you come for a visit. I guarantee you'll see for yourself what a great place it is, how great the people are. They'd do anything for you, Nick." Without taking a breath, Scott went on, "God, I sure miss Jordan. And I haven't even laid eyes on Hutton. I wish I'd been there the day she was born. I hate it Jordan had to go through childbirth without me. She's almost five months old, can you believe it?"

"How does it feel to be a dad?" Nick didn't have a clue about being a father, but it seemed the right thing to say at times like this when Scott got that distant look on his face, that wistful gaze in his eye, the look that said he was homesick and wanted nothing more than to get back home to his family.

"Being a father is great, I think. I'd like to be able to hold her though, you know. Pictures aren't the same thing. You ever thought of having kids, Nick?"

A panicked look crossed his face. "Hell no. I can't even see myself married."

"Marriage is exactly what you need. Might settle you down."

Nick couldn't imagine it. "Marriage would be like a rock around my neck. Too many sweet things out there in the proverbial sea I haven't sampled yet." He wiggled his eyebrows up and down.

"Get yourself in trouble is what you're gonna do. You need to think about finding that special someone. If you ever found a woman like Jordan, you'd change your mind in a heartbeat."

Before Nick could argue, he heard the sound of a rocket blast pierce the air.

Someone yelled, "Look out, incoming!"

Nick heard an explosion, saw a blast of fire, and then a wave of smoke surrounded the vehicle so thick, he could barely see or breathe anything but fire and heat. Soldiers started running toward the lead Hummer. He heard more yelling. His lungs burned.

"Go. Go. Go!" someone shouted.

Chaos reigned as Nick watched the Humvee just ahead of theirs disintegrate into pieces. He saw burned metal fly through the air before he realized it wasn't the lead Hummer at all. He turned to where Scott had sat beside him and saw his buddy's face twisted in pain. Nick heard screaming.

"Promise me, Nick…"

also by Vickie McKeehan

The Evil Secrets Trilogy
JUST EVIL Book One
DEEPER EVIL Book Two
ENDING EVIL Book Three

The Pelican Pointe Series
PROMISE COVE
HIDDEN MOON BAY
DANCING TIDES
LIGHTHOUSE REEF
STARLIGHT DUNES
LAST CHANCE HARBOR
SEA GLASS COTTAGE
LAVENDER BEACH
SANDCASTLES UNDER THE CHRISTMAS MOON
BENEATH WINTER SAND

The Skye Cree Novels
THE BONES OF OTHERS
THE BONES WILL TELL
THE BOX OF BONES
HIS GARDEN OF BONES
TRUTH IN THE BONES

The Indigo Brothers Trilogy
INDIGO FIRE
INDIGO HEAT
INDIGO JUSTICE
THE INDIGO BROTHERS TRILOGY BOXED SET

Exclusively at Amazon in print and Kindle format

ABOUT THE AUTHOR

    Vickie's novels have consistently appeared on Amazon's Top 100 lists in Contemporary Romance, Romantic Suspense and Mystery / Thriller. She writes what she loves to read—heartwarming romance laced with suspense, heart-pounding thrillers, and riveting mysteries. Vickie loves to write about compelling and down-to-earth characters in settings that stay with her readers long after they've finished her books. She makes her home in Southern California.

Find Vickie online at
https://www.facebook.com/VickieMcKeehan
http://www.vickiemckeehan.com/
https://vickiemckeehan.wordpress.com